Phineas T. Barnum

scandalized the stuffy diehards of a Victorian society. His bombastic swindles; his second wife, forty years his junior; the shocking behaviour of his daughter; his allegedly illegitimate son —all provided meat for a gossip-hungry society entrenched in Calvinism, puritanism, and prudery.

In this fascinating biography, Irving Wallace exposes the fabulous life of the world's greatest showman. Here are the full and detailed stories of Tom Thumb, the Siamese Twins, Jumbo, Jenny Lind, the incredible woolly horse, the fossil known as the Cardiff Giant. Here are all the wonder and hokum of P. T. Barnum, the man who began the ballyhoo known as modern advertising, discovered the million-dollar exclamation point, gave America its first zoo and its first beauty contest, and infected millions of people with his uninhibited love of the Fantastic and the Wonderful.

". . . unremittingly entertaining."—*New Yorker*

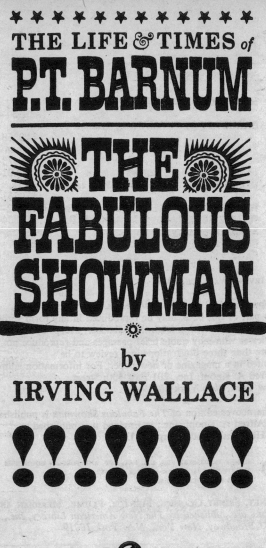

THE LIFE & TIMES of
P.T. BARNUM
THE FABULOUS SHOWMAN

by

IRVING WALLACE

A SIGNET BOOK from
NEW AMERICAN LIBRARY
TIMES MIRROR

A hardcover edition of *The Fabulous Showman* is published
by Alfred A. Knopf, Inc.; in England it is published
by Hutchinson and Company, Ltd.

 SIGNET TRADEMARK REG. U.S. PAT. OFF. AND FOREIGN COUNTRIES
REGISTERED TRADEMARK—MARCA REGISTRADA
HECHO EN CHICAGO, U.S.A.

SIGNET, SIGNET CLASSICS, MENTOR, PLUME, MERIDIAN AND NAL
BOOKS *are published by The New American Library, Inc.,
1633 Broadway, New York, New York 10019*

FIRST SIGNET PRINTING, MARCH, 1962

8   9   10   11   12   13   14

PRINTED IN THE UNITED STATES OF AMERICA

FOR
DAVID AND AMY
with love

"He will ultimately take his stand in the social rank . . . among the swindlers, blacklegs, blackguards, pickpockets, and thimbleriggers of his day."

—TAIT'S EDINBURGH MAGAZINE
1855

"I consider him the greatest genius that ever conducted an amusement enterprise in this country, a man of superlative imagination, indomitable pluck and artistic temperament."

—ROBERT EDMUND SHERWOOD
1926

Contents

List of Illustrations

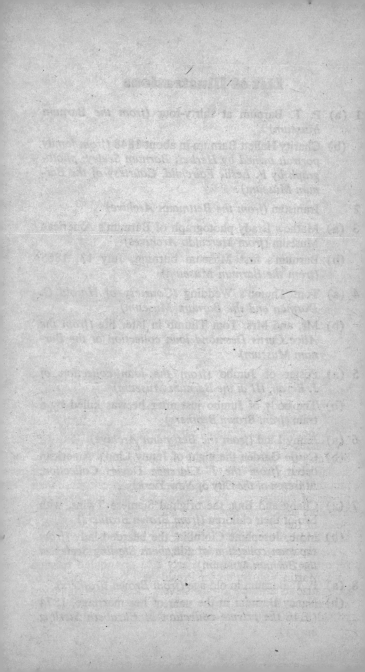

EXHIBIT ONE
Gen. Washington's Nurse

On an early August morning in 1835 a literate majority of New York City's 270,000 citizens awakened to learn of a new phenomenon in their midst. A new age was upon them—the age of showmanship.

In the weeks and months before that fateful morning, all classes of New Yorkers—the old-fashioned Knicker-bockers, the *nouveaux riches* or Shoddyites, the professional people and artists—had prided themselves on the fact that they possessed and patronized more churches than places of amusement. Laws were blue, and life was gray. Theaters and exhibitions were regarded by most as outposts of the devil. Sport was confined to intoxication, assault and battery, and discreet fornication.

Newspapers, as yet inhibited, were devoted to chaste reportage: the Democratic Party had nominated bantam cock Martin Van Buren for President; Oberlin College, to dramatize its attitude toward slavery, was accepting Negro students; a British chemist named James Smithson had willed £100,000 to establish an American institute, "for

the increase and diffusion of knowledge among men"; the
National Trades' Union deplored child labor in the cotton
and wool industries; the frigate *Constitution* had recently
returned from Europe, bearing as its most distinguished
passenger Edward Livingston, United States minister to
France; General Sam Houston had been made the com-
mander of the Texan army; the season's best-seller was
Edward Bulwer-Lytton's *Rienzi,* and *The Letters and Papers of Washington,* edited by Jared Sparks, had just been
published.

But of curiosity and wonder and sensation there was
little until that early August morning when New Yorkers
awakened to read in press advertisements, on street posters,
in pamphlets hawked at six cents a copy, that a colored
woman 161 years of age, who had been President George
Washington's nurse and nanny, was being placed on public
exhibit in Niblo's Garden. The ancient's name was Joice
Heth, the name of her sponsor Phineas T. Barnum.

The advertisements read: "The Greatest Natural & National Curiosity in The World. JOICE HETH, nurse to
General George Washington, (the Father of our Country). . . . Joice Heth is unquestionably the most astonishing and interesting curiosity in the World! She was the
slave of Augustine Washington (the father of General
Washington), and was the first person who put clothes on
the unconscious infant, who, in after days, led our heroic
fathers on to glory, to victory, and freedom. To use her
own language when speaking of the illustrious Father of
His Country, 'she raised him.' Joice Heth was born in the
year 1674, and has, consequently, now arrived at the astonishing AGE OF 161 YEARS. She weighs but Forty-Six
Pounds, and yet is very cheerful and interesting. She retains
her faculties in an unparalleled degree, converses freely,
sings numerous hymns, relates many interesting anecdotes
of *the boy* Washington, and often laughs heartily at her
own remarks, or those of the spectators. Her health is perfectly good, and her appearance very neat. She is a baptist
and takes great pleasure in conversing with ministers and
religious persons. The appearance of this marvellous relic
of antiquity strikes the beholder with amazement, and con-
vinces him that his eyes are resting on the oldest specimen
of mortality they ever before beheld. Original, authentic,
and indisputable documents accompanying her prove, how-

ever astonishing the fact may appear, that Joice Heth is in every respect the person she is represented."

The announcement was oddly electrifying. It was something different in the drab monotony of everyday routine. Here was a living link to the first President, already in his grave thirty-six years and an austere deity to a new generation. Here was a hoary human whose croaking voice had cooed to the infant Washington and whose wrinkled hands had caressed him. To view this relic excavated from the dim past would be strange fun and even patriotic. And because the advertisements promised that she was a True Believer who chanted "hymns" and took pleasure in "conversing with ministers," a visit to this historic freak would certainly not offend the clergy or break its edicts against frivolity and hedonism.

Even as thousands of New Yorkers, titillated, prepared to invade Niblo's Garden for a day's diversion, thousands more considered the attraction and wondered if it was authentic. After all, who was this P. T. Barnum anyway? Was he reputable enough to stand behind his fantastic find?

Renown and repute P. T. Barnum had not in that late summer of 1835. He was, indeed, a nonentity—almost for the very last time in what was to be a most notorious and spectacular life. Later, of course, he would amass a fortune of four million dollars, and in so doing become a household name in America and throughout the world. He would become the personal friend of Queen Victoria and Abraham Lincoln, of William Ewart Gladstone and Mark Twain, of William Makepeace Thackeray and Horace Greeley. He would introduce to America the modern public museum, the popular concert, and the three-ring circus, all forerunners of vaudeville, motion pictures, and television. He would invent modern advertising and showmanship. And he would make himself an international legend. Once, meeting General Ulysses S. Grant, he would say: "General, since your journey around the world you are the best-known man on the globe," and Grant would honestly reply: "No, sir, your name is familiar to multitudes who never heard of me. Wherever I went, among the most distant nations, the fact that I was an American led to constant inquiries whether I knew Barnum."

But this was 1835, and P. T. Barnum was as yet unsuccessful and unknown. At the time when he promoted Joice Heth, he was only twenty-five, a Connecticut Yankee six foot two inches in height, a bundle of massive energy, with curly, receding hair above wide ingenuous blue eyes, a bulbous nose, a full, amused mouth, a cleft chin, and a high-pitched voice. Until this moment, he had been Jack-of-all-trades and master of none. He had served as a clerk in several retail shops, had conducted legal lotteries, had been proprietor of this own fruit store, had edited a liberal weekly, had sold hats and caps on commission, and, finally, had opened a small grocery store in New York with one John Moody as his partner, supplementing this income by running a boarding house with his wife. Not until his discovery of Joice Heth had he found himself. But in his flamboyant exhibition of this wizened and repulsive nursemaid, he would later admit: "I had at last found my true vocation." Equally important, his eager, waiting public had at last found a way of having fun without the fear of fire and brimstone.

How had the age of showmanship come about?

:•:   :•:   :•:

On an ordinary working day in the latter part of July 1835, young Phineas T. Barnum was morosely tending his grocery store and consulting advertisements of the penny *New York Sun* in the hope of finding some golden opportunity, when an old neighbor and customer named Coley Bartram, of Redding, Connecticut, came calling.

As Bartram made his purchases, he related some of his recent activities, and then, remembering the proprietor's unceasing interest in speculative investments, he told Barnum of the latest project that he had discarded. Bartram explained that recently he and one R. W. Lindsay had purchased a curiosity as a business investment, a slave woman thought to be 161 years old and formerly the nurse of President Washington. They had been exhibiting her at the Masonic Hall in Philadelphia. But Bartram had soon wearied of the project, and had sold his interest in the woman to Lindsay. And now Lindsay, homesick for his native Kentucky and feeling that he had little ability as a showman, wanted to get rid of the woman and was casting about for a buyer. Was this something that might interest Barnum?

At once Barnum was attentive. He vaguely recalled having read several paragraphs about the exhibit in the New York press. Could Bartram refresh his memory? Bartram could, indeed. He handed Barnum a clipping from *The Pennsylvania Inquirer,* dated July 15, 1835:

"CURIOSITY.—The citizens of Philadelphia and its vicinity have an opportunity of witnessing at the Masonic Hall, one of the greatest natural curiosities ever witnessed, viz., JOICE HETH, a negress aged 161 years, who formerly belonged to the father of General Washington. She has been a member of the Baptist church one hundred and sixteen years, and can rehearse many hymns, and sing them according to former custom. She was born near the old Potomac River in Virginia, and has for ninety or one hundred years lived in Paris, Kentucky, with the Bowling family.

"All who have seen this extraordinary woman are satisfied of the truth of the account of her age. The evidence of the Bowling family, which is respectable, is strong, but the original bill of sale of Augustine Washington, in his own handwriting, and other evidence which the proprietor has in his possession, will satisfy even the most incredulous.

"A lady will attend at the hall during the afternoon and evening for the accommodation of those ladies who may call."

Something stirred inside Barnum. He must see this oddity for himself. At the earliest opportunity, he made off for Philadelphia by stagecoach, sought out Lindsay at the Masonic Hall, confirmed the fact that Joice Heth was for sale, and then asked to meet her.

He was solemnly ushered into the presence of the extraordinary ancient. "She was lying upon a high lounge in the middle of the room," he later reported in his autobiography. "Her lower extremities were drawn up, with her knees elevated some two feet above the top of the lounge. She was apparently in good health and spirits, but former disease or old age, or perhaps both combined, had rendered her unable to change her position; in fact, although she could move one of her arms at will, her lower limbs were fixed in their position, and could not be straightened. She was totally blind, and her eyes were so deeply sunken in their sockets that the eyeballs seemed to have disappeared altogether. She had no teeth, but possessed a head of thick bushy gray hair. Her left arm lay across her breast, and she had no power to remove it. The fingers of her left hand were drawn so as nearly to close it and remained fixed and immovable. The nails upon that hand were about four inches in length, and extended above her wrist. The nails upon her large toes also had grown to the thickness of nearly a quarter of an inch."

Gazing at her, Barnum reflected that she could as easily be "a thousand years old as any other age." He began to converse with her. He found her at first "sociable" and finally "garrulous"—especially when she reminisced about her servitude under George Washington's father and her duties in raising "dear little George" to maturity. Eventually she discussed the Baptist Church, and she sang a hymn.

Barnum was enchanted. He took Lindsay aside. Only one point remained to be discussed: proof of her age. Lindsay said that he had this proof. He explained that before George Washington's birth Augustine Washington had sold Joice Heth to his sister-in-law, Elizabeth Atwood, who also lived in Bridges Creek, Virginia. When George Washington was born on February 22, 1732, his father borrowed Joice Heth back from his sister-in-law and retained her to raise the future President. The proof itself was encased in a glass frame. It was a yellowing document, greatly creased and worn, a bill of sale from Augustine Washington to his sister-in-law, Elizabeth Atwood, for "one negro woman, named Joice Heth, aged fifty-four years, for and in consideration of the sum of thirty-three pounds lawful money of Virginia." The document was dated February 5, 1727, and it had been witnessed by William Washington and Richard Buckner.

Barnum was satisfied. Only one more question disturbed him. Why had the existence "of such an extraordinary old woman" not come to light years before? Lindsay had the answer. He replied "that she had been lying in an out-house of John S. Bowling of Kentucky for many years, that no one knew or seemed to care how old she was, that she had been brought thither from Virginia a long time ago, and that the fact of her extreme age had been but recently brought to light by the discovery of this old bill of sale in the Record Office in Virginia by the son of Mr. Bowling, who, while looking over the ancient papers in that office, happened to notice the paper endorsed Joice Heth."

Lindsay, a neighbor of the respectable Mr. Bowling, had

heard of the living antique and purchased her, and now he was prepared to dispose of her to Barnum for $3,000. Barnum, always at his best in a horse trade, reacted unfavorably to the price. The two men haggled, and when they were done Lindsay had agreed to accept $1,000 for his exhibit.

Barnum had only $500 to his name. He took a ten-day option on Joice Heth, and then returned to New York to raise the rest of the money. It was not easy. Barnum convinced his wife that though, true enough, there was the definite risk that Joice Heth might die and they would lose their full investment, the venture held enough promise to warrant gambling their entire savings. Then, dazzling a friend with the marvel of his freak, he borrowed the remaining $500. And finally, because he needed cash for living and incidental business expenses, he sold his half interest in the grocery store to his partner, Moody. Then he rushed back to Philadelphia, paid off Lindsay, and overnight became showman and slaveholder.

The site chosen for the exhibition was all-important. Barnum selected Niblo's Garden. This attractive open-air saloon or refreshment center, profuse with flowers and trees, featured a musical floor show. Once Barnum had applied to William Niblo, the proprietor, for a job as bartender, and now, presenting himself again, he was grateful that Niblo did not remember that occasion.

While Niblo had no desire to display Joice Heth in his saloon, he was agreeable to leasing Barnum a large apartment in the building next door. In return for renting this room, paying for all printing and advertising, and furnishing a ticket-seller, Niblo was promised one half of the gross box-office receipts. Barnum next proceeded to hire an assistant, someone who would help him in promotion and serve as master of ceremonies. The assistant was Levi Lyman, a onetime attorney who had practiced in Penn Yan, New York. "He was a shrewd, sociable and somewhat indolent Yankee," Barnum said, "possessed a good knowledge of human nature, was polite, agreeable, could converse on most subjects." The stage was set for "Aunt Joice," as Barnum liked to call his investment.

Barnum filled the newspapers with advertisements and flooded the metropolis with provocative posters. Levi Lyman wrote a learned pamphlet on Washington's nurse, and this, too, was added to the barrage of publicity. In a single week, New York was made Heth-conscious. Then the building adjacent to Niblo's Garden was thrown open to the public, and the public responded.

Most often, as the customers reverently crowded about the high lounge upon which the ancient one reclined—"an animated mummy," the *Sun* called her; "a loathsome old wench," a later critic decided—Barnum and Lyman jointly conducted the show. According to Barnum: "Our exhibition usually opened with a statement of the manner in which the age of Joice Heth was discovered, as well as the account of her antecedents in Virginia, and a reading of the bill of sale. We would then question her in relation to the birth and youth of General Washington, and she always gave satisfactory answers in every particular. Individuals among the audience would also frequently ask her questions, and put her to the severest cross-examinations, without ever finding her to deviate from what had every evidence of being a plain unvarnished statement of facts."

Joice Heth frequently sang or chatted with members of the audience. Once, an elderly Baptist minister joined her in singing a hymn. When he went on to sing several little-known ones, she continued the duet with him, filling in lyrics when he forgot them. On another occasion, Grant Thorburn, a reporter for the *Evening Star,* caught her placidly puffing at a pipe and asked how long she had been a pipe-smoker. "One hundred and twenty years!" she replied spiritedly.

The press, enjoying her, publicized her lavishly. "Methuselah was 969 years old when he died," stated the *Daily Advertiser,* "but nothing is said of the age of his wife. . . . It is not unlikely that the sex in the olden time were like the daughters at the present day—unwilling to tell their age. Joice Heth is an exception; she comes out boldly, and says she is rising 160." And the *Spirit of the Times* remarked: "The dear old lady, after carrying on a desperate flirtation with Death, has finally jilted him." One optimistic physician was heard to admit that Joice Heth might quite possibly prove to be immortal.

For several months, observed the *Sun,* Joice Heth "created quite a sensation among the lovers of the curious and the marvellous." And for each week of these months, Barnum divided a gross of $1,500 with Niblo. It was more money than he had ever known before, and when business in Manhattan slackened, Barnum determined to take his exhibit on the road.

He presented Joice briefly to the people of Providence, and then, on the heels of a saturation campaign of posters and newspaper notices, moved into staid Boston. He unveiled Joice on her high lounge in the middle of the small ballroom at Concert Hall, and the original sensation was repeated. The proper Bostonians appeared in droves.

Competing with Barnum and Joice in Concert Hall was the even more renowned Johann Nepomuk Maelzel with his Terrible Turk, an automaton chess-player. Maelzel and his thinking-machine occupied the larger ballroom of the Hall, and they had been a popular attraction before the arrival of Barnum.

Immediately, perhaps apprehensively, Barnum attended his rival's show. Maelzel was a short, sixty-three-year-old inventor, mechanic, and musician who addressed his audience in a thick Teutonic accent. His robot, to which he had devoted the greater part of thirty-one years, was more impressive. Barnum has left no description of what next occurred, but Edgar Allan Poe, who saw the exhibit the same year, did. "At the hour appointed for exhibition, a curtain is withdrawn . . . and the machine rolled to within about twelve feet of the nearest of the spectators, between whom and it [the machine] a rope is stretched."

The automaton proved to be a larger-than-life-size Turkish gentleman, carved of wood, attired in plumed turban and flowing Oriental robe. He was seated on a backless chair behind a maple desk or chest three and a half feet wide, two feet four inches deep, and two and a half feet high. A chess board was built into the top of the desk.

Barnum watched closely as Maelzel unlocked the front of the chest and revealed a mass of wheels, levers, cylinders and other complicated machinery. Then, rolling the robot around, Maelzel opened the rear door, held a burning candle inside, and disclosed that this too was filled with machinery.

Next, Maelzel set the chess pieces on the board and invited a spectator to play against the machine. Then, as Maelzel turned a key in the hole at the left of the chest, the machinery noisily began to clank, grind, and whir. Slowly the Turk raised his left arm, moved it toward the chess piece he intended to play, grasped it with stiff fingers, placed it in the proper square, withdrew his arm, and rested it on a cushion. His perplexed human competitor made the next move, as the wooden Turk watched impassively. Then, amid much metallic noise, the automaton resumed. In half an hour the machine had conquered and the match was over.

Undoubtedly Barnum was awed, and perhaps he feared that Washington's nurse would not prove to be as great an attraction as this mysterious thinking-machine. He need not have worried on that score. For an automaton, even one that had defeated Napoleon, Catherine the Great, Frederick the Great, and Benjamin Franklin, could not compete with a creature alive 161 years. Every day thereafter Barnum's smaller ballroom was mobbed to the point of suffocation while Maelzel's larger ballroom was almost empty. At last, Barnum, who had by then become acquainted with his competitor, begged Maelzel to close down his exhibit temporarily (for a sum of money, no doubt) and turn the larger ballroom over to Joice Heth. Maelzel, surprisingly, agreed.

Maelzel, who had been Royal Mechanician to the Imperial Court at Schönbrunn for seven years, had a long record of successful entertainment promotions. Although erroneously credited with inventing the metronome, he had done some work on improving the instrument. In 1812 he had fascinated Beethoven with his musical automata and had actually talked the composer into creating a mediocre but popular symphony, *Wellington's Victory,* for the mechanical wind band that he advertised as the Panharmonicon. For all his accomplishments and experience, Maelzel was still enormously impressed by young Barnum's ability to obtain free publicity. "I see that you understand the press," he told Barnum, "and that is the great thing. Nothing helps the showmans [sic] like the types and the ink. When your old woman dies, you come to me, and I will make your fortune. I will let you have my carousel, my automaton trumpet-player and many curious things which will make plenty of money."

Barnum was grateful for the offer. He regarded Maelzel with respect and considered him "the great father of caterers for public amusement." During many afternoons while Levi Lyman held forth with Joice Heth in the large ballroom, Barnum sat at the master's feet and had "long conversations." He had read something of the incredible automaton chess-player's history and had seen Maelzel work with it, but now he wanted to know every colorful detail. Maelzel obliged. From Maelzel's story, Barnum would learn one great lesson, a lesson that would help him to make his fortune. He would learn the importance of using royalty and the upper classes to build up and exploit an exhibit for the masses. He would also learn from Maelzel the means by which he could make Joice Heth an even bigger success in Boston.

Maelzel confessed that he had not invented the automaton chess-player. This had been done by Baron Wolfgang von Kempelen, a hydraulic engineer who had been a counselor of the Royal Chamber of Hungary. The Baron had built his Turk in Vienna in 1769 for the amusement of the Empress Maria Theresa. He traveled widely with the machine. Once, in Berlin, the Turk received a challenge from Napoleon Bonaparte. Though Napoleon was a notoriously poor chess-player, he faced the Turk with confidence. According to the *Illustrated London News* of the period: "After some half-dozen moves, he [Napoleon] purposely made a false move, the figure inclined his head, replaced the piece, and made a sign for Napoleon to play again. Presently, he again played falsely; this time the Automaton removed the offending piece from the board, and played his own move. Napoleon was delighted, and to put the patience of his taciturn opponent to a severer test, he once more played incorrectly, upon which the Automaton raised his arm, and, sweeping the pieces from the board, declined to continue the game."

The Baron died in 1804, and the automaton was sold to one Anthon, who in turn sold it to Maelzel. In 1826, Maelzel brought the Turk to the United States. He was an immediate hit in New York. He was taken on tour as far west as Cincinnati. And in Baltimore, challenged by Charles Carroll of Carrollton, then eighty-nine and the last surviving signer of the Declaration of Independence, the automaton graciously saw fit to lose the match.

Invariably spectators, Barnum among them, would ask Maelzel: "Is the Automaton a pure machine or not?" And invariably, Maelzel would reply: "I will say nothing about it." Certainly Barnum was unable to learn the secret. There were rumors that Maelzel worked the machine with his feet, others that magnets were somehow employed, but not until two years after Barnum saw Maelzel was something closer to the truth revealed.

In 1837, a drunken chess expert in Paris, M. Mouret, sold a cheap French magazine an exposé of the Turk, and the exposé was reprinted in the *Washington Gazette*. Mouret said that the machinery was a camouflage, and that the Turk was secretly operated by a small man hidden inside the chest. He said that he himself had been one of those hired by Maelzel for this work. The man thus concealed "sat on a lower species of stool, moving on casters, and had every facility afforded him for changing and shifting his position like an eel. While one part of the machine was shown to the public, he took refuge in another. . . ."

In 1859, Robert Houdin, the celebrated magician, elaborated the exposé in his autobiography. During a rebellion in Riga in 1796, an officer named Worousky had tried to escape the Russians and "had both thighs shattered by a cannonball." A sympathetic doctor saved him by amputating his legs and then hiding him. During Worousky's convalescence, Baron von Kempelen paid a visit to the doctor. Fascinated by Worousky's genius at chess, the Baron conceived a means of smuggling the cripple to safety. Within three months, he had built the automaton and secreted the stunted Worousky inside it, thereafter employing him as the Turk's alter ego.

When Maelzel bought the machine and took it to America, Worousky remained behind. Edgar Allan Poe thought that Maelzel employed an Alsatian chess expert named William Schlumberger to the same purpose. "There is a man, *Schlumberger*, who attends him [Maelzel] wherever he goes, but who has no ostensible occupation other than that of assisting in packing and unpacking of the automaton. This man is about the medium size, and has a remarkable stoop in the shoulders. . . . Some years ago Maelzel visited Richmond with his automata . . . *Schlumberger* was suddenly taken ill, and during his illness there was no exhibition of the Chess-Player."

Three years after meeting Barnum, Maelzel took Schlumberger to Havana on a vacation. There Schlumberger died of yellow fever. Returning by boat to the States, Maelzel tried to drown his grief in wine, and himself died in his cabin. The Turk wound up in Philadelphia's Chinese Museum, where it was destroyed in the fire of 1854.

The considerable time that Barnum spent with Maelzel in Boston proved to have been more than mere diversion: he was able to turn it to profit. After several weeks, Joice Heth had begun to lose her appeal, and the crowds had started to thin. Listening to Maelzel, and contemplating his Turk, Barnum was struck with an idea. Why not announce that Joice Heth was also an automaton and start the excitement all over again?

Soon, there appeared in the Boston press an open letter signed "A Visitor." It said in part: "Joice Heth is not a human being. What purports to be a remarkably old woman is simply a curiously constructed automaton, made up of whalebone, india-rubber, and numberless springs ingeniously put together, and made to move at the slightest touch, according to the will of the operator. The exhibitor is a ventriloquist, and all the conversations apparently held with the ancient lady are purely imaginary, so far as she is concerned. . . ."

Curiosity was again piqued. At once those who had already seen Joice Heth were determined to have another look, and those who had not seen her were excited to view a contrivance more unusual than the Turk. Barnum's business boomed, and there was no Niblo to share the gross this time.

After Boston, Barnum and Lyman, with Joice Heth in tow, toured New England from Hingham to Hartford, then returned to Niblo's Garden for a second engagement, then went on to New Haven, Newark, and Albany. Joice was shown at the Museum in Albany, where other exhibits were appearing simultaneously. One of these, an Italian immigrant who spun plates, walked on stilts, and balanced bayoneted rifles on his nose, caught Barnum's attention. The Italian billed himself as Signor Antonio. Barnum sought him out, learned that he was available and unbooked, and promptly signed him to a year's contract, guaranteeing him twelve dollars a week, board, and travel fare.

Returning to New York, Barnum bullied the Italian into taking his first bath in a year, then changed his name to Signor Vivalla, and prepared to sell him. Barnum cornered William Dinneford, manager of the Franklin Theater, and expounded in detail on Vivalla's feats. Dinneford was not interested. Barnum persisted. "You have no doubt seen strange things in your life, but, my dear sir, I should never have imported Signor Vivalla from Italy, unless I had authentic evidence that he was the only artist of the kind who ever left the country. . . . You shall have him one night for nothing." Dinneford succumbed.

For three days Barnum publicized his unique foreign find, and on the opening night the Franklin Theater was packed. Barnum appeared on the stage as Vivalla's assistant, arranging his plates, handing him his muskets, and catching his stilts. The act was greeted with smashing applause. Vivalla was engaged for two weeks and Barnum collected fifty dollars a night.

In January 1836, encouraged by the success of his record venture, Barnum left Joice Heth to the management of Levi Lyman, and himself proceeded to snowbound Washington, D.C., with his juggler. Renting an obscure theater at fifty dollars a night, Barnum was dismayed to learn that his first night's gross was no more than thirty dollars. While Signor Vivalla continued to regale empty seats, Barnum racked his brain for another attraction. And suddenly he remembered one near at hand. He went to call on Anne Royall, one of the most notorious women in all America.

Anne Royall, born in Maryland in 1769, had been raised in the wilderness of the Pennsylvania frontier. After her father fell under an Indian's tomahawk and her stepfather died, she accompanied her mother to the Virginia estate of wealthy Captain William Royall, there to work with her mother as a common domestic. After twelve years, the eccentric Captain Royall married Anne, tutored her, and bequeathed her his fortune. In a legal battle with relatives over the estate, Anne could not prove the validity of her marriage, and was left destitute. She journeyed to Washington to claim Royall's Revolutionary War pension. She began to write travel books. She did publicity for the Masons. She indicted the seamier side of American life and berated politicians in *The Black Book,* a three-volume commentary on the national scene. Embroiled in a feud with Evangelicals, she was arrested as "a common scold," found guilty, sentenced to the ducking stool, and then let off with a fine. At sixty-three, five years before Barnum saw her, she had initiated a weekly scandal sheet called *Paul Pry,* and had managed to corner President John Quincy Adams for an interview while he was swimming in the nude in the Potomac River.

Barnum found her, wrinkled, toothy, dumpy, at her decrepit Ramage printing press. Before he could discuss business, Anne Royall asked him for whom he intended to vote in the impending Presidential election.

"Well, I believe I shall go for Matty," Barnum replied, referring to Martin Van Buren.

Barnum would never forget what happened next. "I have seen some fearful things in my day," he recorded, "some awful explosions of tempestuous passion; but never have I witnessed such another terrible tempest of fury as burst from Mrs. Anne Royall, in reply to my response. . . . 'My God! my God! is it possible? Will you support such a monkey, such a scoundrel, such a villain, such a knave, such an enemy to his country, as Martin Van Buren! Barnum, you are a scoundrel, a traitor, a rascal, a hypocrite! You are a spy, an electioneering fool, and I hope the next vessel you put foot on will sink with you.' "

After a half-hour, Anne calmed down, and Barnum meekly joined her on the floor in wrapping papers to be mailed. Eventually he presented his proposition. "I tried to hire her to give a dozen or twenty public lectures upon Government, in the Atlantic cities; but she was not to be tempted by pecuniary reward, and I was obliged to give over that speculation, which, by the way, I am certain would have proved a profitable one."

Reluctantly, Barnum resumed with Signor Vivalla. The Washington stand proved a complete failure, and Barnum had to pawn watch and chain to reach Philadelphia. The receipts at the Walnut Street Theater were better, but still Barnum was dissatisfied. On the second night, studying the scattered attendance and absently watching Vivalla go through his repertoire on the boards, Barnum received the saving inspiration. "It was evident that something must be done to stimulate the public. And now that instinct—I think it must be—which can arouse a community and make it patronize, provided the article offered is worthy of patronage —an instinct which served me strangely in later years, astonishing the public and surprising me, came to my relief, and the help, curiously enough, appeared in the shape of an emphatic hiss from the pit!"

Vivalla, who had never been hissed before, was incensed. Barnum searched for the heckler, found him, and tried to silence him. The heckler turned out to be a circus juggler

named Roberts, who insisted loudly that Vivalla's act was
of mediocre quality and that he could do anything the Italian could do, and perhaps do it better. An armistice was
finally reached, and Vivalla completed his act, but Barnum's performance was just beginning. Excited, he made
the rounds of Philadelphia's daily newspapers, inserting
advertisements offering $1,000 to any person who could
publicly match Signor Vivalla's feats.

As Barnum foresaw, Roberts came forward to accept the
challenge. Barnum produced the $1,000, which he had bor-
rowed from a friend, but first he insisted that Roberts sign
an agreement—to be published—that he would forfeit the
sum if he could not duplicate *every single one* of Vivalla's
feats. Roberts balked. Now it appeared that he could perform most of Vivalla's tricks, and even some few unknown
to Vivalla, but could not duplicate every one of them, being
inexperienced with stilts and plate-balancing. Barnum insisted that it would have to be all or nothing. Angrily, Roberts insulted him. Barnum took it calmly, pocketed the
$1,000, and offered a new proposition. He would give Rob-
erts thirty dollars to pretend that he was challenging Vivalla
to a juggling duel. It would be rehearsed and stage-managed
by Barnum, though no one was to know this, and Vivalla
would of course emerge the winner. Roberts readily agreed.

Barnum quickly secured the Walnut Street Theater at
the cost of two thirds of the gross receipts. Then, feverishly, he wrote and distributed handbills and advertisements, announcing the juggling duel for the prize of $1,000.
The night of the grudge contest the theater was jammed to
the rafters. Vivalla had drawn receipts of seventy-five dollars the evening of the historic hiss; this night the receipts
added up to $593.

"The contest was a very interesting one," Barnum remembered with relish. "Roberts of course was to be beaten,
and it was agreed that Vivalla should at first perform his
easiest feats, in order that the battle should be kept up as
long as possible. Roberts successively performed the same
feats that Vivalla did. Each party was continually cheered
by his friends and hissed by his opponents. . . . The contest lasted about forty minutes, when Roberts came forward
and acknowledged himself defeated. He was obliged to
give up on the feat of spinning two plates at once, one in
each hand."

Thunderous applause and bravos ensued, and then Barnum had an idea to prolong the feud. He appeared before the curtain to reveal that Roberts, who had been handicapped by a sprained wrist, was challenging Vivalla again. The duel would resume the following week, same place, same prices.

After the return performance, once more won by Vivalla before a filled theater, the combatants were transported to New York by Barnum, where they continued their feud on the stage of the Franklin Theater, and then, for a month more, in neighboring villages.

By this time, Barnum had not two acts, but one: Joice Heth had fallen ill and had been retired to an alcove of his half-brother Philo's home in Bethel, Connecticut. Fully appreciative of the garrulous ancient who had given him a vocation, Barnum supported her and paid for a colored woman to look after her.

On February 21, 1836, Barnum received word from his half-brother that Joice Heth was no more. She had died two days earlier, and her remains were now outside, having been delivered by sleigh over snow-packed roads to the very door of Barnum's boarding house. While making preparations to bury her, Barnum remembered that he had once promised a famous surgeon, Dr. David L. Rogers, permission to perform a post-mortem examination of Joice. Barnum now kept his word.

The following day the corpse of Washington's nurse was transported to the medical hall on Barclay Street where Dr. Rogers and "a large number of physicians, students, and several clergymen and editors" waited. Among the editors was the well-known, British-born Richard Adams Locke, a Cambridge graduate, who had been assigned to the story by Benjamin H. Day, founder and publisher of the *New York Sun*. The thirty-six-year-old Locke, though uncommonly short of stature and possessing a face pitted by smallpox, was an impressive man. "There is an air of distinction about his whole person," Poe observed, "the *air noble* of genius." Along with Locke and the others, Barnum and Levi Lyman were on hand to watch as Dr. Rogers proceeded to dissect Joice's anatomy. When the surgery was completed, Dr. Rogers seemed surprised and disturbed. What surprised him was the absence of ossification of the arteries in the region of the heart.

After the spectators had been dismissed, Dr. Rogers, with his close friend Locke, remained behind to discuss the autopsy with Barnum and Lyman. The surgeon had something on his mind, and now he spoke openly of it to Barnum. He said that "there was surely some mistake in regard to the alleged age of Joice; that instead of being 161 years old, she was probably not over eighty."

Barnum was astounded, or so he always insisted. "I stated to him, in reply, what was strictly true, that I had hired Joice in perfect good faith, and relied upon her appearance and the documents as evidence of the truth of her story." He reminded Dr. Rogers that the doctor himself had been impressed by the first exhibition at Niblo's Garden. Dr. Rogers was adamant. Though her appearance had fooled everyone, himself included, his scalpel had revealed the truth. He told Barnum that "the documents must either have been forged, or else they applied to some other individual."

If Barnum hoped that the hoax would not be made public, his hopes were shattered the following day. Prominently displayed in the *New York Sun* was an editorial by Richard Adams Locke:

"DISSECTION OF JOICE HETH—PREVIOUS HUMBUG EXPOSED. The anatomical examination of the body of Joice Heth yesterday, resulted in the exposure of one of the most precious humbugs that ever was imposed upon a credulous community."

The editorial went on to disclose every detail of the postmortem, and soon all of New York was buzzing about the deceit. Even Philip Hone, the retired onetime Mayor of the city, saw fit to record in his diary the scandal of a "black woman named Joice Heth" upon whom "our inquisitive unbelieving doctors, who have had the impertinence all along to doubt the facts in this case of longevity" had performed an autopsy that "resulted in a conviction that she could not have been more than 75 or 80 years old."

Instead of allowing the scandal to die, Levi Lyman, who possessed a warped funnybone, decided to play a joke on James Gordon Bennett, the cross-eyed Scot who was publisher of the sensational *New York Herald,* as well as to strike back at Locke and the *Sun.* Lyman advised Bennett that he and Barnum had merely played a practical joke on Locke and Dr. Rogers, that Joice Heth was still alive in

Connecticut, and that the corpse dissected was that of an obscure old Negress who had recently died in Harlem.

With great excitement, Bennett featured the revelation in the *Herald* of February 27, 1836, beneath the headline "ANOTHER HOAX!" Bennett assured his readers: *"Joice Heth is not dead.* On Wednesday last, as we learn from the best authority, she was living at Hebron, in Connecticut, where she then was. The subject on which Doctor Rogers and the Medical Faculty of Barclay street have been exercising their knife and their ingenuity, is the remains of a respectable old Negress called Aunt Nelly. . . ."

Locke defended his original story, and though Bennett fought back, he realized at last that he had been duped. When he met Lyman in the street, he castigated him. Lyman apologized for "a harmless joke" and, to make up for it, promised to reveal the true story of Joice Heth, which had never before been published. He accompanied Bennett to his office and dictated the "facts." He said that Barnum had found Joice in Kentucky, extracted all her teeth to make her look older, and taught her the entire Washington's-nurse fable. Once again, Bennett went to bold-faced type, announcing: "THE JOICE HETH HOAX!" He called Barnum's fraud "a stupendous hoax, illustrative of the accuracy of medical science, the skill of medical men, and the general good-nature and credulity of the public."

Barnum admitted the existence of a hoax, but argued that he had been fooled as much as the public, and vehemently denied Bennett's story. Nevertheless, the public appeared to accept it, and, forever after, it was thought that Barnum had purposely rigged the whole absurd exhibit. Almost a decade later the memory lingered on sufficiently so that *Tait's Edinburgh Magazine* would rank Barnum "among the swindlers, blacklegs, blackguards, pickpockets and thimble-riggers of his day" and add: "Compared to Barnum, Cagliostro himself was a blundering novice, or perhaps it would be more just to say that he had the misfortune to be endowed with a more tender conscience. More than any other impostor Barnum has humbugged the world. . . ."

Barnum continued to deny any part in the Joice Heth fake for the rest of his life. It was, he said, "a scheme in no sense of my own devising; one which had been some time before the public and which had so many vouchers for its genuineness that at the time of taking possession of it I honestly believed it to be genuine. . . ." Furthermore, Barnum asked himself, "if Joice Heth was an impostor, who taught her these things? and how happened it that she was so familiar, not only with ancient psalmody, but also with the minute details of the Washington family? To all this, I unhesitatingly answer, *I do not know*. I taught her none of these things. She was perfectly familiar with them all before I ever saw her. . . ."

Privately, Barnum believed that R. W. Lindsay had swindled him in Philadelphia, but he never bore Lindsay any malice. In fact, when he learned that Lindsay had fallen ill and was impoverished, he forwarded a gift of one hundred dollars to the unfortunate man.

It is surprising that there was so much indignation at the time and later over the Joice Heth hoax. Elaborate frauds were nothing new to New York or America. In an age of blue laws the harmless hoax was a safety valve and a means of amusement for the public. Only eleven years before Joice Heth, New Yorkers (at least most of them) had been delighted (for it had cost them nothing) by an amateur hoax of gigantic proportions. In the summer of 1824, two retired businessmen, Lozier and John DeVoe, having nothing better to do, announced to friends that they had been hired to saw off Manhattan Island and turn it around.

The preposterous project might have been laughed out of existence had not Lozier, speaking with the authority of considerable wealth, convinced laborers, contractors, and tradesmen that he had the support of Mayor Stephen Allen. According to Lozier, he and the Mayor had agreed that Manhattan Island was beginning to sag on the Battery or southern end, because of the weight of new business buildings. The situation was dangerous. They had decided to saw off the Island at the Kingsbridge, or northern, end, then float it down past Ellis Island, turn it around, bring it back, and moor it in a more sensible position.

DeVoe appeared with an impressive ledger and began signing on workmen and awarding contracts. During the next eight weeks the pixy pair located a quantity of mammoth saws one hundred feet long with teeth three feet deep, hired three hundred laborers to do the sawing, then found two dozen oars two hundred and fifty feet long, and hired two thousand men to row the Island across the bay. Giant anchors were available to keep the Island firm in the event of a storm. When the carpentry was to begin on the appointed date, nearly a thousand persons, with tools, assembled at Bowery and Spring streets—almost everyone was present except Lozier and DeVoe, who had left town. It would be a long while before they would return or the laughter subside. Manhattan Island remained sagging but intact.

A more admirable and far-reaching hoax, much enjoyed by Barnum at the very time he was first exhibiting Joice Heth and proclaiming her authentic, was perpetrated by Richard Adams Locke, the very man who later would expose Joice in the *New York Sun.*

In August 1835, the *Sun,* then a stripling journal of four sheets, began an exclusive series of four articles headlined: "Great Astronomical Discoveries Lately Made by Sir John Herschel at the Cape of Good Hope." This series, written by Locke, excited New York and America for two months. It disclosed that Sir John Herschel had invented a seven-ton telescope, with a lens twenty-four feet in diameter, capable of magnifying an object forty-two thousand times, so greatly that flora and fauna on the moon seemed to be only five miles from the earth. Sir John, assisted by Sir David Brewster, secretly had transported the telescope to Africa, and, eight months earlier, had seen lunar life as no human had seen it before.

The pair minutely observed fourteen species of animal life on the moon. There were "herds of brown quadrupeds, having all the external characteristics of the bison," with hairy flaps over their eyes to protect them from extreme light; there were "gregarious" monsters, blue and swift, "the size of a goat, with a head and beard like him, and a *single horn*"; there were pelicans, cranes, bears, and "a strange amphibious creature of a spherical form, which rolled with great velocity across the pebbly beach." All of these cavorted over pyramid-shaped mountains of amethyst, among thirty-eight species of trees, or near a lake two hundred and sixty-six miles long.

But the biggest sensation was saved for the final article. Sir John Herschel had seen "four successive flocks of large winged creatures," and later observed them "walking erect toward a small wood." Adjusting his lens so that these creatures were brought but eighty yards from his eyes, he saw them clearly at last. "They averaged four feet in height, were covered, except on the face, with short and glossy copper-colored hair, and had wings composed of a thin membrane, without hair, lying snugly upon their backs, from the top of the shoulders to the calves of the legs. The face, which was of a yellowish flesh-color, was a slight improvement upon that of the large orang-utan. . . ."

These articles were so rich in detail and scientific terminology that the greater part of the public and press swallowed them whole. *The New York Times* thought the articles "probable and plausible," and felt they displayed "the most extensive and accurate knowledge of astronomy." The *New Yorker* regarded the discoveries as "of astounding interest, creating a new era in astronomy and science generally." The *Daily Advertiser* considered the series one of the most important in years. "Sir John has added a stock of knowledge to the present age that will immortalize his name and place it high on the page of science."

Locke was gratified. The daily circulation of the *Sun,* Day's penny newspaper, had been twenty-five hundred. With the report of winged men four feet tall on the moon, circulation climbed to nineteen thousand. And some of these readers, notably a club of women in Springfield, Massachusetts, were stimulated to raise funds for sending missionaries to the lunar planet. In pamphlet form the series of articles sold sixty thousand copies in a month, enriching Locke and Day by some $25,000.

There were a few skeptics. Philip Hone noted in his diary: "In sober truth, if this account is true, it is most enormously wonderful, and if it is a fable, the manner of its relation, with all of its scientific details . . . will give this ingenious history a place with 'Gulliver's Travels' and 'Robinson Crusoe.' " Edgar Allan Poe, aware that no telescope could reveal such detail even at a visual distance of eighty yards, let alone five miles, branded the articles as fiction. He confessed that he found few listeners, "so really eager were all to be deceived, so magical were the charms of a style that served as the vehicle of an exceedingly clumsy invention. Not one person in ten discredited it."

When Locke at last confessed the fraud to a fellow newspaperman on the *Journal of Commerce,* which exposed him, and when Sir John Herschel, informed of Locke's stories, laughingly denied the discoveries, the truth was out, and the "Moon Hoax" was relegated to the history of entertainment rather than that of science. Locke's motive, it turned out, had been more aesthetic than commercial. Bored with the speculations and popularity of Dr. Thomas Dick of Scotland, an astronomer whose books (advocating communication with the moon through use of giant stone symbols arranged on earth) were the rage in American society, Locke had intended to ridicule Dick's pompous pronouncements. Apparently his satire had got out of hand.

Yet, only ten months after his own hoax, Locke had exposed Barnum's first venture in the field of amusement. Shortly after this, Locke left the *Sun* to start a periodical of his own, the *New Era.* Later he became editor of the Brooklyn *Eagle,* and finally a customhouse official. But in the end, his disclosure of the bogusness of Joice Heth did not matter. Barnum gradually came to be more admired than resented, for the people desperately needed what he had to offer.

Other isolated purveyors of pleasure operated at the time as they had before, of course, but their talents were limited and minor and made little impression on their era or on the future. They were not movers, not shakers, not Arthur O'Shaughnessy's "dreamers of dreams." Barnum was. With him, indeed, the age of showmanship and fun had its beginning. More than that, with the Joice Heth fraud, the first great showman in history, perhaps the greatest, was born.

EXHIBIT TWO
Ivy Island

Barnum always regretted that he had not made his appearance on the Fourth of July. He missed it by one day. He was born on July 5, 1810, in Bethel, Connecticut, a few miles outside Danbury, and was christened Phineas Taylor Barnum after his maternal grandfather. Phineas was a Biblical name meaning "brazen mouth."

His father, Philo Barnum, had ten children by two wives in the course of his short life, and Phineas Taylor Barnum was the sixth child and the first by the second wife. Barnum's father was, variously, farmer, tailor, tavernkeeper, and grocer, but his religious mother, Irene, remains a strange shadow creature in all of Barnum's later vast reminiscences, possibly by intent. His paternal grandfather was Captain Ephraim Barnum, a militiaman in the then-recent Revolutionary War.

But the one branch of Barnum's family tree that weighed heavier than the rest and hung happiest over the years of his growth was the branch that bore his maternal grandfather, Phineas Taylor, a mop-headed, bespectacled, boisterous figure who might have been created by Thackeray. The old man adored his grandson, devoting half his waking hours and all his lump sugar to the boy, and Barnum worshipped the old man. "My grandfather," Barnum always remembered, "would go farther, wait longer, work harder, and contrive deeper, to carry out a practical joke, than for anything else under heaven."

Much like the hoax in New York, the practical joke in America, and especially in New England, was a weapon of self-survival, one of the few socially permissible forms of fun. Old Grandfather Taylor was a genius at the sport, and this image of him would forever remain in Barnum's memory.

At the time of Barnum's birth and in the years of his growth, Bethel was a tight little prison of Puritanism, not unlike a thousand villages of the new America, but probably more strict. Bethel subsisted on the manufacture of combs and hats, about three hundred persons being employed in those industries. There were fewer than fifty residences in the village proper.

The Congregational Church dominated the community. Arrest by a deacon, with subsequent fine or imprisonment, awaited the man found riding his carriage or horse on a Sunday. Forty lashes were meted out to a blasphemer. All lived under what has been called "the awful shadow of the Calvinistic doom." According to Harvey W. Root: "Amusement of any sort was considered sinful, anything of the nature of a show or the theater rigorously forbidden by law, and even those found playing a social game of cards were arrested and fined." Barnum's mother conformed to this medievalism, and Barnum was raised, he recalled, "in the fear of hell, and when I went to . . . prayer meetings, at the age of thirteen or fourteen, I used to go home and pray and cry and beg God to take me out of existence if He would only save me."

Grandfather Taylor was the rare dissenter, and it was he who saved Barnum so that his grandson in turn might save America from acute solemnity. Not only was Taylor in revolt against the established church, subscribing to the more liberal Universalism, but he also led his cronies in the only legal amusement available to them: the practical joke.

The most memorable of Taylor's stunts occurred during a routine voyage from Norwalk to New York. The sloop was becalmed for five days, and most of the passengers, among them a tall, blue-nosed clergyman with reddish whiskers, had not brought razors for what they had expected would be an eight-hour journey. All were sorely in need of a shave, and as they approached New York, they resembled a pack of hairy barbarians. Taylor alone had a razor. At least a dozen of his companions asked to borrow it.

"Now, gentlemen, I will be fair with you," Taylor said. "It is evident we cannot all have time to be shaved with one razor before we reach New York, and as it would be hard for half of us to walk on shore with clean faces, and leave the rest on board waiting for their turn to shave themselves, I have hit upon a plan which I am sure you will all say is just and equitable."

"What is it?" he was asked.

"It is that each man shall shave one half of his face, and pass the razor over to the next, and when we are all half shaved we shall go on in rotation and shave the other half."

With the exception of the clergyman, all the passengers agreed to the method. Taylor was insistent, however, and the clergyman, too, was forced to agree. The operation began at once. In ten minutes one side of Taylor's "face and chin, in a straight line from the middle of his nose, was shaved as close as the back of his hand, while the other looked like a thick brush fence in a country swamp." The razor went next to the clergyman and did its work. "The left side of his face was as naked as that of an infant, while from the other cheek four inches of a huge red whisker stood out in powerful contrast. Nothing more ludicrous could well be conceived." Soon all members of the group had shaved half their faces. Taylor suggested that they have a round of drinks on deck before completing the task. All hands agreed. At the height of conviviality, Taylor excused himself. "I will go into the cabin and shave off the other side," he explained. "As soon as I have finished I will come up and give the clergyman the next chance."

In ten minutes, smoothly shaved, Taylor returned with the razor and strop. The clergyman, with the others in line behind him, waited for it. Taylor insisted on sharpening the blade first. Propping his foot on the rail, he began to run the razor over the strop. Suddenly, the razor flew from his hand and plunged into the water below. "Good

heavens!" exclaimed Taylor, "the razor has fallen overboard!"

Shortly thereafter, when the sloop docked, the miserable
tribe of passengers, each half bearded, half shaved, like
monsters from another planet, reluctantly trooped into the
gaping city. The clergyman wrapped a handkerchief around
his face and hurried off in search of succor. And Phineas
Taylor split his sides laughing at the result of his planned
joke, delighted in the knowledge that he would have a
hilarious conversation piece for months to come.

Barnum respected this necessary nonsense, and throughout his life tried to emulate his grandparent. Putting one
over on people when it did no harm and added to merriment was part of what gave life its zest, he believed. Not
everyone, however, would agree to the value of this philosophy. In 1855, reviewing the showman's autobiography,
Tait's Edinburgh Magazine acidly remarked: "Barnum was
nurtured in a bad school. Practical joking, which for the
most part is your practical blackguard's rendering of hu-
mour, and the elements of which are lies acted instead of
spoken—and, in which no man of taste, education or common sense is ever fond of indulging—were the favorite
amusement of his sire and grandsire and their families."
This judgment was, perhaps, more righteous and stuffy than
correct. In the context of his time, Barnum's use of the
practical joke, of hoax and humbuggery, was excusable, for
it was desired and necessary, and it relieved the boredom
and tensions of a nation.

One practical joke was crucial to Barnum's future. It
would not only affect his character, but also in a practical
sense assist his entry into show business. It was begun
shortly after his birth and perpetrated by his grandfather.
In some way, it would seem, this joke came to symbolize
the entire manner of his upbringing.

When Barnum was christened, his grandfather Taylor
presented him with the gift of a deed for five acres of land
in the parish of Bethel. The tract was popularly known as
Ivy Island. From the time Barnum was four until he was
ten, he was continually reminded that he was a landowner.
"My grandfather always spoke of me (in my presence) to
the neighbors and to strangers as the richest child in town,
since I owned the whole of 'Ivy Island,' one of the most
valuable farms in the State. My father and mother fre-

quently reminded me of my wealth and hoped I would do something for the family when I attained my majority. The neighbors professed to fear that I might refuse to play with their children because I had inherited so large a property." Magnanimously, young Barnum assured one and all that his wealth would not go to his head. In his waking dreams, Barnum conjured up visions of himself as potentate of Ivy Island, ruler of a realm and rich beyond all fancy.

In the summer of 1820, when he was ten years old, Barnum begged his father for permission to see Ivy Island, and his wish was granted. For three sleepless nights, awaiting the expedition, Barnum dreamed of "the promised land . . . a land flowing with milk and honey . . . caverns of emeralds, diamonds, and other precious stones, as well as mines of silver and gold."

Accompanying his father and a hired hand, Barnum trudged the distance to Ivy Island. As they approached, he could hardly contain himself. He kept inquiring as to its location. "Yonder," said his father, pointing, "at the north end of this meadow, where you see those beautiful trees rising in the distance."

Rushing across muddy swamps and creeks, through brambles and past hornets' nests, Barnum at last reached the center of his precious domain. It was hot and soggy, at the end of the world. He stood incredulous. "I saw nothing but a few stunted ivies and straggling trees. The truth flashed upon me. I had been the laughing-stock of the family and neighborhood for years. My valuable 'Ivy Island' was an almost inaccessible, worthless bit of barren land. . . ."

The hired hand and Barnum's father roared with laughter, and later, when Barnum returned home, his grandfather gravely congratulated him. Barnum never went back to his domain again. One day Ivy Island would be "a part of the weight that made the wheel of fortune begin to turn in my favor at a time when my head was downward," but now, to the ten-year-old boy, it was a disaster and a humiliation. It was the most protracted practical joke Grandfather Taylor ever staged, and it was the one longest remembered by Barnum.

Van Wyck Brooks analyzed the far-reaching consequences of this episode in *Sketches in Criticism:*
"One seldom hears of a grandfather outwitting an infant

in arms, of a mother conspiring to jeer at her offspring, of a whole family, in fact, inviting the village to make game of its youngest and most helpless member. And when one considers the notorious effect that such experiences in childhood have upon the afterlife of the victim, one cannot fail to draw certain deductions. . . . One is led to suggest, first, that the force of Barnum's dominating motive, to fool others, bore some relation to the degree in which, as a child, he had been fooled himself. And secondly, that the motive of his family, far from being, as one might suppose, consciously malevolent, was to give him such a lesson that he himself would not be fooled again. . . . Barnum had had his education, even if it remained imperfect, and he passed it on. Each time he fooled the public, he was putting the public on its mettle; he sharpened the instincts through which a commercial regime is carried on."

This was the best part of his schooling. He was engaged in the lesser or formal part until what today is known as high school. He was in the upper portion of his class, and he excelled in mathematics. And always, from early childhood on, he worked, usually assisting his then farmer father in the fields. He despised physical labor. "Head-work I was excessively fond of. I was always ready to concoct fun, or lay plans for money-making, but hand-work was decidedly not in my line."

With his first employment, young Barnum had a chance to apply "head-work." In despair over his own agricultural shortcomings, Philo Barnum had, with a partner, built and opened a general store that sold and bartered groceries, hardware, and dry goods. Barnum was installed as chief clerk. Yankee bargaining, in which Barnum was most proficient, was sharp on both sides of the counter.

Barnum liked best to illustrate the morality of business in those days with a story he had often heard and as often repeated.

The story concerned the proprietor of a village grocery store, who was also the town's deacon. Once, before breakfast, he shouted downstairs to his clerk: "John, have you watered the rum?"

"Yes, sir."

"And sanded the sugar?"

"Yes, sir."

"And dusted the pepper?"

"Yes, sir."

"And chicoried the coffee?"

"Yes, sir."

"Then come up to prayers."

When Barnum was fifteen, his father, only forty-eight, died. After the business was liquidated and cash assets balanced against debts, it was found that the Barnum family was bankrupt. There were six children in the house, and Phineas, the eldest, became his family's sole support.

With his experience at clerking, Barnum soon found a job in a general store located in Grassy Plain, a settlement a mile outside Bethel. Quickly enough he asserted himself. A peddler came calling with a wagonload of ordinary green bottles. Barnum traded him unsalable goods, marked at high prices, for the lot.

Barnum's employer was not amused. "You have made a fool of yourself, for you have bottles enough to supply the whole town for twenty years."

Barnum promised to get rid of the lot within three months.

"If you can do that, you can perform a miracle."

Barnum prepared to perform his miracle. Recalling that his grandfather had been manager of a church lottery, and aware that lotteries were still legal, Barnum set out to stage one. A thousand tickets were offered at fifty cents each. Five hundred and fifty prizes were promised, and these ranged from twenty-five dollars to five dollars in goods, to be selected by the store's management.

"The tickets went like wildfire," Barnum said. "Customers did not stop to consider the nature of the prizes. Journeyman hatters, boss hatters, apprentice boys, and hat-trimming girls bought tickets. In ten days they were all sold."

The drawing was held. One of every two tickets was a winner. The victorious customers crowded the store for their prizes of merchandise—and went away with green bottles. "Some of the customers were vexed," Barnum admitted, "but most of them laughed at the joke." And, miracle of miracles, in less than two weeks there were no more green bottles.

Barnum obviously was meant for better things and wider horizons. Having turned sixteen, he removed himself to Brooklyn to clerk in a more cosmopolitan grocery store and spend his spare time promenading down Manhattan's fashionable Broadway between the rows of stately poplar trees, past the magnificent hotels and restaurants, constantly wondering how he might become a part of all this. So well did he acquit himself in Brooklyn that his grandfather offered to establish him in a business of his own if he would return to Bethel. Barnum leaped at the opportunity.

He converted half of his grandfather's carriage house into a fruit and confectionary shop. Also handy, as a happy convenience, was a barrel of ale. In May 1828, he threw open his doors on Military Training Day, during which the militia performed on the green, and soon the ale was gone, and much of the goods, and he had made back almost his entire investment. Encouraged, he imported "pocket-books, combs, beads, cheap finger-rings, pocket-knives, and a few toys" from New York, then added stewed oysters, and took on a lottery agency for a commission of ten per cent.

During these days Barnum had his first vision of his future. Hackaliah Bailey became a customer of his store, and Bailey was one of America's pioneer showmen.

Until then Barnum had had no contact with the sinful world of entertainment. True, once several years before, he had revealed the instincts of a showman. A neighbor just returned from a visit to Litchfield County had dropped into Barnum's store. Barnum wondered what was new in that far place, and the neighbor said that he had seen something curious. "I saw a dog of ordinary size which had two natural tails, one about three feet long." Barnum seized excitedly upon this at once. Here was a perfect exhibit. Was it for sale? "Why, yes, I guess five or ten dollars would buy him." Barnum pressed his neighbor to take him to Litchfield and show him the remarkable dog. The neighbor advised him to go alone. Barnum was mounting to leave, when the neighbor remembered something. "I forgot to mention that the dog with two tails was coming out of a tanyard, and one of the tails was a cow's tail which he carried in his mouth." Barnum sheepishly dismounted amid laughter, but he had disclosed the showman's instinct.

Hackaliah Bailey, on the other hand, was the real thing. No relation to the later Bailey, who was to be Barnum's

partner, Hackaliah Bailey laid the groundwork for the
modern circus with his small traveling menageries. When
Barnum was a boy of five, Bailey was making his mark
with Old Bet, the second elephant ever seen in the United
States. Bailey's brother, a ship's captain, had purchased
Old Bet in London for twenty dollars. Bailey paid his
brother $1,000 for the pachyderm, and became financially
secure by exhibiting her. He and Old Bet would travel only
by night, so that no one would see her without paying the
price of admission. For a dozen years he exhibited Old Bet
at ten cents a head, though sometimes accepting a two-
gallon jug of rum as entry fee for an entire family.

During his latter years with Old Bet, Bailey took on a
partner named Nathan Howes. He sent Howes on the road
with the elephant and waited for his half of the profits.
After many weeks, not a penny had been forthcoming.
When Howes did not reply to his inquiries, Bailey set out
after him and caught up with him in New Bedford, Massachusetts. Bailey demanded his portion of the profits. Howes
claimed that there were no profits.

Bailey, observing the large crowds at the exhibition, was
understandably suspicious. "You shall not travel any longer
in charge of this elephant as long as I own any interest in
him," he told his partner.

"I would like to see you prevent it," replied Howes. "Our
written contract stipulates that I am to have charge of the
elephant, and next fall we are to settle up."

"But it also stipulates that you are to remit to me one
half of the profits as fast as they accrue."

Howes repeated that there were no profits. Bailey told
his partner that he wanted to buy him out. Howes declined.
Bailey then said that he would like to sell out. Howes was
not interested. Bailey warned Howes that he must not
travel another mile with the elephant. Howes defied him.
Bailey threatened to do something about it. Howes told him
to do whatever he pleased.

The following dawn, Howes went to the barn, prepared
to remove Old Bet to the next village. Bailey was waiting
beside the elephant with loaded musket. He lifted the
musket to his shoulder and pointed it at Old Bet.

"Hey!" Howes shouted. "That's half my elephant!"

"I'm only aiming at my half," Bailey said.

Howes quickly paid up half the profits, and the troupe

moved on. In July 1816, Old Bet was being shown in Alfred, Maine. After her exhibit, a farmer attacked her and shot her to death. The murderer's motivation was never clarified. Either he was a fanatical member of a religious sect and mistook Old Bet for the terrible behemoth of the Bible, or, as Dr. William Bentley noted in his diary, "the poor Elephant was destroyed in Maine, because he took money from those who could not afford to spend it." Bailey buried Old Bet in Somers, New York, near the fine Georgian Hotel that he had opened and called "Elephant Hotel." Before the hotel entrance stood a stone pillar with a gold-lacquered wooden replica of Old Bet atop it.

Next to his grandfather, the growing Barnum idolized Hackaliah Bailey—or "Hack," as he came to call him—more than any other man. These were the human heroes he held before him when, later, he groped toward the profession of showman.

Barnum's little store in Bethel was so successful that he was able, for the first time, to turn his thoughts to matters less commercial. He had fallen in love at sixteen. He was working in Grassy Plain at the time, and boarding with Mrs. Jerusha Wheeler, a milliner. One day Charity Hallett, a young girl from Bethel, came in to buy a bonnet from Mrs. Wheeler. By nightfall it had commenced to rain and thunder, and Charity was fearful of the lonely ride back to Bethel. Mrs. Wheeler, remembering that Barnum always returned to Bethel for weekends, summoned him and requested that he escort Charity home. Barnum looked at the young woman: "a fair, rosy-cheeked, buxom-looking girl, with beautiful white teeth," answering to the nickname of Charity. Entranced, he agreed.

He and Charity rode horseback the one mile to Bethel, and storm or no storm, Barnum wished it was twenty. Conversing with her, he found her "affable and in no degree prim," and he learned that she was a tailoress. That night he saw her lovely face in his dreams. The next morning, and almost every Sunday after that for the remainder of the year, he saw her at church.

There were clandestine meetings at first, then open ones, and the courtship took a more serious turn. When Barnum was nineteen and Charity twenty-one, he proposed marriage. She readily accepted. When there was some resistance from both families—Barnum's mother thought that he "was not looking high enough in the world," and Charity's family thought that "she was altogether too good for Taylor Barnum"—the couple determined to elope.

Charity went to New York to visit a favorite uncle, Nathan Beers, who lived on Allen Street. Shortly after, Barnum went to New York to purchase goods for his thriving store. On the evening of November 8, 1829, in the presence of her New York relatives, Barnum and Charity were married by the Reverend Dr. McAuley.

Barnum's mother forgave them, and Barnum, who had moved into the boarding house where his wife lived, brought his bride to dinner. He admitted later that he was young for marriage and that in general he disapproved of early marriages, but added that had he waited twenty years longer he "could not have found another woman so well suited to my disposition, and so valuable as a wife, a mother, and a friend."

For Barnum, inspired by his mate, the next three years were industrious ones. He maintained his store in Bethel, opened lottery offices in Danbury, Norwalk, Stamford and several other villages, and built a modest two-and-a-half-story house. But this was not enough, and by the time he was twenty-one, he had constructed a three-story building in the center of Bethel, using the ground floor as a large general store and the upper two stories as domestic apartments.

Having attained his majority and the right to vote, he became interested in politics. Like his grandfather, he was a staunch Democrat. (Long years later, when he had become wealthy and an acquaintance of Lincoln, he would become a Republican.) It was a period of ferment and excitement. The old established church, with its zealous Puritans, was suffering the defection of liberal Democrats and liberal Universalists—among them Barnum—and now the old church put forth its own political party. The Church and State Party, Christian and narrow, was a momentary threat to freedom. Barnum resisted. He felt strongly that church and state should remain separated.

He was anxious to voice his passionate feelings, to enlighten his fellows. There was no newspaper in Bethel, but there was a mild weekly, the *Recorder,* in Danbury. Barnum posted several emotional letters to this newspaper, expressing his convictions. The editor declined to publish them. Barnum decided that the editor was being muzzled by the rising new Church and State Party. If there was no newspaper to tell the truth, then Barnum would start his own. He bought press and type and a sharpened pencil, and on October 19, 1831, put out the first issue of the *Herald of Freedom*.

Publisher Barnum's well-printed four-page newspaper carried beneath its masthead a quotation from Thomas Jefferson: "For I have sworn upon the Altar of God, eternal hostility against every form of tyranny over the mind of man." In its columns Barnum inveighed against militant Calvinism and religious oppression. Barnum constantly promised his wide audience that he would joust with "bigotry, superstition, fanaticism, and hypocrisy." After examining the earliest issues of the weekly, the conservative Bridgeport *Spirit of the Times* remarked dryly: "Its distinctive character is Masonic and anti-priestcraft. We opine that Mr. Barnum, after a short trial will find that he has been fighting phantoms."

Although the mailed subscription was one dollar and fifty cents a year, the *Herald of Freedom* found regular readers in fifteen states. It was Barnum's fearless invective that attracted them. Reading the *Herald of Freedom* gave one the same sensation as attending a bare-knuckle bout. The Church and State Party, Barnum said, was composed of "bipeds of inferior quality such as *note-shavers, new-made deacons, temperance rum retailers, political and religious weathercocks. . . .*" As to the old order of government: "The hard-working, tax-paying *people* have been governed by the aristocracy long enough [and] are determined to place the government [where it should be], in their own hands."

Barnum was arrested for libel three times in three years. In the first case, a Danbury butcher, accused of spying on a Democratic Party caucus, sued and won several hundred dollars. The second suit was withdrawn before trial. The third sent Barnum to jail.

Barnum had published an editorial accusing a Bethel deacon, one Seth Seelye, of being "guilty of taking usury of an orphan boy." The word *usury* was what brought Barnum to trial. Had he used *extortion* instead, he would have been untouchable, but *usury* was condemned in the Bible, and Bethel lived by the Bible and not by Blackstone.

Judge David Daggett sat on the bench. Barnum called him a "lump of superstition." Gideon Welles, then editor of the *Hartford Times* and a rabid Barnum supporter, regarded the Judge as "the enemy of the friends of civil and religious freedom," one who had "persecuted the Democrats for thirty years."

Barnum was tried before the Superior Court in Danbury. He was found guilty as charged, fined one hundred dollars and the costs of the trial, and sentenced to sixty days in the Danbury jail. Friends of free press and free speech rallied around him. The walls of Barnum's cell were gaily papered and the floor was carpeted for his martyrdom. He ate well, received a stream of well-wishers, and, like Leigh Hunt before him, edited his paper from his cell. He was pleased to note that the furor had increased his circulation by several hundred copies. And he was happy to learn from Charity that she was pregnant for the first time.

Meanwhile many of his supporters were highly vocal. One of the strongest, the Reverend Theophilus Fiske, editor of a liberal religious periodical in New Haven, Connecticut, came to Barnum's defense in print.

"Is it possible an American—a Freeman—a Husband— has been torn from his family hearthstone," wrote the Reverend Fiske, "and by the strong arm of oppression has been incarcerated within the gloomy walls of a Common Jail!!! An American Citizen!! By the iron hand of power shut out from the glorious sunlight—and that too for no crime!!!"

Although Barnum was somewhat depressed by his confinement, he enjoyed the publicity his predicament gave him. As he wrote Gideon Welles: "The same spirit governs my enemies that . . . burnt to death Michael Servetus by order of John Calvin. The excitement in this and neighboring towns is very great, and it will have a grand effect."

After sixty days, Barnum was released. The occasion was made a holiday by his supporters. A festive dinner was held in his honor in the court where he had been tried. Several hundred well-wishers attended, and the Reverend Fiske delivered himself of another impassioned address. The feast was followed by a parade.

"P. T. Barnum and the band of musicians took their seats in a coach drawn by six horses, which had been prepared for the occasion," the *Herald of Freedom* reported on

December 12, 1832. "The coach was preceded by forty horsemen, and a marshal bearing the national standard. Immediately in the rear of the coach was the carriage of the Orator and the President of the day, followed by the Committee of Arrangements and sixty carriages of citizens, which joined in escorting the editor to his home in Bethel.

"When the procession commenced its march amidst the roar of cannon, three cheers were given by several hundred citizens who did not join in the procession. The band of music continued to play a variety of national airs until their arrival in Bethel (a distance of three miles), when they struck up the beautiful and appropriate tune of 'Home, Sweet Home!' After giving three hearty cheers, the procession returned to Danbury. The utmost harmony and unanimity of feeling prevailed throughout the day, and we are happy to add that no accident occurred to mar the festivities of the occasion."

This was heady wine for twenty-two-year-old Barnum. It was his first taste of notoriety, and thereafter he would never be surfeited. Barnum resumed with the *Herald of Freedom,* to the neglect of his varied other enterprises, and even continued to attack Deacon Seth Seelye, his antagonist, for obtaining a retail liquor license. But soon he was confessing in print that his lottery offices had been closed by a new law, that his general store was doing poorly, and that his newspaper was in dire economic straits. He could not continue publication without assistance. Apparently, the assistance was not forthcoming. In 1834, after one hundred and sixty published numbers, Barnum sold the *Herald of Freedom* to his brother-in-law. The general store was sold to two friends. The house was sold. In the winter of 1834, his property almost liquidated, Barnum, accompanied by Charity and their infant daughter, Caroline, born in May, put Bethel behind him forever. He moved to New York—"to seek my fortune," he said.

Reluctantly he worked for a brief period as a salesman of caps and hats. He applied for a job as bartender at Niblo's Garden, but changed his mind when Niblo insisted upon a three-year-employment contract. Still attracted to show business, he replied to an advertisement placed by a Professor exhibiting at Scudder's American Museum. "Immense Speculation on a small capital!" the advertisement had promised. "$10,000 easily made in one year!" The Professor offered to sell Barnum "the great Hydro-oxygen Microscope" for $2,000. Barnum, nearly insolvent, quickly left without the microscope.

Then, overnight, some old debtors in Bethel paid up their past-due bills. Barnum invested these few hundred dollars in the boarding house and the grocery-store partnership with John Moody. And then, at last, when Coley Bartram of Reading, Connecticut, came with the news of George Washington's nurse, Barnum had found a profession: "to cater to that insatiate want of human nature—the love of amusement."

After Locke had exposed Joice Heth, and she had been "respectably" laid to rest in her mahogany coffin in Bethel, Barnum determined to stay in show business. He still had the agile Signor Vivalla under contract. He cast about for a connection, and found himself attracted to Aaron Turner of Danbury, an Englishman who had given America its first full-top-canvas circus. Turner, an uneducated ex-shoemaker, had acquired a small fortune with his trained horses and acrobats, and he was about to go on the road again. Barnum approached him. A deal was made. In return for Vivalla's act and his own services as ticket-seller and book-keeper, Barnum was to receive eighty dollars a month and one fifth of the circus-company's profits.

In April, 1836, Barnum sent Charity and his daughter back to Bethel and took to the road with Turner's gaudy wagons and raucous regiment of three dozen men. Hyatt Frost, manager of the old Van Amburgh Circus, always remembered that as a boy he had seen the Turner troupe arrive in town. "The circus then had just nine horses and four wagons," he said. "Eight hauled the entire show, and one very fine ring horse was led over the road. The bandsmen put up the tent and the performers made the ring. The artists dressed at the hotels and made a procession on horseback. The admission was twenty-five cents, children half price." Barnum remained with Turner almost nine months, and this gestation period produced a more knowledgeable showman. Through New York, Massachusetts, Pennsylvania, Virginia, and North Carolina, Barnum rode beside Turner, watching, listening, absorbing.

An attitude toward showmanship, rooted in the same compulsion that had produced the *Herald of Freedom*, was beginning to crystallize. When a clergyman in Lenox, Mas-

sachusetts, denounced the circus from the pulpit, Barnum
made his way to the pulpit stairs and strongly defended the
freedom to amuse and be amused.

Life with Turner seemed familiar to Barnum because it
was like life with grandfather Taylor. Turner devoted more
creativity to practical jokes than to his circus. In Annapo-
lis, Maryland, business was profitable, and Turner put his
mind fully to celebration. The result was almost the death
of Barnum.

On a Sunday morning, Turner and Barnum were having
refreshments in the hotel bar with twenty other persons.
When Barnum, attired in his formal Sabbath best, took his
departure, Turner suddenly pointed after him and called to
the others: "I think it's very singular you permit that rascal
to march your streets in open day. It wouldn't be allowed
in Rhode Island, and I suppose that is the reason the black-
coated scoundrel has come down this way."

"Why, who is it?" several persons asked.

"Don't you know?" said Turner. "That is the Reverend
E. K. Avery, the murderer of Miss Cornell!"

Three years earlier, Sarah Cornell, a thirty-year-old factory worker, had been found hanging in a stack yard outside Tiverton, Rhode Island, apparently murdered. Her
effects produced a note casting suspicion on the Reverend
Avery, a Methodist minister near by. In May 1833, Avery
was put on trial for murder before the Supreme Judicial
Court. It was the first trial of a clergyman for this offense
in the United States, and it excited much attention. Defended by six attorneys, Avery was acquitted. But public
feeling ran high against him, and eventually he disappeared
from Rhode Island (to reappear, much later, as a farmer
in Ohio).

When Turner pointed Barnum out as Avery, the small
group in the bar gave chase, and by the time they caught
Barnum, they were over one hundred in number. They tore
Barnum's coat off his back, shoved him into the dirt, and
prepared to lynch him. Barnum never talked faster. "I am
not Avery," he pleaded. "I despise that villain. . . . My
name is Barnum. . . . Old Turner, my partner, has
hoaxed you with this ridiculous story."

Barnum was dragged back to the hotel, where Turner
stood on the porch red with laughter. He explained the
joke, and most of the mob joined in the merriment.

Later, Barnum demanded to know why Turner had played so dangerous a trick on him. Turner replied seriously. "My dear Barnum, it was all for our good. Remember, all we need to insure success is *notoriety*. You will see that this will be noised all about town . . . and our pavilion will be crammed tomorrow night."

The pavilion was, indeed, crammed the following night, and Barnum never forgot the point.

In North Carolina, Barnum, twelve hundred dollars the richer, at last parted company with Turner. Retaining Signor Vivalla and a Negro song-and-dance man named James Sanford, Barnum went off on his own. Just before an engagement, Sanford quit. A large crowd expected him as advertised, so Barnum put on blackface, went before the audience pretending to be Sanford, lustily sang "Zip Coon," and was applauded and was asked for an encore.

Meeting Turner again, Barnum purchased horses and wagons from him, hired away his clown and magician, Joe Pentland, named his troupe "Barnum's Grand Scientific and Musical Theatre," and marched off through Georgia and Alabama. Nervous days were spent crossing a Cherokee reservation—hostiles among them had recently stopped a mail stage and slaughtered all aboard—and Signor Vivalla shivered more than the others while blustering that he could handle fifty redskins. To relax the company, Barnum dressed Pentland in an Indian costume and sent him in pursuit of Vivalla. The terrified acrobat almost dropped dead before the joke was exposed.

Along the way, Barnum acquired several partners, then disposed of them, and when Vivalla left him at last to retire to Cuba, Barnum knew that it was time to return home. On June 4, 1838, he reached New York and was reunited with his family.

He had profited from his odyssey, but not enough. He was "disgusted with the life of an itinerant showman" and momentarily longed for "a respectable, permanent business." He advertised in the newspapers that he had $2,500 to invest in a sane enterprise. He immediately received ninety-three propositions: from a pawnbroker who wanted a partner, a patent-medicine man who needed backing, an inventor with a perpetual-motion machine (Barnum found the mainspring secreted in a hollow post), a merchant who thought he could disguise himself as a Quaker and cheat customers with short-measured bags of oats, a counterfeiter who needed $2,500 for new dies, paper, and ink.

One proposition, however, appealed to Barnum. A German named Proler, with letters of the highest recommendation, wanted a partner to join him in manufacturing cologne, boot blacking, and waterproof paste. During the spring of 1839 Barnum and Proler set up shop and shipped their product wholesale to dealers as far away as Cleveland. For several months, the firm prospered. And then Barnum awoke one morning to find that Proler had decamped for Rotterdam with the firm's entire assets.

Desperate and almost penniless, Barnum made another try at show business. He rented a saloon at Vauxhall Garden and presented a variety of acts, but the venture was a dismal failure. Discovering a brilliant Negro dancer named John Diamond, Barnum took to the road, presenting performances in Toronto, Ottawa, and St. Louis. Arriving in New Orleans, he had no more money than when he had started. He remembered the juggling contest between Vivalla and Roberts and revived the stunt by pitting Diamond against a Negro dancer from Kentucky. The box office boomed. In Mobile, Diamond, who owed his employer considerable sums of money, deserted. Dismayed, Barnum once more returned to New York empty-handed.

Barnum was thirty-one and disheartened about show business. But even as he undertook to sell a pictorial Bible published by Robert Sears, he was again leasing the saloon at Vauxhall Garden for a variety program. Neither enterprise was successful, and Barnum was happy to obtain a job writing advertisements for the Bowery Amphitheatre at four dollars a week. He met the leading editors, supplemented his meager income by writing free-lance articles for the Sunday editions, and dreamed of glory.

Then one day in the fall of 1841 it happened. Barnum sets it down almost too nonchalantly in his autobiography. "While engaged as outside clerk for the Bowery Amphitheatre, I casually learned that the collection of curiosities comprising Scudder's American Museum, at the corner of Broadway and Ann Street, was for sale." This was the invitation to greatness. With Joice Heth, the showman had been born; with the American Museum, the showman became successful. "The American Museum," wrote Barnum, "was the ladder by which I rose to fortune."

Here, on the threshold, it might be instructive to reflect briefly on those forces of character, inspired by heredity and environment, that led Phineas T. Barnum so inevitably into his destined role.

What was it, after all, that made Barnum a showman? We know, of course, what made him one of the *greatest* showmen in history. This was talent, or a kind of genius, if you will—the gift of chromosomes or his Maker—the instinctive understanding of what startled, amazed, astonished, titillated, thrilled, the special extra sense of knowing what Everyman was curious about and finding the means by which to exploit this curiosity. Talent made Barnum successful. But what made him a showman instead of anything else he might have been? He might as easily have been Boss Tweed or Daniel Drew or Billy Sunday or Andrew Johnson or William Randolph Hearst, but instead, he became the prototype of all entrepreneurs forever after.

Deeply engrained in Barnum—and this vein has too often been overlooked—was the desire to be amused and to amuse all others, with no understandable motive beyond the sensual pleasure of enjoyment. That this natural desire was the result of his harsh, restricted childhood, or flourished because of that background, can scarcely be doubted. Barnum was attracted to showmanship because, even as newspaper editor, he was seeking a means to combat those forces of religion, government, and commerce which made life drab. Not only New England and New York were stifled by this gloom, but all of America as well. Even in faraway Ohio, the English emigrant and prolific author Mrs. Frances Trollope, mother of Anthony Trollope, had observed: "I never saw any people who appeared to live so much without amusement as the Cincinnatians." There were laws against card games and billiards. There were never dinner parties or concerts; there were rarely dances. The lone theater in Cincinnati was almost unattended. "Ladies are rarely seen there, and by far the larger proportion of females deem it an offence against religion to witness the representation of a play," Mrs. Trollope wrote.

Barnum believed that amusement and sensation were the natural prerogatives of the masses, who had little else, and that those who deprived them of pleasure were evil. As a showman, he could give New York, and then America, and finally the world, the gift of enjoyment. So, against all odds, he fought to make entertainment and amusement respectable. That he succeeded is evident with every circus, concert, legitimate play, motion picture, and television program that we, his heirs, freely and guiltlessly attend.

To ascribe to Barnum only the noblest motives in his choice of career would of course be ridiculous. Certainly he wanted money. Also he wanted fame—perhaps fame even more than money. As Gamaliel Bradford remarked: "Foreigners are always accusing Americans of idolizing the dollar. They misunderstand. In reality the American man of business cares nothing for the dollar. . . . What he idolizes is not money but success. . . . This was eminently true of Barnum." But there was more. His crusade was to make life a sinless carnival, to make mirth and play acceptable as a necessary portion of daily living.

The means he used to accomplish his end were often questionable. Frequently, he was one part Merlin, one part Psalmanazar, one part John Law. Perhaps the elaborate fake, the complicated trick, the exaggerated advertisement were used to enrich him and keep him in the limelight. Certainly, many accused him of being unscrupulous. But the hoaxes were always harmless, and they reflected his attachment to Yankee tomfoolery. And sometimes, possibly, they were necessary in another way—the weapons required by one man in a long fight to make amusement recognized in a relatively cheerless world.

Money, of course. Fame and success, yes. But also, always, the deeper, driving thing. He said it himself at the outset of what was to be a dazzling and thunderous career:

"This is a trading world and men, women and children, who cannot live on gravity alone, need something to satisfy their gayer, lighter moods and hours, and he who ministers to this want is in a business established by the Author of our nature. If he worthily fulfills his mission and amuses without corrupting, he need never feel that he has lived in vain."

This was why Phineas T. Barnum became a showman.

III

EXHIBIT THREE
Mermaid from Feejee

Scudder's American Museum was an imposing five-story marble structure on lower Broadway at the corner of Ann Street, and it was the storehouse for $50,000 worth of "relics and rare curiosities" from every corner of the earth.

In America the small museum as a private enterprise was not new. Because the theater and circus were considered outside the pale, the museum emerged as a devious means of supplying entertainment. The first one of any importance had been established in 1786 by Charles Willson Peale, the genial eccentric who had painted the earliest known portrait of George Washington, and who had named his sons Rembrandt, Raphaelle, Titian, and Rubens. His collection of curiosities and art was displayed in his Philadelphia studio.

In 1790, the Tammany Museum was founded in New York City. It exhibited its jumbled marvels in the west wing of a government building that resembled an old Quaker church. In 1810 John Scudder took over this collection, enlarged it by acquiring numerous oddities from visiting sea captains who had been to far lands, and had his first success with the showing of a giant tortoise. Subsequently, he moved to the City Hall, and finally, in 1830, he leased a five-story building recently constructed on the site of an old amusement park known as Spring Garden. There he opened his American Museum.

Scudder had an eye for oddity and history, but he was no showman. Nevertheless, because places of entertainment were so few, his assembly of stuffed birds and reptiles, his waxworks of villains and great men, his living collection of animals and freaks (ranging from a dog named Apollo who played cards and dominoes to a twenty-year-old midget named Caroline Clarke who was thirty-six inches tall), and the struggling professor he employed to lecture daily on some topic of scientific interest attracted a profitable attendance.

When Scudder died, he left the American Museum collection to his daughters. Women of that period were ill-equipped to manage a large business, and the Museum began to fail. In three years the gross receipts totaled no more than $34,000. At last, in 1841, the Scudder daughters decided to divest themselves of the white elephant. They advised the administrator of their estate, John Heath, and their Museum landlord, a wealthy retired merchant named Francis W. Olmsted, to put their collection and the lease of the building on the market.

When Barnum, struggling with his advertising copy, heard that the American Museum was for sale, he was as strangely stirred as he had been earlier by the availability of Joice Heth.

He wanted to be a showman, and he wanted a permanent showcase. He had every qualification for the undertaking except money. He had visited the Museum many times for relaxation, but now he returned to it with a keener eye. "I saw, or believed I saw, that only energy, tact, and liberality were needed, to give it life and to put it on a profitable footing." To make it the leading attraction of its sort in America one had only to "properly present its merits to the public."

He determined to buy it. When he imparted this decision to a friend, the friend was incredulous: "*You* buy the American Museum? What do you intend buying it with?"

"*Brass,*" Barnum said, "for silver and gold I have none."

Barnum decided that the man to see was Francis W. Olmsted, owner of the Museum building. After considering several approaches, Barnum sat down and wrote Olmsted a letter. With audacity, with every Yankee trading artifice brought to bear in his writing, Barnum composed a letter that disarmed by its frankness.

He wrote that he wanted to purchase the Museum collection on credit and lease the building. He confessed that he had no cash. But, he said, he did have "tact and experience, added to a most determined devotion to business." What he proposed was that Olmsted buy the curiosity collection from the Scudder family, then sell Barnum the collection on payments, and also rent him the building. "In fact, Mr. Olmsted, you may bind me in any way, and as tightly as you please—only give me a chance to dig out, or scratch out, and I will either do so or forfeit all the labor and trouble which I may have incurred." Barnum promised to meet every payment, holding out only twelve dollars and fifty cents a week for his family. He was prepared to present references if Olmsted would give him a personal interview.

Barnum took the letter to Olmsted's residence in Park Place and handed it to a servant. For two days, he waited nervously. And then, suddenly, he had his reply. Olmsted would see him.

Arriving for the appointment, Barnum found Olmsted aloof and aristocratic, yet thought that he detected an amused, good-natured twinkle in the merchant's eyes. Barnum was pleased when Olmsted congratulated him for being punctual, and then, at some length, he answered questions about his background, describing his family in Bethel, his upbringing, his habits. As to experience, he did not mention Joice Heth, but instead dwelt upon the Turner circus and the Vauxhall Garden shows.

Olmsted listened, and finally interrupted. "Who are your references?"

"Any man in my line," Barnum replied. Hastily, he mentioned William Niblo, Aaron Turner, Edmund Simpson, of the Park Theater, Moses Yale Beach, the inventor of news syndication, who had taken over the *Sun* from his father-in-law, Day, and who would lift its circulation to 50,000.

"Can you get any of them to call on me?"

Barnum was sure that he could. Olmsted advised Barnum

to have the men call the following day and to appear for
the verdict the morning after.

In a frenzy of excitement, Barnum left to rally his friends
to his support. Most were agreeable. The next day, William
Niblo visited Olmsted, and he was succeeded by Beach and
several showmen. The morning after that, Barnum reappeared at Olmsted's residence.

Olmsted's face was a mask. Barnum waited.

"I don't like your references, Mr. Barnum," the merchant said suddenly.

Barnum's heart sank. He mumbled that he was sorry.

"They all speak too well of you," Olmsted continued.
Then, he laughed. "In fact they talk as if they were all partners of yours, and intended to share the profits."

Barnum was giddy with delight. Olmsted went on. If he
purchased the Scudder collection and turned it and the
building over to Barnum, he would want a lease of ten years
at a rental of $3,000 a year. Barnum was satisfied, and
prayed that Olmsted would want no more concessions. But
Olmsted demanded one more concession. On this, the entire
deal depended.

He insisted upon security of some sort. Barnum had no
bonds, and the few buildings that he owned in Connecticut
were heavily mortgaged. Olmsted was adamant. "If you
only had a piece of unencumbered real estate that you could
offer as additional security, I think I might venture to negotiate with you."

Barnum knew that everything was at stake. He knew
that he had no real security, but he remembered that once,
in his youth, he had thought himself wealthy. He had
owned Ivy Island. And he owned it still. It had been a joke
on him. Why not play the same joke on Olmsted? Surely
there was no harm in it. And, after all, it *was* a piece of
unencumbered real estate.

"I have five acres of land in Connecticut," he blurted,
"which is free from all lien or encumbrance."

"Indeed! What did you pay for it?"

"It was a present from my late grandfather, Phineas
Taylor, given me on account of my name."

"Was he rich?"

"He was considered well off in those parts."

Olmsted wondered how Barnum could bring himself to
part with so valuable and sentimental a property. Barnum

did not think he would be parting with it, for he expected to make his payments on the Museum punctually.

Olmsted seemed satisfied. "Well, I think I will make the purchase for you. At all events, I'll think it over, and in the meantime you must see the administrator and heirs of the estate—get their best terms, and meet me here on my return to town a week hence."

The week that followed was a week of bargaining. John Heath, administrator for the Scudder family, wanted $15,000 for the collection inside the Museum. Barnum offered him $10,000. They settled on a compromise price of $12,000.

When Olmsted returned to town, he was satisfied. He agreed to buy the collection and turn it and the building over to Barnum. Heath drew up the necessary papers. Barnum appeared on the scheduled morning to sign and take possession. Then Heath blandly informed him there would be no papers: the collection and Museum building were being sold to another bidder. The directors of Peale's Museum, a longtime rival of Scudder's American Museum, had offered $15,000 and already paid down $1,000 in cash.

"I was thunderstruck," Barnum remembered. "I appealed to his honor. He replied that he had signed no writing with me, was not therefore legally bound, and he felt it his duty to do the best he could for the orphan girls." In desperation, Barnum turned to Olmsted and pleaded with him. Olmsted said that he could do nothing. Barnum had always been a risk. The Peale's people were not. Put to a choice, he had to select the more solvent, permanent tenant. He was sorry that Barnum had to be "thrown overboard," but that was business.

Had Barnum despaired and quit, he might have been relegated to obscurity and lost to history forever. But he sensed that this was the crucial moment in his life. And, besides, he was angry. Hopeless though it seemed, he made the decision to fight back and regain his Museum.

Privately, he investigated the directors of the Peale's Museum. He learned that no member of the reputable Peale family was connected with the organization. For a few thousand dollars, Rubens Peale had sold his curiosities to a company headed by an unsuccessful ex-banker. The banker and his cronies were swindlers rather than showmen. Once they had the American Museum, they intended to sell the public $50,000 worth of stock in it, withhold $30,000 of the stock money for themselves, and then abandon the enterprise to the stockholders.

With facts in hand, Barnum met with Beach of the *New York Sun* and half a dozen other leading metropolitan editors. He showed them his exposé. "If you grant me the use of your columns, I'll blow that speculation sky-high." Beach, who three years later would publish Poe's hoax about eight people in a balloon crossing the Atlantic in three days, was always ready for anything. The other editors, sensing a good scandal, also agreed to co-operate. Immediately Barnum began to pour out paragraphs about the low character of the Peale's directors and about their bogus stock issue. In the face of this, the Peale's gang issued their stock—but almost no one bought it.

Meanwhile, Barnum scurried to a meeting with Heath. He wanted to know when the Peale's directors intended to pay the remaining $14,000 for the Museum. Heath replied that the balance had to be delivered in seven weeks, on December 26, 1841, or the down payment would be forfeited and the deal canceled. Barnum was positive that they would never pay the balance on the agreed date; Heath was confident that they would. Barnum explained that he had to leave on an exhibition tour, but that he would postpone it if he had a chance to win back the Museum. "If you will agree with me confidentially," Barnum said, "that in case these gentlemen do not pay you on the 26th of December, I may have it on the 27th for $12,000, I will run the risk, and wait in this city until that date." This arrangement seemed to suit Heath fine, and Olmsted later agreed to it, too.

Feverishly, Barnum resumed his press campaign against the Peale's group. At every turn, he thwarted them, and their stock would not move. Soon enough, as Barnum expected, he heard from the Peale's group. They wanted a meeting at their Museum.

In a few days, Barnum sat opposite his more affluent enemies. The ex-banker and his directors were all smiles and friendship. They were respectful, also. They recognized a fellow pirate in Barnum. Since they could not beat him, they would buy him. They told him that they had watched his career closely. He showed promise. They wanted to hire him to manage both of their museums. They would pay him $3,000 a year. Barnum was all innocence. Gratefully, he accepted the job, to begin on January 1, 1842.

The meeting broke up, and as Barnum had moved to the door, the ex-banker called after him, "of course, Mr. Barnum, we shall have no more of your squibs through the newspapers."

"I ever try to serve the interests of my employers," Barnum said.

Leaving, he knew that they were laughing at his expense. But he knew that the last laugh would be his: "They thought they had caught me securely. I *knew* that I had caught *them*."

Barnum calculated correctly. The Peale's directors, assured that they had eliminated their opposition, relaxed. Because no one would take the American Museum from them, they saw no need to close the deal. They decided to withhold their stock until the bad publicity had been forgotten, then reissue it and buy the Museum. December 26 came and went, and the Peale's group did not bother to call on Heath or to deliver the balance due. December 27 came, and Barnum, accompanied by an attorney, was on hand to meet with Heath and Olmsted. Four hours later, the American Museum was Barnum's American Museum. The age of showmanship, begun with Joice Heth, was about to become a dominant reality on the American scene.

Phineas T. Barnum opened his American Museum on the morning of New Year's Day 1842.

In the week before he took active control, he was able to inspect carefully the Museum's situation, outside and inside. The neighborhood pleased him. He was in the very center of America's largest and fastest-growing city. Horsecars and stagecoach lines disgorged hundreds of potential customers almost at his front door. To one side of the Museum entrance was a billiard parlor that had been converted into living quarters for his family, now obliged to make ends meet on $600 a year until the Museum was paid off. On the other side was a hat shop owned by John N. Genin, whom Barnum would make a national figure, and beyond it a cigar store and a clothing store.

Directly across the street, occupying an entire block, was that granite pile known as The Astor House, built by John Jacob Astor a decade before and headquarters for most visiting statesmen and politicians. Near by stood St. Paul's Church, and beyond it a studio that would soon house the daguerreotype establishment of Mathew B. Brady.

Of all the businessmen in the vicinity, Brady probably fascinated Barnum the most. The lanky, scholarly-appearing Irish photographer was twenty-one years old when Barnum first met him. Brady had studied painting under Samuel F. B. Morse, inventor of the telegraph. Morse had become acquainted with Daguerre in Europe and had returned home to experiment with wet-plate photography. This interested Brady more than painting, and after five years of study, he opened his gallery across from Barnum. Twenty years later, he would take a darkroom wagon and a company of assistants into the field during the Civil War, almost lose his life at Fredericksburg, and become immortal with his stark reproductions of the action at Bull Run, Antietam, and Gettysburg. But now, in business on Broadway, he was content to make stiff daguerreotypes of Abraham Lincoln, Edgar Allan Poe, John Howard Payne, and James Fenimore Cooper. And eventually, too, he would have a picture of his friend Barnum, leering at a brunette ballet dancer who worked in the Museum.

Also in the neighborhood, within short walking distance, were two other celebrities who were to be closely involved with Barnum throughout the showman's life. One, who began as friend and admirer and ended as enemy, was James Gordon Bennett, who had started the raucous *New York Herald* seven years before. By the same flamboyant methods Barnum used in another field, Bennett, a big, forceful immigrant from Scotland, had parlayed a sheet published in a cellar into a national institution. He had covered the great twenty-million-dollar New York fire of 1835 first hand, had obtained European news days ahead of his rivals by sending his own boat out to meet incoming vessels, and had published the earliest stock quotations. By intervening in the murder case of the prostitute Ellen Jewett, and by reporting a play-by-play account of how a former partner had caned him publicly, he swelled his paper's circulation to 9,000, and eventually to 50,000. He ridiculed Catholics, Protestants, and the Bible. "I don't think much of Moses," he wrote. "A man who would take forty years to get a party of young women through a desert is only a loafer."

It was he who sent Stanley to darkest Africa to find Livingston. From the outset, though hoaxed in the Joice Heth affair, he respected Barnum's zest and advertising. He called him "the Napoleon of Public Caterers." Later, he would call him a thief and a rascal.

The other neighboring celebrity who became involved with Barnum, as his lifelong friend (though he saw too much "ugliness and deformity" in the world to enjoy Barnum's freaks), was the thirty-one-year-old New England printer Horace Greeley, an authentic journalistic genius and a part of America's conscience. Months before Barnum took over the Museum, Greeley had opened offices for the *New York Tribune* in an attic overlooking cobbled Ann Street. He was a gangling, wispy-haired, pasty-cheeked man, high-domed and myopic, with the face of somebody's favorite grandmother. Bennett hated him and called him "the most unmitigated blockhead connected with the newspaper press." Bennett insisted that "a large New England squash . . . would make as capable an editor as Horace." But Emerson admired Greeley's mind, and so eventually did 300,000 readers.

Greeley battled monopolies and defended unions. He fought against slavery, but offered to go bail for Jefferson Davis. He sponsored Mark Twain and his innocents abroad, published Edgar Allan Poe's "The Raven," introduced Charles Dickens' writings to America, and hired Karl Marx as a foreign correspondent. He was loved by the poor because he wanted each of them to have a free piece of public land, and he was hated by them for supporting the draft laws. He crusaded for development of the west, reprinting John Babsone Lane Soule's advice, "Go west, young man!" —by which Greeley really meant Pennsylvania, not California. He thought Ulysses S. Grant a disgrace, and to get rid of him ran for president himself. He suffered throughout the campaign, protesting: "I have been so bitterly assailed that I hardly know whether I am running for the President or the penitentiary." He polled forty-three per cent of the total ballot, but lost by 700,000 votes. He graced Barnum's frugal table constantly, and remained his intimate and advisor for life.

Having surveyed the district around his Museum, and having met many of his fellow businessmen, Barnum retired into the dim interior of his cavernous showplace. The entrance led into a large hall decorated with grotesque creatures and ancient relics hung from the walls, propped in glass cases, animated in barred cages, and standing in darkened alcoves. Spacious stairways soared invitingly through the five stories to a barren roof—which Barnum hastily converted into a garden ice-cream parlor surrounded by pots of bright flowers and cedar plants.

On his opening day, Barnum had to be satisfied with showing $50,000 worth of exhibits that he had inherited from Scudder. There were cracked and molding panoramas and dioramas of "A Fairy Grotto" and "The Creation." There were dusty miniature models of Dublin, Paris, and Jerusalem. There was a glass-blowing exhibition, an automaton bird that flapped its wings, a robot, and a curious mechanical knitting machine run by a dog. There were rows of stuffed animals, contrasting with cages of living creatures that included an anaconda, an orangutan, and an alligator. There was the gory arm of a pirate named Tom Trouble. There was the waxwork depicting the pitfalls of intemperance, and then the art gallery with paintings of famous Americans. It was interesting, but it was tame and static. And it had been there too long.

Almost overnight, the Barnum touch became evident. The eager showman sought greater oddity, more action and fun, more variety. "The transient attractions of the Museum were constantly diversified," he said, "and educated dogs, industrious fleas, automatons, jugglers, ventriloquists, living statuary, tableaux, gypsies, albinos, fat boys, giants, dwarfs, rope-dancers, live 'Yankees,' pantomime, instrumental music, singing and dancing in great variety ... the first English Punch and Judy in this country, Italian fantoccini [puppet-plays] ... dissolving views, American Indians, who enacted their warlike and religious ceremonies on the stage—these, among others, were all exceedingly successful."

All this was good and reasonable at twenty-five cents a ticket, half-price for children, but for Barnum that was not enough. He wanted the Museum to excite and thrill. He wanted it talked about. Toward this end, he hunted each new attraction with the fervor of a medieval knight in search of the Holy Grail.

In short weeks Barnum succeeded in making the Museum less musty and pedantic. He transformed it into a carnival. Now, seeking something distinctive to advertise, he came upon an ingenious working model of Niagara Falls, created by a patient artist named Grain. The whole arrangement was only eighteen inches high, but real water sloshed over the tiny Falls, and the surrounding buildings, trees, and crags were built in accurate proportion. Barnum paid the inventor-artist $200 for the model, installed it in a place of honor, and then designed advertisements almost as large as the model itself. "The Great Model of Niagara Falls, With Real Water!" the advertisements screamed. Visitors, including many newlyweds and honeymooners who could not afford a trip to the real Niagara, crowded into the American Museum with high expectations. When they came upon the stunted model, they were usually dismayed. But, explained Barnum, "they had the whole Museum to fall back upon for 25 cents, and no fault was found."

The publicity attracted the attention of the Board of Water Commissioners for the newly opened Croton reservoir. Barnum was summoned to appear before them. He was sternly reminded that his water bill was only twenty-five dollars a year. It was kept that low because it was presumed that he would use ordinary amounts of water—and not enough to send cataracts over Niagara Falls. Barnum, with some embarrassment, told the Commissioners that they should not always believe what they read in the newspapers. He explained that a small pump and a single barrel of water, used over and over again, were all that this Niagara Falls demanded, and he "offered to pay a dollar a drop" for all water more than a barrel's worth that he used in a month.

Although customers continued to be attracted to his Niagara Falls, Barnum was eager to keep the critics away from it. When Louis Gaylor Clark, editor of the influential *Knickerbocker,* came calling, Barnum desperately tried to steer him from the Falls. But Clark was curious about the crowds, and insisted upon following them. Nervously, Barnum explained that it was a model of Niagara Falls that was being shown.

"Oh, ah, yes, yes, I remember now," said Clark. "I have noticed your advertisements and splendid posters announcing Niagara Falls with real water. I have some curiosity to see the cataract in operation."

As he began to climb atop a chair to obtain a view over the heads of customers in front of him, Barnum took heart, and quickly began to embellish his exhibit. "I flatter myself it is, in point of originality and ingenuity, considerably ahead of any invention of modern times."

Clark gazed at the miserable, wheezing model a moment, and then peered down at Barnum. "Original! Yes, it certainly is original. I never dreamed of such a thing; I never saw anything of the kind before since I was born——" and he paused, then snapped, "and I hope with all my heart I never shall again!"

Before Niagara Falls had worn out its welcome, Barnum installed wonders physically more in keeping with his advertisements. Extremes in human size had always appealed to him, and whenever he could find a giant, he would hire the Brobdingnagian creature for his Museum. The first impressive colossus he ever showed was Robert Hales, a seven-foot-six-inch Quaker who weighed four hundred and sixty-two pounds. When the public had had enough of this Goliath, Barnum found Eliza Simpson, almost Hales's match in height. Then he contrived to marry the pair legally, on the stage of his Museum.

Later Barnum obtained the services of Colonel Routh Goshen, an Arab born in Jerusalem, who was eight foot two inches in height, and weighed five hundred and ninety pounds. Displayed beside him was a slender Belgian giant, seven foot eight inches tall, named Monsieur Bihin. There was a keen rivalry between the two, and one day, after an exchange of epithets, Goshen and Bihin snatched up club and sword and prepared to lay each other out. A dozen Museum employees intervened until Barnum could be summoned from his downstairs office.

What appalled Barnum was not the impending violence, but the unprofessional action of the participants. "Look here!" he shouted up at them. "This is all right; if you want to fight each other, maiming and perhaps killing one or both of you, that is your affair; but my interest lies here—you are both under engagement to me, and if this duel is to come off, I and the public have a right to participate. It must be duly advertised and must take place on the stage. . . . No performance of yours would be a greater attraction, and if you kill each other, our engagement can end with your duel."

Barnum meant it, and his unswerving loyalty to good showmanship so amused Goshen and Bihin, that they fell on each other, dissolved in laughter, and peace was restored.

Along with giants, Barnum had a true affection for the commercial worth of Indians not yet tamed. The civilized and sedentary East had an overwhelming interest in the attacks and massacres performed by the redskins in the West, especially by the Sioux in the Midwest, so near at hand. At first, Barnum tried to satisfy this curiosity by hiring local actors to make up and play Indian, but audiences soon saw through this clumsy camouflage. At last Barnum was able to import from Iowa a company of real Indians—braves, squaws, papooses—a tribe possessed of only the slightest veneer of civilization. Not one of them had ever seen a railroad or steamer or horse trolley until their trek to New York. Barnum lodged them in the largest room on his fifth floor. They dwelt in communal style, bedding down on the floor and cooking their own meals. Daily, they gave uninhibited war dances on the Museum stage. And often, they were so carried away, so realistic in wielding their tomahawks and knives, that Barnum had to protect the inviting scalps of orchestra and audience by erecting a formidable rope barrier between stage and the public.

After a week, seeking to vary their performances, Barnum suggested an Indian Wedding Dance. He advertised it to take place twice a day. Before the opening dance, the chief of the tribe demanded the traditional "large new red woollen blanket, at a cost of ten dollars, for the bridegroom to present to the father of the bride." The first time, Barnum readily obliged. But when Barnum learned that the Indians demanded a new blanket before each Wedding Dance in keeping with custom, he was appalled. He protested. After all, this was make-believe. The chief was stone. Make-believe the marriage might be, but the Wedding Dance was real enough. When Barnum found himself forced to spend $120 on bridal blankets in a single week, he changed the program. Then, one of the more beautiful squaws of the tribe, Dohumme, unexpectedly died, and the Iowa savages lost heart. They buried her near New York, left food on the roof of the Museum for friendly spirits, and departed for their distant plains.

By then, however, Barnum was onto a dozen other diversions. He began to stage contests as special attractions. There were dog shows, bird shows, poultry shows, flower shows—and finally, a baby show, with cash prizes and medals for winners, and considerable recognition in the press. The baby show was the most successful. Barnum limited the influx of entries to one hundred. When he awarded the first prize in person, there was a near riot of protest from the remaining ninety-nine mothers. Barnum escaped unscathed, but thereafter, with each new baby contest, he announced the winner in writing—from a safe distance.

While Barnum enjoyed his work, he had little personal interest in the original exhibits and promotions. "I myself relished a higher grade of amusement," he confessed, "and I was a frequent attendant at the opera, first-class concerts, lectures and like; but I worked for the million and I knew the only way to make a million from my patrons was to give them abundant and wholesome attractions for a small sum of money."

He lived economically, obsessed with the need to pay off Olmsted and be his own man. One noon, six months after he had taken over the Museum, he was sitting in his ticket office nibbling at corned beef and bread, when Olmsted came upon him.

Olmsted was surprised. "Is this the way you eat your dinner?" he asked.

"I have not eaten a warm dinner since I bought the Museum, except on the Sabbath," said Barnum, "and I intend never to eat another on a week-day until I am out of debt."

Olmsted clapped him on the shoulder with delight. "Ah! you are safe, and will pay for the Museum before the year is out."

Actually, it took Barnum eighteen months to pay Olmsted the $12,000 owed on the Scudder collection. The exhibit that made this possible, and one of his steadiest sources of income, was the Museum's Lecture Room.

Scudder's Lecture Room had been "narrow, ill-contrived, and inconvenient." Its performers were dull. It was opened only one afternoon a week. Barnum determined to make something more of it in every way. He wanted a theater, really, but all about him the theater was condemned as a tool of Satan.

The theater in New York was at a low ebb. Less than

a half-dozen halls were considered even halfway respectable. A woman without escort was unable to attend even in a box or orchestra seat. The gallery, or third tier, in every theater was the hunting ground for prostitutes and an arena of assignation for sporting bloods and their dates. Except in three houses, the boards were devoted to dramas of the penny dreadful variety.

Barnum set about to mend all this and to have his theater, too. He rebuilt his Lecture Room into "one of the most commodious and beautiful amusement halls in the city of New York." He eliminated the third tier. He sold no liquor on the premises, and when he learned that ticket-holders were leaving his theater for drinks between acts, he barred their free re-entry. His stage plays were moral, educational, often religious, with "all vulgarity and profanity" banned. He made a big point of inviting women and children to attend. He assured them that his plays and sketches were for "all those who disapprove of the dissipations, debaucheries, profanity, vulgarity and other abominations, which characterize our modern theatre."

On the stage of Barnum's Lecture Room, *The Drunkard* began its long run. Here was held one of the earliest showings of *Uncle Tom's Cabin,* pilfered from Mrs. Stowe's widely read novel. "Christian Martyrs" introduced the spectacle, featuring vistas of pagan Rome, believers cast to the lions, and Constantine's cross illuminated in the sky. "Moses in Egypt" was yet another popular spectacle despite James Gordon Bennett's objections to glorification of "a loafer."

Even the lusty dramas and comedies of Shakespeare were found palatable after Barnum had arranged to have them "shorn of their objectionable features when placed upon my stage."

Many actors who later became famous made their debuts on Barnum's puritanical boards. The best-known of these was the Englishman Edward A. Sothern, who endeared himself to the proprietor with his propensity for the practical joke and who became popular in *Our American Cousin.*

The Lecture Room was also given over to clean vaudeville. The incredible Dan Rice, a jockey who became America's first clown, began his career by exhibiting an educated pig named Lord Byron, and then devoted himself for a period to jesting and singing on Barnum's stage. The clown had not yet evolved into wig, bulbous nose, white greasepaint, and baggy pants. Rice appeared as the bewhiskered Uncle Sam.

When Rice felt that he had outgrown the Museum, he took to the road with his own troupe. At his peak, he made $100,000 annually, was given the rank of colonel by President Zachary Taylor, and counted Stephen A. Douglas and Robert E. Lee among his best friends. After his wife left him, his luck turned. He became a drunkard and incurred unpopularity by supporting the Southern cause. He published a newspaper, was defeated for Congress in Pennsylvania, and campaigned for nomination to the presidency of the United States. He died broke and embittered, a ward of New Jersey relatives, in his seventy-seventh year.

Another graduate of Barnum's Lecture Room was Tony Pastor, who escaped from his father's farm to do a song-and-dance act at the age of nine. Inspired by Barnum's example, Pastor became a showman at twenty-four. He moved ever onward and upward, from a cheap Broadway theater to a large Bowery beer hall and then to the justly respected Tony Pastor's New Fourteenth Street Theater, where Lillian Russell made her first public appearance. With the passage of years, the blubbery, mustached Pastor, who had committed fifteen hundred songs to memory, competed with his mentor, presenting the most popular variety shows in New York and inventing bank night.

Eventually, Barnum's success with his Lecture Room enabled him to enlarge it beyond the immediate premises of the Museum. Often, three thousand persons jammed into the moral theater daily, and on holidays there was a full turnover every hour of the afternoon and evening. Most of these persons, a theatrical biographer has remarked, "would have been horrified at the suggestion that they had attended the theater."

Barnum's showmanship was evident not only in a canny instinct that enabled him to give the masses what they wanted, but also in his ability to dictate to them a desire for what he thought they should want. Modern high-pressure advertising was Barnum's most lamentable contribution to history.

"If there is a canon of advertising saints," Philip Guedalla wrote, "a Roll of advertising Honour, a hierarchy of those supreme Boosters before whose stately (and well displayed) images the innumerable Babbitts of two continents prostrate themselves, one may be sure that the figure of Mr. Barnum is somewhere near the top. . . ." On a recording of Barnum's voice reissued in 1940 Professor William Lyon Phelps called Barnum "the greatest psychologist who ever lived . . . the Shakespeare of advertising."

Every man has his star. Barnum's star was an exclamation mark. "I thoroughly understood the art of advertising," he wrote, "not merely by means of printer's ink, which I have always used freely and to which I confess myself so much indebted for my success, but by turning every possible circumstance to my account. It was my monomania to make the Museum the town wonder and town talk." Whenever he was asked his secret, Barnum replied: "Advertising is like learning—a little is a dangerous thing." He contended that the only liquid a man could safely use in excess was printer's ink. His advertising blurbs not only accented the unusual, but also bludgeoned readers into submission by persistent reiteration. When an advertisement first appears, said Barnum: "a man does not see it; the second time he notices it; the third time he reads it; the fourth he thinks about it; the fifth he speaks to his wife about it; and the sixth or seventh he is ready to purchase."

His publicity began with the Museum itself. One morning it was a hulking, drab, marble building, and lo, the next, it was a breath-taking rainbow, a kaleidoscope of color and curiosity. Overnight Barnum mounted monstrous oval oil paintings of outlandish "birds, beasts and creeping things" around the fourth story of his building. To this he added, as Lyman Abbott remembered observing it outdoors, "a collection of highly colored and illuminated glasses . . . kept by some contrivance boiling and bubbling on the walls of the Museum" to attract the night traffic. "A gaudy painted box," someone acidly remarked of the Museum, but Barnum preferred to call it his "great pictorial magazine," and estimated that it added a hundred dollars a day to his profits.

On the third-story balcony overlooking the street, Barnum seated a large, inharmonious band to serenade pedestrians. Flowing banners read: "Free Music for the Million." Crowds jostled to hear the concerts, and then recoiled. "I took pains to select and maintain the poorest band I could find," said Barnum, "one whose discordant notes would drive the crowd into the Museum, out of earshot of my outside orchestra." Then, defensively, he added: "Of course, the music was poor. When people expect to get 'something for nothing' they are sure to be cheated."

When a trumpet-player applied to Barnum for a job in the band, he was surprised to be hired on the spot. But when he had received no salary for several weeks, he was even more surprised. He approached the young showman. "Pay!" boomed Barnum. "I pay you? Nothing of the sort. You are to pay me. You seem not to understand, my young friend, that my band is made up of men who are learning their instruments, and want a good outdoor place for practice and to get the hang of playing together. They are glad enough to pay, and of course they ought to be, for there is no such chance in America for an industrious musician to advance in his art as in the band of Barnum's great American Museum."

Often, especially on holidays, Barnum strung banners and flags across the street. On the occasion of his first Fourth of July in the Museum he ran a rope of American flags across Broadway and secured it to a tree in the yard of St. Paul's Church. As crowds gathered before the Museum for holiday music, two vestrymen of the Church grabbed Barnum in the street and protested the use of their property for his publicity. If he would not take the rope of flags down, they would cut it down. Barnum gauged the temper of the gathering spectators, and turned on the vestrymen. "I should just like to see you dare to cut down the American flag on the Fourth of July," he shouted. "You must be a 'Britisher' to make such a threat as that; but I'll show you a thousand pairs of Yankee hands in two minutes, if you dare to attempt to take down the stars-and-stripes on this great birthday of American freedom!" The spectators began to grumble menacingly, and the vestrymen fled to the sanctity of the church.

To supplement his garish displays, Barnum set powerful calcium floodlights—the first known to New York—atop the roof of his Museum, making darkness into daylight every evening, and the bright lights drew more customers than moths.

Barnum's publicity sense often turned the most chance encounter into a public advertisement. One day a plump beggar came by for a handout. Instead, Barnum offered him a job at a dollar and a half a day. He handed the puzzled beggar five ordinary bricks.

"Now," said Barnum, "go and lay a brick on the sidewalk at the corner of Broadway and Ann Street; another close by the Museum; a third diagonally across the way at the corner of Broadway and Vesey Street, by the Astor House; put down the fourth on the sidewalk in front of St. Paul's Church, opposite; then, with the fifth brick in hand, take up a rapid march from one point to the other, making the circuit, exchanging your brick at every point, and say nothing to anyone."

The poor man was bewildered. "What is the object of this?"

Barnum advised him not to worry about the purpose. "It is a bit of my fun, and to assist me properly you must seem to be as deaf as a post; wear a serious countenance; answer no questions; pay no attention to anyone; but attend faithfully to the work and at the end of every hour by St. Paul's clock show this ticket at the Museum door; enter, walking solemnly through every hall in the building; pass out, and resume your work."

The beggar moved off with his five bricks, and began his idiot's play. Within half an hour, more than five hundred curious people were following him. In an hour, the crowd had doubled. When the brick-toting pied piper entered the Museum, dozens bought tickets to follow him. This continued throughout the day for several days, and Barnum's business showed a satisfying increase. But when police learned of the publicity stunt, they forced Barnum to withdraw his bricklayer, calling him a public nuisance and an obstruction to traffic.

Above all, of course, Barnum used the press. "I printed whole columns in the papers, setting forth the wonders of my establishment," Barnum said. "Old 'fogies' opened their eyes in amazement at a man who could expend hundreds of dollars in announcing a show of 'stuffed monkey skins'; but these same old fogies paid their quarters, nevertheless. . . ." Barnum threw most of his first year's profits into paid advertisements. The newspapers were not unappreciative. They opened their news columns to him free of charge, and it was there that he had his greatest successes. Among the first of these successes was the Feejee

Mermaid, one of the most deliberate and carefully plotted hoaxes in the annals of show business.

The saga of the Feejee Mermaid had its beginnings in Calcutta in 1817. There, the captain of a sailing ship out of Boston came upon "a preserved specimen of a veritable mermaid, obtained, as he was assured, from Japanese sailors." So impressed was the captain with this shriveled nautical wonder, an agonized human face with the scaly, finned body of a fish, that he appropriated $6,000 of his ship's funds to purchase it. Abandoning his vessel to a mate, the captain traveled with his acquisition to London to seek his fortune.

He showed his mermaid in a Piccadilly coffee house, and, for a time, three hundred onlookers a day were attracted to it. What they saw was reported by the Reverend Dr. Philip in the *Gentlemen's Magazine* of July 1822:

"The head is almost the size of a baboon. It is thinly covered with black hair, hanging down and not inclined to frizzle. The head is turned back and the countenance has an expression of terror, which gives it the appearance of a caricature of the human face. The ears, nose, lips, chin, breasts, nipples, fingers and nails, resemble those of a human figure. The appearance of the teeth afford sufficient evidence that it is full-grown. . . . The length of the animal is three feet.

"The resemblance to the human species ceases immediately under the mammae. . . . From the point where the human figure ceases, which is about twelve inches below the vertex of the head, it resembles a large fish of the salmon species. It is covered with scales all over. . . . The figure of the tail is exactly that which is given in the usual representation of the mermaid. It was caught somewhere on the north of China by a fisherman."

When receipts abruptly fell off, the captain returned with his mermaid to Boston. He insured the curiosity, placed it in safekeeping, and went to sea again to repay his employer the balance of the $6,000 borrowed from ship's funds. When he died, the only property he left his sailor son was the mermaid. The sailor son preferred cash to a curio, and he sold the thing to Moses Kimball, proprietor of the Boston Museum. But Kimball, possibly afraid of ridicule, decided against displaying it, and in the early summer of 1842 took it to New York to show it to Barnum.

Barnum liked the mermaid at once, but Joice Heth was still fresh in memory. He brought in a naturalist whom he trusted and asked him if the thing was genuine. The naturalist examined it and could find no evidence of hoax. The mermaid was perfect. He could not imagine how it had been manufactured.

"Why do you suppose it is manufactured?" Barnum asked.

"Because I don't believe in mermaids," the naturalist replied.

But Barnum did believe in mermaids. He acquired the thing from Kimball at once, and then mulled over the means by which he might sell the object to the general public. For he was sure that the public would be as skeptical as the naturalist had been. The mermaid could not be placed in the Museum and simply advertised. The public must be made receptive first. It required a build-up. Analyzing the problem, Barnum immediately solved it and went to work.

In a few weeks, a newsletter appeared in the *New York Herald* from a correspondent in Montgomery, Alabama. It was a report on local doings, crops, politics, and then, quite incidentally, a paragraph concerning "Dr. Griffin, agent of the Lyceum of Natural History in London, recently from Pernambuco, who had in his possession a most remarkable curiosity, being nothing less than a veritable mermaid taken among the Feejee Islands, and preserved in China, where the Doctor had bought it at a high figure for the Lyceum of Natural History." Ten days later, a similar newsletter from Charleston, South Carolina, appeared in another New York newspaper. Shortly after that, a third letter in a third New York newspaper, with the dateline Washington, D.C. The last correspondent added one note: he hoped "the editors of the Empire City would beg a sight of the extraordinary curiosity before Dr. Griffin took ship for England."

By slow stages, the honorable and mysterious Dr. J. Griffin was nearing New York. He paused in Philadelphia a few days, and was so grateful for his hotel manager's accommodation that he permitted him a peek at the mermaid. Excitedly, the manager begged to summon several of his friends, some of them editors, to view the wonder. Dr. Griffin was obliging. The editors came and were conquered. The press was filled with the Feejee Mermaid, and the New York newspapers waited anxiously.

Dr. Griffin checked into the Pacific Hotel in New York. He was besieged by reporters. Not one recognized in his dignified British countenance the familiar face of Levi Lyman, lawyer, practical joker, and collaborator with Barnum on the Joice Heth hoax. As Lyman permitted the awed press to peer at his rare specimen, Barnum toiled industriously behind the scenes. He had three romantic woodcuts of a mermaid prepared, and handed them out to three Sunday editors, grumbling that he had hoped to acquire the mermaid and failed, and now the woodcuts were of no use to him. The woodcuts were published with lengthy stories, and the furor mounted. Meanwhile, Barnum printed ten thousand copies of an advertising pamphlet on the Feejee Mermaid and held them in storage.

When the moment was ripe, Barnum distributed his pamphlets at a penny each. Then, leaving himself entirely out of it, he placed in all the newspapers public notices stating that "in accordance with numerous and urgent solicitations from scientific gentlemen in this city, Mr. J. Griffin, proprietor of the Mermaid, recently arrived from Pernambuco, S.A., has consented to exhibit it to the public, *positively for one week only!*" The place was Concert Hall on Broadway, and the admission was twenty-five cents.

Thousands attended the misbegotten creature, while Lyman, in the guise of an English professor, made his scholarly commentary. After a week, the Feejee Mermaid was moved to the American Museum, and no one objected. Across the entrance of the Museum, Barnum raised a huge flag representing a mermaid eighteen feet in length.

When he saw the flag, Lyman, in a rare moment of conscience, or perhaps because it made his task of lecturer more difficult, exploded. He told Barnum that it must be removed at once. "Nobody can satisfy the public with our dried-up specimen *eighteen inches long,* after exhibiting a picture representing it as eighteen feet. It is preposterous."

"Nonsense," replied Barnum. "That is only to catch the eye. They don't expect to see a mermaid of that size."

Lyman would not budge. He prepared to quit. "If you like to fight under that flag, you can do so, but *I* won't."

Cheerfully, Barnum accused him of being a deserter.

"Yes," said Lyman, "I desert false colors when they are too strong."

Regretfully, for the flag had cost him seventy dollars, Barnum hauled down the mermaid.

Before finally deserting New York and Barnum to embrace Mormonism in Nauvoo, Illinois, and to serve as Brigham Young's right-hand man in Salt Lake City, Lyman continued to extol the merits of the Feejee Mermaid. Audiences streamed into the Museum in great number, and receipts were almost a thousand dollars a week. Occasionally, there were dissenters. Once, after listening to Lyman's spiel, a visitor protested: "But I lived two years on the Fiji Islands and I never heard of any such thing as a mermaid." Lyman shrugged. "There's no accounting for some men's ignorance," he replied.

Although Barnum admitted to the hoax three decades later, he insisted that he had not manufactured the Feejee Mermaid. He did not know who had. In later life, he read a work on Japan by Philipp Franz von Siebold, a Bavarian, who wrote that Barnum's mermaid had been created by a Japanese fisherman who "contrived to unite the upper half of a monkey to the lower half of a fish, so neatly as to defy ordinary inspection."

So widely publicized was the Feejee Mermaid that, for the first time, the American Museum became a national institution, and Barnum himself America's first showman.

Now all competition fell before Barnum. He had been threatened briefly by Peale's Museum. The son of the artist-founder of this Philadelphia repository, Rubens Peale, had invaded New York in 1826. He exhibited medals, snuff-boxes, whale's teeth, Seneca Indians, freaks (featuring a five-year-old girl who weighed two hundred and five pounds), copies of such old masters as Leonardo da Vinci, and a menagerie that included a calf with two heads and six legs, a rhinoceros, and an assortment of live tigers, rattlesnakes, and bears. By 1830, he had lost his showplace to creditors, and eventually the ex-banker and his fellow speculators (whom Barnum had outwitted in acquisition of the American Museum) seized control. When their stock swindle failed, they sold out to an exhibitor who tried to appeal to society folk with more "scientific" presentations. When he failed in turn, he sold out to an aggressive showman named Henry Bennett.

Under Bennett's management, Peale's Museum led Barnum a chase for a short time. Bennett cut prices and caricatured Barnum's novelties. When Barnum had the Feejee Mermaid, Bennett answered with the Fudg-ee Mermaid. But it was not enough. A half year after the Feejee Mermaid, Bennett gave up to his landlord, who sold Peale's Museum to Barnum for $7,000. Then Barnum secretly hired Bennett to continue at Peale's so that their rivalry and antagonism could be kept alive. After a while, Barnum tired of the game, absorbed Peale's, and advertised "Two Museums in One."

In the three years before Barnum had taken charge, Scudder's American Museum had grossed $34,000. In the three years after Barnum took charge, the Museum grossed over $100,000. Barnum had paid for it, and it was his own. He had won New York, and then all America. Now, restlessly, he looked abroad—and wondered if the world was possible, too.

IV

EXHIBIT FOUR
Twenty-five-inch Man

It was because of the severity of a winter's day in November 1842, that the thirty-two-year-old Barnum discovered the exhibit that would catapult him to international fame.

Barnum had owned the American Museum almost a year, and he was in Albany, New York, on Museum business. The weather was freezing. When it came time for Barnum to return home by river boat, he learned that travel had been suspended because the Hudson was iced over. Forced to change his plans, Barnum boarded the old Housatonic Railroad for the first leg of his journey to New York. Since the rail terminus was in Bridgeport, Connecticut, where Barnum's half-brother Philo managed the Franklin Hotel, the showman decided to stop overnight.

Bridgeport, a sleepy community of four thousand persons, would seem to have had little to offer Barnum beyond a brief rest. But Barnum's mind was a file cabinet when it came to curiosities. Visitors were always telling him, or correspondents writing him, about new oddities.

Most of these he could not investigate because he was too busy. Yet he never forgot a suggestion or lead. Now, in a Bridgeport hotel room, relaxing with his brother, he remembered that someone had once told him "of a remarkably small child in Bridgeport." Did Philo know of such a one? Philo did indeed. Everyone in town knew of Sherwood Stratton's five-year-old son, who was the size of a small doll and weighed no more than his pet dog.

More interested than ever, Barnum asked his brother if he could convince the Strattons to show him their boy. Philo Barnum thought that a meeting might be arranged, and the very next day returned to the hotel with the miniature boy in hand.

Barnum eyed the boy with incredulity. The child was twenty-five inches in height. He weighed fifteen pounds. His foot was three inches long. "The smallest child I ever saw that could walk alone," Barnum remembered. And the best part of it was that "he was a perfectly formed, bright-eyed little fellow, with light hair and ruddy cheeks, and he enjoyed the best of health. He was exceedingly bashful, but after some coaxing he was induced to talk with me, and he told me that he was the son of Sherwood E. Stratton, and that his own name was Charles S. Stratton. After seeing him and talking to him, I at once determined to secure his services from his parents and to exhibit him in public."

The Strattons were poor, and Barnum had little difficulty in negotiating with them. Barnum wanted only a short-term arrangement. He had no desire to risk much on a child who might suddenly start growing. He offered to hire Charles for four weeks. He would pay the family three dollars a week, travel expenses to New York, and room and board for the boy and his mother. The Strattons considered this a generous offer.

Thus, with a handshake, began the saga of General Tom Thumb. With this midget, Phineas T. Barnum became a giant.

॰॰॰

In the next few months Barnum learned all that there was to know about the short life of Charles S. Stratton. When Cynthia Stratton gave birth to him on January 4,

1838, nothing indicated that he would be anything but normal. The Strattons were descended from solid Revolutionary War stock. There had always been a Stratton male in the militia. Moreover, the Strattons' two daughters, Frances, age four, and Mary, age two, were perfectly normal.

Charles was a strapping infant weighing nine pounds and two ounces at birth. In six months, he had grown to fifteen pounds and two ounces, and there was no apprehension. But at one year, he was still fifteen pounds and two ounces, and he had not grown higher than two feet and one inch. At two years and three he remained the same weight and height, and at four years and five, too. By then, the Strattons knew that they had a midget.

Medical science could do nothing for the Strattons. The reasons for arrested growth were then unknown. Not until three years after Charles Stratton's death, in 1886 to be exact, was the pituitary gland, located at the base of the skull, discovered to be responsible for deficiency in stature: defective pituitary, withholding growth hormones, was found to result in a stunted individual.

Incidentally, Barnum, who knew nothing of physiological refinements, always referred to Charles Stratton as "my dwarf." This was incorrect. His protégé was not a dwarf, but a true midget. In both cases, the problem is diminution, but the distinction exists. The dwarf has a normal upper body, but his lower limbs are misshapen because of a malfunctioning thyroid, and his general aspect is grotesque. The true midget, on the other hand, is perfectly proportioned, the copy of an ordinary human being, done to smaller scale.

There are contradictory versions of Charles Stratton's earliest years. According to some accounts, the midget's childhood was miserable. It was said that his stern, puritanical father regarded him as evidence of God's disfavor. It was said, also, that he was kept a prisoner in the house because public appearances caused too much of a stir. According to other accounts, Charles was a pampered and petted family favorite, always treated as normally as possible. He was given the freedom of the streets and fields, and, according to Barnum, the natives became so used to his size that he was considered neither abnormal nor curious. Whatever the truth, his departure from Bridgeport was a step upward.

When Cynthia Stratton brought her tiny, five-year-old boy to New York on December 8, 1842, she was appalled to learn from handbills and posters about the American Museum that she was the mother of "General Tom Thumb, a dwarf of eleven years of age, just arrived from England."

To pacify Mrs. Stratton, Barnum tried to explain the motives behind the metamorphosis. The name Charles Stratton was too ordinary. Searching for something more striking, Barnum had reached back into history and found the legend of the original Sir Tom Thumb, one of King Arthur's knights, who dwelt in a tiny golden palace with a door one inch wide and rode in a coach drawn by six white mice and was killed in a duel with a spider. Barnum decided that Tom Thumb was infinitely more provocative than Charles Stratton, and so "Tom Thumb" the midget was and would forever remain. As to the pompous military rank of General, the absurdity of it was irresistible.

The updating of the midget's age—a source of constant confusion to his biographers—was felt by Barnum to be a necessity. To exhibit him as a five-year-old would be to make him less a curiosity. Inevitably, people would wonder if he was really a midget and if he might not grow to normal height. But people would realize that as a maturing eleven-year-old, he was retarded and truly different.

As to the fiction of his importation from England, this was a snobbery that the public would like. Connecticut was too near at hand, familiar, and workaday. Marvels did not belong to industrious villages. Marvels came from afar. When Barnum later wrote about the fiction, he did not apologize. "I had observed (and sometimes, as in the case of Vivalla, had taken advantage of) the American fancy for European exotics; and if the deception, practiced for a season in my dwarf experiment, had done anything towards checking our disgraceful preference for foreigners, I may readily be pardoned for the offence I here acknowledge."

Barnum's family, prepared to co-operate in caring for Mrs. Stratton and Tom Thumb, had been enlarged since he had prospered. Installed in the converted billiard parlor next to the Museum were three daughters: Caroline, age nine; Helen, age two; Frances, an infant born eight months earlier (who would die before her second birthday). There was to be yet a fourth girl, Pauline, but she would not appear until 1846. A place for the visitors from Bridgeport was made in the overcrowded quarters, which had the shrill atmosphere of a girls' school. While Mrs. Stratton was made comfortable by the harried, frail Charity, Barnum undertook the education of his midget.

Trying to find a model after whom he might fashion Tom Thumb, Barnum studied the best-known little people of ages past. At last, he fastened on one, an incredible historic midget later much admired by Tom Thumb himself. This idol was Sir Jeffery Hudson.

Sir Jeffery was born in England in 1619. Until he was thirty years of age, he never exceeded the height of eighteen inches. When he was seven, his father, keeper of the baiting-bulls for the Duke of Buckingham, turned him over to his Lord. The Duke, in turn, served Sir Jeffery up to Queen Henrietta Maria in a cold baked pie. The Queen was enchanted with the tiny man, and prevailed upon the King to make him the first and only midget knight in history. Sir Jeffery was a Captain of the horse and the delight of Charles I's court.

In 1630, the Queen sent him to France to fetch her a midwife. Returning, Sir Jeffery was captured by Dutch privateers, but finally was released. His adventures continued. He fought a turkey, and was saved from the bird's talons. He almost drowned in a wash basin, but was rescued by William Evans, the court's eight-foot porter.

In 1644, he followed his Queen into French exile. Teased and insulted by the brother of Lord Crofts, Sir Jeffery challenged the full-grown man to a duel. Crofts appeared with water pistols. Affronted, Sir Jeffery repeated his challenge in stronger terms. They fought with pistols from horseback, and the midget shot his antagonist dead. Sir Jeffery was imprisoned for murder, released at the behest of the Queen, and became her most valiant defender. Once he was captured by the Barbary Turks and sold into slavery. After many privations, he was ransomed. He returned to England, spurted to three feet nine inches in height, and lived on a pension. His best friend was another midget, Richard Gibson, three feet ten, whose paintings of royalty today hang in Hampton Court beside Rembrandts and Leonardo da Vincis. Incidentally, Gibson married a midget named Jane Shephard—Charles I gave the bride away—and had nine normal children by her. Sir Jeffery fared less happily. He was implicated in the Popish Plot, jailed for three years, and died shortly after, at sixty-three.

The study of this singular life proved invaluable to Barnum. He saw to what heights a midget could rise. Further, he saw what he must do with Tom Thumb. Like Sir Jeffery, Barnum's midget must be made autocratic, impudent, regal. There was only a week to prepare. Barnum drilled Tom Thumb day and night, teaching him manners, patter, and a variety of roles. "He was an apt pupil with a great deal of native talent, and a keen sense of the ludicrous," said Barnum. "He made rapid progress in preparing himself for such performances as I wished him to undertake and he became very much attached to his teacher."

On the eve of his debut, Barnum took Tom Thumb on the rounds of the newspaper editors. The General hopped among the papers and inkpots on their desks, and at the home of James Gordon Bennett danced among the plates on the dinner table. The editors were amused and gave "the comical little gentleman" the benefit of their columns.

When Tom Thumb appeared on the stage of the Lecture Room, the auditorium was filled. He opened with a monologue punctuated with Barnum's puns. "Good evening, ladies and gentlemen," he began. "I am only a Thumb, but a good hand in a general way at amusing you, for though a mite, I am mighty. . . . In short, don't make much of me, for making more would be making me less. Though I grow in your favor, no taller I'd be."

This was followed by some banter with Barnum or a master of ceremonies. Barnum, addressing the audience, started it off. "It is only by placing the General in contrast with a very small child that the audience can form a right conception of his real height. Will some little boy step on the stage for a moment?" And then Tom Thumb added, with a squeaky, disgruntled tone: "I would rather have a little miss."

After this began Tom Thumb's main performance, in which he essayed a variety of roles. In flesh-colored tights, holding a bow and carrying a quiver of arrows, he cavorted as Cupid. Then, in the guise of a Revolutionary War soldier, waving a ten-inch sword and chortling "Yankee Doodle Dandy," he went through the paces of a military drill. Later, as the Biblical David, in suitable attire, he staged a mock fight against those Goliaths, Colonel Goshen and Monsieur

Bihin, the Museum giants. Other humorous studies followed: he was a semi-nude gladiator, an American tar in bell-bottomed trousers, Napoleon Bonaparte in full regalia.

Tom Thumb's debut was greeted with gales of laughter and applause. Overnight he became the talk of New York. Twice daily, at three in the afternoon and at seven at night, he appeared on the Lecture Room stage. Between shows he displayed himself alongside the giants, the fat boy, and the fortune teller.

Everyone, it seemed, wanted to see him, including the tireless Philip Hone, ex-Mayor. For July 12, 1843, Hone noted in his diary: "I went last evening with my daughter Margaret to the American Museum to see the greatest little mortal who has ever been exhibited; a handsome well-formed boy, eleven years of age, who is twenty-five inches in height and weighs fifteen pounds. I have a repugnance to see human monsters, abortions and distortions . . . but in this instance I experienced none of this feeling. General Tom Thumb (as they call him) is a handsome, well-formed, and well-proportioned little gentleman, lively, agreeable, sprightly, and talkative, with no deficiency of intellect. . . . His hand is about the size of a half dollar and his foot three inches in length, and in walking alongside of him, the top of his head did not reach above my knee. When I entered the room he came up to me, offered his hand, and said, 'How d'ye do, Mr. Hone?'—his keeper having apprised him who I was."

The four weeks sped by. Barnum was now satisfied that in Tom Thumb he had a tremendous drawing card. He was satisfied, too, that his midget was worth an investment despite the possibility that he might grow in stature. As a consequence, Barnum made a new agreement with Cynthia and Sherwood Stratton. He signed Tom Thumb on for one year at double his old salary—in short, seven dollars a week, with a fifty-dollar bonus at the end of the year.

Under the new contract, Barnum used Tom Thumb in different ways. Sometimes, he would display him at the Museum for several weeks running, then send him out of town with his family and a Museum representative to test him in other cities. In New York and everywhere else, Tom Thumb continued to attract and amuse. After six months, Barnum raised his salary to twenty-five dollars a week and began to consider the future.

Barnum's private dream was Europe. He had never been abroad. He was virtually unknown outside the United States. He wanted to conquer new worlds. In the person of a droll little boy who could walk upright beneath an average table without scraping his head he thought he had, at last, the means by which he might attain international fame.

The European venture, constantly dwelt upon, began to assume reality in Barnum's mind. Suddenly, one day, he decided to chance it. "Much as I hoped for success," he wrote long after, "in my most sanguine moods, I could not anticipate the half of what was in store for me; I did not foresee nor dream that I was shortly to be brought in close contact with kings, queens, lords, and illustrious com-moners, and that such association by means of my exhibi-tion, would afterwards introduce me to the great public and the public's money, which was to fill my coffers. Or, if I saw some such future, it was dreamily, dimly, and with half-opened eyes. . . ."

Once determined, Barnum swiftly put the machinery for his Continental invasion into motion. He negotiated a new contract with the Strattons. He would have Tom Thumb for another year, at fifty dollars a week. He would take abroad not only Tom Thumb, but also his parents and a tutor, and pay all their expenses. Sherwood Stratton agreed to give up his trade of carpenter in Bridgeport to serve as his son's ticket-seller. To this company, Barnum added one more—Professor Guillaudeu, a French natural-ist employed full time at the Museum. It was Barnum's hope that once his midget was launched, he and the Pro-fessor might explore Europe for new curiosities. To make certain that his name might not be forgotten while he was abroad, Barnum arranged to serve as foreign correspond-ent for the *New York Atlas*. He promised regular news-letters from Europe, and before the trip ended, he delivered and had published one hundred of them.

On January 18, 1844, Barnum and his entourage went aboard the *Yorkshire,* a trim new sailing vessel bound for Liverpool. When the anchor was lifted and a band played "Home, Sweet Home," Barnum's eyes were wet. What moved him was not separation from Charity, or his daugh-ters, or his friends, but a sudden sense of isolation and loneliness. For the first time this public man was without a crowd, forced into himself, with only a strange and alien destination ahead. And so tears came. Barnum, more than most, needed people in great number. They were as necessary to his spirit as oxygen to his body.

The crossing was uneventful. At times, the sailing ship ran against heavy seas, and at times it was becalmed, but Barnum was a good sailor, and he found the voyage pleasant. He had recovered from the brief melancholia felt at departure, and now he looked forward to England. After nineteen days the *Yorkshire* docked in Liverpool.

A sizable crowd was on the wharf to greet the Americans —Barnum had been careful to send advance notice of the coming of General Tom Thumb—but Cynthia Stratton, pretending he was an infant in her arms, smuggled the General past the curiosity seekers and into the city.

Barnum had no sooner lodged his company in the Waterloo Hotel than he had a caller. The owner of a cheap waxworks offered Barnum ten dollars a week for the use of Tom Thumb. Barnum sent him packing, and retired to his room to brood. Fear gripped him. He had arranged no itinerary or engagements for Tom Thumb. What if he could obtain none? Or even if he succeeded in obtaining an engagement, what if the public were not interested? The old sense of loneliness returned to oppress him. "I was a stranger in the land," Barnum wrote. "My letters of introduction had not been delivered; beyond my own little circle, I had not seen a friendly face, nor heard a familiar voice. I was 'blue,' homesick, almost in despair." Unashamedly, Barnum wept.

But then came the dawn. Barnum used his letters of introduction. There was friendliness everywhere. He hired a hall and began to show Tom Thumb while trying to formulate his attack on London. Meanwhile, the manager of the Princess' Theater in London appeared to scout Tom Thumb. Apparently he was satisfied. He offered Barnum a long-term contract at a generous figure, but Barnum declined. His old confidence had been restored by his new activity. He countered with the suggestion that Tom Thumb appear at the Princess' Theater in London for three evenings—he had decided that this was a good "means of advertisement"—and the manager agreed.

The troupe proceeded to London. Tom Thumb did his turn on the boards of the Princess' Theater before overflow crowds. The reaction was precisely what Barnum had calculated. Tom Thumb was a hit, and the populace eagerly discussed the talented urchin.

Barnum knew that he could successfully present Tom Thumb on his own, at any time, but still he held back. He remembered Maelzel's example with the automaton chessplayer: obtain the sanction of the noble, the royal, the wealthy. To this purpose, Barnum rented the mansion formerly occupied by Lord Talbot in the fashionable West End, employed a liveried butler, and sent out a limited number of invitations to aristocrats and editors, inviting them to have tea with Tom Thumb. Soon, the crested carriages appeared, and Barnum's parlor was filled with members of the nobility and journalists. Tom Thumb made a favorable impression on one and all.

Barnum still was not ready. Only when Edward Everett, American Minister to England, came calling did the showman make his final move. He told the Minister frankly that he wanted Tom Thumb to be introduced to Queen Victoria at Buckingham Palace. He was persuasive. The twenty-five-year-old Queen, six years on the throne and four married, had been mourning the death of her father-in-law. Now she and her family might appreciate any relaxation. Everett promised to see what he could do. What he did was to arrange to have Charles Murray, Master of the Queen's Household, invite Barnum and Tom Thumb to breakfast. Murray was impressed. He inquired as to Barnum's plans. Barnum said that he expected to leave for France shortly, but that he would delay the departure if Tom Thumb could have his audience with the Queen. Murray promised to do his best.

Meanwhile, Baroness Rothschild, wife of the world's richest banker, invited Barnum and Tom Thumb to her Piccadilly town house. Received by half a dozen servants, the towering Barnum and his miniature boy were led up marble stairs to the presence of the Baroness and a party of twenty ladies and gentlemen. Tom Thumb entertained the group for two hours. As they prepared to depart, Barnum remembered, "a well-filled purse was quietly slipped into my hand. The golden shower had begun to fall. . . ."

Barnum knew that the time was ripe. Promptly he leased the Egyptian Hall in the center of London, poured out his flood of prepared publicity, and placed Tom Thumb on

display. The response was overwhelming. Commoners and
aristocrats alike filled the auditorium to watch the twenty-
five-inch child impersonate Napoleon, Goliath, and Cupid.
And then there arrived the man Barnum most wanted to
see. He was a member of Her Majesty's Life Guards, in full
uniform, bearing a note. The note was from Queen Victoria, and invited General Tom Thumb, and his guardian,
Mr. Barnum to appear at Buckingham Palace.

Some hours later, Murray called to confirm the invitation and to convey the Queen's desire that "the General
appear before her, as he would appear anywhere else,
without any training in the use of the titles of royalty, as
the Queen desired to see him act naturally and without
restraint."

On the night of the command performance, Barnum
proudly hung a placard on the door of the darkened Egyptian Hall. It told all of London: "Closed this evening, General Tom Thumb being at Buckingham Palace by command of Her Majesty."

Upon arrival at Buckingham Palace, Barnum in knee
breeches and Tom Thumb in brown silk-velvet cutaway
coat and short breeches were briefed on how they must
conduct themselves before the Queen. Above all, they were
told, they must remember to answer all of Her Majesty's
questions through the Lord-in-Waiting, never speak directly to the Queen, and retire backwards when the audience was ended.

They were guided through a long corridor, and then
up a spacious flight of stairs, and finally into the royal picture gallery. Across the room, attired completely in black,
wearing no ornaments, stood the young Queen Victoria.
Beside her stood Prince Albert. And, ranged behind them,
the Duchess of Kent and two dozen members of the nobility, dressed in the highest fashion.

Tom Thumb—he looked "like a wax doll gifted with
the power of locomotion," Barnum said—advanced boldly
toward the Queen, bowed, and then chirped to one and
all: "Good evening, ladies and gentlemen!"

The salutation was greeted with hilarity. Smiling, Queen
Victoria took the midget by the hand and showed him
through the picture gallery. Tom Thumb gravely studied
the oils and told the Queen they were "first-rate." When
the Queen inquired about Tom Thumb's career, he amused

her with his witty replies. He glanced about and asked for
her son, the Prince of Wales, the future King Edward VII.
She told him that the boy was asleep and that a meeting
would be arranged in the near future. Then Prince Albert
and the other guests surrounded Tom Thumb, and Barnum
was briefly alone with the Queen. She began to question
him about the midget's family and upbringing. At first
Barnum carefully replied through the Lord-in-Waiting, but
the method was awkward and tiresome, and at last Barnum
conversed with the Queen directly. The Lord-in-Waiting
quivered, but the Queen was not offended.

The visit lasted an hour, most of the time being given
over to Tom Thumb's "songs, dances, and imitations."
When the act was done, Barnum remembered the etiquette
of exit. Rather hastily, he began to back away across the
long gallery, retreating yet always facing the Queen. Tom
Thumb tried to emulate him, but with less success, his legs
being so much shorter. Barnum never forgot what ensued:

"Whenever the General found he was losing ground, he
turned around and ran a few steps, then resumed the position of 'backing out,' then turned around and ran, and so
continued to alternate his methods of getting to the door,
until the gallery fairly rang with the merriment of the royal
spectators. It was really one of the richest scenes I ever saw;
running, under the circumstances, was an offense sufficiently heinous to excite the indignation of the Queen's
favorite poodle-dog, and he vented his displeasure by bark-
ing so sharply as to startle the General from his propriety.
He, however, recovered immediately, and with his little
cane commenced an attack on the poodle, and a funny fight
ensued, which renewed and increased the merriment of the
royal party."

When Barnum and Tom Thumb reached the safety of
the anteroom, the Queen sent her apologies for the poor
manners of her canine. Refreshments were then served in
an adjacent apartment, and at once Barnum was all business again. Learning that the audience would receive a line
or two in the official *Court Journal* and that this would be
seen by all the press, Barnum asked to speak to the editor.
The editor was brought forward. Barnum wondered if it
would be possible to receive a favorable review rather than
a mere mention. The editor suggested that Barnum write
out what he wished printed. Barnum obliged, and accord-

ingly, the next day, not only was the audience noted but Tom Thumb's act was reviewed as well: "His personation of the Emperor Napoleon elicited great mirth and this was followed by a representation of the Grecian Statues after which the General danced a nautical hornpipe and sang several of his favorite songs."

The Queen had taken a fancy to Tom Thumb, and soon invited him to a second audience. This was to satisfy the curiosity of the three-year-old Prince of Wales. The meeting was held in a gold-paneled drawing room. Tom Thumb complimented the Queen on the room's fine "chandelier." The Queen took his hand and said that she hoped he was well.

"Yes, ma'am, I am first-rate," said Tom Thumb.

Queen Victoria then led him to her eldest son. "General, this is the Prince of Wales."

"How are you, Prince?" Tom Thumb said, shaking the boy's hand. He measured himself against the Prince, and then added: "The Prince is taller than I am, but I feel as big as anybody."

There was a third audience in Buckingham Palace, again presided over by Queen Victoria, but also attended by King Leopold of the Belgians. When the Queen requested Tom Thumb to sing a song of his choice, he promptly chose "Yankee Doodle Dandy." There was shocked delight, memories of the revolution in the colonies still being fresh. But Tom Thumb's choice was less patriotic than personal. He had seen a Shetland pony in the courtyard, and he desired it. When he sang, "Yankee Doodle came to town, a-riding on a pony," he sang it with special emphasis, pointing at the Queen. But she missed the point, and Tom Thumb had to be satisfied with a gold pencil.

Royal sponsorship had its effect on the public. Tom Thumb was no longer a curiosity; he was a monument. At once, he became the rage of London. *Punch* called him "Pet of the Palace." Youngsters danced "The General Tom Thumb Polka," and the music halls rang with songs dedicated to him. Everywhere, children played with Tom Thumb dolls and cutouts.

During the spring and summer of 1844, tickets to the Egyptian Hall were at a premium. Celebrities elbowed commoners, and the Duke of Wellington attended several times. On one occasion, when he arrived, Tom Thumb was

doing his impersonation of Napoleon. Brought before the
Duke, the midget, still in the uniform of the recent French
Emperor, appeared very thoughtful. The Duke asked him
what was on his mind. And Tom Thumb replied: "I was
thinking of the loss of the battle of Waterloo." The witti-
cism was spread from one end of the sceptered isle to the
other, and it gave Tom Thumb renewed publicity.

In another section of the Egyptian Hall, Benjamin Robert Haydon, the historical painter and friend of Keats, was
showing his "Banishment of Aristedes" for a modest fee.
Haydon, at sixty, had suffered much from poverty and had
twice been jailed for debt. He set great store by this exhibit, but in a week when Barnum's receipts were three
thousand dollars, Haydon's receipts were only thirty-five
dollars. In despair and bitterness, he scrawled in his journal: "They rush by thousands to see Tom Thumb. They
push, they fight, they scream, they faint, they cry help
and murder! and oh! and ah! They see my bills, my boards,
my caravans and don't read them. Their eyes are open, but
their sense is shut. It is an insanity, a rabies, a madness, a
furor, a dream. I would not have believed it of the English
people." This recorded, Haydon slashed his throat with a
knife and then blew his brains out with a pistol.

So scandal was joined to fame, and the money poured
in. Barnum estimated that his receipts at the Egyptian Hall
were five hundred dollars a day. To this, of course, were
added three generous cash gifts from Queen Victoria. And
at nights and during weekends Tom Thumb entertained at
private parties for a fee of fifty dollars an appearance.
Among those he entertained in this manner were the Queen
Dowager Adelaide, Sir Robert Peel, and Lady Blessington.

During all of this furor, Barnum had not forgotten the
American Museum. He made two hasty visits to Paris early
in 1845, the first to obtain curiosities for the Museum, the
second to pave the way for the arrival of Tom Thumb. It
was during the first visit that Barnum became friendly with
the forty-year-old Robert Houdin, the founder of modern
magic.

Houdin had left his father's watchmaking establishment
in Blois to become a juggler and conjurer. Eventually his
interests turned to the invention of automata. His first profitable gadget was an early alarm clock. "You placed it by
your side when you went to bed," he wrote in his memoirs,

"and at the hour desired, a peal aroused the sleeper, while at the same time, a ready lighted candle came out from a small box." He devoted a year to creating a robot that answered spectators' questions by drawing or writing. As he told Barnum, he concentrated so hard on the construction of this "complicated machine that he lost all mental powers for a considerable period." Now the robot was the hit of the Paris Exhibition. Louis-Philippe, the middle-class liberal King who erased the royal crest from his carriage and was never without his green umbrella, came calling and asked the robot the population of Paris. The mechanical man wrote: "Paris contains 998,964 inhabitants"—and the King conceded that the answer was correct to the last digit. Houdin showed Barnum his robot. Barnum was enthralled, purchased it "at a good round price," sent it to London to be exhibited, and then shipped it on to the American Museum. Barnum visited Houdin's theater in the Palais Royal, watched his brilliant sleight-of-hand, listened to his exposé of illusions and fakes, and afterwards, accepted his advice in buying other mechanical curios as well as a $3,000 diorama depicting the removal of Napoleon's body from St. Helena to Paris. Barnum had great affection for Houdin, and followed his subsequent career closely. The crowning event in Houdin's life occurred in 1857, when he undertook a strange political mission for his government. The Algerian rebels were much excited and influenced by their holy prophets or Marabouts, who employed tricks of conjuring to prove their supernatural powers. The French wanted to pit their wizard Houdin against the fanatical Algerian fakirs, to have him "play off his tricks against theirs, and, by greater marvels than they could show, destroy the prestige which they had acquired."

In the Algiers Theater, before an audience of hostile Arab chiefs, Houdin produced cannon balls from an empty top hat and willed a five-franc piece into a vacant box suspended from the ceiling. His *pièce de résistance* was a small box that "becomes heavy or light at my order; a child might raise it with ease, and yet the most powerful man could not move it from its place." Houdin invited the most muscular of the Arabs to lift the small box. After terrible exertions, the Arab failed to budge it an inch—yet Houdin was able to lift it with a finger. The magic, of course, was in a hidden electromagnet, but the Arabs did not know this, and Houdin successfully wooed the revolutionists from their Marabouts.

On his second visit to Paris, Barnum made preparations for Tom Thumb. With the assistance of Dion Boucicault, the playwright who penned the Joseph Jefferson version of *Rip Van Winkle,* Barnum leased the Salle Musard for his midget, acquired accommodations at the Hotel Bedford for his troupe, and hired a Professor of English named Pinte to tutor Tom Thumb and interpret his patter for French audiences. This done, Barnum called upon William Rufus King, United States Minister to France, and inquired if Tom Thumb might be introduced to Louis-Philippe. The precedent had been set at Buckingham Palace, and the Minister was sure that the Tuileries would be equally receptive.

The exploitation of Tom Thumb in Paris was even greater than it had been in London. The day after Barnum and his troupe arrived, there was a royal summons from Louis-Philippe. Once more the showman and midget pulled on their knee-length breeches. Arriving at the Tuileries, they were escorted into the grand *salon.* The King and Queen, a variety of Dukes and Duchesses, and a dozen well-known citizens, were waiting.

There was less formality here than in London, and everyone conversed freely with Tom Thumb. Louis-Philippe asked countless questions about the United States, and remembered when he himself had lived as an exile in Philadelphia. "He playfully alluded to the time when he had earned his living as a tutor," reported Barnum, "and said he had roughed it generally and had even slept in Indian wigwams." Finally, Tom Thumb did his act, to the delight of all, and the King presented him with an emerald brooch set with diamonds.

The editor of the official *Journal des Débats,* who was witness to the hour-long audience with the King, gave an account of it to his fellow Parisians on May 23, 1845:

"General Tom Thumb accompanied by his guide, Mr. Barnum, has had the high honor of being received at the palace of the Tuileries, by their Majesties the King and Queen of the French, who condescendingly personally addressed the General several questions respecting his birth, parentage and career. . . . The King presented this courteous and fantastic little man with a splendid pin, set in brilliants, but it had the inconvenience of being out of proportion to his height and size. It might answer for his sword. . . .

"Tom Thumb is, in fact, of extraordinary lightness and nimbleness, even as a dwarf. In the King's presence he executed an original dance, which was neither the polka, nor the mazurka, nor indeed anything known. This dance was evidently invented for the General, and no one will ever venture to try it after him. The same may be said of another exercise which, with marked pleasure, he performs. We mean his personations of the Grecian Statues. . . . We prefer seeing Tom Thumb when he appears in the character of a gentleman; he takes out his watch and tells you the hour, or offers you a pinch of snuff, or some pastilles or a cigar, each of which are of uniformity with his size. He is still better when he sits in a golden chair, crossing his legs and looking at you with a knowing and almost mocking air. It is thus that he is amusing; he is never more inimitable than when he imitates nothing—when he is himself. . . .

"We will not mention a celebrated uniform which he wore in London, and which was amazingly successful with our oversea neighbors. The General Tom Thumb had too much good taste to take this costume to the Tuileries. We hope, then, as he possesses such fine feelings, that while he sojourns in Paris, he will leave it at the bottom of his portmanteau."

There were three more audiences with Louis-Philippe, and at one of them the King asked to see the "celebrated uniform . . . at the bottom of his portmanteau." This was, of course, the uniform of Napoleon Bonaparte. In great secrecy, Tom Thumb donned the attire of Napoleon and impersonated him for the King.

In return for this entertainment, Barnum asked one favor of the King. A holiday was approaching, Longchamps day, and Barnum wanted Tom Thumb's carriage in the group reserved for royalty. The King consented.

Tom Thumb's carriage, specially built by Fillingham of London, had been a surprise gift from Barnum. The coach, eleven inches wide and twenty inches high, was painted blue and white. The plate-glass windows were covered by Venetian blinds, and the interior was decorated in brocade. The crest on the doors included the British and American flags and the motto: "Go ahead!" With the coach came four improbable Shetland ponies, almost perfectly matched and thirty-four inches high. The vehicle and ponies had cost Barnum $2,000, but when Tom Thumb rode it through the crowded streets of Paris on Longchamps day, and thousands cheered and roared with delight, Barnum knew that his investment had been worth while.

Barnum's success in Paris was even greater than his success in London. *Figaro* and the rest of the French press publicized Tom Thumb's every move. A café was named after him. Snuffboxes bore his picture on their lids. His plaster statue graced hundreds of shop windows. He inspired poems and lithographs. He was elected an honorary member of the French Dramatic Society. His two shows a day at the Salle Musard were sold out two months in advance. "I was compelled," Barnum said, "to take a cab to carry my bag of silver home at night."

After a long stay in Paris, Barnum took Tom Thumb on a tour of France. This was followed by a journey into Spain, where the midget attended bullfights with Queen Isabella. Crossing into Belgium, Professor Pinte asked Barnum what were the qualifications of a successful showman. Barnum replied: "He must have a decided taste for catering for the public; prominent perceptive faculties; tact; a thorough knowledge of human nature; great suavity; and plenty of 'soft soap.' " In Brussels, the party was entertained by King Leopold. Finally, after visiting the battlefield of Waterloo and buying some relics for his Museum (he later found them to be manufactured yearly in Birmingham), Barnum took his troupe back across the Channel to England. Profitable showings were held in London, in other large cities of England, and in Ireland.

Three years had passed, and it was time to return home. "The General," wrote Barnum, "left America three years before, a diffident, uncultivated little boy; he came back an educated, accomplished little man. He had seen much, and had profited much. He went abroad poor, and he came home rich." Barnum forgot that he might have written almost the same words about himself.

Although Barnum continued his close association with Tom Thumb on an equal partnership basis for more than three decades, he never ceased in his quest for another Tom Thumb.

In 1861, when the General had added a mustache and

ten inches to his stature, and had swelled to fifty-two pounds, a more diminutive midget called upon Barnum at the Museum. His name was George Washington Morrison McNutt, and he was the son of a New Hampshire farmer. He was eighteen years old, twenty-nine inches in height, and weighed twenty-four pounds. Several showmen were interested in him, but Barnum signed him to a three-year contract for $30,000. The new find was christened Commodore Nutt and attired in a naval uniform.

He was an immediate favorite, and Abraham Lincoln invited Barnum to bring him to the White House. A cabinet meeting was interrupted so that the pair might be introduced. The interview was brief but affable. When it was time for the midget to leave, Lincoln took his hand. "Commodore," the President said, "permit me to give you a parting word of advice. When you are in command of your fleet, if you find yourself in danger of being taken prisoner, I advise you to wade ashore." Everyone laughed except the Commodore, who lifted his gaze slowly up Lincoln's long legs, and then replied: "I guess, Mr. President, you could do better than I could."

The year after he had acquired Commodore Nutt, Barnum heard of a remarkable female midget named Mercy Lavinia Warren Bump, who preferred the name Lavinia Warren. Although both of her parents were six feet tall, and seven of her brothers and sisters were of normal growth, she had a younger sister named Minnie who was also a midget. Lavinia, at the age of twenty, was exactly thirty-two inches tall and weighed twenty-nine pounds. Despite her size, she had been a schoolteacher of third-grade pupils in Middleboro, Massachusetts. More recently she had traveled on a Mississippi showboat. Barnum found her to be "a most intelligent and refined young lady, well educated, and an accomplished, beautiful, and perfectly developed woman in miniature." He signed her to a long-term contract at once.

Immediately, Barnum's small world got out of hand. For the advent of the dark-haired, attractive Lavinia created a Lilliputian triangle. Commodore Nutt, who worked beside her, became enamored of Lavinia. Then Tom Thumb, temporarily retired at the age of twenty-three and enjoying the pleasures of his miniature billiard table in Bridgeport and his sailing yacht on Long Island Sound, appeared in

New York, set eyes upon Lavinia, and fell madly in love with her. Competition for her hand became so hectic that the Commodore in a moment of jealousy floored the flabby General with a punch. The Commodore had vigor and strength in his favor. But Tom Thumb had wealth and fame. Tom Thumb begged Barnum to speak to Lavinia on his behalf. Barnum refused. "You must do your own courting," he told the General.

Tom Thumb went ahead. On an evening in the autumn of 1862, he arranged to see Lavinia alone in the sitting room of Barnum's Bridgeport mansion. Without Barnum's knowledge, several house guests secreted themselves and overheard what happened—and Tom Thumb's proposal was saved for history.

The General discussed his property, his trips to Europe, and Lavinia's scheduled journey abroad. He said that he would like to travel with Lavinia.

"I thought you remarked the other day that you had money enough, and was [*sic*] tired of traveling," Lavinia said teasingly.

"That depends upon my company while traveling."

"You might not find my company very agreeable," said Lavinia.

"I would be glad to risk it. . . . Would you really like to have me go?"

"Of course I would."

Tom Thumb slipped an arm around her waist. "Don't you think it would be pleasanter if we went as man and wife?" Lavinia told him not to joke. Tom Thumb replied that he had never been more serious. Lavinia said that it was all so sudden. Tom Thumb replied that marriage had been on his mind for months. "You ought to get married," he told her. "I love you dearly, and I want you for a wife." Flustered, Lavinia answered: "I think I love you well enough to consent, but I have always said I would never marry without my mother's consent."

So it came down to Lavinia's mother. Mrs. Bump disliked Tom Thumb for his mustache and his pomposity. She also feared that the marriage had been engineered by Barnum as a publicity stunt. But letters from Tom Thumb and Lavinia, as well as reassurances from Barnum and George A. Wells, a Bridgeport hotel proprietor who was a friend of the Strattons, softened her, and, at last, she gave consent.

The moment the wedding was announced, New York was agog. Tom Thumb joined Lavinia in the Museum, and thousands poured in to observe them. Receipts were often three thousand dollars a day. Barnum offered the pair fifteen thousand dollars to postpone their wedding one month and continue showing. "Not for fifty thousand dollars," the General cried.

One voice was raised against the wedding. James Gordon Bennett implied that Barnum had arranged it to stimulate business and that people flocked to see the couple because of the freakish sex problem posed. "What class of ideas did Barnum appeal to when he advertised her engagement so extensively?" Bennett asked. "One had only to listen to the conversation of silly countrymen and countrywomen as they stood gaping at the little Queen of Beauty or to open his ears to the numerous jokes in circulation upon the subject in order to receive a sufficient answer to these questions."

Barnum did nothing to encourage the curiosity of the public in the sex life of the midget couple, but the curiosity persisted both before and after the marriage. According to Walter Bodin and Burnet Hershey in *It's a Small World,* most true midgets have normal sexual development consistent with their size. "Though endowed with the sexual desires of mature women of normal size, midget women are virtually always equipped with sexual organs no larger than those of a girl of five or six. . . . The sexual problems of midget men are simpler. They are, in the main, three. These are late potency, early impotency, and the certainty of derision whenever their passions center on women of normal size, which is frequently the case." Lavinia and Tom Thumb were said to be sexually normal.

Two thousand persons were invited to the wedding, and many who were not invited offered as high as sixty dollars for a pew. Gifts came by the hundreds, including Chinese fire screens from the President and Mrs. Lincoln, and a music box (a lever released a warbling bird) from Barnum. On February 10, 1863, in New York's Grace Church, before an assembly that included several governors, army generals, congressmen, and millionaires, Lavinia Bump and Tom Thumb were united in matrimony by the Reverend Junius Willey of Bridgeport.

After the wedding and reception, the tiny couple was

received at the White House. "My boy," Lincoln said, addressing himself to the General, and indicating their respective heights, "God likes to do funny things; here you have the long and the short of it." Respectful of the General's high military rank, the President asked him if he had any advice to offer on the conduct of the Civil War. Tom Thumb nodded. "My friend Barnum," he said to Lincoln, "would settle the whole affair in a month."

Having concluded their meeting in Washington, Lavinia and Tom Thumb retreated to the groom's apartment in the $30,000 Bridgeport house his father had built. The apartment was cluttered with scaled-down furniture constructed by Sherwood Stratton, though the miniature rosewood bed with carved flowers in its headboard was a gift from Barnum. (Once, reciprocating, Tom Thumb gave the showman a gold watch that sounded an alarm every fifteen minutes.) Later, under Barnum's auspices, the newlyweds made a successful three-year, 56,000-mile world tour during which they met Pope Pius IX, Napoleon III, and Victor Emmanuel.

It was generally believed that Lavinia gave Tom Thumb an heir, and that this offspring died of brain inflammation at the age of two. Although the story is still believed, there was no truth in it. The child of the midget couple was Barnum's brainchild, invented for publicity. However, Lavinia's midget sister, Minnie, having married an English fancy skater who was slightly taller than a midget, died in childbirth after bearing a five-and-a-half-pound girl who also died.

Lavinia and Tom Thumb were happily married for twenty years. The General grew portly and attained the height of three feet four inches. He also grew extravagant. He owned a sailing sloop, pedigreed horses, and a carriage and a driver, and he smoked expensive cigars. He was a Thirty-Second Degree Mason and a Knight Templar. On the morning of July 15, 1883, he died of apoplexy at the age of forty-five. More than ten thousand persons attended his funeral service, and he was laid to rest in Bridgeport's Mountain Grove Cemetery, which Barnum had helped to create. Over his grave, atop a forty-foot marble shaft, was placed a life-sized granite statue of himself, a statue he had once commissioned.

Despite the fact that he had made several million dollars

in his lifetime, the General left Lavinia with little but his name. All that remained of the great fortune that he had dissipated was a few pieces of property and $16,000. To still her grief, Lavinia took a troupe on the road. Sharing top billing with her was Count Primo Magri, who had received his title from the Pope and had once worked for her husband. The Count, a piccolo-player and pugilist, was three feet nine inches tall, and eight years Lavinia's junior. After two years of widowhood, Lavinia married him.

Interest in midgets had waned, and Lavinia's life dissolved into a nightmare of one-night stands. She and the Count appeared in a vaudeville act, four motion-picture comedies, and finally a Coney Island side show. At last they retired to a miniature home in Marion, Ohio, and conducted it as a tourist attraction. With old age, Lavinia became fat and garrulous, and much devoted to Christian Science and the D.A.R. She died in 1919, at the age of seventy-eight, and her second husband died shortly after.

To the very end, Lavinia always wore a gold locket containing her first husband's picture. She had loved Tom Thumb more than Magri, and when she died she requested burial beside him. Over her child-sized coffin, in the shadow of Tom Thumb's monument, a small headstone was placed. On it were but two words: "His Wife."

These were the little people who helped make Barnum big. The showman would never forget that of the eighty-two million tickets sold by his variety of attractions, twenty million had been sold by General Tom Thumb alone.

V

EXHIBIT FIVE
Chang and Eng

Barnum returned to New York City from Europe in February 1847. He had two immediate objectives: first, to obtain a stronger hold on the American Museum by renewing his lease; second, "to make the Museum a permanent institution in the city."

Olmsted was dead, and Barnum negotiated with his heirs, demanding a long-term agreement and threatening to construct his own building on Broadway, if he could not have his way. At last, the heirs relented. Barnum acquired a twenty-five-year lease on the American Museum at a rental of $10,000 a year. As his curiosities now grossed in a single day what they had once earned in a week, Barnum could well afford the steep rental.

He concentrated all his energies on making the Museum the city's foremost landmark. How well he succeeded in the next decade may be realized by consulting the leading tourists' guidebook of the period, *New-York* by E. Porter Belden, published in 1849. While its chapter headed "Entertainment and Amusement" makes mention of Castle

Garden, The Lyceum Gallery, The Mechanics' Institute, and the bathing resort of Coney Island, the place of honor is given to Barnum's showcase.

"Of all the institutions of the kind on the continent," Belden's guidebook states, "the AMERICAN MUSEUM of New-York is the most popular. It was founded in 1810 by the late John Scudder, Esq., but it owes its high position in public esteem to the management of its present proprietor, Phineas T. Barnum, Esq., who purchased the establishment in 1842. . . . The American Museum is now supplied with the most novel curiosities, and numerous and valuable specimens in every department of art and natural history. A lecture room is connected with the establishment, where concerts, philosophical experiments, and a variety of entertainments, are given."

In his energetic campaign to make his Museum a synonym for amusement, Barnum brought to bear on the public every perception and strategy and skill at his command. He led off with his best and most publicized attraction: the now cosmopolitan Tom Thumb. Within two weeks of Barnum's return from abroad, newspaper advertisements read:

"GENERAL TOM THUMB, the smallest man in Miniature in the known world, weighing only FIFTEEN POUNDS, who has been patronized by all the CROWNED HEADS of Europe, and been seen by over 5,000,000 persons, has returned to America, in the packet ship Cambria, and will make his GRAND DEBUT at his former headquarters in this city, the American Museum, where the most extensive preparations have been made to receive him."

Barnum promised, of course, the familiar impersonations of Napoleon and the Grecian Statues. But he made it clear that something new had been added:

"He will also appear in his magnificent COURT DRESS presented him by Queen Victoria, of England, and worn before all the principal Courts of Europe. After which he will appear in his BEAUTIFUL SCOTCH COSTUME, in which he will dance the HIGHLAND FLING."

For one month, Tom Thumb performed to large audiences in the Lecture Room. The clamor from the rest of the United States to see the little man was so great that Barnum agreed, at last, to take him on tour. After visiting President James K. Polk in the White House, the showman and the General continued on to Philadelphia, Boston, and Buffalo, then went to Havana, and back to Macon, Mobile, and New Orleans. Barnum's profits were considerable: while his expenses averaged no more than $200 a week on the tour, his box-office receipts averaged better than $3,000 a week.

Once back in his office beside the first-floor staircase of the Museum, Barnum considered new oddities to stimulate business. After brief hibernation, he emerged with a fresh supply of ideas. There was a beauty contest to find "the handsomest women in America" (through daguerreotypes submitted) and to display the pictures for public judgment in a Gallery of Beauty. There was Old Blind Tom, a Negro pianist, who could immediately duplicate on the keyboard anything heard once, even down to mistakes. There was a Negro inventor who had a weed that would turn all colored folk white; Barnum hailed this as the solution to slavery and put the charlatan on exhibit. There was Anna Swan, an intelligent and attractive giantress who was seven feet eleven inches tall and weighed four hundred and thirteen pounds. Upon hearing about her through a Quaker friend, Barnum dispatched an agent to Pictou, Nova Scotia, to bring her back to New York. Eventually, Anna Swan fell in love with another of Barnum's giants, Captain N. V. Bates, a half-inch taller than she and weighing four hundred and seventy-eight pounds, and married him. After many years in show business, they retired to a colossal house, with doors nine feet high, in Ohio. There was Young Herman, the Expansionist, who could inflate his chest from thirty-eight inches to sixty inches. Like his employer, he enjoyed a practical joke. In New York or London, the *English Illustrated Magazine* reported, he enjoyed visiting clothing stores. "Once inside, he makes himself small. The dealer measures him, gives him a thirty-six-inch coat. Finds it too tight. Tries a larger coat; finds that too tight. This process is repeated until the largest coat in the establishment is found, when Herman astounds the dealer by bursting the buttons off." Above all, there was "the most astounding wonder of the nineteenth century," Madame Josephine Fortune Clofullia, comely, feminine, and luxuriantly bearded.

The bearded lady has become a standard attraction of every carnival and circus side show, but in Barnum's day, a bewhiskered female was a rarity, and Madame Clofullia was a pioneer of the species. She had been born Josephine Boisdechene in Versoix, Switzerland. At the tender age of eight, she had a two-inch beard. At fourteen, it was a five-inch beard. And at twenty-five, when Barnum hired her, she sported, according to his advertisements, a "full-grown beard and whiskers that the most fastidious dandy would be proud to wear." In her youth, she had been exhibited by a French showman, and she had received gifts from Napoleon III. A painter named Clofullia had found the beard no bar to romance, and had married her. She had given her husband two children, and the surviving boy—also engaged by Barnum—had a face as hairy as a Yorkshire terrier.

Madame Clofullia might have remained a routine oddity had not a customer at the American Museum, William Charr, gazed at her with disbelief and trotted off to the police to cry swindle. Charr claimed the Madame was "nothing more nor less than a dressed-up man" and that "she and Barnum were humbugs." He had been cheated of his twenty-five-cent entrance fee, and he meant to have his revenge.

The case of fraud came before the Tombs Court in July 1853. Barnum was on hand to testify that a team of reputable physicians had assured him that Madame Clofullia was of the female sex and that her whiskers were not a physical impossibility. The Madame's aged father took the stand to testify that Josephine was indeed his daughter and not his son. Monsieur Clofullia appeared to declare indignantly that the Madame was his legal spouse for two years and that she had borne him two children. Finally, at the initiative of Barnum, Dr. Covil, attached to the Tombs, announced that he and a matron had examined the Madame and found her female in every respect.

The suit was dismissed, and William Charr remained poorer by a quarter of a dollar. And Barnum, by happy accident, had his sensation and his continuing crowds. But was it an accident? One skeptical editor in Connecticut had heard—word had "leaked out," he printed—that Charr had been employed by the astute Barnum to instigate the lawsuit. The editor did not object. He was filled only with admiration. And, apparently, so was the public.

Through the many years of the Museum's life, a variety of 600,000 exhibits, some of them living, some inanimate, many transient, was acquired and presented by Barnum. Of this number, perhaps the most representative of the gallery in its heyday—especially because the name of the exhibit became a part of the American language and found its way into Webster's dictionaries—was the Siamese Twins.

Today, every double monstrosity is labeled Siamese Twins, but Chang and Eng, who were not Siamese, but Chinese, were the originals. Although the joined pair became more renowned than any of Barnum's exhibits except Tom Thumb, Barnum did not care for them. For one thing, they were already world-famous when he took them on. He could claim no credit for their discovery or their drawing power. For another, they were independent and unfriendly. As a matter of fact, the Twins detested and avoided Barnum. Even though they were at odds about many things, they agreed that Barnum was stingy.

Chang and Eng were born in Meklong, Siam, a small village near Bangkok. Their father was an impoverished Chinese fisherman. From birth, they were united by a thick, fleshy ligament covered with skin, like a four-inch arm, connecting their lower chests. At first, this band held them face to face, but as they grew, it stretched to five and a half inches, allowing them to stand and move sideways. The joint was sensitive but strong. If it was touched at the middle, both boys felt the sensation. Yet so sturdy was it that if one of the Twins happened to trip and lose his balance, the ligament held him dangling but firm.

With some difficulty, Chang and Eng learned to walk in step and then to swim with considerable agility in the near-by river. When they were nineteen years old, and a familiar sight to their neighbors, they were seen swimming one day by an American sailing-master, Captain Coffin, of the ship *Sachem*. Amazed at the sight, the Captain consulted Robert Hunter, a Scotch merchant, and together they determined to purchase the boys and exhibit them. They made inquiries. The father of the Twins had recently died, and their mother was prepared to bargain. In due time a contract was signed, money changed hands, and Coffin and Hunter took the Siamese Twins to England.

After being shown on the Continent for many years, Chang and Eng were taken to Boston and then to New York. Advertised as "The Siamese Double Boys," they at once became a center of great interest and controversy.

There was a rumor that they were not genuinely joined. The controversy attracted Barnum. He met them, was satisfied that they were true freaks, and bought up their contract. After that they were shown at the American Museum regularly.

The Siamese Twins were the most temperamental of Barnum's freak family. Nature had played more than one cruel joke on them. For though Chang and Eng were sentenced to each other, they were opposite in every way and disliked one another. Chang, the slightly shorter one on the Twins' own left, enjoyed wine and women; Eng, the more studious and intellectual, liked an evening of chess. Their differences were reported by the *Philadelphia Medical Times* in 1874: "What Chang liked to eat, Eng detested. Eng was very good-natured, Chang cross and irritable. The sickness of one had no effect upon the other so that while one would be suffering from fever, the pulse of the other would beat at its natural rate. Chang drank pretty heavily—at times getting drunk; but Eng never felt any influence from the debauch of the brother. They often quarrelled; and, of course, under the circumstances their quarrels were bitter. They sometimes came to blows, and on one occasion came under the jurisdiction of the courts."

Left alone, they would brood in silence. Sometimes, they would agree to do first what one wanted, then what the other wanted. Their only interests in common were fishing, hunting, and woodcutting. Although their abnormality had made them wealthy, they lived only to be free of one another. Countless doctors were visited, but not one promised them that they could live a single day cut apart.

Once, after a particularly bitter quarrel, they decided to defy medical advice. According to the *Medical Times:* "Chang and Eng applied to Dr. Hollingsworth to separate them; Eng affirmed that Chang was so bad that he could live no longer with him; and Chang stated that he was satisfied to be separated, only asking that he be given an equal chance with his brother, and that the band be cut exactly in the middle. Cooler counsels prevailed."

Enjoying American freedom and American dollars, the Twins agreed to apply for citizenship. At the naturalization office they learned that they must have a Christian or family name. They had no names other than Chang and Eng.

An applicant standing in line behind them, overhearing the nature of the problem, offered his last name. It was Bunker. And so the Siamese Twins became Chang Bunker and Eng Bunker, American citizens.

At last, wearying of the grueling Museum routine, they gave Barnum notice and retired to a plantation near Mount Airy, North Carolina. They relaxed and let their slaves do the work. Then, almost simultaneously, when they were forty-two, they fell in love with the young daughters of a poor Irish farmer in the neighborhood. It was a double wedding. Eng married Sally Yates, and Chang married Addie Yates. Now diplomacy and compromise were required. The Twins built a second mansion, a mile away from the first. Two separate households were established. Chang and Eng and Sally spent three days in Eng's house, and then, Chang and Eng and Addie spent three days in Chang's house. Apparently the arrangement was not inhibiting. The Twins produced twenty-one children.

The Civil War took their slaves and their wealth from them. They were forced back into show business. They asked Barnum to manage them, and he agreed. When their comeback proved unsuccessful in New York, Barnum decided to send them abroad. "I sent them to Great Britain where, in all the principal places, and for about a year, their levees were continually crowded," the showman wrote. "In all probability the great success attending this enterprise was much enhanced, if not actually caused, by extensive announcements in advance that the main purpose of Chang-Eng's visit to France was to consult the most eminent medical and surgical talent with regard to the safety of separating the twins."

Again they were wealthy. And again they took leave of Barnum and retired with their wives to the plantation near Mount Airy. They were sixty-three years old, and though Chang had been unwell, the future was bright. The end came suddenly, and the *Annual Register* reported it in 1874 to the Twins' vast English following:

"They were at Chang's residence, and the evening of that day was the appointed time for a removal to Eng's dwelling. The day was cold and Chang had been complaining for a couple of months past of being very ill. On Friday evening they retired to a small room by themselves and went to bed, but Chang was very restless. Sometime between midnight and daybreak they got up and sat by the fire. Again Eng protested and said he wished to lie down, as he was sleepy. Chang stoutly refused and replied that it hurt his breast to recline. After a while they retired to their bed, and Eng fell into a deep sleep. About four o'clock one of the sons came into the room, and going to the bedside, discovered that his uncle was dead. Eng was awakened by the noise and in the greatest alarm turned and looked upon the lifeless form beside him, and was seized with violent nervous paroxysms.

"No physicians were at hand, and it being three miles to the town of Mount Airy, some time elapsed before one could be summoned. A messenger was despatched to the village for Dr. Hollingsworth, and he sent his brother, also a physician, at once to the plantation but before he arrived the vital spark had fled, and the Siamese twins were dead." Apparently, the fact that Eng had never felt the effects of the alcohol that Chang had consumed did not mean the Twins were separate persons. Probably it meant that Chang possessed less tolerance for stimulants and that his central nervous system was more sensitive. An autopsy revealed that the livers and blood streams of the Twins were one, and that they had been meant to live together or not at all.

Like Tom Thumb, Chang and Eng had enhanced Barnum's reputation for showmanship. He mourned them only briefly, and they received scant notice in his autobiography. His restless mind had long before turned to other wonders.

Few customers in Barnum's lifetime realized how aggressively he searched for oddities. His business had become a big business, and therefore less personalized, and through the years he found it necessary to delegate powers to employees. Instead of waiting to happen upon a curiosity, to hear rumor of one, to investigate one himself, he took to hiring scouts and agents throughout the world. One was a German who owned a fish store in Hamburg in 1848. His name was Gottfried Claus Hagenback. One day he received from local fishermen, along with their regular catch, several live seals. He showed them in wooden tubs, and they attracted more customers than his produce. Encouraged, he turned his shop into an aquarium of living deep-sea oddities. The results justified further investment in animal life. When Barnum heard of Hagenback, he retained him, and gave him thousands of dollars' worth of orders for strange beasts. To satisfy Barnum, his most important client, as well as a hundred zoos, Hagenback sent full-dress expeditions to Bornea, Sumatra, India, and the Congo.

There was no limit to Barnum's expenditure or persistence when he wanted to track down a new oddity. A case in point was recorded by William A. Croffut, for a time one of Barnum's private secretaries. The occult had a fascination for young Croffut, and he asked his employer why he did not send to India for a yogi or two to exhibit. Barnum replied flatly that no such creature as the yogi existed, that the yogi was a myth. Earlier, having heard, from time to time, travelers' tales of the yogi miracle men, Barnum had sent off "two shrewd and learned Yankees who were also Oriental travelers and acquainted with the geography and people of India" to locate for him an assortment of yogis to be employed at fifty dollars a night for one year each.

Barnum's agents had ranged India, but with no luck. "They advertised that they would pay yogis ten thousand dollars a year salary," Barnum told Croffut. "They found no yogi anywhere, although they found sleight-of-hand performers somewhat inferior to our own, and large numbers of mahatmas—the Hindoo priests. . . . Yes, it cost me some thousands of dollars—no matter how many—to prove the wonderful miracle-working-yogi myth. The reason I do not exhibit a yogi is the same as the reason I don't exhibit Santy Claus. I can't catch him!"

Barnum was less and less inclined toward the Feejee Mermaid type of fraud. Still, he could never resist a minor larceny. On one Fourth of July, to accommodate the thousands fighting to get into the Museum when it was already filled, Barnum had his carpenter hastily cut through the wall leading into Ann Street and lay down a temporary staircase in order to empty the building, but only a few people used that egress. The following year, on St. Patrick's day, when thousands of Irish swarmed into the Museum, the new egress was again ready. But Barnum learned that only three persons had used his special exit: most of the Irish families intended to make a day of it, gazing at the sights, having their box lunches, and then making the rounds again. Desperate to admit the customers lined up outside, Barnum grabbed a painter and whispered to him. In fifteen minutes, a canvas four feet square stood over the rear exit. It read: "To The Egress." Hundreds gathered around the sign, wondering. Someone called to someone else: "The Aigress—sure that's an animal we haven't seen." The hundreds filed through the exit into Ann Street —discovering only one marvel, that they had been duped —as new customers pushed into the main entrance.

A later fraud within the confines of the Museum was only a harmless practical joke much enjoyed by all and widely publicized. One autumn day, Barnum advertised "a mysterious novelty." Readers could rarely resist enigma. They appeared in gratifying numbers before the Museum stage. They saw a table to which was nailed a white sack with the legend: "The cat let out of the bag."

Barnum made his entrance, and then his spiel. While he had been on vacation, he stated, his assistant manager, John Greenwood, Jr., an Englishman, had spent twenty-five dollars to purchase from a farmer a "cherry-colored cat." When the curious cat had been delivered, Mr. Greenwood had been dismayed. But, added Barnum, "I thought he had received his money's worth." Barnum signaled to an assistant, who opened the bag and plucked from it an ordinary, scrawny, frightened black cat. The audience looked on blankly. Barnum continued. When the farmer had promised a "cherry-colored cat," he had meant, of course, a "cat of the color of black cherries," and here it was. Instead of threats of lynching, the audience greeted the fraud on Mr. Greenwood and themselves with a sudden burst of laughter, and nicknamed the cat "Black Crook." Once again, Barnum had calculated correctly. People wanted fun—even at their own expense.

The greater hoaxes were usually staged outside the precincts of the Museum. Barnum perpetrated them, by his own admission, for pleasure as well as money and, above all, he said, to publicize the Museum without directly involving it. Attending an anniversary of the battle of Bunker Hill on June 17, 1843, Barnum prepared to listen to an oration by Daniel Webster, but was soon diverted by the contents of an old tent near by. Investigating, Barnum learned that the tent contained fifteen starved and weary buffalo calves about one year old. The buffaloes had been driven from the Far West by C. D. French, an expert rider and lasso artist, who possibly intended to exhibit them. An idea flashed into Barnum's mind. He offered French $700 for the lot, and the offer was accepted. Then he hired French at thirty dollars a month to take care of them, housed the herd in a New Jersey barn, and advised French to cram the spiritless animals with oats.

In his inimitable manner, Barnum went to work. News stories began to pepper the daily press speaking of a horde of wild buffaloes captured in the Rocky Mountains and now en route to New York, whence they would be shipped to Europe. Editors swallowed the bait and wrote notices suggesting that someone should exhibit the beasts, that they would be worth a dollar admission to see, that certainly 50,000 New Yorkers would respond. When interest was thus sufficiently aroused, Barnum released handbills, posters, newspaper advertisements. They read:

"Grand Buffalo Hunt, Free of Charge.—At Hoboken, on Thursday, August 31, at 3, 4, and 5 o'clock P.M. Mr. C. D. French, one of the most daring and experienced hunters of the West, has arrived thus far on his way to Europe, with a Herd of Buffaloes, captured by himself, near Santa Fe. He will exhibit the method of hunting the Wild Buffaloes, and throwing the lasso. . . . Mr. French will appear dressed as an Indian, mounted on a Prairie Horse and Mexican saddle, chase the Buffaloes around the Race Course, and capture one with the lasso. . . .

"No possible danger need be apprehended, as a double railing has been put around the whole course, to prevent the possibility of the Buffaloes approaching the multitude. Extra ferry boats will be provided. . . ."

Nowhere was mention made of the philanthropist who was producing this free entertainment. Behind the scenes, Barnum had negotiated for rental of all ferryboats going to Hoboken on the day of the show. He had also taken over drink and food concessions on the Race Course beside the Hoboken Ferry.

The big day came. The crush was so great that an extra ferry had to be put on the run. In seven hours, 24,000 persons—paying twelve and a half cents round trip each—crossed by boat to witness the free buffalo hunt. As they milled behind the double railing, consuming drink and food, awaiting the ferocious animals, they listened to a brass band. At last, the electric moment was upon them. All eyes were on the central shed. The door opened.

French, on horseback, prodded the footsore, emaciated

buffaloes with a sharp stick. With reluctance, they ambled into the arena. Barnum watched nervously and reported: "He immediately followed them, painted and dressed as an Indian, mounted on a fiery steed, with lasso in one hand and sharp stick in the other, but the poor little calves huddled together, and refused to move! This scene was so wholly unexpected and so perfectly ludicrous, that the spectators burst into uncontrollable laughter."

Startled by the laughter, the fifteen buffaloes broke into a trot. The thousands cheered, and the thunder of their throats so bewildered the buffaloes that they began a disorderly gallop. They plunged through the thin board railings, sending entire families scrambling to safety. Everyone was running now, the scared buffaloes hardest of all. At last, the trembling herd found refuge in a near-by swamp. One was lassoed and dragged back, to the delight of the multitude. Everyone knew that he had been cheated, but no one minded. A good time was had by all.

The indefatigable Philip Hone summarized the affair in his diary:

"A buffalo hunt with the lasso was advertised to take place 'without money and without price' except what was spent in ferriage and groggage. . . . One of the herd being caught by the lasso broke through the enclosure, and followed by the rest dashed into the crowd, overturning everything in their way and occasioning such screaming and scampering among their persecutors as was never before heard of in the peaceful precincts of the Elysian fields. One man was killed by falling from a tree to which he had fled for refuge. The imprisoned buffalo dragged the hunter into a marsh where he left him, and the herd cantered off for the Rocky Mountains for aught that is known to the contrary. So far as the ferry and the tavern were concerned, I presume the speculation turned out as well as was anticipated."

The Honorable Philip Hone need not have worried. Barnum had made $3,500 by the venture. After a few days, Barnum announced that "the proprietor of the American Museum was responsible for the joke, thus using the buffalo hunt as a skyrocket to attract public attention to my Museum. The object was accomplished and although some people cried out 'humbug,' I had added to the notoriety which I so much wanted and I was satisfied. As for the cry of 'humbug,' it never harmed me, and I was in the position of the actor who had much rather be roundly abused than not to be noticed at all."

After recovering the buffaloes from the swamp, Barnum repeated the free entertainment in Camden, New Jersey, with the same success. Finally, he exported half the buffaloes to England and sold the rest to meat markets at fifty cents a pound.

A hoax that better represented Barnum's talent for showmanship, and revealed his ability to use a topical event to his own purposes, occurred in the acquisition and showing of his Nondescript or Woolly Horse.

During the summer of 1848, when Barnum was in Cincinnati with Tom Thumb, he picked up a handbill that invited the public to an exhibition of a "woolly horse." Barnum went to see the curiosity. What he saw was an undersized, Indiana-foaled horse, with neither mane nor hair upon its tail, but with its entire body covered by what resembled tightly curled sheep's wool. The animal was so strange that Barnum promptly bought it, shipped it to Connecticut, and had it secreted in a barn. He knew that some use might be made of it, but in precisely what manner, he was not certain.

Soon enough, an opportunity presented itself. The intrepid John Charles Frémont, recently court-martialed Governor of California and soon to be the presidential candidate for the radical Republicans, was on his fourth expedition in the Rocky Mountains. Working for private interests who wanted a railway route to the west, Frémont became lost in the blizzards and was the subject of widespread front-page interest. Suddenly, he reappeared in California, more dead than alive, his equipment gone and eleven of his party dead. Headlines were bigger than ever, and the public spoke of little else. Barnum seized the moment.

Out of hiding came the woolly horse. Carefully clad in blankets and leggings to cover all but eyes and hoofs, he was carried to New York and placed in a shed behind the Museum. Next Barnum invented a news story, had it arrive by stagecoach from the far west, had it delivered to the leading newspapers. According to the news story, which disclosed Colonel Frémont's adventures in the snow, the Colonel and his party "had, after a three days' chase, succeeded in capturing, near the river Gila, a most extraordinary nondescript, which somewhat resembles a horse, but which had no mane or tail and was covered with a thick coat of wool. . . . The Colonel had sent this wonderful animal as a present to the U.S. Quartermaster."

Several days later it appeared that the clever P. T. Barnum had obtained the animal from the United States Army and was prepared to exhibit it in a building near the Museum. "Col. Frémont's Nondescript or Woolly Horse will be exhibited for a few days at the corner of Broadway and Reade street, previous to his departure for London," the advertisements announced. "Nature seems to have exerted all her ingenuity in the production of this astounding animal. He is extremely complex—made up of the Elephant, Deer, Horse, Buffalo, Camel, and Sheep. It is the full size of a Horse, has the haunches of the Deer, the tail of the Elephant, a fine curled wool of camel's hair color, and easily bounds twelve or fifteen feet high. Naturalists and the oldest trappers assured Col. Frémont that it was never known previous to his discovery. It is undoubtedly 'Nature's last,' and the richest specimen received from California. To be seen every day this week. Admittance 25 cents; children half price."

The mangy equine did moderate business in New York and fair business in neighboring towns, but was, briefly, an immense drawing card in Washington, D.C., largely because of the irritation it caused Colonel Frémont's father-in-law.

The powerful Senator Thomas Hart Benton of Missouri had objected when his sixteen-year-old daughter Jessie had fallen in love with Frémont. But after their marriage seven years before, he had taken Frémont under his wing. When Senator Benton heard of Barnum's showing, he attended it and was dismayed. Immediately, he sued Barnum's agent for taking twenty-five cents from him under "false pretences." Senator Benton argued that he had received many letters from Frémont, and that there had been no mention of a woolly horse. The suit went to court, and as Colonel Frémont was in far-off California, all evidence was inconclusive. In the end, the suit was dismissed, and Barnum profited at the box office. In a short time, the woolly horse was turned out to pasture near Barnum's Bridgeport residence—where he continued to advertise his promoter to passing carriages and trains.

Seven years later, Barnum duplicated the stunt of having an unusual animal on his private estate, and this time to even greater effect. He had imported from Ceylon a herd of ten wild elephants, and for four profitable years made them the featured attractions of "Barnum's great Asiatic Caravan, Museum, and Menagerie"—actually a means of putting the American Museum on wheels.

When he had tired of this, Barnum disposed of Caravan and stock except for a single elephant. This lone elephant was settled on the six-acre farm beside Barnum's home. Its keeper, in Oriental attire, with railroad timetable in hand, set it to plowing Barnum's fields whenever the New York and New Haven train puffed into view.

Reporters came on the run. The most credulous articles were published, saying that the elephant built Barnum's fences and stone wall, that it planted his corn, that it sprinkled his lawns, that it picked his fruit, that it milked his cows. During the two months of its labor, the plowing elephant drew a deluge of hundreds of letters. Everyone wanted to know if the elephant was a profitable agricultural animal. Barnum assured one and all that it was the best of farm help.

A fellow farmer and friend of Barnum's, Gideon Thompson, came calling. He observed the huge beast for fifteen minutes, tested the terrain, and turned a cynical eye on Barnum.

"What is your object, sir, in bringing that great Asiatic animal on to a New England farm?" Thompson asked.

"To plow," replied Barnum innocently.

"To plow? Don't talk to me about plowing! I have been out where he has plowed, and the ground is so soft I thought I should go through and come out in China. No, sir, you can't humbug me. You have got some other object in bringing that elephant up here. Now what is it?"

Barnum doggedly insisted that the elephant was just another beast of burden, employed to do the heavy work. Thompson doubted that the beast could be profitable, considering what it probably ate every day. Barnum answered that it ate no more than a quarter of a ton of hay and four bushels of oats daily.

"Exactly, that is just what I expected," said Thompson. "He can't draw so much as two pair of my oxen can, and he costs more than a dozen pair."

"You are mistaken, friend Thompson. That elephant is a powerful animal. He can draw more than forty yoke of oxen, and he pays me well for bringing him here."

"Forty yoke of oxen!" exclaimed Thompson. "I don't want to tell you I doubt your word, but I would just like to know what he can draw."

"He can draw the attention of twenty millions of American citizens to Barnum's Museum," the showman replied with a grin.

There was little more to add except what Barnum himself added in his autobiography when he discussed the plowing elephant, the woolly horse, the wild buffalo hunt, the cherry-colored cat, and the terrible egress. Wrote Barnum:

"It will be seen that very much of the success which attended my many years' proprietorship of the American Museum was due to advertising, and especially to my odd methods of advertising. . . . I studied ways to arrest public attention; to startle, to make people talk and wonder; in short, to let the world know that I had a Museum."

Not all of Barnum's efforts to obtain the most spectacular attractions were successful. Sometimes, his requests were met with firm resistance by persons reticent and shy of publicity. Often, in the case of his more outlandish requests, Barnum did not expect to obtain what he was after. Rather, by his audacity, he wanted only more and more free copy. But there was a hard core of insensitivity in Barnum, and almost nothing on earth was too impossible to demand or expect.

When he was in England with Tom Thumb, Barnum attempted to negotiate for purchase of the gabled cottage at Stratford-on-Avon where, in 1564, William Shakespeare was born. The cottage had been sadly neglected, and the living room was a butcher's shop. Barnum hoped to ship the cottage in sections to New York and reassemble it inside the American Museum.

When word got out, the English were horrified. Several prominent and wealthy Londoners banded together to buy the cottage for three thousand pounds, then turned it over to the Trustees of Shakespeare's Birthplace, who eventually, in 1857, restored the property and dedicated it as a national monument. "Had they slept a few days longer," said Barnum, "I should have made a rare speculation, for I was subsequently assured that the British people, rather than suffer that house to be removed to America would have bought me off with twenty thousand pounds."

While in London, Barnum became interested in the popular Madame Tussaud's waxworks, located in Baker Street. Marie Tussaud, a native of Switzerland, had learned the art of modeling in wax from an uncle, who had established the original waxworks in Paris. During the French Revolution, Marie Tussaud made death masks of beheaded royalists and added these, together with an actual used guillotine that she had acquired, to her uncle's collection of such figures as Louis XVI, Voltaire, and Benjamin Franklin, all done from life. Later, Marie Tussaud made models of the dead Robespierre and the living Napoleon Bonaparte. Removing herself to London in 1802, at the age of forty-two, she fashioned in wax a remarkable gallery of celebrated sitters —Queen Caroline, Mrs. Siddons, William Hare (of the infamous team of Burke and Hare), Sir Walter Scott, Lord Byron, the Duke of Wellington—until there were several hundred by the time Barnum came calling.

Although, in 1844, Marie Tussaud was still alive at eighty-four (she would live another six years in the house adjoining her establishment), Barnum negotiated with her sons Joseph and Francis for the waxworks. Contracts were actually drawn up and ready to sign, when the sons had a change of heart. The exhibition remained in Baker Street. Barnum's association with the Tussaud family did not end there. Madame Tussaud's great-grandson, John Theodore Tussaud, recalled in his memoirs: "Barnum sat for me in the spring of 1890, about a year before he died, and I think I must give him the palm for being the most entertaining of all my subjects. . . . As I modelled him he gave me some gentle hints not to be too attentive to the wrinkles on his face, from which I inferred that the old showman possibly thought he looked older than he felt. . . ."

Undismayed by his failure to acquire the waxworks, Barnum offered $2,500 for an historic tree on which Lord Byron had carved his name—possibly the oak that the young lord had planted in the park at Newstead, and to which he later wrote a poem—but this offer was also refused.

On another occasion, learning that the English had captured King Cetewayo, monarch of the Zulus, Barnum was immediately fascinated. The robust, stocky Cetewayo had earlier achieved a curious notoriety. An English company in Natal had been ambushed and massacred by the Zulus. In 1879, an avenging detachment of British troops, under the command of a Captain Carey, and including the twenty-three-year-old Prince Napoleon, only son of the deceased Louis-Napoleon and the then exiled Empress Eugénie, rode into the African bush to punish the rebellious natives. This company, too, was surprised by Zulus under Cetewayo. Captain Carey and his men fled, abandoning the unmounted young Napoleon, who was struck down, killed, stripped, and mutilated. Later, in Durham, Captain Carey stood court-martial, was found guilty, reprieved at the request of Eugénie, and went off to die in India.

After the Zulus were suppressed, and Cetewayo captured, Eugénie visited Natal to contemplate mournfully the ravine where her beloved son had fallen and to hear Cetewayo's report, from his prison, of her son's bravery. In 1883, Cetewayo was restored to his old throne, though Zulu enemies overthrew him within a week and sent him into exile. But the publicity, at the time of his capture, was too much for Barnum to resist. The showman offered Queen Victoria's government $100,000 to exhibit the Zulu leader for five years. The British government indignantly turned Barnum down.

When Giuseppe Fiorelli and his crew of five hundred and twelve men abandoned their excavations of the ruins of Pompeii, Barnum proposed to continue these diggings if he could retain for five years all classical ruins of antiquity and preserved skeletons buried under the soft pumice of Vesuvius. The Italian government was not amused. On another occasion, there was talk of placing Niagara Falls and the surrounding countryside on the market. Barnum offered to buy the 167-foot-high American Falls, fence it in and charge admission to the sightseers, but nothing came of it. Later, Barnum denied that he had made this offer seriously, explaining to a friend that he had "too much reverence for those places to make a vulgar exhibition of them." However, he did seriously consider towing an authentic iceberg from the vicinity of the North Pole to an area just outside New York harbor, and there conducting excursions to the floating glacial fragment. He gave the project up only when he was convinced that an iceberg would not long survive the warmer climate.

At the end of the Civil War, the President of the Confederacy, Jefferson Davis, was trapped in Georgia, and it was falsely rumored that he had tried to escape dressed as a woman. Barnum at once snatched at the chance to have a song, "Jeff in Petticoats," sung on his stage, and then offered five hundred dollars for the feminine garments to the imprisoned Davis and the Fourth Michigan Cavalry which had captured him. As Davis had not used female attire other than his wife's raglan, which he had grabbed by mistake instead of his own cloak, none was forthcoming.

In 1858, the first cable across the Atlantic Ocean—a strand over 1,950 miles long laid two miles deep—was successfully spliced. Barnum, in Liverpool, offered five thousand dollars for the privilege of sending the first twenty-word message from London to his Museum in New York by this cable. His high fee was rejected, and Queen Victoria did the honors with a message to President James Buchanan. Apparently, Barnum had been quite serious. After the event, he remarked: "There would have been no especial value in the message itself, but if I had secured the notoriety of sending the first words through the cable, instead of five thousand dollars the message might have been worth a million to me."

If one means of publicity failed, there was always another. In 1874—it was eleven years since Jules Verne had published his first science-fiction book, *Five Weeks in a Balloon*—Barnum told the press that he was prepared to finance the flight of a gas balloon from New York to Paris. A Professor Hodsman of Dublin, who had flown a balloon across the Irish channel the year before, had assured Barnum that the project was not dangerous. The Professor had inflated a test balloon with gas, and after thirty days it showed neither a leak nor a break.

Convinced that a balloon of tulle silk, eighty feet in diameter, could cross the Atlantic in forty-eight hours, Barnum began to draw up plans. The project, he learned, would cost him $30,000. While Barnum had no desire to risk his own neck in the pioneer flight, he had a famous volunteer, John Wise, of Philadelphia, who was prepared to pilot the balloon. Wise had made 440 ascensions in his life, and was a firm believer in air travel. "If the speed of mechanical progress keeps pace with the onward march of the human intellect," he stated, "our children will travel to any part of the globe without inconvenience, smoke, sparks or sea sickness—and at the rate of 100 miles an hour!" The year before meeting Barnum, Wise, after failing to get $15,000 from Congress to support a trans-Atlantic flight, had persuaded the *New York Daily Graphic* to back him in such a venture. His huge balloon, filled with 400,000 cubic feet of gas, carried a whaleboat for a passenger car. When Wise had a last-minute disagreement with his publisher-backers, he was replaced by three other men, one of whom was Washington H. Donaldson, later Barnum's favorite aeronaut. The great gas bag took off from Brooklyn and crashed in Connecticut forty-one miles away. Undiscouraged, Wise offered himself to Barnum. But in the end, after columns of publicity, the showman gave up the project, explaining that he had no wish to endanger the lives of Wise and other passengers.

When Barnum valued an exhibit enough, he would sometimes not accept refusal. Such was his attitude in the case of the Cardiff Giant. On October 15, 1869, two laborers digging a well on the farm of William Newell, near Cardiff, New York, came upon the intact body of an enormous fossilized man, ten feet four and a half inches in height and weighing 2,990 pounds. Three days later, a Syracuse newspaper ran the headline "A Wonderful Discovery," and soon all the world was alerted.

Experts of every variety congregated about the Cardiff Giant. Two professors from Yale, one a paleontologist and the other a chemist, pronounced the Giant a true fossil. Ralph Waldo Emerson agreed. The director of the New York State Museum decided that the Giant was a statue, but ancient, and "the most remarkable object yet brought to light in this country." Oliver Wendell Holmes agreed.

But there were those who disagreed. The President of Cornell University thought that the Giant was concocted of gypsum and that he detected the marks of a sculptor's chisel. A renowned sculptor was summoned, and he declared the whole thing a hoax. While the controversy continued, the happy farmer, Newell, pitched a tent over the Cardiff Giant and dispensed tickets, first at five cents each, then at fifty cents, and later at a dollar.

Barnum hurried an agent to the scene to look things over. The agent was less interested in the Giant or its authenticity than in the 3,000 persons, many having arrived by special trains from Syracuse, pushing and shoving to view the attraction. Informed of the Giant's prowess, Barnum was aroused. He offered Newell $60,000 for a three-month lease of the object, but the farmer refused. Barnum cajoled; the farmer remained immovable.

Annoyed, Barnum hired a Syracuse sculptor, Professor Carl C. F. Otto, to duplicate the Giant in every detail. When a syndicate finally brought out Newell's discovery and prepared to show it to New York in 1871, the syndicate learned that Barnum was already displaying his own version of the Cardiff Giant under canvas in Brooklyn.

The syndicate went to court for an injunction. Barnum fought back. He stated that he was only showing the hoax of a hoax, and that there was no crime in this. The court sided with Barnum, and thereafter the two massive fossils battled it out for public attention a short distance apart. Desperately, the hapless syndicate tried to match Barnum's stentorian announcements with a huge banner proclaiming: "Genuine. CARDIFF GIANT. Original. Taller Than Goliath Whom David Slew . . . P. T. Barnum offered $150,000 for the Giant. THE MOST VALUABLE SINGLE EXHIBIT IN THE WORLD TODAY."

Meanwhile, reporters were learning that a former Binghamton cigar-maker, George Hull, had been Newell's partner in the showing of the Cardiff Giant. Tracing Hull's history, the reporters found that he had once purchased a great block of gypsum in Fort Dodge, Iowa, had employed a stonecutter in Chicago, and had shipped a tremendous box of machinery to Cardiff. Confronted with the mounting evidence of fraud, George Hull broke down and confessed the truth.

Irritated by clergymen (and one Methodist preacher in particular) who were always quoting the line from Genesis about a super-sized race—"There were giants in the earth in those days"—Hull decided to ridicule them. He bought a twelve-foot block of gypsum near his sister's place in Iowa, sent the five-ton stone to the shed of a friend in Chicago, employed a stonecutter, Edward Salle, to carve the Giant, then aged it with ink, sand, and sulphuric acid, and punctured it full of pores by hammering darning needles across it. He shipped it in the guise of machinery to his cousin's farm—Newell was the relative—buried it for a year, and then dug it up. The entire hoax had cost Hull $2,200, and had earned him $35,000. Barnum's hoax of this hoax—at one point the showman was calling his replica of the Cardiff Giant the original, and the original a fake—had cost Barnum considerably less and earned him much more.

In the quarter century of its existence, the American Museum became exactly what Barnum hoped it would be—a permanent institution. For grown children it remained forever a happy, fairyland memory of youth. For visitors to New York from far corners of the broad land and from distant foreign parts, it was an island of wonder and merriment. For celebrities and nonentities, white men and men of every color, rich and poor, it was the leveler, an enjoyment and enchantment to one and all equally.

Henry James remembered that when he had been a shy youngster, in the years before becoming an expatriate in England and world-famous for novels like *The Ambassadors,* the "joy and adventure" of his childhood stretched "from Union Square to Barnum's great American Museum by the City Hall." Tagging after his older brother, William, who was to become the great psychologist and philosopher, Henry James never forgot "the weary waiting, in the dusty halls of humbug and bottled mermaids, 'bearded ladies' and chill dioramas, for the lecture room, the true center of the seat of joy, to open" and, once inside, the thrill of watching *Uncle Tom's Cabin* and having the secret love affair with Emily Mestayer, "who gave form to my conception of the tragic actress at her highest. She had a hooked nose, a great play of nostril, a vast protuberance of bosom and always the 'crop' of close moist ringlets." Although he would become legend long after, remote and sophisticated, Henry James would not forget that "the Barnum picture above all ignoble and awful, its blatant face or frame stuck about with innumerable flags that waved, poor vulgar-sized ensigns, over spurious relics and catchpenny monsters in effigy" was somehow the "flower of the ideal . . . the ideal day."

And there were others, too, who could not forget, typical among them being young Chauncey M. Depew. He would become United States Senator and President of the New York Central Railroad, but first, he had been an awed lad from Peekskill, in the big city for a glimpse of red savages in the American Museum.

"There had been an Indian massacre on the Western

plains," Depew remembered. "The particulars filled the newspapers and led to action by the government in retaliation. Barnum advertised that he had succeeded in securing the Sioux warriors whom the government had captured, and who would re-enact every day the bloody battle in which they were victorious.

"It was one of the hottest afternoons in August when I appeared there from the country. The Indians were on the top floor, under the roof. The performance was sufficiently blood-curdling to satisfy the most exacting reader of a penny-dreadful. After the performance, when the audience left, I was too fascinated to go, and remained in the rear of the hall, gazing at these dreadful savages. One of them took off his head-gear, dropped his tomahawk and scalping-knife, and said in the broadest Irish to his neighbor: 'Moike, if this weather don't cool off, I will be nothing but a grease spot.'"

Eminent foreigners were as children when they entered the Museum. Among the first of these, arriving in America just three weeks after Barnum had taken over the showcase, was thirty-year-old Charles Dickens, with *Pickwick Papers* and *Oliver Twist* behind him.

During his first visit, Dickens was in New York for three weeks. He was lionized everywhere. Three thousand people in full dress attended the Boz Ball given in his honor. He enjoyed drinks with Washington Irving, a play at the Bowery Theater, and visits to the Lunatic Asylum and the city jail, which smelled like "a thousand old mildewed umbrellas wet through." Everywhere, there was much that troubled Dickens. Not only the lack of international copyright law, but lesser things. Pigs roamed Broadway, and men ate with their knives and expectorated streams of tobacco juice. True, Americans were "by nature frank, brave, cordial, hospitable, and affectionate," and the women with their colored parasols were pretty, but still, Americans were "not a humorous people, and their temperament always impressed me as being of a dull and gloomy character." This last bothered Dickens most.

In his *American Notes,* he wrote: "But how quiet the streets are! Are there no itinerant bands; no wind or stringed instruments? No, not one. By day, are there no Punches, Fantoccini, Dancing-dogs, Jugglers, Conjurers, Orchestrinas, or even Barrel-Organs? No, not one . . . Are there no amusements? Yes. There is a lecture room across the way. . . ."

And so Dickens proceeded to the Lecture Room of the Museum and met the man who was trying to teach fun to Americans. Barnum was his guide. When they made their way around the main hall, they stopped before Zip, The Man Monkey, an African pinhead who grunted and grinned, ate the cigars that visitors gave him, and made their coins vanish permanently. Actually, Zip was an intelligent Negro named William Jackson who created a career out of a deformed, cone-shaped skull. Dickens blinked up at him, and turned to Barnum. "What is it?" asked the English author. Barnum clapped his hands with delight. "That's what it is—a What-is-it!" And forever after, Zip, christened by the creator of Scrooge and Fagin, remained the "What-is-it?"

Among the last of the eminent foreign visitors to the Museum was the eighteen-year-old Edward, Prince of Wales, who arrived in America almost two decades after Dickens. The unhappy Prince, a fugitive from Oxford and his exacting mother (Queen Victoria openly judged that he had "defective mental qualities"), enjoyed the Ball at the Academy of Music which was attended by 5,000 persons. But most of all, he wanted to see the American Museum.

On October 13, 1860, the Prince of Wales and his considerable entourage entered the Museum. The assistant manager, Greenwood, had hidden a terrible wax replica of Queen Victoria in the nick of time. Now, scraping and bowing, Greenwood led the Prince through the halls. The Prince inspected Chang and Eng, the aging Zip, Anna Swan, the Albino family, the living skeleton, the Aztec children, and the fat boy (who kissed his hand). But the Prince seemed to be casting about for some other sight. At last he asked to see Barnum, whom he remembered meeting with Tom Thumb. He was told that Barnum was out of town. The Prince shook his head regretfully. "We have missed the most interesting feature of the establishment," he said.

So it had come finally to that, after all: America's permanent institution for amusement was not the Museum, but Phineas T. Barnum himself.

VI

EXHIBIT SIX
Swedish Nightingale

To stand before the world as its foremost showman was gratifying, but somehow not enough. In his secret heart Phineas T. Barnum held one last ambition. He wanted to be heralded as more than an entrepreneur of freaks and oddities. He wanted to be known as impresario of an artistic attraction.

His own private tastes, he had often confessed, leaned more to music than to the Museum. With coarse, crude stunts and exhibits, he had painted in rainbow colors a new and broader horizon of entertainment for America and the world. But the picture remained incomplete. One summit was missing. It was known as culture.

Agonized mermaids and curly-haired horses and miniature men were fine, but in no way elevating. Barnum sensed that the artistic and the aesthetic could, and should, against all prejudice, be made part of the American scene. Mingled with this selfless wish was the selfish obsession that he be recognized not merely as a wily promoter of the strange and the unusual, a brash, shouting peddler of monstrosity, but also as a refined purveyor of polished and civilized artists. This, in October 1849, was the challenge.

But how precisely to transform himself from showman into impresario? And in what tangible terms, what personification, to translate showmanship from vulgar to artistic curiosity? Reviewing all this, considering the improbability of making the transformation successfully, he suddenly thought of Jenny Lind, a Swedish singer whom he had never heard or met or seen.

In his mind, Jenny Lind represented culture. She might also make money for him, but that was not the point. Even if she failed, he would succeed in gaining prestige. "Inasmuch as my name has long been associated with 'humbug,'" he reflected, "and the American public suspect that my capacities do not extend beyond the power to exhibit a stuffed monkey-skin or a dead mermaid, I can afford to lose fifty thousand dollars in such an enterprise as bringing to this country, in the zenith of her life and celebrity, the greatest musical wonder in the world. . . ."

That he hit upon the idea of Jenny Lind at that moment was not in the least surprising. Three months after Barnum had departed London with Tom Thumb, the old city had been stirred again by the arrival of Jenny Lind. Fresh from a triumph at Bonn, where Queen Victoria, Prince Albert, and King Leopold of the Belgians had been overwhelmed by her voice, fresh from victories at Vienna, where she had earned twenty-five curtain calls and spectators had tried to unharness her horses so that they might draw her carriage, and from Stuttgart, where students ripped apart her bedsheets for souvenirs, Jenny Lind took London by storm. After her operatic debut at Her Majesty's Theater on May 4, 1847, as the vast crowd that included Felix Mendelssohn and Fanny Kemble stamped and cheered, Queen Victoria threw her bouquet of flowers at the soprano's feet.

During three of the hectic days that followed, the House of Commons was unable to assemble a quorum because its members had been swept up in the Lind fever and were paying homage to her at the theater. "What a ravishment about Jenny Lind there was that season throughout London," David Masson, biographer of Milton and professor of English literature at the universities of London and Edinburgh, recorded in his memoirs. "Crammed houses every night to hear her and adore her in public; and the old Duke of Wellington hanging about her at private concerts like an enamoured grandfather, and forgetting Waterloo as he put her shawl round her after songs!" The press was almost of a single voice. "We have arrived at a new stage of our theatrical experience," stated the *Illustrated London News.* "A new perception of musical art has burst upon us; it is as though we now learned, for the first time, what singing really is. . . . All conventionalisms are overthrown, all traditions of the operatic stage turned into contempt—and, by what? By the appearance of Mdlle. Jenny Lind at Her Majesty's Theatre."

Although little of this excitement had been transmitted across the Atlantic to the American public, Barnum was fully aware of it through correspondence with his agents and friends.

As he dwelt on the importation of the twenty-nine-year-old woman nicknamed the "Swedish Nightingale" by *Punch,* he began to realize that the venture might even be profitable. To have prestige with profit was almost too much to expect. Yet, sitting with pencil and ledger, figuring possible costs and potential income, he realized that the bold speculation could add up to an "immense pecuniary success."

But he recognized, too, that the odds were against him. With Tom Thumb, the investment had been as small as the object shown, and the promotion had been within the limitations of his proved abilities. Jenny Lind would be costly, the entire enterprise strange to his talents. "It was possible, I knew, that circumstances might occur which would make the enterprise disastrous," Barnum stated. " 'The public' is a very strange animal, and although a good knowledge of human nature will generally lead a caterer of amusements to hit the people, they are fickle, and ofttimes perverse. A slight misstep in the management of a public entertainment, frequently wrecks the most promising enterprise."

Nevertheless, he would risk it. He would accept the challenge and play impresario. One step remained. He had convinced himself about Jenny Lind. Now he must convince Jenny Lind about Barnum.

He decided against traveling to Europe himself, and sought a representative. He found the proper one in an Englishman, John Hall Wilton, who had been touring the

United States as manager of an orchestra. He offered Wilton "a large sum" if he succeeded in signing Jenny Lind, but only expenses if he failed. When Wilton accepted the arrangement, Barnum outlined the terms he must repeat to the singer. She was to have her choice of either a box-office percentage or $1,000 a night for any number of nights up to 150. Barnum also promised to pay for three musical assistants, as well as all expenses for her secretary and servants. If she wanted a guarantee of payment, he would deposit the entire lump sum with Baring Brothers and Company, his London bankers.

On November 6, 1849, armed with contracts and written instructions signed by Barnum, Wilton sailed for England. Upon arrival, he learned that Jenny Lind had taken off for a rest cure in Lübeck, Germany, where she was considering concert engagements in Berlin and Moscow. Immediately, using Barnum's personal stationery, Wilton wrote to Jenny Lind explaining his employer's entire proposal.

It was Barnum's luck that Wilton's letter arrived in Lübeck at an opportune moment. The Swedish vocalist was just recovering from an unfortunate romance and planning a change of scene. And, though her earnings were high, she was eager to acquire a large sum in a short time, both to facilitate her retirement and to enable her to endow schools and hospitals in her native Sweden. She had no desire to travel to Russia, but she was curious about America. She considered Barnum's offer "brilliant" and an answer to her prayers. She wrote Wilton to come to Lübeck at once.

When Wilton met her in her suite at the Hotel du Nord, she was frank and businesslike. She said that four persons had been negotiating with her for a tour of America: a London opera manager; a Manchester theatrical agent; the orchestra conductor of Her Majesty's Opera in England; and the American-born lawyer and dilettante, Henry Wikoff, who had once—substituting for a manager friend who had suddenly died—successfully sponsored the dancer, Fanny Ellsler, on a tour of the United States. Jenny Lind said that she had leaned toward the charming and persuasive Wikoff. At the time, though the singer did not know it, Wikoff, made a Chevalier by the Queen of Spain and leading the life of a wealthy, retired playboy, was a secret agent for the British, having earlier served as a magazine editor in

New York and a United States diplomat in London. When Jenny Lind had mentioned Barnum's substantial offer to Wikoff, he had derided Barnum as "a mere showman" who would "put her into a box and exhibit her through the country at twenty-five cents a head."

Jenny Lind admitted to Wilton that Wikoff's warning had troubled her. Promptly, she had written to Joshua Bates of the Baring Brothers' bank in London, making inquiries about Barnum. The financier assured her that Barnum was an individual of "character, capacity, and responsibility." Further reassurance—though she did not mention this to Wilton, but rather to Barnum himself, later—she had felt from studying the showman's stationery on which Wilton had written her. The letterhead featured an engraving of Barnum's magnificent Oriental house in Bridgeport. "It attracted my attention," Jenny Lind confessed to Barnum. "I said to myself, a gentleman who has been so successful in his business as to be able to build and reside in such a palace cannot be a mere adventurer." One last consideration swayed her. The other managers who wanted her insisted that she must work on a percentage basis, subjecting her to losses as well as profits. Barnum, on the other hand, was prepared to handle her for a flat fee without any risk on her part.

On January 9, 1850, Jenny Lind affixed her signature to an agreement in which she promised to appear in 150 "concerts or oratorios" for $150,000, but kept the right to cut off the contract after seventy-five appearances and with the right to sing for charity whenever she pleased. Also, she would have expenses and salary for a maid, a valet, a secretary, and a friend. Finally, she would be accompanied by Sir Julius Benedict, the German-born composer, pianist, and conductor, who would be paid an additional $25,000, and Giovanni Belletti, the Italian baritone, who would be paid $12,500. The total salaries of $187,500 were to be deposited in the Baring Brothers bank in advance. It might be added that Chevalier Henry Wikoff, having lost Jenny Lind to Barnum, tried to forget his grief in a marriage to an American heiress. The night before the wedding, the heiress had a change of heart and fled from London to Genoa alone. Wikoff followed her, attempted to kidnap her, and had his ardor rewarded by a sentence of fifteen months in an Italian jail.

With Jenny Lind's agreement in his pocket, the jubilant Wilton started home. It took him six weeks to reach New York, and when he did, Barnum was off in Philadelphia on a business trip. Wilton wired the wonderful tidings in a prearranged code. He informed Barnum that the deed was done, and that Jenny Lind would be in Manhattan within eight months. Barnum admitted that he was "startled by this sudden announcement." He telegraphed Wilton to keep the news secret until he could determine the best way to make it public.

Returning to New York the following day, Barnum bought newspapers in Princeton and was disturbed to see that his engagement of Jenny Lind had leaked out and was in the columns. Now, at once impatient to know how the general public reacted to the news, Barnum asked the train conductor what he thought of Jenny Lind's imminent appearance.

"Jenny Lind?" asked the conductor. "Is she a dancer?"

The conductor's answer, Barnum would always remember, "chilled me as if his words were ice." He suddenly realized that though Jenny Lind was the toast of Europe, she was known in the United States to only a handful of "musical people, travellers who had visited the Old World, and the conductors of the press." The millions upon whom he must depend for success were totally ignorant of her.

Even as he puzzled over a means of enlightening the masses, so deficient in culture, he scurried about busily, trying to raise the $187,500 expected in London. His cash assets were not enough. He tried to obtain a loan from his own bank, offering some second mortgages he owned and his Jenny Lind contract as collateral, but he met a stone wall. "Mr. Barnum," said the bank president, "it is generally believed in Wall Street that your engagement with Jenny Lind will ruin you."

Angrily, Barnum went from bank to bank with no better success, until at last an investment firm that thought highly of both the showman and the vocalist came forward with a substantial loan. Still, Barnum was short. He sold some property that he possessed, but $5,000 more was needed. Mentioning his desperate need to a clergyman friend from Philadelphia, he received a loan from that gentleman for the last amount required.

After sending off to London in the form of bonds and a

letter of credit this total of his liquid assets, Barnum reviewed his enterprise in the cold light of reality. Jenny Lind? Is she a dancer? The words still struck a chill through him. His entire future teetered on the voice of a fragile Nordic unknown to most of the New World. Suddenly, eight short months seemed too few to educate an entire nation. Yet educate the masses he must so that soon they would do nothing but think Jenny Lind, talk Jenny Lind, want Jenny Lind.

But first, he knew, he must educate himself. Who, really, was this Swedish Nightingale? What was her story, and what in this story would excite and thrill? He began to investigate.

Jenny Lind was fourteen years old when her parents finally married.

She had been born out of wedlock in Stockholm, on October 6, 1820, and her illegitimate birth shaped her entire life. Her harsh mother, Anne-Marie Fellborg, an unhappy neurotic, had married an army captain named Radberg when she was eighteen, only to divorce him when she learned that he had once been unfaithful to her. Later, she became the mistress of a twenty-two-year-old accountant five years her junior named Niclas Jonas Lind, but did not marry him until almost two decades later, after her former husband had died.

Burdened through childhood with the brand of bastard, Jenny Lind was reared in an atmosphere of excessive poverty and piety, feeling always persecuted and undesired. As a result, she reached maturity suffering from inferiority, introversion, and aggressive morality. But her hated heritage provided her with one compensation: a siren's voice.

One day the maidservant of an opera-dancer named Lundberg happened to hear the Lind child singing to her pet cat, and at once reported to her mistress the discovery of a genius. Nine-year-old Jenny Lind was taken to the Stockholm Royal Theater, where the nobleman in charge, at first repelled by her gawkiness, was moved to tears by her song. She was offered an operatic career at the government's expense. Her mother regarded the stage as Satan's pit, but was finally convinced that Jenny's voice was God's own gift.

She appeared in her first opera at sixteen. It was composed by Adolf Fredrik Lindblad, and eventually Lindblad and his wife Sophie became her mentors and encouraged her to board with them. At eighteen, she had her first success as Agatha in Weber's *Der Freischütz*. At twenty-one, she realized with shock that Lindblad, twice her age, was in love with her, and she flew to Paris.

Actually her visit to Paris had more purpose than mere seeking after a refuge. Her reputation in Sweden, she realized, had been built more on a talent for histrionics than on an ability to sing. But it was as a vocalist that she wished to excel. Though she despised French immorality, she was prepared to bear it if she could study with Manuel Garcia, son of a renowned tenor who had composed forty-eight operas. Garcia had been recommended to her by Giovanni Belletti, with whom she had worked in Sweden. Unlike most instructors, Garcia was fascinated by the physiology of singers, and was later honored for inventing an instrument through which one could study their vocal cords. Garcia had so successfully trained his eldest daughter, Madame de Malibron, for a singing career, that she was immortalized as a figure in Madame Tussaud's waxworks.

Trembling with fear, Jenny Lind appeared for an audition before Garcia. She sang scales and then launched into an aria from *Lucia di Lammermoor* which she had sung in Sweden thirty-nine times the year before. During the aria, her voice cracked and gave out. She was horrified. Garcia shook his head. "It would be useless to teach you, Mademoiselle," he said. "You have no voice left." She entreated him to give her one more chance. He agreed to hear her again in six weeks.

When she reappeared, Garcia was satisfied by her performance. He accepted her for two lessons a week at a fee of twenty francs an hour. Jenny Lind studied with Garcia for one year. While he respected her intelligence and her accurate ear, he saw no promise in her future and thought her soprano voice—which ranged from low D to high F—inferior to that of another pupil named Henriette Nissen who would later sing at the Théâtre Italien.

After study hours, when Jenny Lind was not practicing her scales or her breathing, she would attend the Paris theater. Like Charlotte Brontë and Emerson and most of Europe, she had great admiration for that incomparable tragic actress, Rachel, who gave Count Alexandre Walewski, illegitimate son of Napoleon and Marie Walewski, an illegitimate son of his own. Comparing herself to the actress, Jenny Lind wrote to Sweden: "The difference between Mademoiselle Rachel and myself is, that she can be splendid when angry, but she is unsuited for tenderness. I am desperately ugly, and nasty too, when in anger; but I think I do better in tender parts. Of course, I do not compare myself with Rachel. Certainly not. She is immeasurably greater than I. Poor me." Later, it was Jenny Lind's success in the United States in 1850 which determined Rachel to conquer America in 1855. But Rachel's scandalous personal life preceded her, militating against her in New York, Boston, and Charleston, and she drew two-thirds less at the box office than the virtuous Swede.

When Jenny Lind's lessons with Garcia were completed —and they had been invaluable, though years later she told a Stockholm editor that she followed not Garcia's method or anyone's method, only "that of the birds (as far as I am able); for their Teacher was the only one who responded to my requirements for truth, clearness and expression"— she left Paris with relief. Never, in the soaring career that followed would she sing publicly in Paris. She explained that her "potato nose" would not have been attractive to the Parisians, and she knew that their sinful society was not attractive to her. Only once did she appear in France at all, and then, at the age of forty-six, for a hospital charity on the Riviera.

Now, at her peak, she went from triumph to triumph. Stockholm again, then Copenhagen, Berlin, Vienna, and London fell before her. And everywhere, it seemed, her subjects thought her more beautiful than she really was. At a dinner party in Berlin, Lady Westmorland, wife of the English Ambassador to Prussia, came upon Jenny Lind seated beside the piano, "a thin, pale, plain-featured girl, looking awkward and nervous." Yet when later she sang, there was "the wonderful transfiguration—no other word could apply—which came over her entire face and figure, lightening them up with the whole fire and dignity of her genius." After the party, the Ambassador, who had remained home, asked his wife: "Is she so very handsome?" And Lady Westmorland replied: "I saw a plain girl when I went in, but when she began to sing her face simply and literally shone like that of an angel. I never *saw* anything or *heard* anything the least like it." At the Theatre Royal in Copenhagen, that ugly, gangling Ichabod Crane, Hans Christian Andersen, a shoemaker's son who entranced children with his fairy tales but himself disliked children, saw and heard her sing and fell in love with her.

"No books, no men, have had a more ennobling influence upon me as a poet than Jenny Lind," Andersen wrote. And again: she "showed me art in its sanctity." Stimulated by her, he created *The Emperor's Nightingale*. He called her one of art's "Vestal Virgins" and three times proposed marriage, but she laughingly fended him off and always referred to him as "brother."

Another who loved Jenny Lind, but made no move to compromise her, being newly and happily married, was the charming Felix Mendelssohn. "He is a *man*," she wrote her guardian in 1846. Mendelssohn spoke to her often about life and music, and enjoyed accompanying her at the piano. She responded to his warmth, though the very thought of a serious relationship with him was hopeless. "There will not be born, in a whole century, another being so gifted as she," Mendelssohn told Hans Andersen. Mendelssohn considered her as a singer "the greatest I have known," and it was for her that he composed the oratorio of *Elijah*.

The Jenny Lind legend spread throughout the Old World. A perfume bearing an engraving of her face on the bottle was popular, and her profile graced candy containers, soap packages, and cigar boxes. The geniuses in her field were lavish in praise of her voice. Frédéric Chopin said: "Her singing is pure and true; the charm of her soft passages is beyond description." Hector Berlioz, who liked little, approved of the acclaim. "Her talent is really high above anything one ever hears in the French and German theater." Richard Wagner and Giacomo Meyerbeer, who composed *The Camp in Silesia* for her, joined in the praise of the golden voice.

But it was not all so one-sided. Thomas Carlyle came and was not conquered. Her voice had "little richness of tone," he thought, and her program was "mere nonsense to sing and act. . . . I do not design to hear Lind again." William Makepeace Thackeray was bored while she was "jugulating away," and wanted to leave at the end of the first act. Nathaniel Hawthorne was as little impressed. Henry F. Chorley, one of London's foremost critics, thought the upper half of her register "rich, brilliant and powerful," but the lower half "not strong, veiled, if not husky and apt to be out of tune." Wilkie Collins, author of *The Moonstone,* admired her voice but not her character. He regarded her as insincere. He believed the story, then making the rounds of London, that when Jenny Lind had watched the crowds pouring into Her Majesty's Theatre from an upper window, she had remarked: "What a pity to think of all these people wasting their time in going to hear me sing, when they might be doing so much good with it."

Nevertheless, she had won the people of London, and among these was Captain Claudius Harris, recently of India, handsome, but prim and much attached to his mother. Even though, after meeting the Captain, Jenny Lind had exclaimed, "Oh! what a dull young man!" she was pleased when he pursued her to Edinburgh, Glasgow, and Dublin. She had recently broken an engagement, in which rings had been exchanged, with Julius Günther, a tenor in Stockholm, and now, on the rebound, she reacted favorably to the Captain's courtship. Their betrothal was announced. But when he made it clear to her that he considered public entertainment an evil thing and demanded her signature on a document promising that she would not again appear on the stage after their marriage, she took leave of impending matrimony and hastened to Lübeck. There Barnum's agent found her.

Barnum in New York was satisfied that her career had been remarkable; yet his fellow Americans knew nothing of it. To them she was known less than the lowliest burlesque performer on the local stage. To educate his countrymen to her successes and fame would be simple enough, Barnum realized. But he sensed that more was needed. Other performers had been toasted in Europe. What made Jenny Lind special?

Examining her career and character, Barnum settled on something that would appeal to the temper of the times. The something was virtue. Then he was struck by something else. Jenny Lind did not use her income for self-indulgence, but for charity. The amount of her benevolences was staggering. Why, she was mainly coming to America to raise funds for a Stockholm children's hospital! This was the right note, then: a chaste, unblemished, virgin creature using God's gift of voice in the repelling sink of hell that was the theater, to raise money for the poor and unfortunate.

Accordingly, Barnum released to the New York press the official announcement of Jenny Lind's advent. It was printed in all newspapers on February 22, 1850, and copied by dailies throughout the United States. It read in part:

"Perhaps I may not make any money by this enterprise; but I assure you that if I knew I should not make a farthing profit, I would ratify the engagement, so anxious am I that the United States should be visited by a lady whose vocal powers have never been approached by any other human being, and whose character is charity, simplicity, and goodness personified.

"Miss Lind has numerous better offers than the one she has accepted from me; but she has great anxiety to visit America. She speaks of this country and its institutions in the highest terms of praise, and as money is by no means the greatest inducement that can be laid before her, she is determined to visit us. In her engagement with me (which includes Havana), she expressly reserves the right to give charitable concerts whenever she thinks proper.

"Since her *debut* in England, she has given to the poor from her own private purse more than the whole amount which I have engaged to pay her, and the proceeds of concerts for charitable purposes in Great Britain, where she has sung gratuitously, have realized more than ten times that amount."

Thousands of readers greeted the statement with righteous approval and self-satisfaction. Slowly, gradually, persistently, Barnum began to build the legend of the Swedish Nightingale until her arrival was anticipated with greater fever than the Second Coming.

From a Swedish artist, Barnum acquired a romanticized portrait of Jenny Lind for fifty dollars. He had it reproduced in newspapers, periodicals, and handbills. He hired an English journalist who had once heard Jenny Lind sing, and instructed him to grind out weekly news stories stressing her chastity, charity, and European triumphs. These stories were released to the press under a London dateline. Barnum encouraged publishers to bring out biographical pamphlets on his vocalist. Monthly magazines devoted completely to her were put on sale. There was even a song contest.

The contest for lyrics to be used as a finale at Jenny Lind's debut not only produced an acceptable ode, but also gave Barnum a colorful and lifelong friend in the person of the winning composer. More than seven hundred poets submitted appropriate lyrics, under the title of "Greeting to America," for the $200 prize. Barnum's five judges awarded first place to a twenty-five-year-old poet, novelist, and vagabond named Bayard Taylor. His lyrical effusion began: "I greet with a full heart the Land of the West, / Whose Banner of Stars o'er a world is unrolled; / Whose empire o'ershadows Atlantic's wide breast, / And opens to sunset its gateway of gold!"

Fortunately, Taylor's personality and activity were of higher quality than his verse. Before becoming Barnum's poet laureate, he had published a newspaper, taught at a girls' school, and represented Horace Greeley's *Tribune* in Europe. At the time he won the $200 from Barnum, Taylor felt prosperous enough to marry a childhood sweetheart. She died of tuberculosis two months later. After that, Taylor was never still. He was master mate on one of Commodore Matthew Perry's four warships that opened Japan to the West in 1853. He roved the earth from Lapland to China, from Arabia to India, spewing forth thirteen travel and literary books. After serving as a consular official in Russia, he taught German literature at Cornell University, and spent his last years as American Minister to Germany. Though he remained Barnum's friend, he always felt remorse about having written *Greeting to America*. In the years to follow, it was remembered better than most of his serious accomplishments, until at last he wondered if that song alone would "save my name from oblivion?"

In all, the volume of publicity accorded Jenny Lind was awesome, and it made her name magical and wondrous. The spark generated by Barnum had caught hold and become wildfire. Joel Benton, biographer of Emerson and a close friend of Barnum, summarized the campaign in 1891: "Never, in the history of music or in the history of entertainment in America, has the advent of a foreign artist been hailed with so much enthusiasm. A large share of this public interest was natural and genuine, and would, in any event, have been accorded to Miss Lind. But a considerable portion of it was due to the shrewd and energetic advertising of Mr. Barnum. Under any auspices the great singer's tour in America would have been successful; but under no other management would it have approximated to what it was under Barnum."

On the morning of August 21, 1850, after being personally wished Godspeed by Queen Victoria, Jenny Lind boarded the steamship *Atlantic* in Liverpool harbor. Following her up the gangplank were Sir Julius Benedict, Giovanni Belletti, Barnum's agent John Hall Wilton, the singer's best friend, Josephine Ahmansson, her cousin and secretary, Max Hjortsberg, a maid, and a valet.

The steamer paddled across the Atlantic in eleven days. One evening Jenny Lind gave a paid concert for her one hundred and fifty fellow passengers, the receipts being turned over to the ship's crew. The piano that accompanied her had been purchased by Barnum. On other evenings Jenny Lind danced, and one night during a storm she alone of her company was not seasick and remained on deck. Meanwhile, in New York, Barnum's daily handouts to the press whipped up public enthusiasm over her progress.

The *Atlantic* was expected to dock on September 1, a Sunday, when the citizenry was free and feeling festive. The night before, restless and nervous, Barnum removed himself to Staten Island, where he slept in the house of his friend Dr. A. Sidney Doane, Health Officer of the Port. The great day dawned fair, and Barnum outfitted himself in his formal best and impatiently waited. The steamship came into view at noon.

With Dr. Doane, Barnum was rowed out to the incoming vessel. Then, holding tightly to a large floral bouquet, he ascended the ship's ladder to the deck. In a moment he found Jenny Lind conversing with the owner of the steamship line, who had managed to get aboard earlier with a bouquet that dwarfed Barnum's. The showman elbowed past the businessman and warmly took the singer's hand. At last they were face to face.

Perhaps it surprised Barnum that she was not beautiful. What he saw was a small, thirty-year-old brunette, no more than five feet four, with a plain, almost peasant face. The blue eyes were amused and expressive, the nose and cheekbones broad; the mouth was wide, the dark complexion devoid of make-up. Her figure, the full, deep bosom, and the wasp waist, was nearly perfect. But only when she sang, Barnum would learn, was she transformed into something ethereal and exquisite.

And Jenny Lind, what did she see? Before her stood a massive man, a kind of St. Nicholas, prematurely semi-bald and stout at forty. His face, though enormously round and fleshy, seemed to be the face of all newborn infants. His eyebrows were bushy, his eyes penetrating; his nose was as prominent as a fist, his mouth bracketed with the lines of laughter, and his jaw full.

He released her hand and they exchanged the formal amenities. At last she wanted to know where and when he had heard her sing.

"I never had the pleasure of seeing you before in my life," said Barnum.

Jenny Lind was taken aback. "How is it possible you dared risk so much money on a person whom you never heard sing?"

"I risked it," Barnum said simply, "on your reputation, which in musical matters I would much rather trust than my own judgment."

Thousands of persons shouted and cheered from other anchored ships and piers as the steamer made its passage to the dock. The wharf was black with screaming humanity. Reporters estimated that there were thirty thousand people on hand. Jenny Lind, on the ship captain's arm, descended the carpeted gangplank to a private carriage. Barnum was right behind, and boarded the vehicle with her. They were driven through two triumphal arches decorated with greenery and flowers, one surmounted by an eagle and bearing the legend, "Welcome to America!" and the other inscribed, "Welcome, Jenny Lind!"

At their destination, the Irving House on Broadway, the tumult and frenzy were repeated. Five thousand persons were waiting to hail the Swedish Nightingale. Police cleared a path to the hotel. Even after she was in her suite, the din below continued. She emerged on the balcony and waved her handkerchief, but the noise did not abate.

Once inside, Jenny Lind asked Barnum to dine with her. When the meal was served, she lifted her glass of wine to toast their venture. She was surprised when Barnum made no move to lift his goblet. "Miss Lind," he explained, "I do not think you can ask any other favor on earth which I would not gladly grant; but I am a teetotaler, and must beg to be permitted to drink your health and happiness in a glass of cold water." And so, though she remained puzzled, he touched her wine goblet with his glass of water.

By midnight the excitement outdoors had increased. The crowd in the streets had swelled to twenty thousand, and now three hundred red-shirted firemen carrying blazing torches, followed by a musical band of two hundred representing the New York Musical Fund Society, tramped to the hotel entrance to serenade the Nightingale. A chorus of voices demanded the appearance of Jenny Lind, and at last Barnum, who had been with her all the day and evening, led her out on the balcony to listen for an hour to "Hail Columbia" and other patriotic airs.

The second day was a repetition of the first. The Mayor and celebrities came calling. The leading milliners, dressmakers, and accessory shops bombarded her with gifts of their wares. The newspapers were filled with her, and reporters crowded her corridor. With difficulty Barnum managed to get her out, heavily veiled, to inspect various sites for her concerts. The most impressive site of all was Castle Garden, an abandoned brick fortress standing like a circular isle in the water off the Battery and reached by a wooden bridge connected to the mainland, which had been converted into an opera house with the largest seating capacity in the nation. Here the old Marquis de Lafayette had been welcomed in 1824, and here Samuel Morse had demonstrated his telegraphic code in 1835. Quickly Jenny Lind concurred with Barnum that Castle Garden must be the place of her debut.

On the third day after the prima donna's arrival, a change was made in her contract. According to Barnum, he suggested it. He saw that she would be a success beyond his fondest hopes and he wanted to prevent any discontent. He suggested that she continue to receive $1,000 a performance and all expenses, but that after he had been paid $5,500 a night for his services and outlay, the balance of profits be divided equally between them. Barnum remembered that his Nightingale was so astonished that she held his hand, told him that he was "a gentleman of honor," and exclaimed: "I will sing for you as long as you please; I will sing for you in America—in Europe—anywhere!"

However, the Jenny Lind version of this story, or rather the version given by her advisers, was that she had initiated the revision of the contract. When she realized her potential in America, she openly disclosed her dissatisfaction with the original terms. If forced, she would abide by the old agreement. But she would not be happy. One of her attorneys, Maunsell B. Field, wrote: "Again and again Miss Lind desired changes made in the contract to her own advantage, and every time Mr. Barnum yielded. Whatever his motive, he was most obliging. . . ."

Rehearsals were begun in Castle Garden. Jenny Lind proved surprisingly temperamental. Barnum had invited music critics and reporters to preview his attraction and they in turn invited hordes of their friends. The large number of guests dismayed the diva. She protested, and Barnum was obliged to turn out all but the critics themselves.

The critics who attended the rehearsals were ecstatic. Their advance praise helped churn up added anticipation. Representative of these advance notices was the promise published in the *New York Herald* on the eve of the Nightingale's debut: "We speak soberly—seriously—calmly. The public expectation has run very high for the last week—higher than at any former period of our past musical annals. But high as it has risen, the reality—the fact—the concert—the voice and power of Jenny Lind—will far surpass all past expectation. Jenny Lind is a wonder, and a prodigy in song—and no mistake."

Four days before her debut, Barnum held a public auction of tickets for Jenny Lind's opening night. Three thousand persons braved a downpour and paid twelve and a half cents each to enter Castle Garden to participate. Competition for the very first ticket was frenzied. At last the auctioneer's gavel hammered his pulpit three times and awarded the prize to John N. Genin, the proprietor of the hat store next to the American Museum, for $225.

Earlier, Barnum had advised Genin to go to any price for the first seat. He assured his neighbor that the publicity value would be incalculable, and he was right. Overnight, Genin, who looked like a Roman senator and eventually published a history of headgear, became famous. Almost every newspaper in the land featured Genin's name. A man in Iowa found the Genin label in a battered old hat and was able to auction it from the local post-office steps for four-

teen dollars. Customers flocked to Genin's shop prepared
to pay a dollar extra for their hats just to possess his merchandise and have a glimpse of him. In the twelve months
that followed, he disposed of 10,000 more hats than he had
in the previous year. No one ever recorded whether or not
he enjoyed the concert.

The bidding continued and tickets went at around twenty
dollars for a short time, though later the standard prices for
seats ranged from one to seven dollars. The average price
paid for a ticket at both this auction and another that followed two days later was between six and seven dollars.
Castle Garden was entirely sold out and the gross take was
$17,864. The thrifty Jenny Lind was so appalled at the
prices paid that she felt "it a duty" to turn every penny of
her share over to charity secretly.

The day of the concert, Wednesday, September 11,
1850, was welcomed by press and public as a holiday.
Tension and suspense grew throughout the day and by
five o'clock in the afternoon, three hours before the program was to begin, Barnum found it necessary to open
Castle Garden to clamoring customers.

The two-hundred-foot wooden bridge leading to the
Garden had been lighted and covered with an awning. A
ceaseless stream of carriages clattered over it to be met by
sixty police maintaining order. People passed into the vast
hall, Barnum said, "with as much order and quiet as was
ever witnessed in the assembling of a congregation at
church." Inside, illuminated by rows of gas lights, the Garden was divided into four sections. Each section was lighted
in a different color, and its ushers wore badges and carried
wands of that color. Customers merely displayed the color
of their tickets and were promptly led to the right section.
On the dimmed stage stood a wooden arch painted with
white-and-gold arabesques and hung with the flags of the
United States and Sweden. From the balcony was suspended a bank of flowers garishly spelling out the legend:
"Welcome, Sweet Warbler."

At eight o'clock, when Sir Julius Benedict and his sixty-
piece orchestra appeared to play the overture to Weber's
Oberon, only one third of the auditorium was occupied.
All through the overture, people continued to arrive, while
shouting and yelling and tooting from one thousand row-
dies and drunks in two hundred boats in the water were

heard from outside. For two hours they drowned out the music for listeners in the rear balcony; then they were finally dispersed. By the time the overture was done and Belletti had finished his solo, the Garden was crammed with five thousand eager ticket-holders, seven eighths of them male.

"Now came a moment of breathless expectation," reported the *New York Tribune,* as Barnum waited anxiously, his whole future in the balance. "A moment more, and JENNY LIND, clad in a white dress which well became the frank sincerity of her face, came forward through the orchestra. It is impossible to describe the spontaneous burst of welcome which greeted her. The vast assembly rose as one man and for some minutes nothing could be seen but the wavings of hands and handkerchiefs, nothing heard but a storm of tumultuous cheers. The enthusiasm of the moment, for a time beyond all bounds, was at last subdued . . . and the divine songstress, with that perfect bearing, that air of all dignity and sweetness, blending a childlike simplicity and half-trembling womanly modesty with the beautiful confidence of Genius and serene wisdom of Art, addressed herself to song. . . ."

She began with *"Casta Diva"* from Bellini's *Norma.* "Towards the last portion of the cavatina," Barnum noted, "the audience was so completely carried away by their feelings, that the remainder of the air was drowned in a perfect tempest of acclamation." Next followed a duet with Belletti from Rossini's *Il Turco in Italia,* and later a Swedish number, the "Herdsman's Song," and the applause was even greater. As Jenny Lind continued, each song being greeted with more rapture than the last, Barnum knew that he had won. "Enthusiasm had been wrought to its highest pitch," he wrote, "but the musical powers of Jenny Lind exceeded all the brilliant anticipations which had been formed, and her triumph was complete."

The final number was Bayard Taylor's "Greeting to America," set to music by Benedict in less than a week. When Jenny Lind finished, Castle Garden was a madhouse. Three times she was called back to bow and wave. Then shouts went up for the impresario. Barnum held back in an atypical suffusion of modesty, but at last joined his Nightingale. He quieted the audience and made a little speech. He said that Jenny Lind had begged him not to reveal her secret, but now he must. All of the nearly $10,000 she would profit this night, he said, she was turning over to a long roll of American charities—including the Fire Department Fund, the Musical Fund Society, the Colored Orphan Asylum, and the Home for Indigent Females. There would even be a contribution to Harriet Beecher Stowe, to assist the author in freeing slaves.

The next morning, fearing a press reaction against his diva, Barnum waited for the newspapers in a sweat. But a glance at the lead in the *Tribune*—an unsigned review probably written by George W. Curtis, an authority on Syria who had helped Thoreau build his hut at Walden Pond—dissipated all of Barnum's worries. "Jenny Lind's first concert is over, and all doubts are at an end. She is the greatest singer we have ever heard, and her success is all that was anticipated from her genius and her fame." The other newspapers were equally transported. A weary but pleased Barnum would record: "The people were in ecstasies; the powers of editorial acumen, types, and ink, were inadequate to sound her praises. The Rubicon was passed. The successful issue of the Jenny Lind enterprise was established. I think there were a hundred men in New York, the day after her first concert, who would have willingly paid me $200,000 for my contract. I received repeated offers for an eighth, a tenth, or a sixteenth, equivalent to that price. But mine had been the risk, and I was determined mine should be the triumph."

There were discordant voices, of course. Walt Whitman wrote in the *New York Evening Post:* "The Swedish Swan, with all her blandishments, never touched my heart in the least. . . . I wondered at so much vocal dexterity; and indeed they were all very pretty, those leaps and double somersets. But even in the grandest religious airs, genuine masterpieces as they are, of the German composers, executed by this strangely over-praised woman in perfect scientific style, let the critics say what they like, it was a failure; for there was a vacuum in the head of the performance." Washington Irving was pleased, but more by the woman than the singer. And Chief Oshkosh and his Menominee braves, visiting New York after treating with President Millard Fillmore, were invited by Barnum to hear Jenny Lind. Oshkosh was unable to appear, but his braves attended. Upon being asked their opinion of her, one replied: "She made a very big noise and then a little noise. The white man must have a great deal more money than he needed to pay so much to hear this lady sing."

But the few adverse criticisms were drowned in a tide of Lindomania that blanketed New York and the nation. Songs, poems, and polkas were dedicated to her. Bonnets, gloves, shawls, and robes were given her name. There were Jenny Lind pipes, pianos, cigars, vest buttons, stoves, playing cards, sofas, and whiskeys. A clipper ship was named after Jenny Lind, and a race horse, too. Mathew Brady, over Barnum's objections, made a daguerreotype of her which the press called "unrivaled." New Yorkers paid $87,055 for her first six concerts, and $282,216 for the full thirty-five performed over a period of nine months.

Now, Barnum took his wonder on the road: Philadelphia, Boston, Baltimore, Washington, D.C., St. Louis, Cincinnati, Memphis, New Orleans, Havana. Sixty concerts were held outside New York, and everywhere the scene at Castle Garden was repeated.

The largest newspapers carried regular reports, in standing columns that appeared daily, on her movements and actions. Rarely did she disappoint. In Boston, where she received Henry Wadsworth Longfellow and grossed $70,-388 at the box office for seven performances, she was most impressed by Daniel Webster. The Secretary of State dazzled her, as once Mendelssohn had, and she said to her manager: "Ah, Mr. Barnum, that is a man; I have never before seen such a man!" In Boston, too, her secretary, Hjortsberg, told her of a girl at the box office who had bought a ticket for three dollars, remarking: "There goes half a month's earnings, but I am determined to hear Jenny Lind." The singer, easily moved, sent Hjortsberg scampering downstairs with a twenty-dollar gold piece for the girl. Before departing Boston, she wrote her family in Sweden that she missed her native herring, potatoes, and milk soup, that she was becoming bored with the impact of so many new faces, and that Barnum remained "extremely generous, and reasonable; and seems to have made it his first object to see me satisfied."

In Philadelphia, thousands gathered below her hotel window. Jenny Lind had a headache and refused to appear. Barnum hastily placed her bonnet and shawl on her companion, Miss Ahmansson, and the crowd was deceived but happy. In Baltimore, Barnum took his daughter Caroline, who had joined the troupe, to church. When Caroline sang in the choir, the faithful were certain that they had heard the Swedish Nightingale free of charge. In Washington, President Fillmore came around to visit Jenny Lind at her hotel. She was out. He left his card. And the next day, on Barnum's arm, she returned the compliment, spending an entire evening with the Chief Executive and his family in the White House.

From Charleston, Barnum, his diva, and her entourage, took the steamer *Isabella* to Cuba for three appearances. After New York, Havana proved the greatest trial of all. An air of hostility greeted Barnum everywhere. Most theatergoers, used to the low prices charged by the Tacón Opera House which the impresario had hired for Jenny Lind, resented the higher prices he was posting. Havana newspapers branded him a "Yankee pirate." Further, an Italian opera company was in Havana at the same time, and half the city considered the Latin singers superior to the heralded Nordic talent of Miss Lind. The antagonism disturbed Barnum, but he kept all knowledge of it from his Nightingale.

On opening night, the Tacón Opera House was filled, but the air was charged. Sir Julius Benedict's overture and Belletti's solo were met with a foreboding silence. Then, led forward by Belletti, Jenny Lind was presented to the Cubans. "Some three or four hundred persons clapped their hands at her appearance," reported an attending correspondent of the *New York Tribune*, "but this token of approbation was instantly silenced by at least two thousand five hundred hisses. Thus, having settled the matter that there should be no forestalling of public opinion, and that if applause was given to Jenny Lind in that house it should first be incontestably earned, the most solemn silence prevailed."

For the first time in her tour, Jenny Lind stood stunned. Her face revealed that she was unnerved. For Latins this was the moment of truth. If she wavered, quit, she was done. If she continued, she must penetrate, with her tremulous soprano, the thick curtain of skepticism. She wavered only a moment, then advanced to the footlights. "Her countenance changed in an instant to a haughty self-possession," the *Tribune* continued, "her eyes flashed defiance, and, becoming immovable as a statue, she stood there, perfectly calm and beautiful. She was satisfied that she now had an ordeal to pass and a victory to gain worthy of her powers. In a moment her eyes scanned the immense audience, the music began and then followed—how can I describe it?—such heavenly strains as I verily believe mortal never breathed except Jenny Lind, and mortal never heard except from her lips. . . . The stream of harmony rolled on till, at the close, it made a clean sweep of every obstacle, and carried all before it. Not a vestige of opposition remained, but such a tremendous shout of applause as went up I never before heard."

Five times in the din, she was brought back to curtsy. And then, at last, Barnum was beside her. "God bless you, Jenny," he exclaimed, "you have settled them!" Sobbing with delight, she was in his arms. "Are you satisfied?" she asked. He was satisfied. "Never before," he said later, "did she look so beautiful in my eyes as on that evening."

Before leaving Havana, Barnum had a reunion with Signor Vivalla, the juggler of the early Joice Heth days. Vivalla had suffered a stroke—the left side of his body was paralyzed—and he lived from hand to mouth, employing a trained dog to turn a spinning-wheel and perform acrobatics. Moved by his story, Jenny Lind sent him $500. Deeply touched, Vivalla replied with a basket of fruit and insisted on amusing her with his dog. "Poor man, poor man, do let him come," Jenny Lind told Barnum. In her parlor the singer warmly welcomed Vivalla. She went to her knees to pet his dog and questioned the juggler about his past. Later she applauded his little act, and then sang for him. It was Vivalla's farewell appearance. A few months later he was dead, the names of Jenny Lind and Barnum the last on his lips.

As the tour progressed, Barnum began to understand his Nightingale. Her moods were mercurial: at times, she was withdrawn and aloof, at others excessively joyful and gay. At a party, she antagonized a French editor by refusing to dance, socialize, or converse in anything beyond monosyllables. For long periods she would receive no callers. When the daughter of a wealthy Georgia planter bribed a maid to allow her to wear the maid's habit and carry Jenny Lind her tea, the singer was not amused. Barnum thought such admiration should please her. "It is not admiration—it is only curiosity, and I will not encourage such folly," Jenny Lind snapped.

"With all her excellent, and even extraordinary good qualities, Jenny Lind was human. . . ." Barnum wrote, "She had been petted, almost worshipped, so long, that it would have been strange indeed if her unbounded popularity had not in some degree affected her to her hurt. . . . Like most persons of uncommon talent, she had a strong will which, at times, she found ungovernable." In fact, a friend of the Nightingale, Le Grand Smith, congratulated Barnum for having contrived to keep only "Jenny's 'angel' side" before the public.

Yet with her inner circle, and especially with Barnum, she could be outgoing and delightfully feminine. At a New Year's Eve party in her suite, she was effervescent. She invited Barnum to dance with her. He warned her that he had never danced in his life. "That is all the better," she cried. "Now dance with me in a cotillion. I am sure you can do it." He took her in his arms, and was more on her toes than on the floor. She laughed at the fun of his awkwardness. "She said she would give me the credit of being the poorest dancer she ever saw!" Barnum confessed ruefully.

Whenever there was privacy, she loved to relax outdoors. "She would come and romp and run, sing and laugh, like a young schoolgirl," Barnum observed. Her favorite sport was playing catch with an India-rubber ball. Often, she tried to inveigle Barnum into the game. After a while, puffing like a porpoise, he would throw up his hands. "I give it up." And she would laugh and shout: "Oh, Mr. Barnum, you are too fat and too lazy; you cannot stand it to play ball with me!"

Of course, their proximity encouraged rumors of love and marriage. The gossip reached her ears. She was amused. She went to Barnum with it. "I have heard that you and I are about to be married," she told him. "Now, how could such an absurd report ever have originated?" Barnum grinned. "Probably from the fact that we are 'engaged,' " he said.

But this was the best of the tour. The rest of it was temper and tension. By the time the small company returned to New York for another series of concerts, the friction was beginning to show. Sir Julius Benedict, his health weakened by the travels and his sensitive nature irritated by the circus aspects of Barnum's arrangements, pleaded a previous commitment at Her Majesty's Theatre in London and quit the company for England. At once, Jenny Lind sent to Europe for Otto Goldschmidt, an intense young pianist who had often accompanied her in Germany and who was considered second only to Mendelssohn on the keyboard, as replacement for Benedict.

Barnum thought Goldschmidt "a very quiet, inoffensive gentleman, and an accomplished musician." Jenny Lind thought him somewhat more. She fell madly in love with him, and her love was reciprocated, much to the distress of Giovanni Belletti, who was also in love with her. Earlier in the tour, Belletti had made no secret of his passion, and Jenny Lind had acknowledged it by making him her walking companion and confidant. But with Goldschmidt's arrival, Belletti became just another baritone. Jenny Lind's first lawyer, Maunsell B. Field, recorded that Belletti "used to lie in bed all day, weeping and howling over his unrequited affection." At last, in despair, he, too, quit the company.

Meanwhile, Barnum was having his own troubles with his Nightingale. Writing Joshua Bates, the banker in London, he bared his problems: "In this country you are aware that the rapid accumulation of wealth always creates much envy, and envy soon augments to malice. Such are the elements at work to a limited degree against myself, and although Miss Lind, Benedict, and myself have never, as yet, had the slightest feelings between us, to my knowledge, except those of friendship, yet I cannot well see how this can long continue in face of the fact that, nearly every day, they allow persons (some moving in the first classes of society) to approach them, and spend hours in traducing me; even her attorney, Mr. John Jay, has been so blind to her interests, as to aid in poisoning her mind against me, by pouring into her ears the most silly twaddle, all of which amounts to nothing and less than nothing—such as the regret that I was a 'showman,' exhibitor of Tom Thumb, etc., etc."

Jenny Lind's circle did, indeed, try to prejudice her against Barnum. They argued that his management was poor, his publicity undignified. They said that his concerts, such as one at Fitchburg Depot in Boston, where the acoustics were poor, the heat unbearable, and the floor rumored

unsafe, were greedily oversold without consideration of
her health and nerves. In Philadelphia, Jenny Lind's secretary, whose ambition it was to become her impresario, prej-
udiced her against the National Theater, a former circus
arena rented by Barnum. According to Field, the indignant
singer told Barnum "that she was not a horse, and, therefore, would not appear there." Too, she had wearied of the
showman's excessive exploitation of her name. Field, who
found her "rather calculating than emotional," remembered: "She detested *humbug*—a word which was constantly in her mouth." And steadily, John Jay, who had
succeeded Field as her attorney, reminded her that Barnum
was an albatross around her neck, that she could make and
deserved to make the additional profits that would incur
if she were on her own.

At last, early in June 1851, on the eve of her ninety-third
concert, Barnum brought the conflict to a head. He offered
to release her from her contract if she would pay him
$7,000 for the seven concerts not yet held and return to
him $25,000 that he had deposited in London against a
longer tour. All politeness and affability, Jenny Lind
agreed, and prima donna and impresario parted company
at long last, after a partnership of nine months and nine
days.

It had been a success beyond his wildest fancies. The
series of concerts had grossed $712,161. The gamble on
Jenny Lind, a talent almost unknown in a country that had
never before accepted an exhibit of foreign culture in this
way, had grossed $176,675 for the singer and $535,486 for
the newly crowned impresario.

Above all, because of Barnum, the path was now open
for the appearance of Melba, Patti, Paderewski, Caruso,
Kreisler, and Schumann-Heink.

Thereafter, Jenny Lind's career was an anticlimax.

She continued her American tour alone with lessening
success. Business details bothered her. Running into Barnum on several occasions, she told him: "People cheat me
and swindle me very much, and I find it very annoying to
give concerts on my own account." Without Barnum's
showmanship, her appeal decreased. A Philadelphia newspaper reported that she showed "ill temper and vexation"

on the stage and was as angry "as a hive of wasps and as black as a thundercloud, and all because the house was not crowded."

Worst of all, she was so blindly in love with Goldschmidt that she began to force him upon a resisting public. The German pianist was overly formal and colorless, yet she made him appear twice at each concert, whereas Sir Julius Benedict had been confined to one appearance. She led him on the stage, and she led him off the stage, and when he played she sat near by, gazing at him with moon eyes and encouraging the audience to applause. It was all romantic and heart-warming for Jenny Lind, but it did not stimulate attendance.

On February 5, 1852, Jenny Lind became Madame Otto Goldschmidt, and so advertised herself from that day on. The decision to marry the man she loved had been difficult. For one thing, he was Jewish, and that disturbed Jenny Lind, and for another, he was nine years her junior. But then, he had refinement, solidity, talent, and, above all, a deep love for her begun in their childhood. She could not resist, and they were married in Boston, at the house of a banker, in the rites of the Episcopal Church.

On a rainy night, four months later, she gave her farewell appearance in Castle Garden. The receipts were less than half of what they had been at her debut under the auspices of Barnum. The showman had a complimentary ticket and came to say good-by backstage. He reminded her that God had given her a voice beyond all others and that she must never cease using it. "Yes," she agreed, "I will continue to sing so long as my voice lasts, but it will be mostly for charitable objects, for I am thankful to say I have all the money which I shall ever need."

Jenny Lind and Goldschmidt settled in a home at Malvern Hills, in the Victorian England she so much admired. This home was the only personal luxury she bought out of her considerable American earnings; the rest remained in a fund to be expended on Swedish charitites and scholarships. Within seven years, she gave birth to a boy, Walter, who grew up to become an army officer; a girl, Jenny, who inherited some of her mother's musical gifts and married a government official named Maude; and a second boy named Ernest.

Although she rarely sang for personal gain in the years

that followed, she was far from retired. Before and after the births of her children, she gave concerts for every needy cause. She sang for her church. She sang to raise money for her friend Florence Nightingale, who had her nursing fund. She sang to further her husband's career—in fact, her last public concert, given when she was fifty, was to promote an oratorio, *Ruth,* composed by Goldschmidt, which she had introduced three years before. It is possible that she sang too long. Toward the end, the critics noted, her tones were "veiled and weak," and powerful passages were accomplished with grim effort.

Her good friends were many. Sir Arthur Sullivan, whose *H.M.S. Pinafore* had run seven hundred nights, was one; Queen Victoria was another. Jenny Lind was still ungracious, even tart, with curiosity hunters. When a group of American tourists came calling, she asked them what they wanted. Their spokesman said they merely wanted to see her. "Well, this is my face," she said sharply, and then, turning on her heel, "and this is my back. Now you can go home and say you have seen me." And she slammed the door.

She was outspoken about her contemporaries and her role of wife, in a way that made Goldschmidt shudder. Once, when the formidable Viennese music critic Eduard Hanslick came visiting, she told him: "Present-day singers all lose their voices at thirty years of age; they have studied so little and scream so much. I myself never had much voice, but I have kept it intact; indeed, I sing now with much less effort than formerly. . . . At home, I never sing a note, for I am a housewife and work like a dog."

At a resort, an English friend found her sitting on the beach late one afternoon, staring off at the horizon, with a Lutheran Bible open on her lap. The friend wondered why she had abandoned her career at its height. Jenny Lind thought about her career a moment, then replied: "When, every day, it made me think less of *this*"—and she indicated her Bible—"and nothing at all of *that*"—and she pointed off at the setting sun—"what else could I do?"

When she was sixty-three, the Prince of Wales asked her to become Professor of Singing at the new Royal College of Music. She accepted. On November 2, 1887, after a cerebral hemorrhage and six weeks of paralysis, she died at the age of sixty-seven. Hearing the news in New York, Barnum remembered their enterprise: "the glorious voice of the Nightingale, not alone in the raptures of unrivaled singing, but low and soft, with pitying, tender words, as she sought to comfort one in trouble; or ringing out in the hearty laughter of blithe and vigorous young womanhood." To Goldschmidt, the showman cabled his sympathies, and then noted: "So dies away the last echo of the most glorious voice the world had ever heard."

But the press would not let her rest. Three years later the *New York Tribune,* reprinting a London story, announced that Goldschmidt had lost interest in Jenny Lind before her death and was now neglecting her grave. At once, Barnum refuted this. He had just dined with Goldschmidt in London. The German had fresh flowers sent to her grave daily. And in life he had loved her dearly. In the *North American Review,* Barnum wrote that Goldschmidt was "a most delightful and worthy man . . . instead of squandering his wife's money, as was alleged, it was doubled in amount in his hands. Everything else that was said unfavorably of him was also utterly without foundation."

Barnum had once told her that they were "engaged." For him, that had meant for life, and after.

VII

EXHIBIT SEVEN
Iranistan

The Jenny Lind venture had occupied ten intense months of Barnum's life. With its success, he had reached the highest peak of celebrity in his career as showman. Now he was tired. "After so many months of anxiety, labor, and excitement, in the Jenny Lind enterprise," he said, "it will readily be believed that I desired tranquility."

For almost four years Barnum devoted more of his time to home and family in Connecticut than to his Museum. He would visit New York only once or twice a week. Finally, even his interest in the Museum, which had dominated his life for thirteen years, began to flag.

At last, in the summer of 1855, Barnum decided to retire completely. He sold the Museum collection of curiosities to John Greenwood, Jr., his assistant manager, and Henry D. Butler, for $24,000. And the long-term lease on the building, which he had signed over to his wife, he sublet to Greenwood and Butler for an annual rental of $29,000.

In 1855, unencumbered, wealthy, renowned, and only

forty-five, Phineas T. Barnum sat back to enjoy the fruits of his imagination and labor. For the first time since he had become a vertical man, he had stopped running. He was left with himself and his private life. But of this aspect of his existence, Barnum, publicist and advertiser, spoke little.

Few persons knew in his own time, and few have found out in the century since, just what were Barnum's personal interests outside show business, his habits, his prejudices, his beliefs, his character, his relationship with his wife and three daughters. It would be difficult to find another public figure in modern times who has had so little known or written of his private self. Constance M. Rourke, in *Trumpets of Jubilee*, remarked with wonder upon it. "Almost nothing substantial about him emerges from the ruck of contemporary evidence; scarcely another figure of equal proportions had left so little behind him by way of personal print. Necessarily he becomes legend—an outcome he would have relished."

Yet, behind the elaborate façade of showman was a man stripped of show. What manner of man?

Perhaps he had a bond, a strange affinity, with Coleridge. Perhaps he read: "In Xanadu did Kubla Khan, / A stately pleasure-dome decree. . . ." Prosaic Bridgeport was no Xanadu. But Barnum's stately palace in this New England city would have seemed properly familiar and exotic to Coleridge and Kubla Khan. The showman's palace was Iranistan. Behind its Oriental walls the real Phineas T. Barnum lived.

As long before as 1846, Barnum and Charity had selected Bridgeport as their place of residence. It was near enough to New York by rail and water to enable Barnum to commute to his business, but far enough removed to give him the feeling of country living. Too, the city gave promise of growth and expansion, which made any real-estate investment seem sensible. Accordingly, Barnum purchased seventeen acres less than a mile west of the city. The site was choice. It overlooked Long Island Sound. The surroundings were sylvan. And, important consideration, the railroad ran near by: "I thought that a pile of buildings of a novel order might indirectly serve as an advertisement of my Museum," Barnum said.

Not until he had visited England with Tom Thumb did Barnum decide what architecture his "buildings of a novel order" would reproduce. In Brighton, he was enchanted by the Oriental Pavilion that had been built by George IV in 1787. He had seen nothing like it before in either Great Britain or America, and he instinctively knew that it was what might be expected of him. Forthwith he employed a London architect to draw up a blueprint of the actual Pavilion, so that he might duplicate it on his seventeen acres outside Bridgeport.

Barnum's showy mansion—Iranistan, he named it, which meant "Oriental villa" or "Eastern country place" —was two years in the building, and cost $150,000. Part Byzantine, part Moorish, part Turkish, the three-story main building was capped by a center dome rising ninety feet above the ground. Flanking this were lesser minarets and piazzas. The house was one hundred and twenty-four feet wide at its entrance. It faced a park containing a huge fountain and tame elk, all enclosed within an iron fence.

The interior dazzled and bewildered the unprepared visitor. A great staircase rose to the second story, and along it were niches filled with marble statues imported from Italy. The furniture in each room was of a different period. The drawing room, its ceiling white and gold, its paneling covered with murals of the four seasons, its folding doors mirrored, featured rosewood furniture. The library was Chinese, though the tortoise-shell table was often graced by china and silver purchased from a Russian prince. Barnum's private study was hung in orange satin with "furniture of corresponding elegance." Adjacent to it was that wonder of the period, a bathroom with a shower that ran hot and cold water. The dome above the structure, sixty feet in circumference, was outfitted as an astronomical observatory.

The landscape around the house, once barren, soon contained an orchard planted full-grown, a stable for horses, several barns filled with livestock, and a complete private waterworks. On November 14, 1848, these grounds, and the house itself, were crowded with one thousand guests, including Tom Thumb and his parents—"the poor and the rich," Barnum said proudly—invited to attend the formal housewarming. It was a long way from the boarding house and the billiard parlor next to the Museum. Iranistan was destined to remain Barnum's refuge for almost a decade. The housewarming party set the note of hospitality.

Barnum liked people, especially listeners. Joel Benton, a frequent visitor, regarded Barnum as the perfect host. "As a host he could not be surpassed. He knew the sources of comfort—what to omit doing, as well as what to do, for a guest. He had the supreme art of making you really free, as if you were in your own house." Among the guests who shared Barnum's table, at Iranistan and at later homes, were Colonel George A. Custer, Matthew Arnold, Horace Greeley, and Mark Twain. Barnum constantly tried to encourage Mark Twain to write about him and his enterprises, but without success.

When no house guests were present, Barnum followed a rigid, unvarying routine. He rose at seven o'clock in the morning. He devoted the entire morning to his littered desk in the orange study where, quill in hand, he answered letters or conducted business affairs. Commercial callers were usually received briefly during these morning hours, but after these appointments were out of the way, Barnum would permit no further interruption from friends or family. Shortly after the noon hour, he would emerge to take a ride in his carriage. Returning to Iranistan, he had a large midday meal, sometimes with members of the family. This was followed by a five-minute nap, after which, he said, "I am as much refreshed as if I had slept for hours." Another outing in the carriage followed before nightfall.

Evenings at Iranistan were short. Except when he went to the theater, Barnum liked to read for an hour or listen to piano or string music. Best of all, he enjoyed having a few neighbors in for several games of whist, cribbage, or chess. By nine-thirty, visitors were expected to leave. If they forgot, Barnum bluntly reminded them that he intended to be in bed by ten o'clock sharp. Once, asked to what habits he owed his vigorous health, Barnum replied: "Primarily, regularity; secondarily, abstinence from things that tend to shorten life."

When he still had his Museum collection, he devoted the greater part of his mornings to corresponding with paid oddity-hunters scattered throughout the world. Freed of the Museum, he was able to give more time to his other mail. Every post brought him hundreds of letters. Some of these were fan letters, but the greater number were money-making schemes. Correspondents offered him partnerships in new inventions, in land investments, in issues of mining stocks. For the most, said Barnum, the schemes were "as wild and unfeasible as a railroad to the moon, while perhaps once in a thousand times something reasonable is suggested."

For business callers who had a speculation to suggest, one that might make him a fortune, Barnum had a set reply. Before the visitor could disclose his idea, Barnum would abruptly state: "You are much mistaken in supposing that I am so ready or anxious to make money. On the contrary, there is but one thing in the world I desire—that is, tranquility. I am quite certain your project will not give me that, for you probably would not have called upon me if you did not wish to draw upon my brains or purse—very likely on both. Now, of the first, I have none to spare. Of the second, what I have is invested, and I have no desire to disturb it." When his visitor protested that what he had to offer was special, Barnum usually interrupted in a firm tone. "If you should propose to get up a stock company for converting paving stones into diamonds, with a prospect of my making a million a year, I would not join you. If your speculation therefore is not something better than that, you need not divulge it, for I certainly should not engage it."

This frontal attack usually kept Barnum's appointments brief. Rarely were the schemes heard of again, though one of the wildest speculations ever offered Barnum was actually carried out later. A man had approached Barnum with the suggestion that camels be imported to carry passengers overland to California. Barnum dismissed the visionary with a sarcastic remark: "I told him that I thought asses were better than camels, but I should not be one of them."

Nevertheless, in 1853, a group of New York businessmen organized "The American Camel Company." Shortly after, at the instigation of Secretary of War Jefferson Davis, Congress appropriated $30,000 for the "importation of camels and dromedaries to be employed for military purposes." In 1856, the American vessel *Supply* left Smyrna with thirty-three camels, and after three months landed at Indianola, Texas. Lieutenant Edward Beale, a friend of Kit Carson, was assigned the task of leading the camels across the arid Southwest, from Texas to California, to establish a new military transport route. Using Turkish drivers, Beale guided his strange caravan—further purchases had swelled the number of beasts to seventy-five—through Indian country to Los Angeles, and back again, four thousand sweltering miles in a year, to prove its worth. But the outbreak of the Civil War finally buried the scheme, and Barnum was satisfied not to have been part of this colorful but costly diversion in American history.

On the several occasions when Barnum did speculate on projects outside show business, he failed to make profits. He owned seventeen per cent of the *North America,* a steamship controlled by Commodore Cornelius Vanderbilt, who had a hundred other steamers servicing the East Coast, and who would one day accumulate one hundred million dollars. The first time Barnum and Vanderbilt met, the crusty Commodore roared: "Is it possible you are Barnum? Why, I expected to see a monster, part lion, part elephant, and a mixture of rhinoceros and tiger!" Almost coincidental with the *North America's* sinking in the Pacific, Barnum sold his share in the vessel to another millionaire, Daniel Drew, and thus emerged unscathed.

At about the same time, Barnum became interested in an English invention, the Philipps' Fire Annihilator, which was supposed to be more effective than water in dousing a blaze. Barnum put $10,000 into this scheme, but in its first test against a burning building, the Annihilator failed to annihilate and the showman's investment went up in flames.

Again, speculating in a field with which he was more familiar, Barnum exchanged $20,000 for a one-third ownership of a new pictorial weekly to be called *Illustrated News.* His partners were two brothers named Beech. For his editor, Barnum hired the untrustworthy Rufus Wilmot Griswold, maligner of Poe, and Griswold selected, for an assistant, Charles Godfrey Leland, a lawyer turned journalist who had been educated at Princeton, Heidelberg, Munich, and the Sorbonne.

Of the pair, Barnum admired Leland more because Leland was a man much like himself. According to Van Wyck Brooks, Leland was "famous for two generations as a lover of the marvellous, the forbidden, the droll and the wild. . . . He was drawn naturally to sorcerers and fakirs, wizards, tinkers, tramps and those who dwell in tents and caravans." Leland loved Barnum for his essential innocence, his practical jokes, and his infectious smile. For a short time, the two conducted a humor column in the weekly.

Leland recalled later that Barnum "would come smiling in
with some curiosity of literature such as the 'reverse' [a
sentence that reads the same forward and backward]—
'Lewd did I live & evil I did dwel'—or a fresh conundrum
or joke, with all his heart and soul full of it, and he would
be delighted over the proof as if to see himself in print was
a startling novelty. We two had 'beautiful times' over that
column, for there was a great deal of 'boy' still left in Barnum. . . . On that humorous column Barnum always de-
ferred to me, even as a small schoolboy defers to an elder
on the question of a game of marbles or hop-scotch. There
was no affectation or play in it; we were both quite in
earnest. I think I see him now, coming smiling in like a
harvest-moon, big with some new joke, and then we sat
down at the desk and 'edited.' "

Within a month of its publication, the *Illustrated News*
climbed to a circulation of 70,000, and soon after it reached
150,000. Griswold, entangled in a domestic crisis, quit his
job, and Leland was left in full charge. Though Leland
fretted over his small salary, objected to a single cramped
office "half-portioned off from the engine room," protested
his lack of help, and deplored the "wretched scrimping" of
the entire operation, he stayed on loyally because he liked
Barnum. But, much as he liked his employer, Leland stead-
fastly refused to publicize him. "I never would in any way
whatever write up, aid, or advertise the great show or museum, or cry up the elephant," Leland said. "I was resolved
to leave the paper first. . . . The entire American press
expected, as a matter of course, that the *Illustrated News*
would be simply an advertisement for the great showman,
and as I represented to Mr. Barnum, this would ere long
utterly ruin the publication. I do not now really know
whether I was quite right in this but it is very much to Mr.
Barnum's credit that he never insisted on it and that in his
own paper he was conspicuous by his absence." Because
Barnum and the Beech brothers were too busy to devote
full time to the periodical, and too close-fisted to make it
more than a repository for reprints, the *Illustrated News*
soon languished from this lack of love and money. After a
year, said Leland, it "came to grief," but Barnum and his
partners managed to sell out to a Boston publishing firm
without loss.

In the years to come, Leland led a varied life. Emanci-

1(a)
Barnum at thirty-four, during his second year as owner of the American Museum.

(b)
Charity Hallett Barnum, the showman's first wife, about 1848, when she was forty.

2. Iranistan, Barnum's first great home in Connecticut, was a $150,000 replica of George IV's Oriental Pavilion.

3(a). A rare Mathew Brady photograph of Barnum's American Museum, the world's foremost showcase, visited by thousands including Charles Dickens, Henry James, and Edward, Prince of Wales. Here Tom Thumb and *The Drunkard* made their debuts.

(b). Barnum's American Museum burning, July 13, 1865. Forty thousand spectators watched the $400,000 loss.

4(a). Tom Thumb's wedding to Lavinia Warren, a school-teacher. The attendants are Commodore Nutt, who competed for the bride's hand, and Miss Minnie Warren, the bride's sister.

(b). Mr. and Mrs. Tom Thumb in later life. He was a prosperous Mason, and she a Christian Scientist and member of the D.A.R.

5(a). Poster of Jumbo, who carried a million children on his back, including the young Winston Churchill.

(b). Photograph of Jumbo after he was killed by a freight train in Canada on September 15, 1885.

6(a). Jenny Lind, the illegitimate Swedish soprano, whose voice was praised by Mendelssohn, Chopin, Wagner, and criticized by Carlyle, Hawthorne, Walt Whitman.

(b). Jenny Lind's debut at Castle Garden, New York City, the night of September 11, 1850. Five thousand persons, mostly men, bought tickets at auction. One bid reached $225.

7(a). Chang and Eng, the original Siamese Twins, who hated each other and Barnum, shown here with two of their twenty-one children.

(b). Mme. Josephine Clofullia, the bearded lady who went to court to prove she was not a man.

8(a). Barnum in old age, the millionaire friend of Queen Victoria and Abraham Lincoln.

(b). Nancy Fish Barnum, second wife of P. T. Barnum, in the year of their marriage, 1874, when he was sixty-four and she was twenty-four.

pated by the inheritance of his father's estate, he became an expatriate. In Heidelberg he spent long hours with the older cousin of Shelley, Thomas Medwin, who had studied Arabic with the poet at Pisa and had ridden with Lord Byron. In Munich, Leland fell in love with the uninhibited Lola Montez, but later refused to elope with her. He tramped the Old World to study gypsy life in Brussels, Moscow, and Cairo. An amazing linguist, he acquired knowledge of Icelandic, Romany, Provençal, pidgin English, Illyrian. He was made Honorary Fellow of the Royal Society of Literature for his discovery of Shelta, a forgotten Welsh-Irish dialect. He published twenty-three books on such diverse subjects as gypsies, Abraham Lincoln, industrial education, slang, and Virgil, and he was never out of touch with his admirable "Uncle Barnum."

The periodical had been fun, but of all Barnum's outside investments, real estate alone gave him huge profits. Acquisition of more wealth was not his primary motive. He speculated in land because he could not stand idleness. More important, he wanted to build a city where none had been before.

He had been in Iranistan three years when he determined to establish an industrial community a half-mile across the river from Bridgeport. In 1851, in partnership with William H. Noble, a wealthy neighbor, Barnum acquired two hundred and twenty-four acres of beautiful level land. This was the beginning of what was to be called East Bridgeport.

On this property, Barnum and Noble laid out the outlines of a city, complete with streets, trees, and a seven-acre park. Then they began to sell every second lot as a home residence or a business. In order to encourage growth, they financed some of the dwellings themselves, demanding only small monthly payments. The total cost of a single house and lot ranged from $1,500 to $3,000. Barnum insisted upon certain restrictions. All houses had to be built a specified distance from the streets, all had to have their architecture approved by Barnum himself, all had to be fenced in and kept clean and neat. And every owner, in return for the right to build in East Bridgeport and receive financing from Barnum, had to sign a contract that promised he would no longer drink whiskey or smoke. Despite these restrictions—from a man who had long jousted against all blue laws—families began to construct homes. A carriage factory was the first of many businesses to appear.

In ten years Barnum had his city flourishing. East Bridgeport displayed three churches, a horse railway, and a Barnum School District. Sewing-machine factories and other industries employed thousands of workmen. And the workmen, with their large families, lived in neat little houses, each with porch and green shutters, each free of the curse of liquor and nicotine, on streets named Barnum, and Hallett, and Caroline, and Helen, and Pauline.

But Barnum had more than a city. He had a sinecure and a profit. For years he and Noble had retained every second lot in the tract for themselves. "We looked for our profits," said Barnum, "solely to the rise in the value of the reserved lots, which we were confident must ensue." Rise in value they certainly did. Barnum had paid an average of $200 for each acre of East Bridgeport; a decade later, each acre was worth $4,000.

Barnum's personal idiosyncrasies were frequently reflected in his business dealings. The stern edict against stimulants and tobacco on his tract was merely a reaction against his old habits. There is no evidence that Barnum was ever an alcoholic, but there is every evidence that until middle age he drank heavily.

When he built Iranistan, he was prouder of the well-stocked wine cellar than of any other room in the mansion. He did not care for Scotch or bourbon, but daily at lunch he consumed an entire bottle of champagne. Sometimes, instead of the champagne, he drank a bottle of port or its equivalent in ale. He was usually drunk by early afternoon —which probably accounted for his habit of concentrating all work in the morning—and eager to have fresh air and a nap. When Mrs. Hannah Hallett, his mother-in-law, who lived beneath his roof, would accuse him of being "heady," he would lose his temper. He would blame overeating and not champagne for his sluggishness. If mother-in-law or wife lectured him, he would threaten to replace his wine diet with hard whiskey to show them what drunkenness really was like.

One autumn day, attending the State Fair at Saratoga Springs, New York, Barnum was shocked to see several prominent millionaires and intellectuals staggering about drunk. It worried him. Might he, too, become an alcoholic? He vowed never to touch whiskey, but to confine himself to the less harmful wine bottle. As he did not care for whiskey anyway, the sacrifice was not great. Still, his intoxication bothered him. He decided to inform himself more on the habit. He invited his friend the Reverend E. H. Chapin, a temperance crusader, to lecture at the Baptist Church in Bridgeport.

The Reverend Mr. Chapin appeared, and for his subject, significantly, he chose "The Moderate Drinker." Apparently, the Reverend was a persuasive evangelist, for his audience listened spellbound. The real problem, said the speaker, was "not the drunkard in the ditch" but the "moderate drinker" whom young people looked to as an example. The moderate drinker gave the whole habit a dangerous air of respectability, and his influence was the most evil of all.

The Reverend Mr. Chapin repeated the words with which he always privately addressed all those who pleaded that they only consumed wine. "Sir, you either do or you do not consider it a privation and a sacrifice to give up drinking. Which is it? If you say that you can drink or let it alone, that you can quit it forever without considering it a self-denial, then I appeal to you as a man, to do it for the sake of your suffering fellow-beings."

All the long night that followed, Barnum did not sleep. He rose red-eyed at dawn with a new resolve. After dressing, he summoned his coachman. Together they descended into the beloved wine cellar where over seventy bottles of champagne lay on the shelves. Barnum and his servant carried the bottles outside, knocked the neck off each, and poured the sparkling contents on the lawn. Then Barnum sent the port wine to neighboring families who might use the bottles medicinally, and returned the whiskey to the grog shops.

When the cellar was bare, Barnum hastened off to find the Reverend Mr. Chapin. He begged for the teetotal pledge. The Reverend did not hide his surprise. He had assumed that the showman had sent for him because he was already an abstainer. Quickly, he produced the pledge, and Barnum signed it.

Returning to Iranistan, Barnum revealed his act of prohibition to his wife. She wept with joy. Confused, he wanted to know why his pledge provoked tears. She told him, he said, "that she had passed many a weeping night, fearing that my wine-bibbing was leading me to a drunkard's path. I reproached her for not telling me her fears, but she replied that she knew I was self-deluded, and that any such hint from her would have been received in anger."

At lunch, the happy champagne bottle was missing, and wife and mother-in-law beamed on the reformed inebriate with contentment. After eating, Barnum felt sufficiently self-satisfied and sober to pass the revelation on to others. That day he talked twenty friends into signing teetotal pledges. For the remainder of his life, he was a useful—or possibly insufferable—temperance man.

He lectured everywhere on the evils of alcohol. He spoke throughout New England an entire winter and spring at his own expense. He went into New York City, in a year when twenty-one thousand men and eleven thousand women had been arrested for intoxication, and tried to get its citizenry to boycott the seven thousand liquor shops and saloons. He harangued the moderate drinker in Toledo, St. Louis, and Montreal. He invaded Wisconsin in an election year to support the prohibitionists, and he addressed a female audience in the ladies' lounge of the steamer *Lexington*. In New Orleans, he filled the Lyceum Hall, and when a heckler interrupted his tirade on the destructive force of alcohol with the question, "How does it affect us, externally or internally?" Barnum shouted back, "E-ternally."

Tobacco was more difficult to give up. Barnum smoked ten cigars a day. Several times, for the sake of economy, he tried to give up cigars. On those tortured days, he chewed camomile flowers instead, but confessed that "they almost killed me" and went back to tobacco. Not until he was fifty did he quit. One day he arrived at the Museum with a fit of choking and palpitations of the heart. Certain that he was having a heart attack at death's door, he made his way to his doctor. He was told that his heart was fine. "Nicotine is all that is the matter with you," the doctor said. "Stop smoking." Barnum stopped. Henceforth, cigars and cigarettes were coffin nails. He chewed bits of calamus, the root of sweet flag, to make him forget.

His chief hobby was farming. Although he hated physical labor, he occasionally enjoyed planting potatoes or flower beds. His green thumb was awkward. Once, observing his gardener cut away useless shoots and limbs from his maples, he tried to emulate him and instead destroyed all the grafts. In 1848, and for three years after, he was President of the Fairfield County Agricultural Society and liked to buttonhole all who would listen to talk on the values of manure. During his tenure of office, he sponsored six county fairs, handling them like the showman that he was. One he enlivened with a plowing competition. Thousands of spectators came to watch plowmen and their teams lay hasty furrows over staked-out plots thirty-six rods square. At another fair, just when receipts were falling off, the sheriff caught an English pickpocket in the act of pilfering a purse. Barnum convinced the sheriff that the thief should be put on display at the fair for the purposes of further identification. When the sheriff consented, Barnum quickly distributed handbills promising one and all that they could view "a live Pickpocket." Hundreds came from great distances to cluck over the handcuffed culprit.

Barnum was a sedentary person. He had no interest in athletics or games beyond an occasional billiard match with Henry Ward Beecher at Irving Hall. Except for two horse races that he had seen in England, even spectator sports bored him. As he told the editor of the *New York Standard* at the very time when Charles "Old Hoss" Radbourne was winning twenty-six successive games for Providence with his underhand pitch and when Paddy Ryan was winning the heavyweight title in eighty-seven rounds: "I never witnessed the 'great and glorious' national game of baseball, and I never expect to. I never saw a boxing or sparring match, a boat race, or a cock fight."

Indoor sports appealed to him more. He had a gift for mimicry, and liked to imitate many celebrities he knew. He enjoyed practicing ventriloquism, at which he was poor, and performing parlor tricks of magic, at which he excelled. He enjoyed reading as much as playing cards, and, wearing those spectacles rarely seen by outsiders, he read widely. Among his favorite authors were Emerson, Whittier, Oliver Wendell Holmes, Shelley, Smollett, and Thomas Moore. Among his most treasured books were an anthology entitled *Library of Choice Reading,* a reference volume entitled *Positive Facts,* the *Encyclopedia of English Literature,* and a set of the *Pictorial History of England.* Also, he frequently consulted bound sets of the *Annual Report* of the Smithsonian Institution, and the *Illustrated London News.*

In later life, Barnum was partial to religious and inspirational works. He claimed to read the family Bible regularly, and next to it, he enjoyed a slender anthology of prose and verse by "wise and holy men of many times" entitled *Daily Strength for Daily Needs*. He said that he read a page of the latter volume every morning, and on the flyleaf of one of his two copies, he wrote: "This book I believe teaches the philosophy of Life and death. . . . I wish every person would daily read it." Another book that Barnum read every morning was *Manna—Daily Worship* by J. W. Hanson, D.D., a collection of prayers published by the Universalists. "Its Bible lesson and prayers afford great consolation to those who desire to love God and practice the Gospel teaching thru Living conscientious, honest, and as far as possible unselfish lives," wrote Barnum in this book.

He was an inveterate collector of oil paintings. The pursuit of art gave him pleasure, though it pained his friends. Barnum's taste was abominable. He had frequently visited London and Paris when the works of Turner, Rossetti, Whistler, Constable, Ingres, Corot, Delacroix, and Courbet were available, many of them for a song—yet the oils that graced his favorite walls were an Adirondacks scene, a portrait of Columbus, and two views of Niagara Falls, all by artists who did not survive their time. Also, in Iranistan, he hung commissioned portraits of Charity, his three daughters, and himself, and in later residences an oil of his grandson Clinton H. Seeley as a child.

But even more than art and reading, the practical joke still gave him his greatest pleasure. When one of his daughters left Bridgeport to spend her wedding night in Boston, Barnum sat casually waiting in Boston the next morning to embarrass bride and groom at breakfast. Sometimes his jokes were more elaborate. During the Jenny Lind tour, his daughter Caroline traveled with him and kept a diary, and for April 1, 1851, she noted: "Well this is All Fool's Day and I think we have all had our share of jokes. Father has perpetrated one of the best jokes today that I ever heard of. He procured some blank telegraph papers and envelopes and wrote some of the most astounding news by telegraph to all our company. I received one saying that Mother would meet us at Louisville on Monday and I believing it true was very happy. Soon I received another saying that Minerva [Philo Barnum's daughter] was coming with her which made me quite wild with joy. Also stating that Mrs. Lyman's father [Mrs. Lyman, a Bridgeport widow, was Caroline's companion on the tour] had sold his house and purchased one in Trumbull, she was very unhappy about it. Soon Mr. Wells [the Bridgeport hotel proprietor] came in with a telegraph that the old Franklin Hotel, Sterling Hotel, etc., were burned, that the wind was high and that the new Presbyterian Church was then burning. Imagine our consternation. Mr. Wells and Mrs. Lyman looked as though they had lost all the friends they ever had. After Mr. Wells went away, however, we thought it over and Mrs. Lyman came to the conclusion that it was *April Fool. . . .*"

Although Barnum imported thousands of animals for the masses and countless pseudoscientific gimcracks for the curious, he had no fondness for household pets and no interest in scientific experiments or discussions.

He liked to talk, or rather to propound. He had a carefully nursed reputation for wit, but he was neither witty nor clever. Sometimes when inspired, he would get off a bright retort. When the Bishop of London bade him farewell and assured him that they would meet again in Heaven, Barnum replied: "If your Lordship is there." On another occasion, he remarked: "Every crowd has a silver lining." Invited by friends to dine in a restaurant, he was sated two thirds through the feast. When heaping platters continued to appear, he held up his hand. "No, thank you," he said. "I will take the rest in money, if you please."

His conversation was colorful rather than quick. The best-known comment attributed to him was: "There's a sucker born every minute." He was said to have uttered this cynicism in a speech, yet no record has ever been found of the speech or of any evidence that Barnum spoke the words. In fact, Robert Edmund Sherwood, who worked for Barnum twenty years, denied that the remark was made at all. "The great impresario never expressed himself in this manner," Sherwood wrote. "Primarily, the word 'sucker' as a slang slogan was not in use during Barnum's lifetime. His favorite expression was 'the American people like to be humbugged.'" Rather proudly, Barnum had named himself the "Prince of Humbugs."

In his book *The Humbugs of the World,* published in

1865, Barnum discoursed on the sin of cynicism. "The greatest humbug of all is the man who believes—or pretends to believe—that everything and everybody are humbugs. We sometimes meet a person who professes that there is no virtue; that every man has his price, and every woman hers; that any statement from anybody is just as likely to be false as true and that the only way to decide which, is to consider whether truth or a lie was likely to have paid best in that particular case. Religion he thinks one of the smartest business dodges extant, a first-rate investment, and by all odds the most respectable disguise that a lying or swindling businessman can wear. Honor he thinks is a sham. Honesty he considers a plausible word to flourish in the eyes of the greener portion of our race. . . . Poor fellow! he has exposed his nakedness. Instead of showing that others are rotten inside, he has proved that he is."

Like Polonius, Barnum was given to banal profundities. In the year he retired to Iranistan, he was asked his advice on how to get ahead in business. Whereupon he issued the following ukase in the form of maxims: "Select the *kind* of business that suits your natural inclinations and temperament. . . . Let your pledge word ever be sacred. . . . Whatever you do, do with all your might. . . . Sobriety. Use no description of intoxicating drinks. . . . Let hope predominate, but be not too visionary. . . . Do not scatter your powers. . . . Engage proper employees. . . . Advertise your business. Do not hide your light under a bushel. . . . Avoid extravagance; and always live considerably within your income, if you can do so without absolute starvation! . . . Do not depend upon others."

Barnum meant every word of this. He sincerely believed what he publicly preached. In the privacy of his memorandum notebook, under the date of April 15, 1889, he summarized his credo of The Compleat Man: "The noblest art is that of making others happy, honesty, sobriety, industry, economy, education, good habits, perseverance, cheerfulness, love to God & good will toward men. These are the pre-eminent requisites for securing Health, Independence, or a Happy Life, the respect of Mankind and the special favor of our Father in Heaven."

Although Barnum was always satisfied with, even proud of, his profession as showman, he often fancied that his forensic talents might have served him better in another capacity. Once when he was crossing the Atlantic, a mock trial was staged on shipboard for the amusement of the passengers. Barnum acquitted himself well as prosecutor. Flushed with the success of his performance, he later told Joel Benton: "I have the vanity to think that if my good fortune had directed me to that profession, I should have made a very fair lawyer."

Beyond his boundless egotism, his passion for the pronoun *I*, and his continuing love affair with himself, beyond this and his self-advertised generosity, little else was known of Barnum's character traits in his lifetime. But careful consultation with friends, enemies, and employees, who left obscure memoirs of him, reveals something more.

He was good-natured, as well as thoughtful and kind in most of his personal relationships. Lyman Abbott, who knew him, wrote: "If I am right in defining a good-natured man as a man who desires to make other people happy, then the word good-natured would adequately describe him." Joel Benton remembered an incident when a poor boy had fallen ill just before Barnum's circus parade was to appear, and was inconsolable because he must miss it. In childish scrawl, the boy wrote Barnum asking "if he would not change the route of the parade to a certain direction that he named, so that it would pass his house, as he could then be taken to the window to see it go by." Despite all inconvenience, Barnum changed the direction of the parade and did not publicize his thoughtfulness.

Benton always felt that the showman's ego was more a matter of hardheaded business than vanity. "When he found his celebrity was a tremendous factor in his success, he did everything that he could think of to extend the exploitation of his name. This was not to nourish vain imaginings or because he felt exalted; it was to promote business."

The great majority of those who worked for Barnum were unrestrained in their admiration of him as human being and careerist, even when they were not in his employ. In 1893 Charles Godfrey Leland recalled: "Of all the men whom I met in those days in the way of business, Mr. Barnum, the great American humbug, was by far the honestest and freest from guile or deceit or 'ways that were dark, or tricks that were vain.' He was very kind-hearted and benevolent and gifted with a sense of fun which was even stronger than his desire for dollars. . . . He was a genius like Rabelais, but one who employed business and humanity for material instead of literature, just as Abraham Lincoln, who was a brother of the same band, employed patriotism and politics. All three of them expressed vast problems, financial, intellectual or natural by the brief arithmetic of a joke." As late as 1926, Robert Edmund Sherwood was nominating Barnum as the foremost showman in history. "I consider him the greatest genius that ever conducted an amusement enterprise in this country, a man of superlative imagination, indomitable pluck and artistic temperament."

Some persons, of course, found less attractive traits in Barnum. He was a poor loser at whist, and often embarrassed guests with his lack of sportsmanship. Although he could invest a fortune in a Jenny Lind or a Commodore Nutt, or volunteer large sums to charities, he was niggardly about the most minor household expenses. The Siamese Twins had considered him parsimonious, and they were not alone in this.

Major James Burton Pond, the Civil War veteran who made lecturing a big business with his management of Mark Twain, Henry Ward Beecher, and Henry M. Stanley, always remembered Barnum with mixed emotions. "A more plausible, pleasant-speaking man was never heard," wrote Pond. "It was as good as the show itself to listen to him in conversation." Yet, Pond added, "I think I never knew a more heartless man or one who knew the value and possibilities of a dollar more than P. T. Barnum."

In his youth, Pond represented Barnum during a temperance speaking tour of New England. Barnum, who was to receive $2,000 and all expenses for twenty talks, was met at the Boston depot by Pond. The showman refused a carriage because of the cost, and insisted on walking to his hotel. "He was the most prudently economical man that I have ever known," Pond said.

Barnum hired the cheapest rather than the best musicians for his orchestras. His colored posters were prepared so that they could be used again year after year. For his sideshow double acts, he preferred married couples because he refused to provide more than one sleeping berth to a pair on the road. According to Pond, the showman, who knew that his ticket-seller often shortchanged customers and did not mind, freely admitted that his ticket-seller had paid him $5,000 to obtain the job.

Pond saw Barnum as a cold, emotionless promoter in his relations with employees. Human beings were forever subordinate to the success of the show. Once, during a circus performance, a giantess was run over by a chariot and instantly killed. Barnum watched without visible reaction. Pond turned to him in horror. "That is dreadful, isn't it?" Barnum shrugged. "Oh, there is another waiting for her place. It is rather a benefit than a loss."

Barnum believed in God and the Universalist creed, and he attended church regularly with his wife, but he did not become a member of the church until late in life. He suffered few superstitious beliefs except in the ominous number thirteen, which he felt plagued him in every way during his life and caused him bad luck.

Even less known than his private personality was his private life as husband, father, and lover. Although he was constantly in the headlines, he was able to suppress most domestic news and gossip, even from the prying scandal sheets that infested New York.

In 1855, his wife of more than a quarter of a century, Charity, was forty-eight years of age. She was prematurely old. Her face bore the ravages of the trying and lonely years spent as mate of a public man. She wore her hair in ringlets. Her high forehead, narrow eyes, long straight nose, tight thin lips, and receding chin line made her countenance a startling contrast to her husband's big, merry, expansive face. Little is known of the elusive Charity Barnum, of her personality or her relationship with the showman, because little was ever recorded. Even in his voluminous autobiography, Barnum gave her entire life less lineage than the Feejee Mermaid, and no more than he gave to a single dance and frolic with Jenny Lind.

Charity had been raised in poverty, and even after she married Barnum she knew how to economize. When he had undertaken the Museum, and was determined that the household be managed on six hundred dollars a year, Charity had come forth with a proposed budget of four hundred dollars. She had born Barnum three daughters before they had means and one when he was becoming wealthy, and she had suffered to see the third of the four girls, Frances, die at the age of two in 1844.

After the children had appeared, Charity became increasingly ill and weakened. Barnum built a greenhouse for her, and there she puttered among her "rare and beautiful flowers." One of her few outside interests was a membership in the exclusive Bridgeport Charitable Society. She was almost never consulted by Barnum about personal affairs. In March 1851, while in St. Louis with Jenny Lind, Barnum abruptly told his daughter Caroline that he was selling Iranistan and moving the family to an estate near Philadelphia. Caroline burst into tears. "Father has not written yet to Mother about it," she complained in her diary. "I expect she will be perfectly miserable for she is as much attached to Bridgeport as I am, and after having so much trouble with our house and grounds I think it is abominable to have to leave them. . . ." Later, it was Caroline and not Barnum who revealed the news to Charity. In the end, however, Barnum decided against the move.

Except for two visits to London with her daughters in 1844 and 1857, there is no evidence that Charity ever traveled abroad or in the United States with her husband. When Barnum was staging his Jenny Lind concerts in Havana, he invited Charity to make a sea voyage to Cuba. At the last moment she declined, explaining that "she had not the courage" to face seasickness. For the most part, her role was that of mother, hostess, and homebody. Barnum rarely wrote of her or spoke of her in public, though once, at the Museum, he told an audience, "Without Charity I am nothing"—but this may have been merely a pun, since he was then recovering from a period of hardship, and all his money was in his wife's name. When she died, his grief was great, he said, yet it was of brief duration.

Being in show business, Barnum was regularly exposed to the charms of other women, and all of them were not freaks. He consorted with a wide variety of attractive actresses and ladies of society and title, not only in America but also in England. The proximity of these women, their awe and flattery, and the showman's long absences from home, gave rise to rumors of infidelity.

If Barnum had love affairs, they did not find their way into the newspapers in his lifetime. But tongues wagged, nevertheless, at least enough so that his friend Sherwood was still trying to silence them in another century. In *Here We Are Again* Sherwood wrote: "Another untruth . . . is the declaration that he was a libertine, and consequently lived unhappily with his family. These scurrilous and scandalous assertions are made for sensational reasons only and embrace not a trace of truth. There never lived a man more lovable in his family than Mr. Barnum."

On January 17, 1897, six years after Barnum's death, the *New York World* published a sensational exposure of the showman's extramarital sex life, as revealed by the newspaper's "Special Correspondent" in Bridgeport. "Besides the three daughters Barnum had a son," the *World* reported. "That circumstance is not generally known, but it is none the less a fact. He does not bear the name of Barnum because he is not entitled by law to do so. His mother was a French actress who was one of the attractions at the old Barnum Museum, when that notable landmark was at the corner of Ann Street and Broadway, New York, where the new Havemeyer skyscraper now towers. The paternity of this son Barnum never denied. He cared for him in childhood and educated him as a physician, and at the present day, under a name that affords only an indirect hint of his ancestry, he is holding an honored place among the medical practitioners of an important city of the Union. . . .

"Not long after Barnum married his last wife [Nancy Fish, Barnum's second wife], this illegitimate son made a sudden and by no means welcome descent upon Bridgeport. There was a more or less remote possibility of a male heir to the Barnum millions—something the old showman very much desired—and the real but unrecognized son came to demand that his father settle some property upon him. Barnum drew up a cast-iron contract by which the son received $60,000 on condition that he never attempt after Barnum's death to annoy the heirs or claim anything from the will. The son has kept the contract faithfully."

In 1904 Julian H. Sterling, a Barnum relative, corroborated the exposure by writing that, sometime between 1851 and 1855, the showman had "brought over to Franklin house . . . a circus woman who shortly gave birth to a boy. Barnum educated the boy and late in life gave him a fortune. He turned out well and now lives in Richmond."

Old Bridgeport families still remember that a Mrs. Candee, whose husband edited the *Bridgeport Daily Standard,* used to speak of "a dashing young man named Phineas

Taylor, who was said to be P. T. Barnum's illegitimate son." His mother was thought by some to have been Ernestine de Faiber, an actress and dancer at the Museum.

Barnum's three daughters were his greatest domestic pleasure and possibly his greatest trial. In 1855, Caroline was twenty-two years old, the next, Helen, fifteen, and the youngest, Pauline, nine. "They had been brought up," Barnum said a little regretfully, "in luxury; accustomed to call on servants to attend to every want; and almost unlimited in the expenditure of money." In short, they were spoiled.

Caroline, a tall, slender, dark-eyed brunette, was Barnum's favorite daughter. She was said to have a first-rate business sense, considerable linguistic ability, and a talent for conversation. On October 19, 1852, a thousand guests arrived for her wedding to David W. Thompson, a twenty-one-year-old Episcopalian who shared a prosperous Bridgeport saddlery business with his father. Most of the guests were driven outdoors when a portion of Iranistan caught fire. The groom was deeply upset, but Barnum assured him: "Never mind! We can't help these things; the house will probably be burned; but if no one is killed or injured, you shall be married tonight, if we are obliged to perform the ceremony in the coach-house." Fortunately, a bucket brigade quenched the flame and the wedding took place as scheduled.

Caroline bore Thompson a daughter and son, but the boy died in his infancy. The girl, Frances Leigh, who died in 1939, was Barnum's last surviving granddaughter. In Thompson's later years, he went into the coal business, became vice-president of a Bridgeport bank, and accepted a government job with the custom-house in New York City. During the Civil War he incurred Barnum's wrath for his secessionist sympathies, and when he ran for the state senate in 1865 as a Copperhead, and was soundly beaten, Barnum was delighted. Thompson died in 1915; Caroline had died four years earlier, when she was seventy-eight, as the result of a fall and brain concussion. At her death, she was worth one and a half million dollars.

Helen, a shapely brunette, grew up to marry Samuel H. Hurd in 1857, when she was but seventeen. Not Iranistan but Caroline's home was the scene of the wedding. Hurd, whom Barnum loved as he might his own son, was shareholder in a company that sold goods brought east from

California. He also conducted a leather business. After his marriage to Helen, he accepted employment as Barnum's treasurer. The union between Helen and Hurd produced three daughters. Of all his brood, Barnum considered Helen the most extravagant. "She was a warm-hearted, generous girl, but knew literally nothing of the value of money and the difficulty of acquiring it." Shortly before her marriage, when she was still attending an exclusive French boarding school in Washington, D.C., Helen learned that her father was in desperate financial straits. She offered to return home and give piano lessons to help him. Barnum was deeply moved and thought her concern "worth ten thousand dollars."

Pauline, Barnum's youngest daughter, was a large, buxom girl of considerable beauty. She developed a first-rate singing voice, and it is said that several times her father sponsored her in vaudeville shows on the road. Finally, in 1866, she gave up her career to marry Nathan Seeley, a stockbroker. Five hundred guests, including three Congressmen and John N. Genin, of hat fame, attended the formal wedding in Bridgeport. A *New York Times* correspondent praised Barnum's management of the affair. "It was the wedding of his last daughter and his last child, and its celebration was conducted nobly. I may properly refer to the fact that no stimulants were present, and I have no doubt that to this excellent feature is due the complete success of the affair."

Pauline's marriage to Seeley resulted in two sons and a daughter. Her early death, in 1877 when she was thirty-one, was blamed on "diphtheria and measles," and her passing struck Barnum cruelly. "This blow would have been unsupportable to me," he said, "did I not receive it as coming from our good Father in Heaven, who does all things right." Seeley remarried later, and died in 1917.

Not all of Barnum's daughters, according to the *New York World* exposé, led exemplary lives. Apparently, ardent Helen was unfaithful to Hurd, and finally left him for another. "The career of a certain one of Barnum's daughters was about as sensational as anything in the Barnum family history," said the *World*. "This daughter married and she and her husband lived in the handsomest house in Fairfield Avenue, this city, which was called Lindenhurst, a house which Barnum had built for himself after

Iranistan was burned. There were gay times at Lindenhurst while the Hurds lived there. A good-looking tailor's clerk was one of the favored guests, so much favored that his wife left him. The clerk died soon after so there was an end to that scandal.

"But the daughter soon developed another and even more sensational one. She ran away from her husband with a doctor, and the two lived openly together in Chicago. Poor old Barnum, whose chickens were coming home to roost with a vengeance, tried hard to suppress this scandal, but a New York newspaper printed it and gave a diagram of the apartment in Chicago.

"The much-abused husband started in to get a divorce, but Barnum induced him to abandon it on account of his two other daughters. Some years later the eloping daughter quietly got a divorce out West and married the doctor. She, too, like the irregular son, made a descent upon Bridgeport soon after Barnum married his last wife, and there was a terrible scene at 'Waldemere,' as Barnum called his home in Seaside Park. Barnum was just about to take his great show to London and had made his will. The daughter was entirely cut off, her name not even being mentioned in it. After much bitter wrangling Barnum agreed to give her a tract of land, but insisted on leaving her name out of his will."

Certain elements of this lurid account are confirmed by what is known of Helen's activity and Barnum's will. To the best recollection of the oldest Bridgeport families, Helen did indeed run off with a physician, and live openly with him as his mistress. Helen did divorce Hurd, who retained custody of their children and remained in Bridgeport to work for Barnum. According to a living relative, "Barnum was furious about the divorce—he was so very fond of Hurd." Helen did take a doctor for her second husband. On March 22, 1871, at South Bend, Indiana, she married Dr. William Harmon Buchtel, an Ohioan who had served in the Civil War and was a practicing physician. Shortly after the ceremony, Helen and Dr. Buchtel moved to Denver, Colorado, where he became Professor of Obstetrics at Gross Medical College, and later its president, before the school was incorporated with Denver University. By her second husband, Helen had two daughters, the elder dying before the age of three. In Barnum's will, while Helen

was mentioned by name several times, she was finally left
no cash, but rather "a tract of land" near Denver.

In Barnum's original will, written on January 30, 1882,
eight years after he had taken a second wife, Helen was
promised "the gold watch worn by her mother, and the
ivory Madonna, also the two old tapestry pictures in parlor,
and one gilt vase bought with gold set in Paris." She was
also bequeathed $1,500 a year for the remainder of her
life. But seven years later, in 1889, Barnum wrote the first
codicil to the will and amended his legacy to Helen: "By
a mutual and friendly agreement entered into between my
daughter, Helen M. Buchtel, and myself, on the second day
of May, 1884, I conveyed valuable property to her, which
property she has accepted in full satisfaction of any and
all claims and demands upon my estate after my decease,
and she has agreed to forever acknowledge the same as a
just and liberal provision by me for her out of my estate,
and of as much thereof as she ought to expect or desire as
my daughter. Now, therefore, I hereby revoke and annul
all the provisions, annuities, gifts, legacies, and devices contained in my will, or other testamentary documents, to, or
for her benefit in any way, and declare each and all of the
same to be void, excepting always the gilt vase given to her
in this codicil. (This is already delivered to her. P.T.B.)"

Barnum privately considered the so-called "valuable
property" he had conveyed to Helen as "worthless." He
justified his deceit as proper punishment for the disgrace
she had brought upon the family. But the last laugh was
Helen's own. For, ironically, after Barnum's death the
"worthless" property was discovered to be rich in mineral
deposits, and it made Helen more prosperous than all the
other Barnum heirs combined.

Between 1882, when he offered gifts and annuity, and
1884, when he revoked them for the real-estate settlement,
Barnum may have had that "terrible scene at 'Waldemere' "
with Helen. Yet, the year before his death, Barnum accompanied by his second wife who had insisted upon the
reconciliation, traveled west to call upon Helen and Dr.
Buchtel.

Helen, said the *World,* always blamed her passions and
misfortunes on Barnum's example. When he severely chas-
tised her for her affair with the tailor's clerk before she
took off with her doctor lover, she rebuked him with the

words: "How could I help it? Am I not P. T. Barnum's daughter?"

Of his numerous grandchildren, Barnum favored the two boys, Pauline's offspring, Clinton H. Seeley and Herbert Seeley. Barnum left behind him a $4,100,000 estate. After liberally providing for his second wife, his friends, and his charities, he bequeathed one third to Clinton, Herbert, and their sister Jessie, one third to two of the daughters Helen had abandoned to Samuel H. Hurd—Helen B. Rennell and Julia H. Clarke—and one third to his eldest daughter Caroline. Clinton H. Seeley was also left three per cent of the profits (not to exceed $10,000 a year) of Barnum's show business enterprises, and an additional $25,000 if he would co-operate in keeping Barnum's name alive.

"Whereas I have no son," Barnum wrote in his will, "and therefore my name of Barnum will not otherwise be continued in my family, except by my wife, and as I would like to perpetuate my surname, and I have a deep love and respect for, and confidence in the strict integrity of my said grandson, Clinton H. Seeley, who I am sure will honor the name, therefore I give my grandson, Clinton H. Seeley, Twenty-five Thousand Dollars ($25,000), on this express condition, that he shall in a legal and proper way change his name, or cause his name to be changed to that of Clinton Barnum Seeley, and that he shall habitually use the name of Barnum, either as Clinton Barnum Seeley, or C. Barnum Seeley, or Barnum Seeley in his name, so that the name Barnum shall always be known as his name." Quickly enough, the eldest of the boys became C. Barnum Seeley.

However, Barnum's certainty that C. Barnum would "honor the name" might have been sorely shaken had he lived a short time longer. For in the last month of 1896, Barnum's two grandsons were involved in a scandal that rocked and amused New York. To celebrate C. Barnum Seeley's impending marriage to Florence Tuttle, the younger Herbert, who had recently departed from West Point after two unhappy years, threw a stag dinner for him in an upstairs suite of Sherry's restaurant. Twenty gentlemen of society participated in what the *World* later called "the pigsty revel at Sherry's" and the Reverend A. H. Lewis called a scene to be likened "to the most licentious periods of Pompeii."

The Seeleys' entertainment featured a shapely young lass

named Catherine Devine, more popularly known as Little Egypt—probably the very same who had, three years before, exhibited her unsheathed charms and wiggle at the Columbian Exposition in Chicago, side by side with such attractions as John Philip Sousa, Sandow, Susan B. Anthony, John Brown's house, Swami Vivekanada, and the stuffed horse Comanche, only survivor of Custer's Last Stand. Little Egypt, it appeared, cavorted in the nude on a table top while the Seeleys and other guests, hot with wine, snatched at her bare legs.

Police Captain George Chapman and two detectives, performing on a tip, raided the bacchanalia, but the Seeleys had been forewarned and had secreted their dancer in time. Later they protested the invasion of privacy, and Captain Chapman was placed on trial. At the same time the Grand Jury indicted Herbert Seeley for "conspiring to induce the woman known as Little Egypt to commit the crime of indecent exposure." Eventually this indictment was dropped, as were charges against Captain Chapman. Thereafter, Little Egypt advertised herself as the veteran of "the Awful Seeley Dinner" (until she died in 1908, leaving behind almost a quarter of a million dollars); Captain Chapman was congratulated by the Woman's Purity Association; and C. Barnum Seeley was happily married in New York's Trinity Chapel (the ceremony, reported the *New York Tribune*, being unhappily attended by a large number of "unbidden" and "unwelcome" guests who had heard of "an incident which happened at a dinner").

Although Barnum had wanted Clinton to carry his name, it was grandson Herbert who eventually most resembled the showman. "Herbert seems to have been the only Barnum descendant with a circus flair like P. T.," a member of the Barnum family said recently. "Herbert was a carefree bachelor, who served in the Spanish-American War, and did not marry until just before his death at forty-three. His older brother, Clinton Barnum Seeley, worked with the circus only a short time after P.T.'s death. In 1907, Clinton set up residence in Bridgeport, headed the Bridgeport Trust Company, and served as member and then President of the Park Board for thirty-one years. He devoted himself to the Union League Club, the New York Yacht Club, genealogy, and golf. He died in 1958. The rest of the Barnum descendants led quiet, humdrum lives, far from the bright lights, the tinsel, the sawdust, and all seemed rather ashamed of their circus money."

Thus Barnum, grandfather as well as human being and mere mortal. William Roscoe Thayer called him "the typical American" of the latter half of the nineteenth century. Many other writers concurred. But in 1923, Robert C. Benchley dissented. "To point to Barnum as a 'typical American' is like pointing to a cat as a typical mouse. The 'typical American' was Barnum's meat. . . . You can never call a genius 'typical' anything."

VIII

EXHIBIT EIGHT
Jerome Clock Company

If Barnum re-read his Old Testament in his retirement, he may have found a strange portent in Genesis. For in its pages, Pharaoh revealed to Joseph a dream: "There come seven years of great plenty throughout all the land of Egypt, and there shall arise after them seven years of famine, and all the plenty shall be forgotten."

Barnum had known the years of plenty, ten or more of them, and now came the years of famine. In 1855, secluded in Iranistan, he had seemed unassailable, mighty, utterly indestructible. Before the year was out, his life was a shambles. All that he had so laboriously built through the American Museum, the Tom Thumb tour, the Jenny Lind enterprise—reputation, wealth, haven—was brought tumbling down in a decade of disaster. Some of it he might attribute to an unkind fate or accident, but much of it he invited upon himself.

The disintegration began in a small way, and was of his own making. It began with the writing of a book, his autobiography, a common act of vanity overlaid with a

desire for immortality. Until this book reached the public,
his reputation in America and Europe had been relatively
unblemished. With the appearance of the book, he became,
overnight, a rascal and blackguard. He had committed the
incredible folly, out of some insensitivity or further need
for sensation, of letting his vast public come backstage—
where they might learn, for the first time, the extent and
detail of his occasional trickery. By this act, the prophet
of the new showmanship made his flock feel foolish—and
there were many who would not forgive him.

During most of 1854, he scratched away at the autobiography—"being assured by publishers that such a work
would have an extensive circulation, and by personal
friends that it would be a readable book"—and at last,
in 1855, the 404 pages were put before the public by J. S.
Redfield, of New York, who also published Fitz-Greene
Halleck and Edgar Allan Poe. It was entitled: *The Life
of P. T. Barnum, Written by Himself.*

Barnum insisted that he had, indeed, written it by himself though Charles Godfrey Leland, the editor of Barnum's defunct *Illustrated News,* thought that it was ghost-
written. Leland said that Barnum had asked him to write
the book, and that he had refused. "This would have been
amusing work and profitable," Leland admitted, "but I
shrunk from the idea of being identified with it." It was
Leland's opinion that Barnum had then turned to Rufus
Wilmot Griswold, another editor on the periodical.

Griswold was the most unsavory character in Barnum's
circle. A onetime Baptist minister, he had worked as editor
on twenty magazines and produced forty books. On several
occasions he had been dismissed for dishonesty. A psycho-
pathic liar and plagiarist, he maligned Catholics and
Thomas Jefferson. Appointed Edgar Allan Poe's literary
executor, he viciously slandered Poe in print the moment
that he was dead. Of Poe, he wrote: "Irascible, envious—
bad enough, but not the worst, for these salient angles were
all varnished over with a cold, repellant cynicism, his passions vented themselves in sneers. There seemed to him
no moral susceptibility; and, what was more remarkable
in a proud nature, little or nothing of the true point of
honor. He had, to a morbid excess, that desire to rise
which is vulgarly called ambition. . . ." Griswold was a
capable hack, and it is possible that he did secretly write

Barnum's autobiography. But the style of the published book is so perfectly the showman's own that either Griswold was a remarkable literary ape or Barnum actually wrote the book.

Barnum's bulky confession, advertised as the success story of a self-made man and a guidebook to riches, was startlingly frank. "It will be seen that I have not covered up my so-called 'humbugs,'" Barnum wrote, "but have given a full account even of such schemes as 'Joice Heth,' the 'Feejee Mermaid,' and the 'Woolly Horse.' . . . Though a portion of my 'confessions' may by some be considered injudicious, I prefer frankly to 'acknowledge the corn' wherever I have had a hand in plucking it."

It was sold, as were most serious books at that time, by subscription. Door-to-door salesmen trudged about the nation extolling its virtues and quoting its contents. Too, it was for sale at the American Museum. Soon enough, it was competing as a best-seller with Charles Dickens's *Hard Times,* Henry Thoreau's *Walden,* and T. S. Arthur's *Ten Nights in a Barroom.*

The critics fell on it and belabored Barnum sorely. In the United States, the *New York Times* led the pack. "The great fact which Mr. Barnum sets forth in this biography of himself, is that his success has been achieved—his wealth acquired—his reputation and consideration established, by the systematic, adroit and persevering plan of obtaining money under false pretences from the public at large. . . . Nothing in this book is more remarkable than the obvious insensibility of Mr. Barnum to the real character of its disclosures. He takes an evident pride in the boldness and enormity of the impositions by which he has amassed his fortune. He does not confess them, he boasts of them. . . . The book will be very widely read, and will do infinite mischief. It will encourage the tendency, always too strong in the young men of this country, to seek fortune by other means than industry. . . ." To this, Severn T. Wallis added an amen. "Lie and swindle as much as you please—says the voice from Iranistan—but be sure you read your Bible and drink no brandy!"

But these reviews were as caresses compared with the reception awaiting Barnum in England. *Blackwood's Magazine,* which had once tried to destroy that "Cockney," John Keats, now had its knives out for Barnum. "We find but few instances of rogues openly congratulating themselves upon the success of their roguery, and confidently demanding from the public applause and congratulation. . . . Mr. Phineas Taylor Barnum is, we are thankful to say, not a native of this country. . . . We have not read, for a long time, a more trashy or offensive book than this. . . . If we could enter, with anything like a feeling of zest, into the relations of this excessively shameless book, we should be inclined to treat its publication as the most daring hoax which the author has yet perpetrated upon the public. But it has inspired us with nothing but sensations of disgust for the frauds which it narrates, amazement at its audacity, loathing for its hypocrisy, abhorrence for the moral obliquity which it betrays and sincere pity for the wretched man who compiled it. He has left nothing for his worst enemy to do; for he had fairly gibbeted himself. No unclean bird of prey, nailed ignominiously to the door of a barn, can present a more humiliating spectacle than Phineas Taylor Barnum, as he appears in his autobiography."

Tait's Edinburgh Magazine characterized Barnum as a swindler and villain whose career was "a living libel upon all that is manly in humanity." The periodical railed at him for his "wretched conceit," and then went on: "How much of Mr. Barnum's revelations is to be believed, and how much of them is sheer lies and moonshine? That is the question. Who shall say that when this autobiographical spec. has served its purpose, and brought the anticipated addition of dollars to the showman's coffers, another volume may not be forthcoming in which the writer shall renounce all claim to the nauseous depravity in which he has thought fit to clothe himself in this book, and stand forth in a new light. Positively, we have our suspicions whether this candid confession be not after all as much an imposture and humbug as Old Mother Heth, the mermaid, and Tom Thumb. Sure we are that it has been muckraked together for the same special purpose—to wit, to subserve the greedy, money-getting propensities of the author."

The Edinburgh critic was right in one respect: another volume was forthcoming, one in which the author did try to soften some of "the nauseous depravity" evident in his first book. Fourteen years later, after buying back the plates of his first book and destroying them, Barnum produced a new version of his autobiography with a new title. In

1869, J. B. Burr and Company of Hartford published *Struggles and Triumphs; or, Forty Years' Recollections of P. T. Barnum, Written by Himself*. This version, almost twice the length of the first and three pounds in weight, was over 700 pages long and sold for three dollars and fifty cents.

Certain sections of *Struggles and Triumphs* were understandably expurgated or condensed. The years had mellowed Barnum. He wanted respectability. And he did not wish to be burned by a new generation of reviewers. As a consequence, many episodes that might show him in a bad light were played down. Certain details of the Feejee Mermaid trickery were omitted, as was his falsification of Tom Thumb's age and birthplace. Added were the stories of his most recent successes and an indignant account of his eventual downfall.

Again, the autobiography sold well, though it was still disdained by critics. After a few years, Barnum bought the plates and copyright back from Burr and decided to publish it himself. Using some of the old plates and joining with them new plates of smaller type, Barnum had a condensed edition of 300 pages printed in Buffalo. Each volume cost him nine cents and sold for one dollar. Until 1888, he continued to fiddle with the book, regularly adding accounts of his latest activities as if it was a personal yearbook or almanac, and periodically turning these new editions loose on the public. Nine versions of the autobiography are known, though possibly as many as twenty were published.

By 1884, desiring publicity more than profit, Barnum put the book in the public domain, offering its contents royalty free to any publishers who wished to reprint it. One Chicago publisher obliged at once, retitling it *How I Made Millions*. In 1883, Barnum claimed that half a million copies had been sold; six years later, he claimed over one million copies. It was hawked at the Museum, and then at the circus. Wherever Barnum went, the book went with him.

He considered his autobiography the best gift any human being could receive. In 1920, George Conklin, one of Barnum's lion-tamers, disclosed that Barnum had kept a large packing box, nailed tight, in the Bridgeport office of his circus's winter quarters. On the box was painted the warning: "Not to be Opened Until After the Death of P. T.

Barnum." An English elephant-keeper who had once been keeper of Jumbo, a senile soul named Matthew Scott, took it into his head that this mysterious box contained his cash inheritance from Barnum. "When after Mr. Barnum's death the box was opened it was found to be full of copies of his life written by himself and each of the old men round the show was given a copy." Scott went to pieces from sheer disappointment. He could not understand that, in giving this book, Barnum was offering him the greatest treasure that he possessed.

Barnum's autobiography continued to be issued after his death, well into the twentieth century. As recently as 1927, both The Viking Press and Alfred A. Knopf brought out editions of the book, in each case combining the best of Barnum's many revisions. George S. Bryan, who edited the two-volume Knopf publication, regarded the book as "a full, leisurely narrative, done with vast relish. The style is, as one might expect, facile, in a high-spirited and careless way. The story, bulk considered, well maintains its interest. . . . Who so touches this book, touches a human being— touches a career of a peculiarly rich, varied, and entertaining pattern."

Yet, in 1855, there had been the savagery of the critics. They did not understand Barnum's intent, Joel Benton argued in *The Century Magazine* in 1902. The book "was not meant to be taken as literal truth; but it was so taken, and the criticism of it was very bitter. The soberer matter-of-fact public of that day did not see the Pickwickian sense and the orientalism of statement that pervaded it. The cold type could not carry with it the twinkling of the author's eye." What stabbed Barnum deepest was that everywhere he was accused of having built his career on trickery instead of on industry and by the use of his intelligence.

Before he could recover from this blow, another of far more drastic consequences occurred. This time, it was not his pride that was damaged, but his pocketbook. Late in 1855, because he was overly ambitious for East Bridgeport and gullible in most matters outside show business, he found himself thrown into bankruptcy.

The man so recently branded swindler by the reviewers was, in his own words, "cruelly swindled and deliberately defrauded." It was incredible to all. Barnum later tried to explain his vulnerability to an audience: "Many people have wondered that a man considered so acute as myself should have been deluded into embarrassments like mine, and not a few have declared, in short meter, that 'Barnum was a fool.' I can only reply that I never made pretensions to the sharpness of a pawnbroker, and I hope I shall never so entirely lose confidence in human nature as to consider every man a scamp by instinct, or a rogue by necessity. 'It is better to be deceived sometimes, than to distrust always,' says Lord Bacon, and I agree with him." Apart from the fact that Lord Bacon had not originated that statement, the sentiment was appropriate. Barnum, ever impressed by wealth and position, did not consider Chauncey Jerome or his son, respectively president and secretary of the Jerome Clock Company, a scamp or rogue—and he suffered for it.

According to Barnum, Chauncey Jerome visited him in September 1855 at Iranistan. Later, in his own autobiography, Jerome denied this. "I wish to have it understood that I never saw P. T. Barnum, while he was connected with the company of which I was a member." Jerome declared that he was retired at the time, and it may have been his son who called upon Barnum. No matter which, *a* Jerome came calling. A proposition was suggested to Barnum. The Jerome Clock Company would gladly move from New Haven to the showman's beloved East Bridgeport if, in return, Barnum made the firm a loan. The company was worth $587,000—there were ledgers to prove it—but this had been a poor season. Unless the company could raise another $110,000 immediately, it would have to lay off a large number of workmen.

Barnum was interested. In exchange for a temporary loan to an established and reputable firm, he would have its factories permanently in East Bridgeport. At once he investigated Chauncey Jerome. He learned that Jerome had made his fortune by inventing brass clockworks eighteen years before. Through mass production of standardized brass parts from steel dies, Jerome was able to sell an all-metal timepiece for four dollars, thereby undermining the market for wooden clocks selling at twelve dollars. Jerome's clocks were used as far away as China, where the innards were removed so that the cases could be used as temples for the Gods—"proving that faith was possible without 'works,'" Barnum added while he could still be merry. Jerome had given a $40,000 church to New Haven and a large clock to a church in Bridgeport. Barnum was satisfied. "So wealthy and so widely known a company would surely be a grand acquisition to my city," he decided.

And so Barnum made his ill-fated deal with the Jerome Clock Company. He signed a series of notes vouching for the loans the Jeromes needed. On some notes he left the date of payment blank, allowing the firm to use them as required, but they were never to total in excess of $110,-000. A whole series of complex financial transactions followed, in which Barnum's old canceled notes were returned to him for new ones. Assured by Jerome's son that the prospering company would soon be able to "snap its fingers at the banks," Barnum relaxed, and in so doing, made his final mistake. He continued to cosign new notes, without bothering to see if all of the old ones had been canceled.

At the end of three months he learned the truth—"the frightful fact that I had endorsed for the clock company to the extent of more than half a million dollars, and most of the notes had been exchanged for old Jerome Company notes due to the banks and other creditors. My agent who made these startling discoveries came back to me with the refreshing intelligence that I was a ruined man!" Not only was the Jerome Company bankrupt, but so was Barnum himself.

He was incredulous. He could scarcely believe it. He had been on the summit, safe against all emergencies, secure, and now suddenly he was poor.

"What a dupe I had been!" he cried in anger. "Here was a great company pretending to be worth $587,000, asking temporary assistance to the amount of $110,000, coming down with a crash, so soon as my helping hand was removed, and sweeping me down with it. It failed; and even after absorbing my fortune, it paid but from twelve to fifteen per cent of its obligations, while to cap the climax, it never removed to East Bridgeport at all, notwithstanding this was the only condition which ever prompted me to advance one dollar to the rotten concern!"

The distraught Barnum briefly contemplated suicide. But, after much soul-searching, he concluded "that the blow was wisely intended for my ultimate benefit" and that a higher authority wished to teach him the lesson "that there is something infinitely better than money or position or worldly prosperity. . . ."

Except for Charity's possession of the Museum lease, which profited her $19,000 a year, all was lost. Iranistan and all personal property fell into the hands of his creditors. Barnum rented a furnished house in New York City, removed his family there, and tried to restore method to the madness. But swarms of creditors, impatient to recover some part of their depressed notes, kept him in court to face a series of separate judgments until he was exhausted and in despair.

In one of these many trials, a stunted, waspish attorney, representing a creditor who had bought a thousand-dollar note for $700, baited Barnum until the showman had all that he could endure.

"What is your business?" the attorney demanded.

"Attending bar," said Barnum quietly.

"Attending bar? Attending bar! Why, don't you profess to be a temperance man—a teetotaler?"

"I do."

"And yet, sir, do you have the audacity to assert that you peddle rum all day, and drink none yourself?"

"I doubt whether that is a relevant question," said Barnum softly.

"I will appeal to his honor the judge, if you don't answer it instantly."

Barnum considered, then replied, "I attend bar, and yet never drink intoxicating liquors."

"Where do you attend bar, and for whom?" the attorney snapped.

"I attend the bar of this court, nearly every day, for the benefit of two-penny, would-be lawyers and their greedy clients," Barnum replied.

The trials were fewer after that.

No longer high and mighty, he was the target of every kind of attack from press, clergy, and fair-weather friends. The press gloated over the debacle of "Barnum and the Jerome Clock Bubble." To Barnum, the sadistic slanders were unbelievable. For years, the press had been his friend, his collaborator, his very life blood. Now, it was his rack.

"I was taken to pieces," he said, "analyzed, put together again, kicked, 'pitched into,' tumbled about, preached to, preached about, and made to serve every purpose to which a sensation-loving world could put me."

It was an age-old lesson, and he would never forget it. "There were those who had fawned upon me in my prosperity, who now jeered at my adversity; people whom I had specially favored made special efforts to show their ingratitude; papers which, when I had the means to make it an object for them to be on good terms with me, overloaded me with adulation, now attempted to overwhelm me with abuse. . . ." Worst of all, as with the book, were the preachers and moralists who announced that Barnum was getting just retribution for his "ill-gotten gains." This, when he had labored day and night for what was achieved and deserved.

His enemies, of course, had a field day. James Gordon Bennett, who strongly disliked him, was in the vanguard of the calumniators. On March 17, 1856, the *New York Herald* piously editorialized:

"THE FALL OF BARNUM—The author of that book glorifying himself as a millionaire from the arts and appliances of obtaining money upon false pretenses is, according to his own statements in court, completely crushed out. All the profits of all his Feejee Mermaids, all his woolly horses, Greenland whales, Joice Heths, negroes turning white, Tom Thumbs and monsters and impostures of all kinds, including the reported $70,000 received by the copyright of that book, are all swept away, Hindoo palace, elephants and all, by the late invincible showman's remorseless assignees. It is a case eminently adapted to 'point a moral or adorn a tale.' "

Bennett did not bother him. It was the defection of so many friends that really hurt. More than a year later, they were still treating him as a leper. "Oftentimes in passing up and down Broadway," he recalled, "I saw old and prosperous friends coming, but before I came anywhere near them, if they espied me they would dodge into a store, or across the street, or opportunely meet someone with whom they had pressing business, or they would be very much interested in something that was going on over the way or on top of the City Hall."

Bitterness turned finally to secret and sardonic amusement. He vowed to himself that once he had escaped the "bewilderment of broken clock-wheels," he would remember his "butterfly friends."

Then, on the late night of December 17, 1857, came another crushing blow.

Iranistan had been vacant for two years while realtors attempted to sell it on behalf of Barnum's creditors. But its weird design and ungainly size deterred all prospective buyers. At last, the creditors agreed that Barnum could move himself and his family back into it until a purchaser was found or an auction held.

At once, with what funds he had, Barnum sent painters and carpenters into the mansion to refresh and mend it. He gave strict orders that workmen should not smoke inside the building. Nevertheless, when the painters and carpenters climbed to the observatory dome to sprawl on the circular seat during lunch hour, they usually smoked as they conversed after their meal. On one such noon, it was surmised afterwards, a laborer absently left his glowing pipe on the cushion of the curved divan. The pipe rolled to its side, dumping burning tobacco on the tow with which the cushion was stuffed. How many hours or days the tow smoldered could not be determined. But an hour before midnight, in the week before Christmas, all Iranistan was aflame.

The exertions of the bucket brigade were futile as the flames from the wooden pyre lit the frozen grounds and the dark sky. In two hours Barnum's Oriental palace was a grotesque heap of smoking embers. Nothing but its memory and scattered pieces of charred furniture survived the fire.

With heavy heart, Barnum's half-brother, Philo, wired him the news in New York. When Barnum awakened in his room at Astor House the next morning, the telegram was waiting. "My beautiful Iranistan was gone!" he wrote. "This was not only a serious loss to my estate, for it had probably cost at least $150,000, but it was generally regarded as a public calamity. It was the only building in its peculiar style of architecture, of any pretension, in America, and many persons visited Bridgeport every year expressly to see Iranistan."

Financially the loss was cataclysmic. Barnum, in his difficulty, had allowed the property insurance to lapse from

$62,000 to $28,000. This relatively meager sum was swallowed by the creditors. Now the seventeen acres, unencumbered by the eccentric dwelling, was easily disposed of by these same creditors. The land was purchased by a close friend of Barnum's, Elias Howe, Jr., whose invention of the sewing machine twelve years before had eventually made him wealthy enough to pay personally the salaries of a company of his comrades in the Army of the Potomac during the Civil War. Once, in fact, he even chartered a special train to bring these men home on furlough. Howe paid $50,000 for the estate, intending to construct another mansion on it, but his long litigation with Isaac Merrit Singer and others over the sewing-machine patent, as well as his enlistment in the war as a private, delayed his plans, and he died without developing the property.

Much of the period of Barnum's greatest travail coincided with the agonizing fratricide by which his country was gripped from 1861 to 1865. At the outbreak of hostilities, Barnum was fifty-one years of age and too old to enlist. Instead, as was the custom, he paid for four substitute soldiers to represent him at the front. Because he opposed slavery, he contributed generously to the Union cause.

All too soon he became personally involved in a homefront struggle to prevent sabotage and treason. Connecticut was well populated with advocates of peace at any cost and Southern sympathizers. After the Federal defeat at Bull Run, many of these peace groups began to propagandize openly. When Barnum heard that one such group was going to hold a rally at Stepney, ten miles north of Bridgeport, he joined Elias Howe, Jr., in attending the meeting to investigate disloyalty.

Arriving at the rally, Barnum and Howe were accompanied by two omnibuses filled with curious Union soldiers home on leave. When a white peace flag was run up to replace the stars and stripes, and the leading orator, a preacher, began to speak of Northern aggression, the soldiers present charged the platform. In the ensuing melee, the speaker fled to a cornfield, while his confederates drew revolvers and brandished muskets. One pacifist fired a shot before being chased out of town. The others were quickly disarmed. The soldiers carried Barnum on their shoulders to the platform, where "he made a speech full of patriotism, spiced with the humor of the occasion." A Union officer made another speech, then "The Star-Spangled Banner" was lustily sung, and finally Elias Howe, Jr., mounted the platform to shout: "If they fire a gun, boys, burn the whole town, and I'll pay for it!"

Returning to Bridgeport, the soldiers muttered of burning the offices of the *Farmer,* a local newspaper with secessionist sympathies. Barnum warned them to remain law-abiding citizens and refrain from violence. But the moment Barnum went to telegraph the story to New York newspapers, the soldiers rushed the newspaper office, smashed the presses, and scattered the type in the street. Distressed, Barnum offered to raise money for the editor, but the editor was not interested and ran off to Georgia.

In 1863 Barnum was a prominent member of the "Prudential Committee," one of the home-front vigilante organizations. His life was often threatened, and he was provided with rockets to shoot in case his home was ever besieged. Several times he was given Federal troopers to guard his premises.

One of the less well-known sidelights of the Civil War was the Confederate plot to burn and take over New York in retaliation for General William T. Sherman's savage march of attrition to the sea. Barnum was, as it turned out, one of the minor victims of the plot, for the American Museum, now in his hands again, turned out to be a prime target.

Greenwood and Butler, lacking the master's showmanship, had done poorly with the Museum, and five years after the Jerome Clock disaster, Barnum offered to buy the collection back. Greenwood and Butler were only too glad to oblige. Barnum had been in possession of the Museum, which again was flourishing, for four years when the Confederate raiders almost turned it into cinders. It was, in a way, a forewarning of the Museum's eventual fate.

The great Confederate arson plot was master-minded by Jefferson Davis to boost sagging morale in the South and to terrorize the North into ending the war. Davis wired Jacob Thompson, in Mississippi, to execute the plan. Thompson, wealthy lawyer, Congressman, and Secretary of the Interior under President Buchanan, left at once to establish headquarters in Toronto, Canada. His private war chest contained one million dollars in Federal currency.

Results were immediate. Two steamships on the Great

Lakes were captured and sunk. Several boats were burned at St. Louis. St. Albans, Vermont, was successfully raided, and three banks there were emptied of $200,000. But the big plan was, in Thompson's words, "a corps to burn New York City." The mustached, twenty-six-year-old Colonel Robert Maxwell Martin, a Kentuckian who had slashed through Ohio as commander of Morgan's guerrilla cavalry, was selected to lead the task force of eight. Three of his more prominent aides were the hard-drinking Robert C. Kennedy, of Louisiana, Lieutenant John W. Headley, of Kentucky, and Lieutenant John T. Ashbrook.

The scheme relied heavily on the co-operation of those peace groups in the metropolis which were allied with the very groups Barnum was combating in Connecticut. Thompson and Colonel Martin had been assured that the Sons of Liberty, a secret society that supported the right of secession by any state at any time, had a membership of 300,000, of which 85,000 were in Illinois, 50,000 in Indiana, and 20,000 in New York City itself. At the given signal—the firing of New York hotels and places of amusement—the Copperheads would rise up and panic the citizenry, thus blocking off troop movements. With muskets and bombs, the Sons of Liberty would take over City Hall and the Superintendent of Police's offices and blow up Fort Lafayette in New York harbor.

Colonel Martin, Captain Kennedy, and six others, slipped into New York on the eve of the 1864 Presidential election in which Abraham Lincoln was to defeat General George B. McClellan by 400,000 votes. Election day, when various peace groups from New Jersey and Connecticut were convening with their fellow subversives in New York, was to be the day of the firing and revolt. The entire city was absorbed in the impending vote. The campaign had been bitter. The cocky, thirty-eight-year-old McClellan had even called Lincoln "the original gorilla . . . a well-meaning baboon."

The eight rebel invaders met with three representatives of the Sons of Liberty in a piano store owned by one of them. The New York contacts were Henry W. McDonald, proprietor of the piano store, James A. McMasters, publisher of the *Freeman's Journal,* and Captain E. Longuemare, who had drawn up the list of hotels to be burned and had arranged for the production of a large number of incendiary bombs filled with the chemical known as Greek fire. But the following morning, before the rebels could act, pudgy General Benjamin Butler marched into New York with 10,000 troops. This was the same Butler who, when administrator of New Orleans, was despised by all Southern womanhood. When the belles turned their backs to him, he remarked admiringly: "These women know which end of them looks best." Butler, obviously, was a man who brooked no nonsense. He promptly let it be known that he was aware some plot was afoot, and that he was out to arrest the conspirators. Much later, the rebels learned that they had been betrayed by a man named Godfrey Hyams, who knew of their plans made in Canada, and who sold his knowledge to the Union for $70,000.

The arrival of Union troops made the eight raiders delay their sabotage. Then, suddenly thinking it all too romantic and unfeasible, the publisher and piano dealer withdrew their support. Discouraged, Captain Longuemare also gave up. Now, divested of aid from the Sons of Liberty, the rebels might have returned to Canada except for reading the news that Sherman had burned Atlanta. Stirred by Colonel Martin's demands for retaliation, six of the eight agreed to remain and reduce New York to ashes. Lieutenant Headley visited an elderly chemist in Washington Square and picked up a valise, two by four feet in size, containing 144 four-ounce bottles of incendiary Greek fire. Sixty of the bottles were divided, and the six men separated to register under false names in nineteen hotels.

On the evening of Thanksgiving Day, November 25, 1864, the plot to burn New York went into motion. "I went to my room in the Astor House at twenty minutes after seven," Lieutenant Headley said. "I hung the bedclothes over the footboard, piled chairs, drawers, and other material on the bed, stuffed newspapers into the heap and poured a bottle of turpentine over the whole mass. I then opened a bottle of 'Greek fire' and quickly spilled it on top. It blazed instantly. I locked the door and went downstairs. Leaving the key at the office, as usual, I passed out. I did likewise at the City Hotel, Everett House and United States Hotel."

Simultaneously, Colonel Martin was igniting the Hoffman House and Fifth Avenue Hotel. By nine o'clock, all nineteen hotels had been set aflame. Meanwhile, Lieutenant

Ashbrook, assigned to the giddier avenues of holiday New York, heaved a bottle of Greek fire into the audience at Niblo's Garden and another into the Winter Garden where three thousand persons were enrapt by John Wilkes Booth's performance as Marc Antony in *Julius Caesar*. Headley, taking the sea air at the North River wharves, deposited several incendiary bombs among the moored shipping and sank one hay barge and damaged two other vessels.

The metropolitan fire department, alerted at once, caught most of the sputtering combustions in their earliest stage. Mobs of people in confusion and fear began to fill Broadway. Captain Kennedy, having committed arson at three hotels and reinforced his waning courage with a drink, found himself caught in the milling crowd before Barnum's brightly illuminated American Museum.

Hugging his half-filled valise, fearing recognition and consequent lynching, Kennedy hastily paid twenty-five cents and ducked into the safety of the Museum. Once inside, he mingled with the customers, examining several exhibits. Suddenly, moved again by a memory of the wicked Sherman, he realized that he was in the perfect place for a spectacular act of demolition. Eliminating the world-famous Barnum's Museum would be an immense demoralizing factor. Descending the main staircase, he halted, opened his valise, extracted a glass bomb, and hurled it at the steps. There was a sudden sheet of flame, and the Museum was afire.

As Kennedy hastened into the street, the Museum became the scene of the night's most effective conflagration. In the Lecture Room, twenty-five hundred persons were being lulled by one of Barnum's morality plays. The assistant manager, Greenwood, burst in, shouting warnings of fire. At once, the auditorium was in chaos as playgoers scrambled and fought for means of egress. There were injuries, but no fatalities.

Now, the Museum's main entrance was thick with smoke. Thousands in the street fell back as firemen charged in to smother the blaze. A female customer trapped on the second floor was rescued by ladder. One of Barnum's freaks, a seven-foot giantess, possibly Anna Swan, stumbled to the entrance suffocating and hysterical. When Greenwood and three firemen tried to assist her, she sent the pygmies sprawling. She was subdued by six men, and was soon asleep under sedation.

Gradually the wild animals were ushered out of the Museum onto Broadway, where they were closely guarded. In a few hours, the fire was out. Barnum estimated the damage at $1,000. It had been a close call.

By daybreak, after nine valiant hours, the red-shirted fire fighters had quenched every rebel blaze. Except for a report from one hotel of a $10,000 loss, the damage had been light. What saved the city was not the efficiency of its fire department alone, but the ineffectiveness of the bottles of Greek fire. With the exception of the glass bottle used in the Museum, all the bombs had been weak and fizzling. As a result, the desperate foray had ended in utter futility. Informed of the result in Toronto, Thompson made the following notation: "Their reliance on the Greek fire had proved a misfortune. It cannot be depended on as an agent in such work. I have no faith whatever in it and no attempt shall hereafter be made under my general directions with any such materials."

Two days later, with a reward on their heads, the arsonists sneaked out of New York on a train for Albany, and finally reached Toronto safely. Sometime later, Kennedy, who had ignited Barnum's Museum, and Ashbrook boarded a train in Detroit with the object of returning to the South. Detected by Union secret-service agents, Ashbrook escaped through a window. Kennedy was trapped and arrested by two officers. Charged with arson and espionage, he was returned, manacled, to New York. There, in March 1865, he was tried by a military court and found guilty. He was hanged at Fort Lafayette. Barnum had his precious Museum and giantess intact—but, as it turned out, not for long. Misfortune still had him by the coattails.

The last severe blow fell on July 13, 1865. What the Confederacy had started was now finished by the unkindest Fate. In the engine room of the American Museum, there was machinery that furnished steam to rotate the large fans cooling the building and to pump fresh water into the recently installed aquarium. This machinery sparked a fire. The flames took hold of the adjacent manager's office— usually occupied by Greenwood and his assistant, the unhappy Samuel H. Hurd, Barnum's son-in-law—and spread swiftly through the first floor and then to the floors above.

It was a major holocaust. Even as the fire brigades of the metropolis were hastily summoned, Hurd staggered to his burning desk and rescued several thousands of dollars in receipts. Fearing to expose the cash to the unruly crowds gathering outside, he placed the money in Barnum's metal safe.

From Maiden Lane to Chambers Street, Broadway was lined with forty thousand people watching a blaze worthy of Nero's art. Although the Museum rapidly became a torch, no human being died. Barnum was in Hartford, and Greenwood was also away. Hurd, having secreted the money, barely reached the safety of the street. The few visitors escaped easily, but the freaks had a harder time. Great billows of smoke invaded the upper stories, and many freaks were overcome. Fortunately, innumerable fire engines clanged up before the building just in time.

Among the heroic firemen was John Denham, of Hose Company Number Fifteen, who dashed inside time and again to rescue victims. He led the Albino woman to safety, and again, by some surprising reserve of strength, he carried out the fat lady, whose weight was advertised as four hundred pounds. From a room across the street, Nathan D. Urner, reporter for Greeley's *New York Tribune,* witnessed the rescue of Anna Swan, the seven-foot-eleven-inch giantess from Nova Scotia.

Miss Swan, who lost her entire savings of $1,200 in gold and her wardrobe to the fire, was found at the top of the third-story staircase, nearly unconscious. "There was not a door through which her bulky frame could obtain a passage," reported Urner. "It was likewise feared that the stairs would break down, even if she should reach them. Her best friend, the living skeleton, stood by her as long as he dared, but then deserted her, while as the heat grew in intensity, the perspiration rolled from her face in little brooks and rivulets, which pattered musically upon the floor. At length, as a last resort, the employees of the place procured a lofty derrick which fortunately happened to be standing near, and erected it alongside the Museum. A portion of the wall was then broken off on each side of the window, and the strong tackle was got in readiness, the tall woman was made fast to one end and swung over the heads of the people in the street, with eighteen men grasping the other extremity of the line, and lowered down from the third story, amid enthusiastic applause. A carriage of extraordinary capacity was in readiness, and entering this, the young lady was driven away to a hotel."

Firemen reached the upstairs cages of tropical birds, and a great number of cockatoos and parrots were set free to fly over the city. A condor, and several vultures and eagles (one of the latter locked in a death battle with a snake, which he vanquished) were also freed.

But two frenzied lions who burst the bars of their confinement were soon overcome by smoke. A massive bear tried to escape through a second-story window, but failed and was lost to the flames. A thirty-foot python writhing with pain on the roasting floor was compassionately put out of his misery by volunteer fireman George Collyer.

Some animals got into the streets and created small panics. Several serpents made their way up Broadway, forcing spectators to scatter. A Bengal tiger leaped from the second story to the thoroughfare below. Police emptied their pistols at the cat without effect until fireman Denham killed the tiger with a single blow of his ax. A sociable orangutan made his way to the near-by office of James Gordon Bennett and tried to effect an interview. "The poor creature," wrote Urner, "but recently released from captivity, and doubtless thinking that he might fill some vacancy in the editorial corps of the paper in question, had descended by the waterpipe and instinctively taken refuge in the inner sanctum of the establishment." It took the muscles of Bennett and his entire staff to suppress the potential journalist.

By nightfall the American Museum was a mound of charred ruins. During the progress of the fire, realizing that all was lost, Hurd sent a telegram to Barnum, who was then serving as an elected representative in the state legislature at Hartford. At the very moment the telegram arrived, Barnum was speaking against railroad monopoly. He paused in his address to glance at the wire, and then, without the slightest hesitancy or change of expression, went on to finish his speech.

When he was done, Barnum showed the telegram to his colleagues. His leading rival in the railroad fight took his hand in sympathy. "Mr. Barnum," he said, "I am really very sorry to hear of your great misfortune." With not unexpected bravado, Barnum retorted: "Sorry? Why, my dear sir, I shall not have time to be sorry in a week! It will take me at least that length of time before I can get over laughing at having whipped you all so nicely in this attempted railroad bill."

But Barnum was deeply distressed. The following morning, standing before the still-smoldering debris of what had once been the mainstay of his career, he felt an infinite sadness. "Here were destroyed," he wrote, "almost in a breath, the accumulated results of many years of incessant toil, my own and my predecessor's, in gathering from every quarter of the globe myriads of curious productions of nature and art—an assemblage of rarities which a half million of dollars could not restore, and a quarter of a century could not collect."

Not even a thousand dollars of personal property had been saved. Of course, the metal safe with the cash receipts was intact. A trained seal, a bear, the journalistic orangutan, some monkeys, snakes, and birds had been spared. And a portion of the waxworks, including statues of President Buchanan, Tom Thumb, and Barnum himself, all somewhat melted, had been rescued, whereas priceless Revolutionary War relics had been left to burn. And finally, of course, Anna Swan and the freaks were alive. But out of 600,000 exhibits, Barnum was left with pitifully few. His total loss was at least $400,000. His insurance was worth only $40,000.

His first instinct was to quit. The clock scandal, the destruction of his home, and this final accident weighed heavily upon him. He was no longer wealthy, but he had enough potential income from the Museum real estate and the East Bridgeport investment to retire.

He consulted his close friend Horace Greeley and asked his advice. What should he do?

"Accept this fire as a notice to quit," said Greeley, "and go a-fishing."

"A-fishing?"

"Yes, a-fishing. I have been wanting to go a-fishing for thirty years, and have not yet found time to do so."

Barnum considered. He knew that Greeley's advice was "good and wise," but felt that the editor did not really mean it or expect it. He remembered Greeley's editorial in the *New York Tribune* the day after the fire. The editor had publicly deplored the death of a showplace that had been "a fountain of delight," a wonder "as implicitly believed in as the Arabian Night's Entertainment," a site that "amused, instructed, and astonished."

The editorial had concluded: "We mourn its loss, but not as without consolation. Barnum's Museum is gone, but Barnum himself, happily, did not share the fate of his rattlesnakes. . . . There are fishes in the seas and beasts in the forests; birds still fly in the air and strange creatures still roam in the deserts; giants and pigmies still wander up and down the earth; the oldest man, the fattest woman, and the smallest baby are still living, and Barnum will find them."

Barnum's course was clear and his decision made. Fishing would have to wait. Somewhere, "the oldest man, the fattest woman, and the smallest baby" were waiting, and he would find them, he would show them, and he would rise from defeat at last.

EXHIBIT NINE
White Whale

After the failure of the Jerome Clock Company, Barnum took stock of his position. He had paid all his personal debts, but he still owed a half-million dollars on notes bearing his signature. The Clock Company was paying fifteen cents on the dollar to creditors. Barnum decided to pay thirty-three cents on the dollar for the sums that were his responsibility.

He sent the following word to a conclave of creditors in New Haven: "I was induced to agree to indorse and accept paper for that company to the extent of $110,000—no more. That sum I am now willing to pay for my own verdancy, with an additional sum of $40,000 for your cuteness, making a total of $150,000, which you can have if you cry 'quits' with the fleeced showman and let him off."

Most creditors, apparently, agreed to let Barnum off with this compromise. But others wanted their notes settled in full, and some sold their notes at reduced prices to speculators. At any rate, Barnum's total indebtedness was soon fixed in his mind, and he knew what he must earn to stand independently on his feet again.

Even as he determined to fight back, and searched his weary brain for a means of squaring himself, large numbers of persons rallied to his support. In June 1856, a letter signed by one thousand prominent New Yorkers was sent to Barnum. The letter stated: "The financial ruin of a man of acknowledged energy and enterprise is a public calamity. The sudden blow, therefore, that has swept away, from a man like yourself, the accumulated wealth of years, justifies we think, the public sympathy." The one thousand signers offered "a series of benefits." From Bridgeport a group of businessmen begged Barnum to accept a loan of $50,000. And dozens of people in show business, from Laura Keene, the actress, to William Niblo, proprietor of the Garden, suggested "receipts of their theatres for one evening."

Barnum was deeply moved. "While my enemies and a few envious persons and misguided moralists were abusing and traducing me," he said, "my very misfortunes revealed to me hosts of hitherto unknown friends who tendered to me something more than mere sympathy. Funds were offered to me in unbounded quantity for the support of my family and to re-establish me in business." These offers, one and all, Barnum gratefully declined. "I declined these tenders because, on principle, I never accepted a money favor. . . ."

Among the many offers of assistance that he received, one touched and interested the showman most of all. Written on the stationery of the Jones' Hotel in Philadelphia, it was signed by General Tom Thumb:

"My Dear Mr. Barnum,—I understand your friends (and that means 'all creation') intend to get up some benefits for your family. Now, my dear sir, just be good enough to remember that I belong to that mighty crowd, and I must have a finger (or at least a 'thumb') in that pie. . . . I have just started out on my western tour, and have my carriage, ponies and assistants all here, but I am ready to go on to New York, bag and baggage, and remain at Mrs. Barnum's service as long as I, in my small way, can be useful. Put me into any 'heavy' work, if you like. Perhaps I cannot lift as much as some other folks, but just take your pencil in hand and you will see I can draw a tremendous load. I drew two hundred tons at a single pull to-day, embracing two thousand persons, whom I hauled up safely and satisfactorily to all parties, at one exhibition. Hoping that you will be able to fix up a lot of magnets that will attract all New York, and volunteering to sit on any part of the loadstone, I am, as ever, your little but sympathizing friend. . . ."

At first, Barnum refused his onetime miniature partner. And Tom Thumb, under his own management, continued west. Barnum, who still had hopes for East Bridgeport, occupied himself with persuading the prosperous Wheeler and Wilson Sewing Machine Company to take over an empty factory. When the move was made, Barnum finally agreed to borrow $5,000, without security, from the Sewing Machine Company. Adding this to his wife's private savings, Barnum bought back many undeveloped acres of his East Bridgeport property which were being sold at public auction by his creditors. Though the investment gave him no immediate relief, he admitted that eventually it put "more money into my pocket than the Jerome complication had taken out."

Meanwhile, less than a year later, Tom Thumb had concluded his western tour and again offered himself to his discoverer. This time, determined to return to show business, Barnum accepted. But he wanted another novelty to bolster Tom Thumb. He did not have to search far.

At the time, the nine-year-old Cordelia Howard was scoring a hit as Little Eva in *Uncle Tom's Cabin*. When Mrs. Stowe's novel had first appeared, Cordelia's father, who managed a stock company, had learned that the dramatic rights were not reserved. He assigned an actor in his troupe, his cousin George L. Aikin, to convert the novel into a play. The entire Howard family—father, mother, and five-year-old Cordelia as Little Eva—opened in the play in July 1853, and were soon on the road to riches. They had been performing *Uncle Tom's Cabin* for four years when Barnum signed the company for his European tour. Now, in 1857, Cordelia was one of Barnum's hopes. Satisfied with his prodigy and his midget, Barnum sailed for England. (Shortly after returning from abroad, at the age of twelve, blonde Cordelia retired from the stage; eight years later, she married a Cambridge bookbinder. She died in 1941, at ninety-three.)

The publication of his autobiography and news of his business failure made Barnum uncertain of the reception that awaited him in London. But his mind was soon put at ease. An old friend, Dr. Albert Smith, a former dentist and author now successfully presenting melodramatic lectures on his conquest of Mont Blanc in 1851, welcomed Barnum with open arms and invited him time and again to the Garrick Club. Sir Julius Benedict and Giovanni Belletti came calling with invitations to dinner. Otto Goldschmidt, on behalf of Jenny Lind and himself, appeared and proffered financial aid. Joshua Bates, of Baring Brothers and Company, and George Sala, a foreign correspondent who had worked for Dickens, feted Barnum at their homes.

Best of all, the forty-six-year-old William Makepeace Thackeray, whose *Vanity Fair* was running monthly in *Punch,* and who was making a losing attempt to be elected to the House of Commons, renewed his acquaintance with Barnum. They had first met five years before. According to Barnum: "He called on me at the Museum with a letter of introduction from our mutual friend Albert Smith. He spent an hour with me, mainly for the purpose of asking my advice in regard to the management of the course of lectures on 'The English Humorists of the Eighteenth Century,' which he proposed to deliver, as he did afterwards, with very great success, in the principal cities of the Union. I gave him the best advice I could as to management, and the cities he ought to visit, for which he was very grateful." However, according to Eyre Crowe, Thackeray's secretary and business manager, Barnum heard that the novelist was in New York and sent for him. When they met, Barnum asked Thackeray to write a series of articles on his impressions of the United States for the *Illustrated News,* which the showman was preparing to publish with Griswold and Leland. Barnum also hinted at other collaborative ventures, but Thackeray replied that he preferred to go it alone.

Now, in London, Thackeray greeted Barnum with warmth. "Mr. Barnum," he said, shaking his hand, "I admire you more than ever. I have read the accounts in the papers of the examinations you underwent in the New York courts, and the positive pluck you exhibit under your pecuniary embarrassments is worthy of all praise. You would never have received credit for the philosophy you manifest, if these financial misfortunes had not overtaken you." Barnum interrupted to express his thanks, but Thackeray went on. "Tell me, Barnum, are you really in need of present assistance? for if you are, you must be helped."

Barnum laughed. "Not in the least," he said. "I need more money in order to get out of bankruptcy and I intend to earn it; but so far as daily bread is concerned, I am quite at ease, for my wife is worth 30,000 to 40,000 pounds."

Thackeray was wide-eyed and impressed. "Is it possible? Well, now, you have lost all my sympathy. Why, that is more than I ever expect to be worth; I shall be sorry for you no more."

Nor had anyone any need to be sorry for Barnum. At work again, bombarding the press with publicity, inundating the city with provocative posters and handbills, Barnum knew that he still had the magic touch. For many weeks, the return of Tom Thumb was welcomed by increasing audiences, and Cordelia Howard as Little Eva was an immediate hit. Barnum thrived.

He moved his troupe to an engagement in Paris, and then to a stand in Strasbourg. In the German city, somewhat apologetically, he went to see a clock. "One would suppose that by this time I had had enough to do with clocks to last me my lifetime, but . . . I did not forget or fail to witness the great church clock which is nearly as famous as the cathedral itself. At noon precisely a mechanical cock crows; the bell strikes; figures of the twelve apostles appear and walk in procession." Next followed visits to Baden-Baden, Ems, Homburg, Wiesbaden, and Frankfurt. "These exhibitions were among the most profitable that had ever been given," said Barnum, "and I was able to remit thousands of dollars to my agents in the United States to aid in re-purchasing my real estate and to assist in taking up such clock notes as were offered for sale."

Though his attractions were less successful in Amsterdam and Rotterdam—"the people are too frugal to spend much money for amusement"—Barnum enjoyed Holland more than any other foreign country he had ever visited, excepting England. He delighted in the cleanliness, industry, and sobriety in evidence everywhere. When he attended a country fair, his old showmanship instinct was again aroused by sight of an albino family, Rudolph Lucasie and his wife and son, all white and pink, though born of Negro parents. He hired them at once, with an eye to the near future.

Returning to New York late in 1857, Barnum learned that he had made inroads on his huge indebtedness. But still more money was needed. So, after Iranistan went up in flames, he decided on a tour of Scotland and Wales with Tom Thumb. As this tour progressed, Barnum realized that the midget did not require his close attention and management. Consequently, he turned Tom Thumb over to several assistants, and, to increase his income, undertook to convert himself into a public exhibit.

At the suggestion of several American friends in London, Barnum agreed to present a series of paid lectures on "The Art of Money-Getting." At first, still licking his clock wounds, he ruefully remarked that the lectures should be entitled, "The Art of Money-Losing." But his friends reminded him that he could not have lost a half million dollars if first he had not earned it.

His debut took place in spacious St. James's Hall, and it was widely advertised for the evening of December 29, 1858. Three thousand English folk paid from fifty to seventy-five cents each to attend, and there was standing room only. Encouraged by the turnout, and the many familiar faces, Barnum was at his best.

"In the United States, where we have more land than people," he began, "it is not at all difficult for persons in good health to make money." Mingling clichés with original humor, making frequent allusions to Benjamin Franklin, Micawber, Madame Tussaud, Henry Ward Beecher, Solomon, Cromwell, Rothschild, Goethe, John Jacob Astor, and Genin the hatter, Barnum sang out for concentration, organization, moderation, advertising, and integrity. Time and again he drew upon his past. "I was born in the blue-law State of Connecticut," he said, "where the old Puritans had laws so rigid that it was said they fined a man for kissing his wife on Sunday. Yet these rich old Puritans would have thousands of dollars at interest, and on Saturday night would be worth a certain amount. . . . On waking up on Monday morning, they would find themselves considerably richer than the Saturday night previous, simply because their money placed at interest had worked faithfully for them all day Sunday, according to law!" Yet, there were pitfalls. "Money is in some respects like fire— it is a very excellent servant but a terrible master." John Randolph, the Virginia eccentric, had the right idea. He had told Congress: "Mr. Speaker, I have discovered the philosopher's stone: pay as you go."

Barnum gave an emphatic warning born of a recent experience. "Don't indorse without security. I hold that no man ought ever to indorse a note or become security for any man, be it his father or brother, to a greater extent than he can afford to lose and care nothing about, without taking good security." And finally: "To all men and women, therefore, do I conscientiously say, make money honestly, and not otherwise, for Shakespeare has truly said, 'He that wants money, means, and content, is without three good friends.'"

The lecture was well received. Nine major London newspapers praised it. The *Times* considered Barnum "one of the most entertaining lecturers that ever addressed an audience on a theme universally intelligible" and approved of his "dry humor," his "sonorous voice," his "admirably clear delivery." Buoyed up by this approval, Barnum delivered the same lecture almost one hundred times throughout England, including riotous appearances at Cambridge and Oxford. He refused $6,000 from a London publisher for the speech, but later included it in his autobiography and in a specially printed pamphlet. He enjoyed lecturing, and in his lifetime addressed an estimated 1,300,000 persons. Leaving England with Tom Thumb, considerably enriched, Barnum was satisfied: "The lecture itself was an admirable illustration of 'The Art of Money-Getting.'"

In New York again, having acquired his collection of curiosities from Greenwood and Butler, Barnum announced that he was back in business. Screaming posters shouted to the populace from every street corner: "Barnum on his feet again!" And in the *New York Herald* an advertisement promised that on the night of March 24, 1860, Barnum would appear on the platform of the Lecture Hall and formally take over the premises. "Between the first and second acts Mr. P. T. Barnum will appear and give a brief history of his Adventures as a Clock maker, showing how the clock ran down and how it was wound up. . . ."

A capacity crowd awaited him. Instead of appearing between acts, Barnum ascended the stage before the morality play commenced. He was met with an ovation greater than any he had ever experienced. He stood facing the deafening applause, tears streaming down his cheeks. At last, with a tremor, he began to speak.

"Ladies and gentlemen," he said, "I should be more or less than human, if I could meet this unexpected and overwhelming testimonial at your hands, without the deepest emotion. My own personal connection with the Museum is now resumed, and I avail myself of the circumstance to say why it is so. Never did I feel stronger in my worldly prosperity than in September, 1855. Three months later, I was so deeply embarrassed that I felt certain of nothing, except the uncertainty of everything. A combination of singular efforts and circumstances tempted me to put faith in a certain clock manufacturing company, and I placed my signature to papers which ultimately broke me down. After nearly five years of hard struggle to keep my head above water, I have touched bottom at last, and here, to-night, I am happy to announce that I have waded ashore. Every clock debt of which I have any knowledge has been provided for."

The announcement of his solvency and resumption in show business was met with thunderous applause by the assembly, and with mingled congratulations and doubts by the press. As if in answer to his skeptical critics, Barnum resumed management of the Museum with a new vigor. Only fifty years of age—"scarcely old enough to be embalmed and put in a glass case in the Museum," he stated—Barnum was out to prove to the world that he was better than ever.

After a week of renovation, the Museum reopened under Barnum's banners and flags and to the accompaniment of his erratic musical band. From the start it was plain that his genius for showmanship had not left him. Newer and more startling novelties, animate and inanimate, were introduced and then whisked off, to be replaced by others. In short months, the daily attendance of the Museum doubled.

Even as Barnum improved his collection, he kept his eye open for outside enterprises. A month after he had resumed business, one such appeared. He was a gray-haired, weather-worn, gnarled, and white-bearded old western hunter attired in a cap made of a wolf's head and a buckskin suit trimmed with animal tails. He introduced himself as James C. Adams, known to most of the west as "Grizzly" Adams.

He told his story as Barnum listened, entranced. For years Adams had defied all dangers to hunt and trap in the Sierra Nevada mountains. He caught the wildest animals, and though much buffeted about by them, had trained them as pets. Now, at last, seeking security for his long-neglected wife and his daughter, he had brought a menagerie of California beasts on the clipper *Golden Fleece* around Cape Horn. He had imported from twenty to thirty huge grizzly bears—their leader he named Old Sampson, and their most delinquent he named General Frémont—as well as six other species of bears, and an assortment of wolves, lions, tigers, buffalo, and elk, and a massive sea lion answering to the name of Old Neptune.

While explaining to Barnum the difficulties involved in domesticating these animals, Adams pulled off his wolf's cap and revealed the top of his head. The skull was badly smashed and, as Barnum observed, his brain exposed "so that its workings were plainly visible." (Modern medical opinion agrees that Barnum may not have been exaggerating when he said "Grizzly" Adams's brain was visible, for, most likely, it was covered by the galea or thick, transparent healing tissue that contains the spinal fluid.) As Barnum studied the gaping wound with morbid fascination, Adams described how the injury had come about. Whenever he trained the bears, they delighted in playfully bashing him on the head. Thus, it had been broken in and healed many times. Recently, the bear known as General Frémont had struck him, and his head had cracked open like an eggshell.

Barnum remarked that it appeared to be "a dangerous wound and might possibly prove fatal." Adams nodded complacently. "Yes, that will fix me out. It had nearly healed; but Old Frémont opened it for me, for the third or fourth time, before I left California, and he did his business so thoroughly, I'm a used-up man. However, I reckon I may live six months or a year yet."

Barnum wondered if he was not worried, in this condition, about undertaking a public appearance with the grizzly bears.

The hunter signified that, worried or not, he had no choice. "Mr. Barnum, I am not the man I was five years ago. Then I felt able to stand the hug of any grizzly living, and was always glad to encounter, single-handed, any sort of an animal that dared present himself. But I have been beaten to a jelly, torn almost limb from limb, and nearly chewed up and spit out by these treacherous grizzly bears. However, I am good for a few months yet, and by that time I hope we shall gain enough to make my old woman comfortable for I have been absent from her some years."

Barnum readily agreed to present the California Menagerie on an equal-partnership basis. He would publicize and manage the show; Adams would put the animals through their paces. Learning that Adams's wife lived in Massachusetts, Barnum brought her to New York to nurse him. He also brought in his physician, who examined the head wound and was appalled. The physician prophesied that Adams would be in his grave within a few weeks, but the battered patient laughed off the prediction.

Taking the physician's words to heart, Barnum hurried to get the show before the public. He threw up a canvas tent on a vacant lot at the corner of Broadway and Thirteenth Street. Then, after a shower of publicity, he inaugurated what may have been the first large circus parade in history. On the morning of the opening, multitudes of spectators gathered on Broadway to view with astonishment James C. Adams, in his bizarre costume, astride the surprisingly docile General Frémont, both being drawn by a wagon. Preceded by a blaring band, followed by cage after cage of animals not familiar to the East, Adams made his way to the show tent.

Daily, though staggering under his infirmity, the hunter lashed the beasts through their acts as thousands watched with awe. After six weeks of performances, the weakened Adams gave in to Barnum's physician. He agreed to quit and sold out to the showman. But when Adams learned that Barnum intended to exhibit the menagerie through Connecticut and Massachusetts using a German trainer named Driesback in his stead, he protested. The animals would trust no one but himself. Moreover, he wanted every penny he could earn. He would handle the traveling zoo, he said, for sixty dollars a week and expenses for his wife and himself. Barnum did not think that he could survive such a tour. Adams snorted. "What will you give me extra if I will travel and exhibit the bears every day for ten weeks?" Barnum laughed. "Five hundred dollars," he said cheerfully. "Done!" exclaimed Adams.

Grimly determined to have his bonus from Barnum, Adams went on the tour, which became a race against death. After five weeks, Barnum visited the hunter in New Bedford. His eyes were glazed, his rough hands trembling, and he complained of the heat. Barnum begged him to quit, and offered him $250 if he would go home. But Adams rejected any compromise. He went on and on with the bears, scarcely able to lift an arm, until the tenth week had ended. Then, with exclamations of triumph, he accepted the $500.

Before retiring to Neponset, Massachusetts, with his wife, Adams spied a new beaver-hunting suit Barnum had ordered for the German trainer. Adams asked to borrow it. Barnum agreed, if it would be returned to him. "Yes," Adams said, "when I have done with it." He accompanied his wife to Neponset, where his daughter waited, went immediately to bed, and never left it alive. In five days, he was dead. His last request was to be buried in the new beaver-hunting suit—for he was not done with it, and would never be, and it would be a capital joke on Barnum. He was laid to rest in the beaver suit, and Barnum grieved his passing.

The grizzly bears, twenty or thirty of them, and the other beasts became permanent attractions of the Museum. Later, Barnum sold all but Old Neptune, the sea lion, who was pampered in a large tank of salt water.

Casting about for further sensations, Barnum proved again that he had lost none of his old cunning. In 1864 he read that a dozen long-feared Indian chiefs, representing four tribes, had been induced to visit Washington, D.C., and parley with President Lincoln. The most prominent member of the delegation was White Bull, nephew of Sitting Bull and high-ranking in his tribe's hierarchy. With him were Yellow Bear, fresh from the Wichita Mountains, and Yellow Buffalo, both Kiowas. Then there was War Bonnet, who, with Black Kettle, had dominated Colorado, and Lean Bear and Hand-in-the-Water, all Cheyennes. At once, Barnum had an inspiration. He met with the Indians' interpreter, and offered him a liberal bribe to bring them to New York to visit the Museum. The interpreter accepted the bribe and agreed to deliver them, but could not promise for what length of time. "You can only keep them just so long as they suppose all your patrons come to pay them visits of honor," he told Barnum. "If they suspected that your Museum was a place where people paid for entertaining, you could not keep them a moment after the discovery."

Presently the dozen chiefs arrived in New York. Barnum was introduced as their host. For several days he guided them about the Museum, always winding up with them on the stage of the Lecture Hall at the hour the performance was to begin. When there was nothing more to see in the Museum, the Indians accompanied Barnum in carriages to meet the Mayor, to visit public schools, to ride in Central Park—returning, at day's end, to the stage of the Museum, where they thought that they were being honored by streams of distinguished visitors.

When on the stage, the Indian chiefs would sit in a row while Barnum went down the line announcing each one's name and giving his background to the packed auditorium. Whenever he reached Yellow Bear, whom he despised for his record of butchery, Barnum would pat him on the shoulder and, in return, be stroked affectionately on the arm by the chief. Knowing that neither Yellow Bear nor his colleagues understood a word of English, Barnum pretended to compliment him. But, as he smiled and patted him, Barnum would tell the audience: "This little Indian, ladies and gentlemen, is Yellow Bear, chief of the Kiowas. He has killed, no doubt, scores of white persons, and he is probably the meanest blackhearted rascal that lives in the Far West." At this point Barnum would pat Yellow Bear on the head, and Yellow Bear would stroke his arm, pleased to have a champion. Then Barnum would resume: "If the bloodthirsty little villain understood what I was saying, he would kill me in a moment; but as he thinks I am complimenting him, I can safely state the truth to you, that he is a lying, thieving, treacherous, murderous monster. He has tortured to death poor, unprotected women, murdered their husbands, brained their helpless little ones; and he would gladly do the same to you or me, if he thought he could escape punishment. This is but a faint description of the character of Yellow Bear." Here, again, Barnum would pat the redskin on the head, and the Indian would rise and bow to the laughter and applause.

To preserve the good temper of his attractions, Barnum tried to satisfy all their whims. When they saw rare shells or relics, they begged for them. "This cost me many valuable specimens," Barnum complained, though he was making a fortune on them at only the price of a bribe. One chief demanded an ancient mail breastplate. It had cost Barnum several hundred dollars, and he resisted. The chief explained that he needed it to fight the Utes when he returned to the Rocky Mountains. Now he was prepared to trade his newest buckskin suit for the armor; Barnum was forced to give in.

After a week, a more inquisitive member of the Indian peace party learned that an entrance fee was being charged to the Museum and realized that he was being used as a lowly curiosity. In great anger, he passed the word to all the chiefs. Insulted, they made after Barnum with "wild, flashing eyes." Discretion being the better part of valor and survival, the showman made himself unavailable. Their nervous interpreter hastily returned the chiefs to Washington the following day.

Two of these same chiefs, shortly after departing from Barnum's stage, became involved in two of the bloodiest massacres of the Far West. When War Bonnet left the American Museum after his pleasant week with the albino family, the giantess, and the living skeleton, he returned to his slumbering village at the bend of Sand Creek in Colorado. There, in November 1864, Colonel J. M. Chivington, a former Methodist preacher, on some minor provocation, led his Second Colorado Cavalry in a savage charge on the peaceful redskins. Three hundred unarmed Indians were killed, and Chivington was officially censured.

As a result of Sand Creek, another veteran of Barnum's Museum was eventually engaged in an act of vengeance. In June 1876, a large horde of Indians engaged Major General George Custer and five companies of the Seventh Cavalry at Little Big Horn. In less than half an hour, Custer and his two hundred and seven men were annihilated. The hero of this greatest of Indian victories was none other than White Bull, who captured twelve cavalry horses, seven cavalrymen's scalps, and shot down two soldiers, one of them possibly Custer himself. Incredibly, White Bull managed to survive the vindictiveness of his paleface pursuers, and died of natural causes in 1947, eighty-three years after treating with Lincoln and performing for Barnum.

In 1861, Herman Melville's *Moby Dick: or The White*

Whale had been before the public ten years, and, though much discussed in literary circles, had not sold well even at a dollar and fifty cents a copy. Melville, in ill health, was eking out a livelihood lecturing in the west. But if his whale had not profited him, it gave Barnum the idea for one of his most popular attractions.

Reading that a live white whale had been captured by fishermen at the mouth of the St. Lawrence River, Barnum was fascinated by the knowledge that Moby Dick existed. He determined to have himself a white whale—two white whales, male and female, for exhibition. To this end, he constructed in the Museum basement a brick and cement tank eighteen feet wide and fifty feet long. This done, he personally set off, like Captain Ahab, in quest of his white whales.

Taking a train from New York to Quebec, and thence going by rail and boat to Hazel Island in the St. Lawrence, he hired twenty-four French-Canadian fishermen. He placed them on a daily retainer, with a sizable bonus promised if they caught two living white whales. The fishermen built a kraal in the river—stakes driven into the mud in the shape of a V—and then they waited for two white whales to swim into the V, which they planned to close quickly with their boats.

For dreary days, Barnum watched spouting whales gambol about the kraal but fail to enter it. At last, disheartened, he returned to Quebec. No sooner had he arrived there than he was informed that two white whales had been trapped—they had swum into the kraal, had been closed inside it, left high and dry by the receding tide, and then had been dragged to seaweed-lined boxes by ropes attached to their tails.

Hastily, Barnum arranged for a private freight car to transport his mammals during the five-day journey to New York. Each white whale reposed uncomfortably in a crate partially filled with salt water and seaweed, where it was attended by a Barnum employee who continually moistened its mouth and spout with a sponge dipped in salt water.

Barnum drummed the progress of the whales into the ears of waiting New York on a ceaseless beat of publicity. Every stop, every depot, from Quebec to New York, was thronged by alerted natives. Hourly dispatches were fed to the press, and a stream of bulletins was posted before the

Museum. Finally the mammals arrived and were lowered into the basement tank filled with fresh water artificially salted, real salt water not being immediately available. "Anxious thousands literally rushed to see the strangest curiosities ever exhibited in New York," Barnum said with satisfaction. "Thus was my first whaling expedition a great success; but I did not know how to feed or to take care of the monsters, and, moreover, they were in fresh water, and this, with the bad air in the basement, may have hastened their death, which occurred a few days after their arrival, but not before thousands of people had seen them."

Tempted by the challenge and the rewards, Barnum prepared to have two more living white whales caught and delivered. This time he planned more carefully for their longevity. Even as his St. Lawrence fishermen kept watch about their kraal, Barnum, at a cost of $4,000, constructed a new tank on the second floor of the Museum. This aquarium was twenty-four feet square, with a floor of slate, and sides made of imported French glass one inch thick. An iron pipe projecting under the street to the bay supplied a steady stream of real salt water. In a short time, two more white whales were there. "It was a very great sensation," said Barnum, "and it added thousands of dollars to my treasury. The whales, however, soon died—their sudden and immense popularity was too much for them."

Undiscouraged, Barnum ordered a third pair. The mammals were duly caught by thirty-five men, and delivered by rail after an expenditure of $10,000. Barnum's advertisements almost matched his marine attractions in size. "I am highly gratified," he announced at the conclusion of one notice, "in being able to assure the public that they have arrived safe and well, a MALE and FEMALE, from 15 to 20 feet long, and are now swimming in the miniature ocean in my Museum, to the delight of visitors. As it is very doubtful whether these wonderful creatures can be kept alive more than a few days, the public will see the importance of seizing the first moment to see them."

A reporter from Greeley's *Tribune* observed them in the seven feet of salt water and gave them much of a column. "Their form and motion are graceful, and their silver backs and bellies show brightly through the water. A long-continued intimacy has endeared them to each other, and they go about quite like a pair of whispering lovers, blowing

off their mutual admiration in a very emphatic manner.
. . . Here is a real sensation. We do not believe the enterprise of Mr. Barnum will stop at white whales. It will embrace sperm whales and mermaids, and all strange things that swim or fly or crawl, until the Museum will become one vast microism [*sic*] of the animal creation. A quarter seems positively contemptible weighed against such a treat."

When cynics labeled the whales as fakes, as being porpoises really, and aired their doubts, Barnum indignantly sent to Harvard University for the eminent Professor Louis Agassiz, the Swiss naturalist whose geological studies of the shores of Lake Superior, Florida, California, and Brazil had made him world-famous. Agassiz stood before the tank, peered through the French glass, and announced that the suspect sea monsters were, indeed, genuine whales. Elated, Barnum had the Professor sign a certificate of authenticity, which he then published far and wide.

But the Museum, apparently, was no just habitat for Moby Dick. First one whale died, and then the other. The *Tribune,* blaming the catastrophe on the foul scent of a resentful grizzly bear, ran a lengthy obituary. "The blow is a severe one. To Mr. Barnum it must be a shocking reminder of the emptiness of all human plans. Enterprise, liberal expenditure, courage—what are they all before the fell destroyer. Even whales have their time to sink and rise no more."

The great tank was not vacant long. A three-year-old hippopotamus from Africa supplanted the whales, to be followed, in turn, by sharks, sea horses, angel fish, and at last porpoises.

The white whales, the grizzly bears, the untamed Indian chiefs were Barnum's valediction to two decades of pioneer showmanship. In June 1865, the American Museum was an ash heap, and with its destruction Barnum's decade of disaster reached its end.

Having disregarded Greeley's advice that he retire to rod and stream. Barnum leased an old building on the west side of Broadway between Spring Street and Prince Street, known as the Chinese Museum. After four intense months of directing carpentry and painting, he filled it with a stock of curiosities purchased from several hundred small collections and exhibits. Quickly he installed his freaks and his old troupe of thespians, and on November 13, 1865, Barnum's New American Museum was open for business.

The one shortcoming was the lack of relics, many irreplaceable ones having been lost in the fire. To acquire more, he obtained passage for $1,200 for John Greenwood, Jr., again his assistant, on an 1,800-ton steamer, *Quaker City,* which was taking sixty-six passengers on the first American Mediterranean cruise in June 1867 and climaxing its grand tour with a pilgrimage through the Holy Land.

On the steamer, Greenwood joined Moses Sperry Beach, proprietor of the *Sun,* whose father had vouched for Barnum when the showman had first tried to buy the Museum, Bloodgood Cutter, the eccentric Long Island poet, and the thirty-two-year-old Mark Twain, as yet known only for *The Celebrated Jumping Frog of Calaveras County.* This pleasant excursion—"Three-fourths of the Quaker City's passengers were between forty and seventy years of age! There was a picnic crowd for you!" Mark Twain wrote—took the weary travelers to Gibraltar, Morocco, France, Italy, Greece, and Palestine. The five-month cruise was celebrated by Mark Twain in his enduring best-seller *The Innocents Abroad,* and valued by Barnum for the great number of relics Greenwood brought back from the Holy Land.

With his collection of bric-a-brac improved, Barnum concentrated on making his menageries the most populous in America. There were lions and tigers in abundance, the only giraffe in the nation, and the smallest elephant found in Africa. Finally, in partnership with the Van Ambrugh Menagerie Company, there was that animal which Barnum desired most of all, a huge, ferocious African gorilla.

Though Barnum wrote that the gorilla was so strong that he "bent the heavy iron bars of his cage" and once grabbed a poker thrust at him and "twisted it as if it had been a bit of wire," other eyewitnesses saw the gorilla in a different light. One of these, Matthew Hale Smith, writing in 1869, saw the beast as being "as ferocious as a small-sized kitten." Large crowds were attracted by the supposedly wild gorilla. A Smithsonian Institution professor visited the exhibit and asked to see Barnum.

"He is a very fine specimen of a baboon—but he is no gorilla," the professor told Barnum.

"What's the reason that he is not a gorilla?" the showman inquired.

The professor explained that real gorillas had no tails.

"I know that ordinary gorillas have no tails," replied Barnum, "but mine has, and that makes the specimen more remarkable."

Later, in his own version, Barnum stated that his agents had been duped into taking a baboon for a gorilla, and that he knew instantly that the animal was only a baboon. Although continuing to advertise the beast as a gorilla, Barnum realized that he would soon be exposed. To anticipate this, he wrote a chiding, humorous letter to Paul du Chaillu, who had first told the world of pygmies and gorillas after his African explorations, saying that "since he had only killed gorillas . . . we had secured a living one, and brought the monster safely from Africa to America. I informed him, moreover, that all the gorillas he had seen and described were tailless, while our far more remarkable specimen had a tail full four feet long!"

Again Barnum fared well. His New Museum was more successful than Niblo's Garden or Wallack's Theater. Casting about for another enterprise, he was not long in finding one. Isaac A. Van Amburgh, a nearsighted lion-tamer whose traveling menagerie featured the largest band wagon in the country, had recently died, and his partners needed someone to replace him. Barnum stepped into the breach, and soon his $2,000,000 Van Amburgh menagerie was a successful drawing card on the road. The nightmare of the Jerome Clock Company receded into a memory. The "butterfly friends" were back. Barnum's popularity was restored. But a hard-bitten few still remained his enemies.

James Gordon Bennett was a perpetual adversary. Perhaps Bennett recognized in Barnum something of his own coarser self, that defect of character which he exploited yet despised the most, and perhaps his hate was self-hate. Barnum did not seem to mind the attacks of his publishing foe. "I always found Bennett's abuse far more remunerative than his praise," Barnum wrote, "even if I could have the praise at the same price, that is for nothing. Especially was it profitable to me when I could be the subject of scores of lines of his scolding editorials free of charge, instead of paying him forty cents a line for advertisements, which would not attract a tenth part so much attention. Bennett had tried abusing me, off and on, for twenty years, on one occasion refusing my advertisement altogether for the space of about a year; but I always managed to be the gainer by his course."

Bennett's feud with Barnum reached its climax shortly after the old Museum burned down. Barnum retained a real-estate agent, one Homer Morgan, to dispose of the eleven years remaining of his lease of the property. Bennett was eager to have the land for a larger newspaper building. He asked the showman his price. Barnum said that the lease was worth $275,000 but that he would sell it to Bennett for $200,000. Bennett, after too brief a consideration, agreed, and gave Barnum his check on the Chemical Bank for $200,000. Then, for $500,000 more, he purchased the land itself.

No sooner had Bennett concluded his deals than he read in rival newspapers "that the sum which he had paid for a piece of land measuring only fifty-six by one hundred feet was more than was ever before paid in any city in the world for a tract of that size." Not only did Bennett suddenly feel that he had been swindled, but also his deeply ingrained Scotch sense of thrift was shaken. He decided that Barnum had falsely assessed the property. He sent his attorney to the showman with a request that the $200,000 be returned. Barnum refused. "I don't make child's bargains," he said.

The following day the advertisements for the New American Museum were dropped from the *New York Herald*. Unable to get satisfaction from Bennett, Barnum lodged protest with the New York Managers' Association. At once every major theater and entertainment center in the metropolis boycotted Bennett's daily. Bennett continued to print the advertisements of Niblo's Garden and Wallack's Theater free of charge, trying to woo them from the league against him, whereupon Niblo and others headed their advertisements in rival newspapers with the legend: "This Establishment does not advertise in the New York Herald."

In a fury, Bennett proceeded to abuse and attack every offending manager, as well as actors, singers, and dancers. To Bennett's astonishment, the bad publicity increased theatrical business everywhere. In his two-year feud with Barnum, the publisher lost $200,000 in advertising and job-printing contracts, and a considerable amount of cir-

culation, especially among readers who wished daily notices
of amusements. At last the feud was resolved, and advertising was restored to the *Herald* by all except Barnum,
who saw that the *Herald* was not necessary to him, and
decided that advertising in it was not worth the price.

A friendlier enemy was the tall, funereal, frock-coated
Henry Bergh, friend of all animals, enemy of some men,
and founder of the American Society for the Prevention
of Cruelty to Animals. The long-standing feud between
Bergh and Barnum had overtones of comic opera.

Bergh, a wealthy graduate of Columbia University, had
served as a diplomat in Russia before he became possessed
by an obsession to protect all dumb beasts. When he was
forty-five, he started his Society. A year later, in 1866,
with the support of Horace Greeley, of the rich merchant,
Alexander Stewart, and of the slaughterer of fur-bearers,
John Jacob Astor, he succeeded in forcing through a law
in New York State allowing the Society to make arrests in
all cases of cruelty to animals. When he saw live turtles
in the market, their flippers tied together, he took the pro-
prietors to court. When he saw emaciated horses pulling
streetcars, he stopped the vehicles. He interfered in cock
fights and dog fights, and he replaced live pigeons with
clay birds in all shooting games. The upper classes supported him until the day when he tried to eliminate fox-
hunting.

Barnum, America's foremost importer of animals, was
Bergh's natural prey. When the showman exhibited a rhinoceros, Bergh demanded that it be given a tank of water
to swim in. Barnum had to prove that the rhino was not
an amphibian. When the showman kept his snakes alive by
feeding them toads and lizards, Bergh's pained outcry
shook the Museum. Barnum had to prove that without
toads the snakes would perish. When the showman fed
his boa constrictors live birds and small mammals, Bergh
called him a "semi-barbarian" and warned him: "On the
next occurrence of this cruel exhibition this society will
take legal measures to punish the perpetrator of it." In
desperation, Barnum appealed to the reliable Professor
Agassiz, and the noble naturalist replied: "I do not know
of any way to induce snakes to eat their food otherwise
than in their natural manner—that is alive. . . . The society
of which you speak is, as I understand, for the prevention

of unnecessary cruelty to animals. It is a most praiseworthy object, but I do not think the most active members of the society would object to eating lobster salad because the lobster was boiled alive. . . ." Before such august authority, Bergh retreated.

The final duel occurred in 1880 over a new act Barnum had publicized widely. A trained horse, Salamander, was to leap through a fiery hoop. Bergh protested "on the grounds of cruelty to the animal." Barnum challenged Bergh to witness the act. Instead, Bergh sent an assistant, Hatfield, and seven aides, as well as twenty policemen. While thousands of spectators sat in tense expectation, Salamander was led into the ring and the fire hoops lighted. In a grand gesture of disdain, Barnum, hat in hand, calmly walked through one of the burning hoops without singeing a hair. He was followed by ten clowns, and then by Salamander. Next Barnum invited Bergh's assistant to test the "cruelty" of the flaming hoop. Hatfield obliged, emerged untoasted, and sheepishly apologized for Bergh.

Despite the annoyance caused by this fanatical gadfly, Barnum had respect and affection for Bergh and his crusade. In his will, Barnum left $1,000 for the erection of a statue in Bridgeport honoring Bergh. But Bergh's real monument was this: at the beginning of his career, no state or territory had a law against cruelty to animals; at his death in 1888, thirty-nine states had such laws in their statute books.

Barnum's comeback in public life—evidence that his popularity had reached its highest peak—was dramatized by his entrance into politics. In 1852 he had declined the Democratic nomination for governor of Connecticut. In 1888 he rejected the idea of running for president of the United States on the Prohibition ticket. Yet, he firmly believed in active political participation. "It always seemed to me," he wrote, "that man who 'takes no interest in politics' is unfit to live in a land where the government rests in the hands of people."

In 1865, as a Republican, Barnum was elected to the Connecticut state legislature from the town of Fairfield. At Hartford, Barnum immediately made his presence felt. Two candidates were up for the job of speaker. One was supported by the railroad lobby. Barnum joined the opposition to him, and for the first time, the previously invincible railroad monopoly was defeated.

When the Fourteenth Amendment to abolish slavery came up for ratification, Barnum supported it vocally and with his vote. "The word 'white' in the Constitution cannot be strictly and literally construed," he stated in a speech. "The opposition express great love for white blood. Will they let a mulatto vote half the time, a quadroon three-fourths, and an octoroon seven-eighths of the time? If not, why not? Will they enslave seven-eighths of a white man because one-eighth is not Caucasian? Is this democratic? Shall not the majority seven control the minority one? Out on such 'democracy'!"

When a Representative from Milford feared that passage of the Amendment would encourage interracial marriages, Barnum replied: "The gentleman may remember that when his sons propose to marry with negroes the black girls may have a word to say in objection to such a proposition. It is a matter of taste, and the tastes of the colored women may not be found sympathetic."

His continuing fight against the New York and New Haven Railroad lobby was watched throughout the state. He strongly opposed a bill to raise commutation rates. And he introduced several bills of his own, including one to do away with capital punishment. His liberality and obvious sincerity won many neutral newspapers to his side. One of them wrote approvingly: "The people of Connecticut are under great obligations to him for breaking down the railroad combinations which have so long infested the legislature and sought in various ways to control it. When the members of the House return to their homes it will be with more exalted ideas of P. T. Barnum and his character for frankness, intelligence, and uprightness. . . . "

So satisfactory was Barnum's record, that a year later he was re-elected to the legislature. In 1867, aspiring higher, he ran as Republican candidate from the Fourth District for the House of Representatives in Washington. Although he disliked "the dirty work" of politics—"to shake hands with those whom I despise, and to kiss the dirty babies of those whose votes were courted"—he was attracted to the important office and campaigned with energy against the local political boss, who was his opponent.

The *Nation,* in its issue of March 7, 1867, came out

against Barnum. The Democrats, said the periodical's editors, already had disgraced the country by electing to Congress from the Fifth New York District—"by the votes of the ignorant foreigners"—that Irish-born, wealthy gambler and ex-pugilist, John Morrissey, who had flattened John C. Heenan in eleven rounds to win the American heavyweight championship, and now the Republicans were no better. Barnum, the editors said, "is the personification —and so far from concealing or denying it, he boasts of it —of a certain low kind of humbug. . . . If it be honorable or instructive to go and see strange or queer things, it is honorable to collect and exhibit them; and if Barnum had confined himself to this, though we might not select him as a legislator or like to see him sent to Congress by a New England State, we should not accuse him as we now do, of having been for twenty or thirty years a depraving and demoralizing influence."

But the *Nation* need not have worried. A Democratic landslide was in the making, and it swept across Connecticut. Barnum was buried under it. His backers shouted fraud, arguing that voters had been bribed and transported from other states, but no fraud was proved, and the election stood. Not until 1877 did Barnum hold another state office, and then he was elected from Bridgeport to the Connecticut general assembly; he was re-elected the year following.

The political venture that gave him the most satisfaction was his election on April 5, 1875, by a margin of one hundred and forty-one votes, as Mayor of Bridgeport. He served one busy, hectic year. The *Farmer,* a Democratic sheet complained: "His forte has been buffoonery and the undignified, unparliamentary, improper interjecting of personal remarks into the debates." But his constituents enjoyed him. Mayor Barnum opposed liquor licenses and enforced the closing of saloons on Sundays. He came out for lower utility rates. He advocated a better water supply and drainage system, and pleaded for public baths. He arranged to have fruit sold by weight instead of measure. He attacked trade-union discrimination against Negroes. He tried to check unemployment by convincing the populace that any work was better than time-wasting devotion to baseball and billiards. "There are too many soft hands (and heads) waiting for light work and heavy pay," he said.

Barnum's fiercest crusade as mayor was against the local houses of prostitution. Peremptorily he ordered his chief of police to shut down all Bridgeport brothels within twenty-four hours. If the chief displayed any hesitancy, Barnum promised to close the houses himself. Plainly irked, the chief visited two of the houses, read Barnum's order aloud, and received the pledge of both madams that their "boarders" would be dismissed at once. However, when the chief's supporters asserted in print that Mayor Barnum himself had owned three houses in New York "which were rented for disreputable purposes," His Honor was enraged. Barnum loudly denied ownership of any brothels, and abruptly turned to other municipal matters. It is to be presumed that the "boarders" of Bridgeport returned to their houses.

At his last council meeting, Mayor Barnum ended his term of office on a characteristic note: "Gentlemen," he said, "as we are about to close our labors in a harmonious spirit and bid each other friendly farewell, we have, like the Arabs, only to 'fold our tents and silently steal away,' congratulating ourselves that this is the only stealing which has been performed by this honorable body."

Ever since his recovery of position and wealth, Barnum had dreamed of reviving the glory that was Iranistan. At last, in 1860, just five hundred yards west of the old grounds where his Oriental palace had stood, he built his new dwelling. At the suggestion of his friend Bayard Taylor, the "delightful place" was named Lindencroft. Compared with what he had known in the past, it was relatively small and conservative. Even though he proudly pointed out that "elegance, pure and simple, predominated," it was plain that his heart was not in this home.

Meanwhile he sought a residence in New York. He preferred to spend his winters in the city. "There is a sense of satisfaction," he said, "even in the well-cleared sidewalks after a snow-storm, and an almost selfish happiness in looking out upon a storm from a well-warmed library or parlor window. One loves to find the morning papers, fresh from the press, lying upon the breakfast-table; and the city is the centre of attractions in the way of operas, concerts, picture galleries, libraries, the best music, the best preaching. ..." To satisfy this need, Barnum spent $80,000 to purchase a brownstone on Fifth Avenue at Thirty-ninth Street.

Soon, Lindencroft was abandoned altogether. Charity's health remained poor, and her physician suggested that she live nearer the water. With delight, Barnum disposed of Lindencroft and planned a mansion more representative of his tastes. In 1869, at Seaside Park, a 210-acre suburb of Bridgeport (Barnum had donated a small portion of it to the city four years before), the sprawling, ornate, gingerbread castle, Waldemere — "Woods-by-the-Sea" — was born.

Waldemere was a product of love. The statue of a pacified Indian met visitors at the outer gate. Beyond the spraying fountain, and between the groves of hickory trees and numerous flower beds, rose the spired, domed building, which resembled a Saratoga hotel.

An Englishman who was a guest at Waldemere in 1877 published his impressions in the London *World*: "The house itself is not easily described, being a curious but pleasant mélange of Gothic, Italian and French architecture and decoration, presenting a front a hundred and sixty feet long to the water, whereby most of the rooms command a very charming view. On entering one is pleasantly struck by the spaciousness of halls and rooms. One can breathe as freely in-doors as out. Nothing is small or contracted. ... Pictures of high merit hang on tinted walls and stand on easels. Chinese vases of quaint and wonderful design guard the fireplaces; busts and statuettes fill nooks and corners; capacious bookcases fail to hold the latest works; while mantels and *étagères* hold costly *bric-a-brac* in artistic confusion. ... On a pedestal in a place of honor, stands a marble bust of Jenny Lind. ... A corner bracket in a cosy sitting-room holds a small Parian Bacchus—a Christmas gift from the Swedish Nightingale to Mr. Barnum, in good-natured ridicule of his firm temperance principles and practice. In an *étagère* in this same pleasant room lie dimpled marble models of Tom Thumb's hand and foot taken when his size was smallest and his fame greatest. ... The mansion is intersected with a very network of waterpipes—there being scarcely a room that has not its bath-room and lavatory attached."

The guest rooms seemed endless, and many were named after their most frequent occupants. One of the most comfortable was the "Greeley room." Horace Greeley came visiting often, and Barnum was much devoted to him. "He once told me," Joel Benton said, "that it pained him to see Mr. Greeley omit those little cares for himself in later life to which he was surely entitled, and so, when he was his guest for many days together, he took care to provide him with a loose morning coat and comfortable slippers, and would not have him drop in an ordinary chair by accident, but secured for him the easiest one."

The kitchen stood outside so that the odors might be kept from the house. Walks led to the specially built cottage, "Petrel's Nest," where Caroline and Thompson resided, and to "Wavewood," the home of Pauline and Seeley. Daughter Helen alone resisted feudal living. A private gasworks supplied illumination to the cottages and the main house. In the barns were cattle shipped from Holland, and in the stables, horses of blood. Magnetic burglar alarms surrounded the property, and there was a direct telephone wire to the police. Like his friend Mark Twain, who was the first author to use a typewriter, Barnum was quick to adopt every modern invention. He had lost no time in installing one of the earliest telephones in America. When the host was at home, a white silk flag bearing the initials "P.T.B." fluttered from the flagpole above the glass cupola.

All was serenity at Waldemere until the morning of March 3, 1868. Barnum was reading the newspaper at breakfast, half-listening to his wife and her female guest across the table. Suddenly, eyes still on the paper, he spoke aloud. "Hallo!" he exclaimed. "Barnum's Museum is burned."

It was true. In the night—a winter night so cold that water from the firehoses froze as it splattered against the granite walls of the city showplace—the New American Museum had gone the way of the old. When the flames were finished, the Museum was a hollow shell of charcoal and icicles. Most of the valuable animals were dead and the collection of curiosities was gone forever. The collection had been worth $288,000. The insurance was $160,000.

No longer did Barnum wish to tempt fate. He was fifty-eight and a millionaire. He decided at last to accept Horace Greeley's earlier advice "and go a-fishing." Short weeks after the Museum loss, he announced his retirement. It would have amazed him to know that ahead waited the final adventure—the one that would make his name immortal in show business.

EXHIBIT TEN
Jumbo

For two years, from the summer of 1868 through the summer of 1870, Barnum rested and avoided all major business entanglements. At first he enjoyed the leisure. He was proud to tell a friend that he had no office in New York, adding: "I have done work enough, and shall play the rest of my life." From the warm recesses of his birch-and-maple octagonal study, he watched his wealthy neighbors, bankers and merchants, drive through sleet and rain to their desks in Bridgeport, and he was pleased that he was not one of them.

But eventually this hibernation wearied him. "Reading is pleasant as a pastime," he decided; "writing without any special purpose soon tires; a game of chess will answer as a condiment; lectures, concerts, operas, and dinner parties are well enough in their way; but to a robust, healthy man of forty years' active *business* life, something else is needed to satisfy. Sometimes like the truant school-boy I found all my friends engaged, and I had no playmate."

He packed Waldemere with guests, but often there were

"evenings quite alone" with the invalided Charity, and these he could not stand. He leaped at every opportunity to lecture, anywhere, on any subject, for whatever cause. But still—"time hung on my hands"—and, in desperation, he tried to absorb himself in travel.

There was a long trip with old friends, to Cuba, and then through the shattered South, and home again by way of Washington. Shortly after, with another small party, Barnum boarded a train for California. He had scheduled three lectures en route, and one was in Salt Lake City.

Two decades before, Brigham Young, the Mormon leader, had courageously led the exodus of his persecuted people from Illinois and had founded Salt Lake City. He had twice been appointed Utah's governor. In 1852, Young had made public the doctrine of plural marriage or polygamy as a tenet of the Latter-day Saints, and for this he was notorious. Once he had received Horace Greeley, who found the despot good-natured and ungrammatical. In their two-hour interview, Greeley asked Brigham Young: "What is the largest number of wives belonging to any one man?" Young replied: "I have fifteen; I know no one who has more; but some of those sealed to me are old ladies whom I regard rather as mothers than wives, but whom I have taken home to cherish and support." At his polygamous peak, Young, who often made vulgar references to women, had twenty-seven wives and, by count of one of his daughters, fifty-six living children, thirty-one of them girls.

When Barnum delivered his lecture in Salt Lake Theatre, a dozen or more of Brigham Young's wives were in the audience. "As I came out of the theatre," Barnum recalled, "one of the Apostles introduced me to five of his wives in succession! The Mormon wives whom I visited in company of their husbands, expressed themselves pleased with their positions; but I confess I doubt their sincerity on this point. All whom our party conversed with (and some of our ladies talked with these Mormon wives in secret), expressed their solemn conviction, that polygamy was the true domestic system sanctioned by the Almighty; although they confessed they wished it was right for a man to have but one wife."

Forever interested in curiosities, Barnum was eager to meet Brigham Young, whom even gentiles considered one of America's foremost colonizers and statesmen. Soon enough he had his invitation. At the presidential mansion, the Bee-Hive, Brigham Young was waiting, all cordiality.

After some inconsequential talk, Brigham Young suddenly inquired lightly: "Barnum, what will you give to exhibit me in New York and the Eastern cities?"

"Well, Mr. President, I'll give you half the receipts, which I will guarantee shall be $200,000 per year, for I consider you the best show in America."

"Why did you not secure me some years ago when I was of no consequence?" asked Young.

"Because," said Barnum, "you would not have drawn at that time."

Continuing westward to San Francisco, where he spent a week, Barnum found his showman's interest intruding on his sight-seeing. When he saw gigantic sea lions, several weighing a ton apiece, gathered on Seal Rock, he thought it would be worth $50,000 to have ten of them. When he met a nine-year-old midget smaller even than Tom Thumb had been at that age—his name was Leopold Kahn, and he spoke German as fluently as English—Barnum could no longer resist. He acquired the midget, christened him Admiral Dot, presented him for three weeks in San Francisco, and then took him east as "The El Dorado Elf." At the same time, Barnum became a silent partner in Lavinia and Tom Thumb's around-the-world venture, and a silent partner, too, in showing Anna Swan and the Siamese Twins in England.

Outwardly he still tried to maintain the fiction of retirement. After three restless months at Waldemere, he joined a group of ten men who were going buffalo hunting in Kansas. His old friend Colonel George A. Custer, seven years before Little Big Horn, was commanding officer at Fort Hayes. He received Barnum as he would have received royalty, gave him horses and rifles and an escort of fifty cavalrymen. Barnum and his friends charged a herd of peacefully grazing buffaloes and killed twenty. When the sport became "wanton butchery," the hunt was called off.

At Waldemere again, Barnum decided that buffalo hunts "cannot be made to order every day," that it was useless to attempt further "to chain down energies peculiar to my nature," that he needed work as a "safety valve." And so, in the autumn of 1870, with the quiet reserve of a shot catapulting from a howitzer, Barnum bolted out of retirement. Not another day, in the next two decades, would he allow himself to vegetate. For his return to show business, he chose not the permanent museum or the single exhibit, but the entertainment that forever after would be associated with his name: the circus.

Barnum, who always considered himself a promoter and "a museum man" rather than "a circus man," had achieved his greatest success before his entry into the circus. Only the last twenty years of his long life were devoted to canvas and sawdust; he did not become a full-time circus proprietor until after his sixtieth birthday. The misconception persists that Phineas T. Barnum invented the circus. Nothing could be further from the truth. He gave the circus its size, its most memorable attractions, and its widest popularity. But, as an amusement form, the circus had existed long before Barnum. In the days of antiquity, in ancient Crete, Egypt, Greece, and Rome, there were circuses. The modern circus was created in England by a tall, handsome cavalryman, Philip Astley, who gave his outdoor arena a riding-ring and equestrian acts in 1768, and later added clown, tightrope walker, acrobats, and a three-piece band. In the United States, the first modern circus was presented in a Philadelphia amphitheater by an English stunt rider named John Bill Ricketts. In 1793, President Washington twice attended Ricketts's circus to enjoy his trained horses, his tightrope walker, and his clown. Shortly afterwards, Washington sold Ricketts a twenty-eight-year-old white horse, a veteran of the Revolution named Jack, for $150. Ricketts earned many times his investment by exhibiting the four-legged relic.

Barnum's only previous experience with a traveling circus had been in his impoverished youth when he had traveled through the South with Aaron Turner, who had given the primitive entertainment its big top. Now, at the invitation of William Cameron Coup, a former roustabout and side-show manager, and Dan Castello, an ex-clown, Barnum prepared to thrill his old public with the biggest outdoor circus in history.

Although lost in the brilliant glare of his senior partner's great name, the natty, bearded Coup was the prime mover of the new enterprise. Indiana born, Coup had been a tramp printer and employee in small circuses. He tried to settle down to a Wisconsin farm, but Castello lured him into promoting a floating carnival shown in the ports of the Great Lakes. It was at this time that Coup conceived the idea of using Barnum's name, money, and genius for hiring attractions to create a circus greater than any known before.

On April 10, 1871, the "great show enterprise" of Barnum, Coup, and Castello opened in Brooklyn beneath three acres of canvas tent. Ten thousand spectators peered through the flickering gaslight at the animals, the freaks, the side-show curios, the parade, and the circus acts themselves. Then, the circus went on the road, from New England through the Midwest to California. Everywhere Esau, the bearded boy, Colonel Goshen, the giant, and Admiral Dot, the twenty-five-inch midget (who would soon desert show business to open a saloon, frequented by John L. Sullivan, in White Plains, New York), were welcomed with amazement. In that first season, the gross receipts were $400,000.

Barnum liked to say that he made the circus bigger and bigger over Coup's frightened protests. "To the horror of my very able but too cautious manager, Mr. W. C. Coup," Barnum wrote in his autobiography, ". . . I so augmented the already innumerable attractions, that it was shown beyond doubt, that we could not travel at a less expense than five thousand dollars per day, but, undaunted, I still expended thousands of dollars, and ship after ship brought me rare and valuable animals and works of art." And then again: "Perceiving that my great combination was assuming such proportions that it would be impossible to move it by horse power, I negotiated with all the railway companies between New York and Omaha, Nebraska, for the transportation by rail, of my whole show, requiring sixty to seventy freight cars, six passenger cars, and three engines."

Coup's version, corroborated by impartial witnesses, was the opposite. It was he who overcame Barnum's timidity, a conservatism apparently acquired with age, in order to make their circus the most richly mounted in America. It was he who added to "Barnum's Great Traveling World's Fair," as the circus was soon called, such expensive attractions as "the lightning ticket seller," Ben Lusbie, who could dispose of six thousand fifty-cent pasteboards in one hour;

the daring aeronaut Washington H. Donaldson, of Maine, who made semi-weekly balloon ascensions (until, accompanied by a Chicago reporter, he disappeared in a storm over Lake Michigan); a rare giraffe; and a half-ton seal; an Italian goat that rode a horse bareback; and four wild Fiji cannibals rescued from an enemy pot (whom Henry Ward Beecher refused to visit at "feeding time").

Furthermore, it was Coup who overcame the horrified objections of both Barnum and the railroad companies to putting the circuses on flatcars. In 1901, Coup wrote: "Previous to 1872 the 'railroad circus' was an unknown quantity. Like all other circuses of that day, the big show of which I was the manager traveled by wagon. . . . Of course we showed in towns of all sizes and our daily receipts ranged from $1,000 to $7,000. Finding that the receipts in the larger towns were frequently twice and three times as much as in the smaller ones, I became convinced that we could at least double our receipts if we could ignore the small places and travel only from one big town to another. . . . This was my reason for determining to move the show by rail the following season. To this end, therefore, I at once telegraphed to the superintendents of the different railroads asking if they could accommodate us. . . ."

Coup was also credited with inventing a more efficient system for loading and unloading the trains, inaugurating half-rate excursions that brought in spectators from outlying districts, installing the tent's center pole, and conceiving a two-ring circus to replace the old one-ring affair. When Barnum, against his own advice given long before, tried to limit advertising, Coup went ahead on his own to plaster billboards and posters within a radius of fifty miles of each show. In its second season, the circus grossed almost a million dollars in six months.

According to Barnum, he had long cherished the idea of a permanent circus structure in New York City, to be called the Great Roman Hippodrome. While in Europe in 1873 to scout new attractions, he heard from Coup that the perfect site, an entire square block between Fourth and Madison avenues, was available. Barnum cabled Coup to lease it and build on it an immense indoor coliseum, 200 feet wide and 426 feet long. According to Coup, however, it was he who suggested the Hippodrome while Barnum was abroad, and Barnum who flatly rejected the extravagance. When

Coup threatened to undertake the project himself, with new backers, Barnum finally relented.

In either case, P. T. Barnum's Great Roman Hippodrome—with Coup the general manager and Castello the director of amusements—was opened to the public in April 1874. For the first performance, the ten thousand seats were filled. A grand procession of triumphal cars, carrying one thousand performers in representations of historical monarchs and rulers the world over, circled the arena. Then followed chariot races, in the Ben Hur manner, around an oval track one fifth of a mile long. Then came the tightrope walkers, the Japanese acrobats, the monkey races, the clowns.

The huge Hippodrome show, later taken on the road, was a success in every way. But now Barnum and Coup, whose health was impaired by overwork, had a falling out. Unwisely, Barnum had leased the use of his famous name to a fellow teetotaler, a fat, asthmatic young Irishman named John "Pogey" O'Brien, proprietor of a cheap circus. On the road, Barnum's show with Coup competed against Barnum's show with O'Brien while rival circuses shouted in print: "Barnum Show Divided!" Coup felt that this lessened the value of Barnum's name, and he was furious. Castello had already sold out his interest to Barnum, and now Coup did the same.

Two years later, in partnership with a German named Charles Reiche, Coup built the $500,000 New York Aquarium on Broadway. When he and his partner disagreed about Sunday shows—Coup was against them—Coup suggested that they part company after flipping a coin to determine which would keep the valuable Aquarium and which receive the consolation of a handful of animals. The coin was spun in the air. Coup lost. He collected his animals, added a white whale, genuine Zulus, and a Zouave drill team, and took to his beloved rails. Ironically, a train accident ruined him, and he died, poor and forgotten, in Florida.

Meanwhile, a radical change in Barnum's personal life had come about. While he was in Hamburg purchasing ostriches and giraffes for the new Hippodrome, he received a cablegram from his son-in-law, Samuel H. Hurd, announcing that Charity was dead.

Barnum's mate of forty-four years, after a paralytic

stroke, had died in their daughter Caroline's New York house at two o'clock in the afternoon of November 19, 1873, at the age of sixty-five. The following day, on page three, the Bridgeport *Daily Standard* noted: "For many years Mrs. Barnum has been an invalid and a great sufferer, and her death, though sudden at last, was not wholly unexpected. She was a woman of superior natural gifts and has been the valued and endeared companion of her husband since 1829, or nearly half a century. Absence in foreign lands precludes his presence at the last scene on earth of the one who has for so long a time sustained to him the nearest and most blessed relation of life."

A sorrowful Barnum managed Charity's funeral services and burial by cable. Embalmed in New York, her remains were shipped to Bridgeport by train. Then, resting in an expensive rosewood coffin with white roses at the head and base spelling out "Mother" and "Charity," she was displayed to children, grandchildren, and friends in a parlor of Waldemere. After those present had sung "Praise God from Whom all blessings flow," she was taken to a vault in the Mountain Grove Cemetery to await the return of her husband.

In Germany, far from his family, among foreigners and strangers, Barnum suffered, he said, "utter loneliness." Of this period, he wrote: "Long accustomed as I have been to feel that God is good, and that His ways are always right, that He overcometh evil with good, and chastens us 'for our profit,' I confess the 'cloud' seemed so utterly black that it was hard to realize it *could* have a silver 'lining.' And my tongue ceased to move when I attempted to say, as surely we all ought unhesitatingly at all times to say, 'Not my will, but Thine be done.' I remained in my room for several days, and on that Saturday on which I felt confident my children and friends were accompanying her remains to our beautiful Mountain Grove Cemetery, my lonely head was bowed, and my tears flowed in unison with theirs. . . ."

Barnum canceled his plans to continue to Italy, and returned to his favorite London, there to spend "several weeks in quiet." It might be added that near London lived the pretty English girl, forty years his junior, whom he loved and would marry within ten months.

Barnum's second wife, Nancy Fish, was eight years old when he met her. He was then forty-eight. Barnum honored her father, one of his most worshipful admirers, with an entire chapter entitled "An Enterprising Englishman" in his revised autobiography. John Fish had been a struggling millhand in Manchester when he came across a copy of *The Life of P. T. Barnum, Written by Himself.* Reading the book, Fish thought that he saw "a pleasant spirit and a good heart" beneath the author's "rougher exterior." Best of all, Barnum's example inspired him. As Fish later told Barnum: "I said to myself, 'Why can't I go ahead and make money as Barnum did? He commenced without money and succeeded; why may not I?' In this train of thought I went to a newspaper office and advertised for a partner with money to join me in establishing a cotton-mill." The partner was found, the 1,000-loom mill built, and Fish was soon a man of means.

In 1858 Barnum lectured in Manchester. John Fish came calling, all gratefulness and awe, and soon they were fast friends. Fish's attractive daughter, Nancy, was no less reverent in the presence of the great showman. When Fish installed a new engine in his mill, and announced that he would name it "Nancy," the child demanded that it be named "Barnum."

Once when Barnum wrote Fish that he wanted an eight-foot French giant investigated, Fish obligingly rushed to Paris with a ruler in his pocket. He learned that the giant was little more than seven feet tall, and that he used springs in his boots to make himself appear taller. The giant was not hired.

In 1868, while Barnum was in retirement at Waldemere, Fish and his daughter made their first visit to the United States. By now, Nancy Fish had matured into a shapely, handsome young lady of eighteen. She was blonde, with wide eyes, an aquiline nose, a prominent chin, and "the most dazzling complexion in the world." Barnum had always fancied Englishwomen. In the *North American Review* he rhapsodized: "They are healthy-looking to an extent that we cannot match in any of our women in America. So rosy and rubicund are the faces of the country women who come into London from their homes that you would make an affidavit almost, if you did not know to the contrary, that they are painted. And they are marvellously well developed in form." Now, in Waldemere, Barnum no doubt contrasted this lively, bursting English girl of eighteen with his withered, invalided wife of sixty.

His visitors wanted to see the United States, and Barnum insisted on being their guide. He took them first to Cuba, and when they gazed at the breathtaking valley of Yumuri, near Matanzas, Barnum was moved "to see the tears of joy and gratitude roll down the cheeks of the young English lady." Together they visited New Orleans, Louisville, Niagara Falls. Perhaps it was Nancy's nearness that made Barnum admit later: "I saw beauty and grandeur in scenes which I had before gazed on unimpressed."

In Liverpool in 1873, Fish met Barnum on his Hippodrome trip. His stately home in Southport, the place of Nancy's birth, was eighteen miles away. Barnum spent several days there with Fish and Nancy, and then continued to the Continent, where he learned that he was a widower. Ten months later, on September 16, 1874, Barnum married Nancy Fish in the Church of the Divine Paternity on Fifth Avenue in New York, with the Reverend Mr. Chapin, enemy of the moderate drinker, officiating. A brief honeymoon followed, and then the second Mrs. Barnum moved into Waldemere. She was twenty-four years old, younger than all three of her married stepdaughters, and Barnum was sixty-four.

The seventeen years that Barnum was to live with Nancy were among the happiest of his life. An English guest, after visiting with Barnum and Nancy, told readers of the London *World:* "The good taste displayed in the ornamentation of Waldemere is due to Mrs. Barnum, who is highly appreciated by the best families of Bridgeport as a charming hostess, an intelligent and agreeable conversationalist, and a kind neighbor and friend. Mr. Barnum's daughters regard her as a treasure added to their enjoyment, and to their father's happiness and comfort. As for Mr. Barnum himself his round, full face beams with extra smiles when he is near her. He never seems quite so happy as when listening to her playing opera music on the grand piano, riding at her side in the family landau to and from church, in Sea-side Park, or on the numerous pleasant avenues in the vicinity of Bridgeport."

In the role of perfect wife, Nancy had to become accustomed to her husband's sense of humor. Many evenings she would sit by "astonished"—the word is Barnum's—at the droll stories exchanged by the showman and his friends, notably the Reverend Mr. Chapin, a chronic raconteur.

Once after the guests had departed, Nancy asked her husband: "Do you suppose that these tales that were told by the Reverend Chapin and others were really true, or were they made up?"

"Oh, of course they are not strictly true," said Barnum. "All funny anecdotes are exaggerated—there would be no fun in them if they were not."

"Well, I do not see any sense in laughing at a lie," Nancy said solemnly.

Barnum quickly dedicated himself to developing his young wife's appreciation of buffoonery. "Before she had lived with me three years," he later wrote, "she became one of the most inveterate of jokers." When her sedate father, John Fish, came visiting from England, and wondered why the eggs served at breakfast were not fresh, Nancy startled him by replying: "Our hens are all old hens, and they are not able to lay fresh eggs."

With pride, Barnum was able to report Nancy's progress in *Murray's Magazine* of London during 1890: "I must say she is quite sharp when any jokes or riddles or conundrums are propounded. She has a faculty for guessing every conundrum that is propounded to her, and when she misses the right answer she usually gives one that is better than the original."

On one occasion, Barnum playfully asked her: "Why is a dog's tail like an old man?" The proper answer was: "Because it is *in firm.*" Instead, Nancy, after brief consideration, replied: "Oh, anybody can see that in a moment; a dog's tail is like an old man because it is *on its last legs.*"

Throughout his second marriage, Barnum was in his second childhood. Hand in hand with Nancy, he attended clambakes and picnics, enjoyed the weekly open-air concerts at Seaside Park, attended the opera and theater in New York, went canoeing at Paul Smith's resort in the Adirondacks. At the resort, he and Nancy once had a mirthful dinner with Grover Cleveland and his wife. The Barnums were together on almost every trip. In 1875 it was Niagara Falls again, in 1877 England for a vacation and series of lectures. Even on his last triumphal visit to London, in 1889, when he was approaching his eightieth year, Nancy was beside him.

Following the showman's death, Nancy Barnum was wealthy. In 1882, Barnum's will had provided her with an annuity of $9,000, the free use of their house for one year, and "the best piano of which I shall die possessed, any and all horses, harness, saddles, carriages and sleighs . . . my diamond pin, chain and holder, usually worn by me, my stereoscope box or instrument with all stereoscopic slides or pictures, and all photographs and albums, except my family album." By 1889, Nancy's legacy had been amended to give her an annuity of $25,000, the ownership of their house and most personal property, and the diamond pin. In 1891, the will was amended a fifth time, and as a result Nancy finally inherited an annuity of $40,000 for life, their last home—Marina—much of Barnum's Bridgeport real estate and personal property, $100,000 in cash, and the diamond pin.

With Barnum gone, Connecticut held few charms for her. She sold Marina to Pauline Barnum Seeley's daughter, Jessie, and her husband Wilson Marshall, the renowned yachtsman. Then, Nancy moved to France and purchased an elegant apartment in Paris, its furnishings a curious blend of Second Empire and New England, and a villa in Cannes.

After a short period of widowhood, Nancy Barnum married Demetrius Callius Bey, a Greek of royal blood. She returned briefly to Bridgeport with her second husband—they were the house guests of a corset manufacturer—and a member of Nancy's family still remembers Bey as "a very presentable young man, nearer Nancy's age than was Barnum, and the real love of her life." Tragically, less than nine months after their wedding, Bey died and Nancy was once more a widow. Her third marriage was to a striking Frenchman named Baron d'Alexandry d'Orengiani. Nancy enjoyed her title, but not her mate. In a short time she was divorced.

As Madame la Baronne d'Alexandry d'Orengiani, Nancy circulated in the best French society. She commuted regularly to her native England, and she became an intimate of the exiled Empress Eugénie. The widowed Spanish wife of Napoleon III had purchased the rambling cottage of Farnborough from Longmans, the publisher, and there Nancy went visiting often, to sip tea or milk with the Empress in the red morning room or in the study where a statue of her dead son stood in a patch of grass brought from Natal. "People come to see me like the fifth act," Eugénie liked to say, and Nancy was among the most faithful of playgoers, not only in Farnborough but in Eugénie's villa known as Cyrnos at Cap Martin, and later in her suite of rooms on the second floor of the Hotel Continental in Paris. Nancy's loyalty was rewarded by numerous gifts from her royal friend, including a bracelet bearing miniatures of the Bonaparte family.

Of her three husbands, Nancy remembered Barnum alone with the affectionate respect accorded a parent. She liked to show new acquaintances a copy of his autobiography, which he had inscribed, "With love forevermore." "I have met many great gentlemen in my time, the most interesting personalities of the Second Empire," she told a visitor, "but not one of them had the intelligence and charm of my husband, P. T. Barnum." For her constant companion, she kept with her to the very end a distant Barnum relative—Caroline R. Leigh, sister-in-law of Caroline Thompson's daughter, Frances Leigh. On June 23, 1927, seventy-seven years of age, Barnum's second wife was dead, and soon after laid to rest in Cannes beside her second husband, Demetrius Bey.

But in 1874, death was far away and Nancy seemed to infuse Barnum with a new zest for living. After auctioning off the Hippodrome, though continuing to maintain his traveling circus, he devoted most of his time to matters outside business. Besides long vacations with Nancy, he lectured on "The World and How to Live in It," under the auspices of the Redpath Lyceum Bureau. And, for some years, he concentrated on politics.

As ever, Barnum's curiosity about the outside world was insatiable. In 1873, he was present in London at the marathon trial of Arthur Bull Orton, the 280-pound butcher from Wagga Wagga, Australia, who claimed to be the long-missing Sir Roger Tichborne and heir to the family fortune. Orton was found guilty of perjury and sentenced to fourteen years' hard labor. In 1874, Barnum was moved by the kidnapping of four-year-old Charley Ross from the front lawn of his home in Germantown, Pennsylvania, by two men in a carriage. Curly-haired little Charley, last seen in a Panama hat and brown linen suit, was never seen again, though his father spent $60,000 to find him and Barnum offered $10,000 reward for his return. In 1882, Barnum was fascinated by the lecture tour of the young Oscar

Wilde, and attended a matinee in New York, sitting in the very first row, to listen to the aesthete deplore American wallpaper and horsehair sofas and praise Pilgrim furniture. In 1886, Barnum followed closely the arrival of a new chess-playing automaton, a turbaned Moor named Ajeeb, who appeared at the three-story Eden Musee in New York and later defeated individually O. Henry, Sarah Bernhardt, and Christy Mathewson.

But, above all, Barnum remained interested in his circus. He was satisfied that "Barnum's Own Greatest Show on Earth" stood alone. Perhaps because he was energized by Nancy, the recent hesitancy and conservatism he had shown in his partnership with Coup disappeared. A revived Barnum began to reveal his renowned flair for showmanship. His circus had "millions of dollars" in attractions, and an overhead of $3,000 a day, but still it must be improved.

At a cost of $30,000 he imported six German stallions from Paris. The animals performed as a drill team and marched erect on their hind legs. He was pleased to acquire the services of an English girl named Rosa M. Richter, known professionally as Mademoiselle Zazel, "the Human Projectile." Zazel, in pink tights, was discharged by a spring from a wooden cannon, flung forty feet into the air, where she was caught by a colleague dangling from a trapeze. Among the most popular of Barnum's new attractions was the self-styled Captain Georgius Constantine, a bewhiskered Greek with the most thoroughly tattooed face and body in the world. Not a quarter of an inch of his skin was unmarked. From hair line and eyelids to genitals and toes, Constantine was covered with three hundred and eighty-eight designs, mostly of wild life. Barnum advertised him as one who had suffered the severe tattooing while in captivity. Sometimes the offenders were ferocious Albanians who hated the victim's Christianity; and other times they were savage Chinese pirates in Burma. Actually, Constantine had hired six tattoo muralists for three months to do the job.

Suddenly, in 1880, Barnum realized that he was being seriously challenged for the first time. A circus known as International Allied Shows, which had bought out Sanger's Royal British Menagerie, was making effective inroads on audiences throughout the nation. Allied Shows was owned by James E. Cooper, James Anthony Bailey, and James L.

Hutchinson. Their most recent success was a two-year tour of Australia, Java, Brazil, and Peru. They had carried their 168,000 yards of canvas, their menagerie of elephants and giraffes, and their performers, 76,000 miles without mishap and had returned to New York with enormous profits. Now they were creating a new sensation by being the first circus to advertise the use of electricity instead of gas to illuminate their two rings.

Of the three men who owned Allied Shows, one was the managerial genius, as Barnum would soon learn, and he was the thirty-three-year-old James A. Bailey. What brought Barnum into direct contact with Bailey was an elephant. On March 10, 1880, in Philadelphia, a female elephant in the Allied Shows named Hebe gave birth to a baby christened Columbia. This was the first instance of an elephant being born in captivity. The publicity was nationwide. Barnum was excited by it and he determined to own the baby elephant. But he made the mistake of regarding Allied Shows as a smaller competitor who could be bought off at a price, rather than as a full-fledged rival. When Hebe's offspring was two months old, Barnum dashed off a telegram to Cooper, Bailey, and Hutchinson offering $100,000 for Hebe and her child. Barnum was shocked when Bailey wired back a refusal to sell and audaciously advised him to look to his laurels. At once, on twelve sheets, Bailey reproduced an enlarged reproduction of Barnum's telegram, and captioned his advertising: "What Barnum thinks of the Baby Elephant."

Barnum knew that he had met his match at last, but he took it good-naturedly and sensibly. If he could not eliminate them, he would join them. "I found that I had at last met foemen 'worthy of my steel,'" Barnum admitted, "and [was] pleased to find comparatively young men with a business talent and energy approximating to my own, I met them in friendly council and after days of negotiation we decided to join our shows in one mammoth combination and, sink or swim, to exhibit them for at least one season for one price of admission. The public was astonished at our audacity, and old showmen declared that we could never take in enough money to cover our expenses, which would be fully forty-five hundred dollars per day."

Barnum's legal representatives in the merger negotiations were the bloated, flashy William F. Howe, and his bald, five-foot junior partner, Abraham H. Hummel. The union of the two circuses was made easier by the fact that Howe and Hummel were retained by Cooper, Hutchinson, and Bailey, as well as by Barnum. It was quite natural that Barnum employed Howe and Hummel as his lawyers. They were as adept at fraud and self-advertisement as he, and the most brazen and notorious legal lights in the land. Their offices, across from The Tombs, were publicized by a sign forty feet long which was illuminated by night. During the greater part of four decades, Howe and Hummel defended in court over a thousand persons indicted for manslaughter or murder. Besides Barnum, they represented at various times such celebrities of entertainment, sport, and society as John L. Sullivan, Edwin Booth, Lily Langtry, Stanford White, John Barrymore, and Lillian Russell. They represented Barnum throughout his circus career and pleased him deeply by including in all contracts a clause that permitted no consumption of alcoholic beverages by freaks in his employ.

A half-dozen years after Howe and Hummel had helped the two circuses merge, Cooper sold out for a large sum. Then Hutchinson, who had once made his living peddling Barnum's autobiography on a percentage basis, also withdrew for a price. At last, for better or for worse, it was Barnum and Bailey.

Like Barnum, the short, thin, nervous Bailey, who wore spectacles, mustache, and goatee, and a professorial air, had lifted himself to success by his own bootstraps. Like Barnum, too, he understood the inflexibility of the times and pleaded the highest morality for the show. Among his promises to the public was the following: "No camp-followers, street fakirs, gamblers, or disreputable or intoxicated persons will be tolerated on its grounds. Everything in the slightest degree calculated to offend or annoy its patrons will be absolutely prohibited. Morality, purity, and refinement will be the rule without exception." At this point, the resemblance between the two partners ended.

Bailey had been born James A. McGinnis, in Detroit during 1847. When his father died in a cholera epidemic, and his mother died shortly after, he found himself in the charge of brothers and sisters whom he intensely disliked. At twelve, he ran away from home, went to work in a Pontiac hotel, and was befriended by two advance agents for the Robinson and Lake circus. One of these agents was Frederick H. Bailey, who gave McGinnis a job in the show. McGinnis took his benefactor's name and was thereafter known as James A. Bailey. He hated his old name. Years later, when he heard that an equestrian, Billy Dutton, was telling everyone that he had once played marbles with Bailey when his name was McGinnis, he fired Dutton on the spot. During the Civil War, Bailey was a civilian sutler's clerk, and when peace came, he resumed touring with a small circus. Soon he joined Cooper and Hutchinson, and his remarkable talent for organization made him a boy wonder. He was only twenty-nine when he successfully guided the Allied Shows circus on its two-year journey around the world.

For a showman, he was extremely retiring. In complete contrast to Barnum, he avoided personal publicity and exaggeration. When celebrities or reporters were on hand, he hid in his personal quarters. He objected to use of his portrait in advertising. He found letter-writing a chore, and maintained almost all his correspondence by wire, often dispatching fifty telegrams in a single day. He wore a perpetual derby hat to screen his growing baldness, and possessed a dozen nervous mannerisms, such as chewing rubber bands and twirling a silver dollar between his fingers. He was too sensitive to fire performers personally, and always delegated the task to an assistant. He meted out justice as sternly to animals as to human beings. When an ill-tempered eight-foot elephant named Mandarin killed one of his keepers in London, Bailey calmly crated the beast for the voyage back to New York. But, in mid-ocean, Bailey weighted Mandarin's crate with pig iron and pushed it into the sea.

Logistics were Bailey's specialty. Fred Bradna, a German who became Bailey's equestrian director, wrote in *The Big Top:* "While I was in the army at Dieuze, the German military staff sent its quartermaster general to travel with Bailey and learn how to move masses of men, animals and equipment by railroad car. His techniques for loading and unloading trains and laying out lots are still, with modern modifications, in use today."

Except for a two-year period when Bailey withdrew from the partnership in protest against Barnum's egotism, the pair remained successful and congenial partners until Barnum's death. At no time was Barnum ever jealous of the younger man. He respected Bailey for his brilliance and originality and continually begged the press to credit Bailey for the success of the circus.

Barnum and his three partners first presented the results of their combined talents—the Barnum and London Circus—to New York City on March 18, 1881. Two nights earlier, the opening had been heralded by a mammoth torchlight parade. A half million people, many paying from five to ten dollars for views from windows, stood dazzled by the golden chariots and tableau cars, some drawn by teams of zebras and deer, the barred cages of leopards and hyenas, the glassed wagons of serpents, the three hundred and thirty-eight horses, twenty elephants, fourteen camels, and the three hundred and seventy costumed circus performers who marched past in review. As the magical procession continued in a seemingly unending stream, four brass bands of the circus, one composed entirely of Indians, and a wheezing steam organ or calliope enlivened the evening.

This first greatest show on earth opened in Madison Square Garden, where once the Hippodrome had flourished. Nine thousand spectators were on hand, including one hundred of the most prominent editors in the east (congregated for four days at the circus's expense), and another three thousand people clamored outside for any available seats. For the first time, three rings were used—"the only drawback," the *Herald* commented, because when the spectator's "head was turned in one direction he felt that he was losing something good in another." But if these multiple rings confused and bewildered, they also contributed to the new circus's appeal. They created an atmosphere of plenitude and riches, of size and wonder. They made every adult child feel as though he was loose in Santa's workshop with only two inadequate hands.

Beneath the new electric lights, the introductory pageant glittered and sparkled. Then followed the memorable attractions that were to make the circus a national institution: General Tom Thumb and Lavinia, the eight-foot Chinese giant named Chang-Yu Sing, the baby elephant Barnum had once tried to buy from Bailey, the harnessed giraffes, the bareback riders, the wire-rope walkers, the daredevil trapeze artists, the drilling elephants, the Japanese jugglers.

Then by rail the show was on the road. Constantly, Barnum added new attractions. The two Wild Men of Borneo, Plutano and Waino, thrilled crowds everywhere, for few knew that they were really Hiram and Barney Davis of Long Island. The Negro two-headed girl, truly twins joined at the back, received $600 a week to dance and sing before fascinated onlookers. Most popular of all was America's first Marimba Band, which Barnum claimed that Henry M. Stanley had brought out of Africa after finding Livingston at Ujiji, but which Barnum had actually recruited from the darkest Bowery.

Wherever the circus went, it was "Barnum Day" and a civic holiday. Advance posters bearing his portrait did not have to identify him by name. "The Children's Friend" was caption enough. In Washington, President James A. Garfield was on hand, as were General Sherman and Robert Todd Lincoln. The President watched the spectacle with disbelief, and later remarked in the showman's presence: "Mr. Barnum is the Kris Kringle of America."

While Barnum had little to do with the active management of the circus beyond lending his name and his accurate intuition for selecting new attractions, he did not like to see his nonparticipation advertised. When the *Philadelphia Sun* asserted that he had merely leased his name to the big show, Barnum sued for $100,000, withdrawing his charges only after the newspaper retracted the story. The truth was that even the publicity, which he had once handled himself, was now in the hands of another. Richard F. "Tody" Hamilton, graduate of Bennett's *Herald,* Wall Street, and Coup's New York Aquarium, was taken on as the circus press agent. To Hamilton an adjective was as vital to human survival as life-giving oxygen. "To state a fact in ordinary language is to permit a doubt concerning the statement," he liked to say.

As Barnum and Bailey went from success to success, a minority believed that the masses would tire of the spectacle. To one such person, Barnum remarked: "As long as there's babies there'll be circuses." And, he added another time, as long as there were clowns and elephants, the circuses would be successful.

Barnum's single great achievement as a circus proprietor, the climax of his sawdust-and-tanbark career, was his brilliant acquisition of an elephant, the internationally famous Jumbo. "It never cost me a cent to advertise Jumbo," Barnum once told Major J. B. Pond. "It was the greatest free advertising I ever heard of."

The pachyderm who came to be named Jumbo was captured as a baby by a band of Hamran Arabs in central Africa. Transported by riverboat to the coast, he was sold to a Bavarian collector of animals, Johann Schmidt, who in turn sold him to the Jardin des Plantes in Paris. He was only four feet high—African elephants mature much more slowly than the Indian species—when the discouraged French traded him to the London Zoological Society for a rhinoceros.

During his seventeen years in the London Zoological Gardens, Jumbo continued to develop. By 1882, he was twelve feet tall at the shoulders, and weighed six and a half tons. With his seven-foot trunk he was capable of reaching an object twenty-six feet from the ground. It was thought that only one other elephant in the world, the member of a maharajah's retinue in India, was larger. Jumbo's daily intake of food included two hundred pounds of hay, fifteen loaves of bread, and an assortment of oats, biscuits, onions, and fruits. Daily, too, he drank five pails of water and a quart of whiskey. He was the Gardens' leading attraction, a favorite of Queen Victoria and the royal family. He was visited by countless celebrities. Theodore Roosevelt saw him among the sights of London, the young Winston Churchill was photographed with him, and Barnum gazed at him many times with envy and once rode on his back.

In January 1882, one of Barnum's many agents abroad, knowing his master's wishes, asked Superintendent Bartlett of the Gardens if he would consider selling Jumbo. At first the Superintendent was outraged at the suggestion. But when the agent confirmed that Barnum was prepared to offer $10,000 for the behemoth, the Superintendent reconsidered.

Jumbo was going through an irritable period, known as "must," common to all male elephants. He was in bad temper, likely to go berserk, and there was the possibility that this time he might have to be destroyed. If he was ever to be sold, this was the moment. After two days of private debate, the Council of the London Zoological Society agreed to sell Jumbo to Barnum. The news was cabled to the showman, who immediately consulted his partners.

Hutchinson, alone, objected to the purchase. "What is the difference between an elephant seven feet high and another eleven or twelve feet high?" he asked. "An elephant is an elephant." But Barnum would not be dissuaded. "I insisted that this was the greatest beast in the world, and urged that, being such, Barnum's Circus couldn't afford to be without him. Finally the objections of my partner were overruled." At once, Barnum sent $10,000 to London by steamer in the form of a £2,000 bank draft, and the deal was concluded. But, the moment the Society made the sale public, a storm of protest broke out the likes of which had been rarely seen in Great Britain.

Queen Victoria, the Prince of Wales, John Ruskin, and *The Times* all demanded that the contract be broken. If Barnum successfully sued the Society, the government was ready to assume all responsibility for damages. The London *Standard* compared the act of separating Jumbo from his British public to that of a Southern slave-owner separating a Negro family at auction. "Surely, to tear this aged brute from a home to which he is attached, and from associates who have so markedly displayed their affection for him, is scarcely less cruel." Thousands of English subjects, adults and children alike, showered the Society and Barnum with letters imploring him to withdraw his bid.

The Editor of the London *Daily Telegraph* cabled Barnum: "Editor's compliments; all British children distressed at Elephant's departure; hundreds of correspondents beg us to inquire on what terms you will kindly return Jumbo. Answer, prepaid, unlimited." Barnum promptly cabled back: "My compliments to Editor Daily Telegraph and British Nation. Fifty-one millions of American citizens anxiously awaiting Jumbo's arrival. My forty years' invariable practice of exhibiting the best that money could procure makes Jumbo's presence here imperative. My largest tent seats 20,000 persons, and is filled twice each day. It contains four rings, in three of which three full circus companies give different performances simultaneously."

In despair, the *Daily Telegraph* reprinted the cable and mourned editorially: "Jumbo's fate is sealed. The disappointing answer from his new American proprietor . . . proves too clear that there is nothing to expect from delicacy or remorse in that quarter. . . . To increase the general regret, the message depicts the sort of life which poor Jumbo has before him. No more quiet garden strolls, no shady trees, green lawns, and flowery thickets. . . . We fear, however, that Jumbo will never come back to us alive. His mighty heart will probably break with rage, shame, and grief; and we may hear of him, like another Samson, playing the mischief with the Philistines who have led him into captivity, and dying amid some scene of terrible wrath and ruin."

Public sentiment continued unabated. "All England seemed to run mad about Jumbo," Barnum said; "pictures of Jumbo, the life of Jumbo, a pamphlet headed 'Jumbo-Barnum,' and all sorts of Jumbo stories and poetry, Jumbo Hats, Jumbo Collars, Jumbo Cigars, Jumbo Neckties, Jumbo Fans, Jumbo Polkas, etc., were sold by the tens of thousands in the stores and streets of London and other British cities." United States Ambassador James Russell Lowell remarked at a banquet in London that "the only burning question between England and America is Jumbo."

At last a legal effort was made to retain Jumbo. Several Fellows of the Royal Zoological Society, led by one Berkeley Hill, in protest against their majority, asked the court for an injunction to halt removal. Their argument was that the Society had no right to sell any article "valuable for the study of natural history," and that it was morally wrong to dispose of a dangerous beast. The hearing was held in the Chancery division of the High Court of Justice on March 9, 1882. It was proved that the Society had sold animals before, in particular a gnu for $750. The Court decided that if Jumbo was dangerous, that was Barnum's problem and not one that involved the Society. In short, the sale to Barnum was held to be proper and valid.

The moment had come to remove Jumbo from the Gardens to Barnum's circus. Barnum had a chartered English freighter, the *Assyrian Monarch,* waiting in the Thames. One full deck of the ship had been cut away to make room for the elephant. When Jumbo's keeper of twenty years, Matthew Scott, reluctantly led the recluse out of the Gardens into the unfamiliar street, the elephant trumpeted his displeasure and settled down on the pavement. All England wept. Barnum's agent cabled the showman: "Jumbo has laid down in the street, and won't get up. What shall we do?" Barnum replied: "Let him lie there a week if he wants to. It is the best advertisement in the world."

Considering the problem, Barnum conceived a ruse to trap the elephant. He ordered an immense van on wheels, clamped with iron, constructed. It had doors on either end. These were left open when Scott led Jumbo through the open van on his daily walk to the exercise ground. "For several days this ruse was repeated," said Barnum, "then, as he entered the cage, the door behind him was swiftly closed, then the door in front of him, and Jumbo was mine."

Jumbo resented the trick briefly and violently, but then settled down. In the night, he was dragged off six miles to the Thames, where crowds had already gathered, then hoisted aboard a lighter by steam crane, moved down river to the steamer, and lifted to the deck by tackle. After being placated with beer, he relaxed in his illuminated crate with Scott snoring beside him. The Atlantic crossing took fifteen days. Jumbo was seasick two of those days, but after that he appeared placid and hopeful. On the morning of Easter Sunday 1882, he arrived in New York City.

As usual, Broadway was thick with people. Jumbo in his wheeled iron van was drawn by sixteen horses to Madison Square Garden, where the circus was playing. The next day he became the star of the greatest show on earth. To emphasize his stature, he was displayed beside a baby elephant known as Tom Thumb. Because he had long led a retired English life, the din from Barnum's four bands and the activity of the circus performers frightened him. But after a while, he became accustomed to the excitement. At no time was he ever dangerous.

The purchase and transportation of Jumbo had cost Barnum and his partners $30,000. Barnum had that amount back in ten days, and in six weeks, Jumbo grossed $336,000 for his owners. In his first season of thirty-one weeks, spent in New York and on tour throughout America, he drew receipts totaling one million seven hundred and fifty dollars. For three and a half years, ridden by an estimated million children, gulping down endless quantities of peanuts and candy, he enriched the lives of America's young and the pocketbooks of the circus.

On the evening of September 15, 1885, Jumbo and his tiny companion, Tom Thumb, had finished their performance in St. Thomas, Ontario, Canada. The show's thirty-one other elephants had already been loaded on the waiting train when, at nine o'clock, Matthew Scott led Jumbo and Tom Thumb to their private car. As they crossed the freight yard, the threesome marched along an unused spur line of the Grand Trunk Railway. Suddenly there was the rising clang of an approaching locomotive. An unscheduled special freight train rounded the bend, and from five hundred yards away its glaring headlights held on the terrified Jumbo. The train, closing the gap at breakneck speed, tried to jam to a halt, but too late. Scott leaped aside in time as the locomotive hit Tom Thumb a glancing blow, breaking his left hind leg, and tossing him aside to safety. Then the engine plowed head-on into Jumbo's towering body. The locomotive and two cars were smashed and derailed, and the engineer was killed. Jumbo, his skull fractured, blood oozing from his mouth, flanks, and feet, went down to his knees and then rolled to his side. His trunk beckoned Scott. In a few moments, he was dead.

Jumbo's end saddened the world. According to Barnum, nine million Americans had seen him. He insisted that his one thought was of those thousands more who would be deprived of the pleasure. Barnum was never one to let sentiment interfere with practical business. "The loss is tremendous, but such a trifle never disturbs my nerves," he told the press. "Long ago I learned that to those who mean right and try to do right, there are no such things as real misfortunes. On the other hand, to such persons, all apparent evils are blessings in disguise." So it was not surprising to anyone that Barnum capitalized on Jumbo's death.

Taxidermists applied their skills to the mammoth carcass. Jumbo's teeth and bones proved that he was still growing before his death. His stomach gave up a small mint of English coins. His skeleton was presented to the Museum of Natural History in New York. But his hide, which in itself weighed 1,538 pounds, was settled on a shaped frame of hard wood, and thus Jumbo continued to serve the circus until, at last, he was turned over to the Barnum Museum at Tufts College in Medford, Massachusetts, a school favored by Barnum because of its Universalist leanings. To this day, Jumbo may be seen at Tufts alongside Barnum's handwritten account of his death and a bust of the showman.

Just as Barnum always sought, but never found, a singer

to equal Jenny Lind, he persisted in trying to locate another elephant to match the box-office appeal of Jumbo. He bought Alice, Jumbo's female companion in the London Gardens, from the Society, and showed her as Jumbo's "widow" beside the stuffed carcass. But this did not satisfy, and Barnum finally gave up.

Even the year before Jumbo's death, Barnum had been attempting to find another colorful elephant. This promotion, which turned out to be a failure, engaged him in the deadliest circus war of his career. It had long been Barnum's ambition to show a genuine sacred white elephant of the Far East. After three years of effort and an expenditure of $250,000, by the showman's estimate, a sacred white elephant named Toung Taloung was secured in Mandalay, through permission of King Theebaw of Siam. Shipped from Rangoon to London, and thence to New York, it arrived aboard the steamer *Lydian Monarch* on March 28, 1884, its appearance celebrated by three prize-winning poems, one written by Joaquin Miller.

Barnum had been advertising the sacred elephant as of purest milk-white hue. But when he went on the steamer, followed by the press, to observe his purchase, he found Toung Taloung's complexion a dirty gray except for a few light pink spots and pink eyes. Appalled, Barnum tried to swallow his disappointment. "Well," he lamely told the reporters, "it's whiter than I expected to find it."

Later, with Bailey beside him, Barnum presided at a reception for the press in the ship's dining room. One young reporter, emboldened by the free beverages, called out to the showman: "Mr. Barnum, I don't think your elephant is so very white." The room was suddenly hushed. Barnum did not bat an eyelash. "My boy," he said, "in my youth I was fond of attending sociables. At one such party I unwisely expressed the opinion that a young lady's extraordinary complexion was not genuine. Unfortunately she overheard my tactless remark. As she passed me she said, without introduction, 'God made these cheeks.' Now, sir, God made that white elephant, but I assure you had he been made by Mr. Bailey or myself he would be as white as the driven snow."

Because the elephant was not white, Barnum went to great lengths to get Siamese experts to authenticate it. Meanwhile, his leading circus rival, the gray-haired, self-centered Adam Forepaugh, began to exploit and exhibit a pure white elephant named Light of Asia.

Forepaugh, a Philadelphia meat dealer turned showman, plagued Barnum for years. He had stolen Madison Square Garden from Barnum by leasing it far in advance. He had hired the nation's foremost clown, Dan Rice, for $1,000 a week. When Barnum had Jumbo, Forepaugh advertised Bolivar, as the "largest and heaviest elephant in the world." Now Forepaugh summoned the press to view another sacred elephant whiter than Barnum's.

While Forepaugh disarmed the reporters with drinks, a sober journalist from the *Philadelphia Press,* Alexander C. Kenealy, sneaked toward the white elephant with a soaked sponge. He rubbed the creature's flank, and removal of the coating of white paint revealed the animal's natural gray beneath. Instead of publishing his exposé, Kenealy sold it to Barnum, who advertised Forepaugh's deception wherever Americans could read. Despite the exposé, Forepaugh's white-coated elephant outdrew Barnum's genuine gray one. When Forepaugh died in 1890, his circus was taken over by Bailey.

Barnum's last great adventure as a showman took place in November 1889, when he and Bailey presented their most expensive circus at the London Olympia, an arena larger than Madison Square Garden. This first invasion of England with a circus was Bailey's idea. Barnum considered it a financial risk, but finally went along with the plan. In advance of animals and personnel, a ship carrying eight tons of advertising material, including 50,000 posters, was sent across the Atlantic. Then, slings loaded the animals on the decks of the *Furnessia.* Because lions and tigers were no novelty in England, Barnum left them behind. "The question of providing so many flesh-eating animals with food during the voyage," *Harper's Weekly* reported in 1889, "was solved by freezing the fresh meat in cubical cakes, and then packing it in refrigerators between layers of ice." Accompanying the animals were 1,240 circus performers. And lastly, somewhat apprehensive aboard the *Etruria,* traveled Barnum and his wife Nancy.

Barnum had every reason to worry. He feared resentment over the Jumbo incident. He and Bailey had spent $350,000 in shipping the circus, and were contracted to pay the Olympia $12,000 a day for one hundred days. But the opening night ended all his fears. Fifteen thousand persons crammed into the Olympia to applaud the spectacle "Nero, or The Burning of Rome," and newspapers were in ecstasies. The *Dramatic News* said: "Barnum, of course, has been the inexhaustible topic in all circles, including theatrical ones, this week. In fact there is very little else talked about."

Almost every one of the one hundred nights was memorable. During most of them Barnum put in a personal appearance. "Whenever my manager advertises that I am to be present," he explained, "he estimates the increase in the receipts to be 200 pounds per day." In the midst of the show, Barnum would arrive in an open carriage drawn by two horses. All activity in the three rings would cease while he made his way slowly around the track to mounting applause, halting several times to call out to the audience: "I suppose you come to see Barnum, didn't you? Wa-al, I'm Mr. Barnum." Then he would continue to the exit, and the lesser attractions in the three rings would come to life again.

No one who was any one in London missed the spectacle. Even Queen Victoria, with the Prince of Wales in tow, attended. When one of Barnum's leading clowns, Robert Edmund Sherwood, pranced out before her, pantomimed the cleaning of his hands, and offered one to the Queen, the old showman, said Sherwood, "was jumping around like a chicken on a hot griddle." But the Queen graciously took the clown's hand, and the applause was deafening. Delighted though he was, Barnum would not permit Sherwood to do an encore. "If you go on again, how do I know you won't invite her out to dinner?"

When former Prime Minister Gladstone attended the circus with his wife and party, Barnum was a guest in his box. They discussed Barnum's autobiography—Gladstone had enjoyed it but objected to the fine print—and then the Roman spectacle taking place before them. "Mr. Gladstone complimented me upon the youthfulness of my appearance," Barnum informed a reporter, "but I want to tell you that I think he looks much younger than I do. You see, he was eighty in December—I shall not be eighty until July."

Returning to Bridgeport from his final triumph, Barnum and Nancy moved into their new house, called Marina by Mrs. Barnum. Nancy had long felt that Waldemere was too large to manage and too old-fashioned. So, a few feet east of it, Barnum had built the considerably smaller Marina in the Queen Anne style. It had modern electricity and plumbing, and the moment it was done, Barnum razed Waldemere and gave the deed of Marina to his wife. According to Harvey W. Root in *The Unknown Barnum,* when a friend wondered why Barnum needed the new house, Barnum wrote him: "My wife is but thirty-eight years old. I must soon leave her a widow. She loves Bridgeport and its people. Waldemere is too large for her, but its site is unequaled. So I said to her, 'You plan and oversee the construction of a solid brick-and-stone house. . . .' So she erected the new house. She said, 'Let it be made,' and it was made."

In 1880 Barnum had been critically ill, but an iron constitution had helped him survive. Now, in 1890, he was failing again. After a last vacation in Colorado with Nancy and a last visit to the circus in Kansas City, he returned to Marina to rest. In November, he was struck down by what was diagnosed as acute congestion of the brain. For three weeks, he hovered between life and death, but once more he recovered.

While Bailey conducted the big show, Barnum remained confined to Marina. He was a national institution, and he gloried in it. When an envelope postmarked Bombay, and addressed only to "Mr. Barnum, America," was promptly delivered to him, he was childishly pleased. When a company that he partially owned constructed a schooner and christened it *P. T. Barnum,* he left his sick bed to wave to it as it passed down the harbor.

He busied himself with his will. To the fourteen-page testament written eight years before, he had added a seventeen-page codicil in the spring of 1889. Now, he added three more codicils, and soon he would add four more, the final one (laying out plans for "The Barnum Institute of Science and History" in Bridgeport) a week before his death.

He fretted about his autobiography. The last version, published in 1888, had ended with the last confession he was to write for print: "As I close this volume I am more thankful than words can express that my health is preserved, and that I am blessed with a vigor and buoyancy of spirit vouchsafed to but few; but I am by no means insensible to the fact that I have reached the evening of life (which is well lighted, however), and I am glad to know that though this is indeed a beautiful, delightful world to those who have the temperament, the resolution, and the judgment to make it so, yet it is happily not our abiding place; and that he is unwise who sets his heart so firmly upon its transitory pleasures as to feel a reluctance to obey the call when his Father makes it, to leave all behind and to come up higher, in that Great Future when all that we now prize so highly (except our love to God and man) shall dwindle into insignificance." He had hoped to append more of his personal story to this, but now he knew that it was too late. And so he asked Nancy to write the final chapter of his book, after he had gone, and this she solemnly pledged to do.

Daily he rose from his bed, dressed, sat for a few hours at his bay window overlooking the Sound, then received business callers and friends. Although Nancy knew better, he continually reassured her: "Now I feel that I am really getting well." Because he subscribed to Greeley's *Tribune* and the Bridgeport papers, scanning them always for comments on his condition, Nancy was forced to ask the press to avoid speculating on his death. For the most part, the press obliged. As 1890 gave way to 1891 and he entered his eighty-first year, he was aware that his favorite newspapers were filled with new names: David Belasco, Edward Bellamy, George Eastman, Marie Corelli, DeWolf Hopper, Eugene Field, James J. Corbett, Walter Camp, William Jennings Bryan, Nellie Bly, Rudyard Kipling, Charles Bolden, Clyde Fitch—all entertaining the sixty-three million Americans whom he had prepared for a new century of fun.

The reality of an end to life was unthinkable. Perhaps, he thought, he was not merely mortal. Nancy Barnum later wrote: "I do not think that, until the last two weeks of his sickness, Mr. Barnum gave up his hope of getting well. There was nothing to show when he gave up clinging to the life he so much enjoyed and loved so well. Of his own death he would not speak; of death in the abstract, he said: 'It is a good thing, a beautiful thing, just as much so as life; and it is wrong to grieve about it, and to look on it as an evil.'"

Three physicians were in attendance upon him, and, to allay Barnum's growing claustrophobia, two of them, Dr.

C. C. Godfrey and Dr. John Lynch, alternated in sleeping in his bedroom with him. Near at hand, always, were Nancy, a colored valet, Wyatt Roberts, and a nurse. When he knew that the end could no longer be postponed, Barnum made arrangements for a modest funeral—he had had enough of shows and parades and spectacles—but in making the concluding arrangements, at no time mentioned the word death. He wondered what the newspapers would say of him after he was gone. Learning of this, *The Evening Sun* of New York asked permission to publish his obituary in advance, so that he might enjoy it. He gave his permission, and on March 24 he reveled in the headline: "GREAT AND ONLY BARNUM. He Wanted To Read His Obituary; Here It Is." According to the *Sun,* Barnum had told a friend that he would be happier if he had "the chance to see what sort of lines" would be written about him after his death. "Mr. Barnum has had almost everything in this life, including the woolly horse and Jenny Lind," the *Sun* explained, "and there is no reason why he should not have this last pleasure which he asks for. So here is the great showman's life, briefly and simply told, as it would have appeared in *The Evening Sun* had fate taken our Great and Only from us. It will be read with as great interest by the public as by Mr. Barnum." There followed, then, four biographical columns of newsprint illustrated with woodcuts of Barnum at his present age, of Barnum at the age of forty-one, of his mother, of Charity, and of Jenny Lind.

Briefly, he rallied. And then again he sank. Through the dark morning of April 7, 1891, his heart beat grew more feeble. Nancy sent telegrams summoning members of the family. The night before, he had inquired about the box-office receipts of the circus. It was his last business request. At two o'clock in the morning, he told his wife: "My last thoughts are of you." At four o'clock, he was asked if he wanted a glass of water. "Yes," he replied. He slept until eight in the morning. Then, upon being told some election news, he said: "I am glad."

"All that weary day," Nancy Barnum wrote, "as his sorrowing children and grandchildren gathered at his bedside, a faint word of tenderness, faint as a breath, fluttered forth to greet each one.

"Morning wore into afternoon, and afternoon into the dusk of early evening. Death was kind, and no physical pain disturbed the quiet figure on the little bed. Quicker and quicker beat the tired heart, then slower and still slower; and at 6:34, with undaunted heart and unclouded brain, passed out of this place of being which we call life, one of the most remarkable and best loved men of the country."

Long, long before, as a boy of ten, he had dreamed of a shimmering, magical place known as Ivy Island. It had disappointed him. But still he held the dream, and eventually all the wide world became the fairyland he had cherished on that hot, sunny day in childhood. The dream he had made a reality, and now he needed to dream no more.

Thousands who had known Barnum crowded about the South Congregational Church while inside the Reverend Robert Collyer, bent and gray, with tears rolling down his face, spoke the eulogy over Barnum's body.

"P. T. Barnum was a born fighter for the weak against the strong, for the oppressed against the oppressor. The good heart, tender as it was brave, would always spring up at the cry for help and rush on with the sword of assistance. This was not all that made him loved, for the good cheer of his nature was like a halo about him. He had always time to right a wrong and always time to be a good citizen and patriot of the town, State, or Republic in which he lived."

The funeral cortege wended slowly over the long, last mile, past flags at half-mast, to the beautiful Mountain Grove Cemetery, where he was laid to rest beside Charity. Later, his statue in bronze, the work of Thomas Ball, was presented to Bridgeport by Bailey and members of the circus, and mounted in Seaside Park at the edge of the Sound.

His last notices would have pleased him. *The Times* of London led them all:

"Barnum is gone. That fine flower of Western civilization, that *arbiter elegantiarum* to Demos . . . gave, in the eyes of the seekers after amusement, a lustre to America. . . . He created the *metier* of showman on a grandiose scale, worthy to be professed by a man of genius. He early realized that essential feature of a modern democracy, its readiness to be led to what will amuse and instruct it. He knew that 'the people' means crowds, paying crowds; that crowds love the fashion and will follow it; and that the business of the great man is to make and control the fashion. To live on, by, and before the public was his ideal. For their sake and his own, he loved to bring the public to see, to applaud, and to pay. . . .

"When, in 1889, the veteran brought over his shipload of giants and dwarfs, chariots and waxworks, spangles and circus-riders, to entertain the people of London, one wanted a Carlyle to come forward with a discourse upon 'the Hero as Showman.' . . . There was a three-fold show— the things in the stalls and cages, the showman, and the world itself. And of the three perhaps Barnum himself was the most interesting. The chariot races and the monstrosities we can get elsewhere, but the octogenarian showman was unique. His name is a proverb already, and a proverb it will continue."

His immortality lay in the age he spawned. Because of his break-through of the social barriers against entertainment and his uses of curiosity and sensation, a diversity of heirs was born to walk in his footsteps: Tony Pastor, Oscar Hammerstein I, Charles Frohman, Richard D'Oyly Carte, Florenz Ziegfeld, John Ringling, John Ringling North, C. B. Cochran, Sol Hurok, Mike Todd, Billy Rose, C. C. Pyle, Tex Rickard, the brothers Shubert, and a hundred more, offering every variety and type of fun.

He had wanted the last chapter of his autobiography written. Faithfully, before departing for France, Nancy Barnum wrote it with affection and grace. She published it in a nineteen-page pamphlet, and her adieu was a farewell from one and everyone.

"But a better fame is his, for, though the busy hands are folded, the cheery voice stilled, and the kindly smile hid forever, he lives in the love of his devoted family; in the hearts of all who came within the circle of his wonderfully magnetic personality; and, it will be long ere the world forgets P. T. Barnum."

ACKNOWLEDGMENTS AND BIBLIOGRAPHY

I am deeply indebted to Martin Jurow, of Los Angeles, California, and Richard Shepherd, of Beverly Hills, California, for suggesting to me the subject of this biography. Without their continued encouragement and enthusiasm, this book could not have been written.

I am especially grateful to Helen Gladys Percey and Dorothy R. Robinson, both of Los Angeles, for assuming so large a burden of the research.

I wish to thank Elizebethe Kempthorne, of Arlington, California, for her editorial assistance; Margaret Solensten, of Los Angeles, for her untiring stenographic aid; Jay D. Barnes, President of the Yates County Genealogical and Historical Society, in Penn Yan, New York, for his cooperation.

My heartiest appreciation must go to Elizabeth Sterling Seeley, curator of that remarkable showcase and archive of Americana, The Barnum Museum in Bridgeport, Connecticut, for her thorough investigation of elusive facts and her detailed replies to all the difficult questions that I asked of her. Too, I am beholden to Miss Seeley for putting at my disposal information from Phineas T. Barnum's private journal, address books, circus route books, last will and testament, as well as portions of Caroline Barnum Thompson's unpublished diary.

My thanks, also, to E. P. Dutton and Company, New York, for their permission to let me reprint an extract from *Sketches in Criticism* by Van Wyck Brooks.

Above all, I suppose, I owe gratitude to Phineas T. Barnum himself. This volume represents the first new biography of the showman written for adults in over three decades. It could not possibly have been accomplished with any degree of completeness without the collaboration of Barnum, whose autobiography and numerous magazine articles remain the prime research sources on his long and varied life.

Between the years 1855 and 1888, there were published at least nine new versions or revised editions of Barnum's autobiography. I have relied mainly on one edition brought out when he was sixty-one: it proved more comprehensive than his first edition and less expurgated than his last. It was entitled *Struggles and Triumphs: or, Forty Years' Recollections of P. T. Barnum Written by P. T. Barnum,* American News Company, 1871. Two editions printed after the showman's death combined material from all of Barnum's autobiographies, and they proved most valuable. One was *Struggles and Triumphs: or, The Life of P. T. Barnum, Written by Himself,* edited by George S. Bryan, brought out in two volumes by Alfred A. Knopf, 1927. The other was *Barnum's Own Story* by P. T. Barnum, edited by Waldo R. Browne, The Viking Press, 1927.

Of the full-length biographies written about Barnum, I found most interesting the *Life of Hon. Phineas T. Barnum* by Joel Benton, Edgewood Publishing Company, 1891, which was largely a paraphrasing of the autobiography into the third person, but which contained a few personal observations of the author who knew Barnum well; *Barnum* by M. A. Werner, Harcourt, Brace and Company, 1923, which was the first scholarly and witty effort successfully to challenge and supplement material in the autobiography; *The Unknown Barnum* by Harvey W. Root, Harper and Brothers, 1927, which provided excellent source material on Barnum's publishing and political careers. The most readable of the several juvenile books concerned with Barnum was *The World's Greatest Showman* by J. Bryan III, Random House, 1956.

Curiously, in no biography of Barnum has there been any organized or sustained attempt to examine his personal life—that is, his personality and habits, and his relationship with both of his wives and his three daughters. I have attempted, as well as I could, to rectify this omission. Besides covering the more or less standard facts of the showman's life in sources employed by previous biographers, I have tried to shed a little more light on his career in the American Museum and the circus, his advertising methods and hoaxes, his involvement with his numerous prodigies, through use of sources overlooked or ignored in his lifetime and later.

Finally, it was my definite intent to illuminate, in a small way, the lives of those people who surrounded Barnum: friends, enemies, business associates, odd acquaintances, employees. Perhaps every man's circle, studied closely, is curious. But more than most, Barnum attracted a veritable zoo of strange and fascinating characters. His life was as well populated with human curiosities as was his American Museum, and I have gone far afield in my research to put them all on display alongside the hero of this work.

The bibliography that follows is by no means complete. In the interests of space conservation, I have confined myself to the most serviceable books and periodicals on Barnum and his circle and his time. To their authors and publishers in two centuries, my sincere thanks.

Nineteenth-century Books

Anonymous: *The Great Eccentric Characters of the World.* New York: Hurst; n.d.

Anonymous: *Portrait and Biographical Record of Denver and Vicinity.* Chicago: Chapman; 1898.

Arnold, Matthew: *Letters of Matthew Arnold.* 2 Vols. New York: The Macmillan Company; 1895.

Barnum, Phineas Taylor: *The Humbugs of the World.* New York: Carleton; 1866.

Barnum, Phineas Taylor: *Struggles and Triumphs; or, Forty Years' Recollection.* New York: American News Co.; 1871.

Barnum, Phineas Taylor, and Sarah J. Burke: *P. T. Barnum's Cirkus,* Text und Illustrationen eingerichtet für kleine Leute. New York: White and Allen; 1888.

—— *P. T. Barnum's Museum.* New York: White and Allen; 1888.

Belden, E. Porter: *New-York Past, Present, and Future.* New York: Putnam; 1849.

Benton, Joel: *Life of Honorable Phineas T. Barnum.* Philadelphia: Edgewood; 1891.

Browne, Junius H.: *Great Metropolis.* Hartford, Conn.: American Publishing; 1869.

Dickens, Charles: *American Notes.* Philadelphia: Gebbie; 1895.

Field, Maunsell B.: *Memories of Many Men and of Some Women.* New York: Harper & Brothers; 1874.

Greenwood, Isaac J.: *The Circus; Its Origin and Growth Prior To 1835.* New York: Dunlap Society; 1898.

Hall, Frank: *The History of the State of Colorado.* 4 Vols. Chicago: Blakely; 1890.

Haswell, Charles Haynes: *Reminiscences of an Octogenarian.* New York: Harper & Brothers; 1897.

Holland, Henry Scott, and W. S. Rockstro: *Memoir of Madame Jenny Lind-Goldschmidt.* 2 Vols. London: Murray; 1891.

Houghton, Walter R. ed.: *Kings of Fortune.* Chicago: Davis; 1886.

Leland, Charles Godfrey: *Memoirs.* New York: Appleton; 1893.

McCabe, James D., Jr.: *Lights and Shadows of New York Life.* Philadelphia: National Publishing; 1872.

Orcutt, Samuel: *The History of the Township of Stratford and the City of Bridgeport.* 2 Vols. New Haven: Tuttle, Morehouse, and Taylor; 1886.

Parton, James: *Famous Americans of Recent Times.* Boston: Ticknor and Fields; 1867.

Robert-Houdin, Jean Eugene: *Life of Robert Houdin, the King of Conjurers. Written by Himself.* Tr. by Dr. R. Shelton Mackenzie, Philadelphia: Henry T. Coates; 1859.

Smith, Matthew Hale: *Sunshine and Shadows in New York.* Hartford, Conn.: Burr, 1869.

Stowe, Harriet Beecher: *Lives and Deeds of Our Self-made Men.* Hartford, Conn.: Worthington, Dustin: 1872.

Tomes, Robert: *War with the South.* 3 Vols. New York: Virtue and Yorston; 1862.

Valentine, David T.: *History of Broadway.* New York; n.d.

Vickers, William B.: *History of the City of Denver.* Chicago: Baskin; 1880.

Walsh, William S.: *A Handy-book of Literary Curiosities.* Philadelphia: J. B. Lippincott Company; 1892.

Nineteenth-century Periodicals

Blackwood's, of London, February, 1855; *Bridgeport Farmer* and *Bridgeport Daily Standard,* issues from 1866 through 1899; *English Illustrated,* of London, Vol. 18; *Harper's Weekly,* February 13, 1864, March 21, 1868, October 29, 1870, January 11, 1873, March 27, 1875, September 27, 1879, July 17, 1880, February 18, 1882, December 3, 1887, November, 2, 1889, April 1, 1891; *Harper's Magazine,* December 1881; *Illustrated London News,* issues from 1845 through 1891.

Leslie's Illustrated Newspaper, May 20, 1871; *Littell's Living Age,* Vol. 44, 1855; *Murray's Magazine,* of London, January 1890 (an article by P. T. Barnum); *Nation,* March 7, 1867; *New York Evening Sun,* March 1891; *New York Herald* and *New York Tribune,* issues from 1841 through 1891; *New York Evening Telegram,* November 1873; *New York World,* January 1897; *North American Review,* June 1891 (an article by P. T. Barnum); *Scientific American,* April 1, 1899; *Tait's Edinburgh Magazine,* Vol. 22, 1855.

Twentieth-century Books

Abbott, Lyman: *Silhouettes of My Contemporaries.* Garden City: Doubleday, Page; 1921.

Adams, James Truslow, ed.: *Album of American History.* 5 Vols. New York: Charles Scribner's Sons; 1944–9.

Aldrich, Richard: *Musical Discourse.* New York: Oxford; 1928.

Asbury, Herbert: *All Around the Town.* New York: Alfred A. Knopf; 1929.

Aswell, James R., ed.: *Native American Humor.* New York: Harper & Brothers; 1947.

Aubry, Octave: *Eugénie.* Philadelphia: J. B. Lippincott Company; 1931.

Bailey, J. O.: *Pilgrims through Space and Time*. Mohegan Lake, N. Y.: Argus Books; 1947.

Barnum, Phineas Taylor: *Animal Stories*. Akron, Ohio: Saalfield Publishing Company; 1926.

—— *Barnum's Own Story*, edited by Waldo R. Browne. New York: Viking; 1927.

—— *Forest and Jungle*. Akron, Ohio: Saalfield Publishing Company; 1907.

—— *Struggles and Triumphs: or, The Life of P. T. Barnum. Written by Himself*, edited by George S. Bryan. 2 Vols. New York: Alfred A. Knopf; 1927.

Barschak, Erna: *The Innocent Empress*. New York: E. P. Dutton & Co.; 1943.

Barton, Margaret, and Osbert Sitwell, ed.: *Sober Truth*. London: MacDonald & Co. (Publishers); 1944.

Basso, Hamilton: *Mainstream*. New York: Reynal & Hitchcock; 1942.

Bishop, Morris: *A Gallery of Eccentrics*. New York: Minton, Balch & Co.; 1928.

Bodin, Walter, and Burnet Hershey: *It's a Small World*. New York: Coward-McCann; 1934.

Bonte, George W.: *America Marches Past*. New York: D. Appleton-Century Company; 1936.

Bradford, Gamaliel: *Damaged Souls*. Boston: Houghton Mifflin Company; 1922.

Bradna, Fred, and Hartzell Spence: *Big Top*. New York: Simon and Schuster; 1952.

Brierly, J. Ernest: *Streets of Old New York*. New York: Hastings House; 1953.

Britt, Albert, ed.: *The Great Biographers*. New York: Whittlesey House; 1936.

Brooks, Van Wyck: *Sketches in Criticism*. New York: E. P. Dutton & Co.; 1932.

—— *The Times of Melville and Whitman*. New York: E. P. Dutton & Co.; 1947.

Brown, Henry Collins: *Brownstone Fronts and Saratoga Trunks*. New York: E. P. Dutton & Co.; 1935.

—— *Fifth Avenue Old and New*. New York: Fifth Avenue Association; 1924.

Brown, Henry Collins, ed.: *Valentine's Manual of the City of New York*. New York: Valentine's; 1926.

Bryan, Joseph: *The World's Greatest Showman*. New York: Random House; 1956.

Bulman, Joan: *Jenny Lind*. London: J. James Barrie, Publishers; 1956.

Butterfield, Roger: *The American Past*. New York: Simon and Schuster; 1947.

Callender, James H.: *Yesterdays in Little Old New York*. New York: Borland; 1929.

Carlson, Oliver: *The Man Who Made News*. New York: Duell, Sloan & Pearce; 1942.

Carmer, Carl, ed.: *Cavalcade of America*. New York: Lothrop, Lee & Shepard Co.; 1956.

Chidsey, Donald Barr: *John the Great*. New York: Doubleday, Doran; 1942.

Clarke, John S.: *Circus Parade*. London: B. T. Batsford; 1936.

Coad, Oral Summer, and Edwin Mims, Jr.: *The Pageant of America*. New York: Oxford; 1929.

Conklin, George: *Ways of the Circus*. New York: Harper & Brothers; 1921.

Cooke, Charles: *Big Show*. New York: Harper & Brothers; 1938.

Coup, William Cameron: *Sawdust and Spangles*. Chicago: Stone; 1901.

Cowles, Virginia: *Edward VII and His Circle*. London: Hamilton & Co.; 1956.

Croffut, William A.: *An American Procession*. Boston: Little, Brown & Company; 1931.

Croft-Cooke, Rupert, ed.: *Circus Book*. London: Sampson Low, Marston; n.d.

Cutter, William R., and others, eds.: *Genealogical and Family History of the State of Connecticut*. New York: Lewis Historical Publishing Company; 1911.

Davidson, Marshall B.: *Life in America*. 2 Vols. Boston: Houghton Mifflin Company; 1951.

Desmond, Alice Curtis: *Barnum Presents: General Tom Thumb*. New York: The Macmillan Company; 1954.

Dibble, Roy F.: *Strenuous Americans*. New York: Boni & Liveright; 1923.

Dowdey, Clifford: *Experiment in Rebellion*. New York: Doubleday & Co.; 1946.

Dulles, Foster Rhea: *America Learns to Play*. New York: D. Appleton-Century Company; 1940.

Dumas, Alexandre: *The Last King*. 2 Vols. London: Paul; 1915.

Dunshee, Kenneth H.: *As You Pass By*. New York: Hastings House; 1952.

Durant, John, and Alice Durant: *Pictorial History of the American Circus*. New York: Barnes; 1957.

Earle, Alice M.: *Home Life in Colonial Days*. New York: The Macmillan Company; 1913.

Edwards, Frank: *Strangest of All*. New York: Citadel Press; 1956.

Fellows, Dexter, and Andrew Freeman: *This Way to the Big Show*. Garden City: Halcyon House Publications; 1938.

Foster, Freling: *Keep Up with the World*. New York: Grosset & Dunlap; 1949.

Gilbert, Douglas: *American Vaudeville*. New York: Whittlesey House; 1940.

Godden, Rumer: *Hans Christian Andersen*. New York: Alfred A. Knopf; 1956.

Gray, Wood: *The Hidden Civil War*. New York: The Viking Press; 1942.

Guedella, Philip: *Supers and Supermen*. Garden City: Garden City Publishing; 1924.

Hamid, George A.: *Circus*. New York: Sterling Publishing Company; 1950.

Hart, James D.: *The Popular Book*. New York: Oxford; 1950.

Hibben, Paxton: *Henry Ward Beecher*. New York: Readers Club; 1942.

Hone, Philip: *Diary of Philip Hone, 1828-1851*, edited by Allan Nevins. 2 Vols. New York: Dodd, Mead & Company; 1927.

Horan, James D.: *Confederate Agent*. New York: Crown Publishers; 1954.

—— *Mathew Brady*. New York: Crown Publishers; 1955.

Hornblow, Arthur: *History of the Theatre in America*. 2 Vols. Philadelphia: J. B. Lippincott Company; 1919.

Hunt, Mabel Leigh: *"Have You Seen Tom Thumb?"* Philadelphia: J. B. Lippincott Company; 1942.

James, Henry: *Autobiography*, edited by Frederick W. Dupee. New York: Criterion Books; 1956.

Johnson, Edgar: *Charles Dickens*. 2 Vols. New York: Simon and Schuster; 1952.

Kouwenhoven, John: *Adventures of America, 1857–1900*. New York: Harper & Brothers; 1938.

—— ed.: *Columbia Historical Portrait of New York*. Garden City: Doubleday & Co.; 1953.

Kunitz, Stanley J., and Howard Haycraft: *American Authors 1600–1900*. New York: Harcourt, Brace & Company; 1936.

Lesley, Lewis B., ed.: *Uncle Sam's Camels*. Cambridge: Harvard University Press; 1929.

Lewis, Lloyd, and Henry Justin Smith: *Oscar Wilde Discovers America*. New York: Harcourt, Brace & Company; 1936.

Lloyd, James: *My Circus Life*. London: Douglas; 1925.

Masson, David: *Memories of London in the Forties*. London: Blackwood; 1908.

May, Earl Chapin: *The Circus from Rome to Ringling*. New York: Duffield and Green; 1932.

Meredith, Roy: *Mr. Lincoln's Camera Man*. New York: Charles Scribner's Sons; 1946.

Miller, David Humphreys: *Custer's Fall*. New York: Duell, Sloan & Pearce; 1957.

Miller, Francis Trevelyan, ed.: *Photographic History of the Civil War*. 10 Vols. New York: Review of Reviews; 1911.

Miller, Francis Trevelyan: *The World in the Air*. 2 Vols. New York: G. P. Putnam's Sons; 1930.

Mott, Frank Luther: *Golden Multitudes*. New York: The Macmillan Company; 1947.

Mussey, June B., ed.: *Yankee Life by Those Who Lived It*. New York: Alfred A. Knopf; 1947.

Nicolson, Marjorie: *Voyages to the Moon*. New York: The Macmillan Company; 1948.

O'Brien, Frank M.: *The Story of The Sun, 1833–1928*. New York: Appleton; 1928.

O'Higgins, Harvey, and Howard H. Reede: *American Mind in Action*. New York: Harper & Brothers; 1924.

Paine, Albert Bigelow: *Mark Twain*. 3 Vols. New York: Harper & Brothers; 1912.

Pearson, Edmund: *Murder at Smutty Nose*. New York: Sun Dial Press; 1938.

Pearson, Hesketh: *Dickens*. New York: Harper & Brothers; 1949.

Pergament, Moses: *Jenny Lind*. Stockholm: P. A. Norstedt & Söner; 1945.

Poe, Edgar Allan: *Works*. New York: Harper & Brothers; n.d.

Pond, James B.: *Eccentricities of Genius*. New York: Dillingham; 1900.

Rhodes, James F.: *History of the United States*. 8 Vols. New York: The Macmillan Company; 1909.

Robinson, Kenneth: *Wilkie Collins*. London: Bodley Head; 1951.

Root, Harvey W.: *The Unknown Barnum*. New York: Harper & Brothers; 1927.

Rourke, Constance Mayfield: *Trumpets of Jubilee*. New York: Harcourt, Brace & Company; 1927.

Rovere, Richard H.: *Howe and Hummel*. New York: Farrar, Straus; 1947.

Sedillot, René: *An Outline of French History*. New York: Alfred A. Knopf; 1953.

Seitz, Don C.: *Uncommon Americans*. Indianapolis: The Bobbs-Merrill Company; 1925.

Sherwood, Robert Edmund: *Here We Are Again*. Indianapolis: The Bobbs-Merrill Company; 1926.

—— *Hold Yer Hosses!* New York: The Macmillan Company; 1932.

Sothern, Edward H.: *Melancholy Tale of Me*. New York: Charles Scribner's Sons; 1916.

Stoddard, Henry L.: *Horace Greeley*. New York: G. P. Putnam's Sons; 1946.

Stone, Irving: *They Also Ran*. New York: Doubleday; 1943.

Stowe, Lyman Beecher: *Saints, Sinners, and Beechers*. Indianapolis: The Bobbs-Merrill Company; 1934.

Strachey, Lytton: *Queen Victoria*. New York: Harcourt, Brace & Company; 1921.

Thornton, Willis: *Fable, Fact and History*. New York: Greenberg; 1957.

Trollope, Frances: *Domestic Manners of the Americans*, edited by Donald Smalley. New York: Alfred A. Knopf; 1949.

Turner, Katherine C.: *Red Man Calling on the Great White Father*. Norman, Okla.: University of Oklahoma; 1951.

Tussaud, John Theodore: *The Romance of Madame Tussaud's*. New York: Doran; 1920.

Vail, Robert W. G.: *Random Notes on the History of the Early American Circus*. Barre, Mass.: Barre Gazette; 1956.

Webster, Samuel C., ed.: *Mark Twain, Business Man*. Boston: Little, Brown & Company; 1946.

Wellman, Paul I.: *Death on Horseback*. Philadelphia: J. B. Lippincott Company; 1947.

Wellman, Rita: *Eugénie*. New York: Charles Scribner's Sons; 1941.

Wells, Helen Frances: *Barnum, Showman of America*. New York: David McKay Company; 1957.

Werner, Morris Robert: *Barnum*. New York: Harcourt, Brace & Company; 1923.

—— *Brigham Young*. New York. Harcourt, Brace & Company; 1925.

—— *It Happened in New York*. New York: Coward-McCann; 1957.

Wildman, Edwin: *Famous Leaders of Industry*. 2 Vols. Boston: Page; 1920.

Wilson, Rufus R.: *New York*. 2 Vols. Philadelphia: J. B. Lippincott Company; 1902.

Winwar, Francis: *American Giant.* New York: Harper & Brothers; 1941.

Twentieth-century Periodicals

American Heritage, Vol. 5, Fall 1953; *Bridgeport Post,* issues 1915 through 1958; *Century,* August 1902 (an article by Joel Benton); *College Art Journal,* Fall 1952; *Collier's,* April 29, 1944 (an article by Dorothy Meserve Kunhardt); *Current Opinion,* June 1923; *Denver Post,* December 1915; *Everybody's,* of London, January 12, 1952; *Forum,* July 1923; *Freeman,* May 16, 1923; *Harper's Magazine,* September 1925 (an article by Harvey W. Root); *Hobbies,* October 1946; *Holiday,* March 1949; *Literary Digest,* October 12, 1918, and January 29, 1927; *Mentor,* March 1922; *The New York Times,* June, November, and December 1927, August 1941; *The New York Times Magazine,* May 4, 1952 (an article by Jorge Joveyn).

The New Yorker, January 6, 1932 (an article by Lucius Beebe), September 2, 1933 (an article by Homer Croy), August 25, 1934 (an article by Kenneth Campbell), April 11, 1936 (an article by Clara de Morinni), November 2, 1943 (an article by John Kobler); *Outlook,* January 12, 1921 (an article by Lyman Abbott); *Popular Science,* November 1935; *The Saturday Evening Post,* February 14, 1920 (an article by George Conklin) and December 8, 1923 (an article by Kin Hubbard); *System,* January 1924; *The Trail,* October 1912; *Theatre,* February 1904; *True,* April 1951 (an article by Alan Hynd).

General Works

Century Dictionary; Proper Names; Dictionary of American Biography; Encyclopedia of American Facts and Dates; Encyclopedia Britannica; Encyclopedia Americana; Handbook of American Museums; New Century Cyclopedia of Names; New International Encyclopedia; Reader's Encyclopedia; Webster's Biographical Dictionary.

INDEX